Too Good to Be True

Too Good to Be True

a novel

Taunia L. Bean

Covenant Communications, Inc.

Cover design copyrighted 2004 by Covenant Communications, Inc.

Published by Covenant Communications, Inc.
American Fork, Utah

Printed in Canada
First Printing: March 2004

12 11 10 09 08 07 06 05 04   10 9 8 7 6 5 4 3 2 1

ISBN 1-59156-449-2

Prologue

"You did it, huh?"

"Yeah." Morgan sighed and dropped her coat on her friend's bed.

"He really left then, actually got into the car and drove up there and signed in?" Julia wondered if she shouldn't tease Morgan about this, but it was her natural reaction. Sometimes a little humor went a long way.

"Of course! He was raring to go. He didn't even seem real last night. It was like he was already gone. Almost like he'd never been here." Morgan sat down on the bed and fell backward, her long, blonde hair fanning out. "Man!"

"He's probably just excited. I mean, Italy is a big deal, across the ocean and everything. It's not like he's being sent to Oklahoma or somewhere."

"I know, but it wasn't as romantic as I'd thought." Morgan sat up on the bed and put her hand to her heart. "It was pretty much, 'See ya, Morgan. I'm off to fulfill my destiny.'" They both laughed.

Julia leaned back, tilting the chair away from her desk. "You mean he didn't ask you to wait or anything?"

"No," Morgan replied. "He can't; he's a missionary. He basically wanted to write me off so he could have a clear conscience."

"What?" Julia drew back in mock horror. "You mean you're not secretly wearing an engagement ring on a chain around your neck?"

Morgan threw her a dirty look and continued, "But what I really can't believe, you know, what really kills me, is that he didn't even get me a Christmas present! I mean, I know that going on a mission is a big deal and everything and that he was nervous and excited and busy, but he's always been so great before."

Julia heard her mother start the vacuum downstairs, so she stood up and closed the door. Her dad had planned a Christmas party for tonight, and her mom was vacuuming a perfect pattern into the already clean carpet. "Well, I guess it's going to be tough, losing all that masculine attention. Aaron Jenner is incredible! Sensitive, kind, funny . . . and usually so *generous.*"

"Hey. Don't bug me. It's not that I wanted a gift—well, I did . . ." Morgan paused here, sat up, and gave her pure American-girl smile. "But it's just that it meant that he wasn't thinking about me, you know, didn't care."

"Morgan, he's not supposed to be thinking about you." Julia was exasperated. "This is his mission. He's been thinking about going his whole life. You know he likes you, but it can't—it really can't—be about you."

Morgan fell back onto the bed again. "You make me sound so shallow. I know all that stuff! I just can't help how I feel sometimes."

Morgan didn't seem to be able to help how she felt most of the time, and Julia usually had to listen to all the heart-rending problems. Most of the time it was very entertaining, but she got sick of always talking about Morgan. Julia knew it was selfish, but sometimes she wanted to talk about *her* life, *her* problems. Okay—so maybe her life wasn't as exciting as Morgan's. Maybe she didn't have guys lying in wait for her in school hallways, ringing the phone off the hook, and begging for dates, but she did have a life. But then, as Morgan continued to talk, the old sympathy began to creep in. It was like when she was watching a really engrossing movie or reading a novel. She felt drawn in, almost like she was living the role herself.

As the familiar drama began to fill the room, Julia attempted to change the subject. "So . . . did you get registered for next semester before we came home?"

"What?"

"Did you get the classes you wanted for winter semester?"

"Oh . . . no. I didn't get a chance to go over there. I was killing myself with that stupid paper and making up those couple of assignments, not to mention finals. Who's had time to worry about *next* semester? This first one's been hard enough." Morgan sat up and began looking through Julia's CD collection.

Who had time? Julia had registered on the first day it was possible—in the morning! There was no way she was going to take the chance of missing some of the core classes she needed for the pre-science programs. She didn't know what she was majoring in yet, not exactly, but her advisor assured her that taking some heavy physics, chemistry, and math would prepare her for anything she wanted to do.

"But seriously, Julia, what am I going to do? Two years . . . two whole years!" Morgan fell back onto the bed again, knocking some of the CDs onto the floor and leaving them there.

"You're going to survive." Julia bent down to pick up the CDs and replace them in the tower.

"I don't think you understand how much . . . well, I know that I flirt around with other guys . . ."

Julia sucked in her cheeks in order to swallow that one. It was the understatement of the year.

". . . but you know, Julia, I mean it with Aaron. I really do."

"I know." Julia looked steadily at Morgan, her long, blonde hair, blue eyes, slim body, and wondered how long it would last.

Part One

Chapter 1

Julia hit the ball hard and sent it bounding off the front wall, ceiling, and back of the court. The ball ricocheted around her as she swung the racket. The echoing smash of the little blue ball exactly matched the furious angles of her thoughts.

She'd been excited when the dark, good-looking guy had drifted over to her when it was time for assigning lab partners. Finally, her fourth semester into school, maybe she'd get someone decent to work with. The teacher paired them up because they were standing next to each other, and Julia looked at the boy and smiled. He laughed with her and joked about the teacher, and Julia felt lucky—until they actually started to work.

When Julia spread open the workbook and began to read down the list of instructions, her partner had fiddled with the burner and the lighter and acted like he was on a field trip. She let him measure one of the liquids, and he did it quickly, carelessly, then dumped it into the flask with the other elements before she could check the level. Then he turned the burner up too high and made it boil too soon, and the glass of their flask turned black and had to be scrubbed. And then he was clowning around and knocked into the entire apparatus, and she had to lunge to save it. Naturally the lab hadn't turned out like it was supposed to. Her frustration was unbearable—they'd probably get a B.

Why is that stupid guy in Organic Chemistry anyway? Did he mean to sign up for 101? And I'd been so flattered. Julia pushed her dark bangs out of her eyes and backhanded the ball explosively. Man, that guy was an idiot. And she felt like one too.

Okay, she'd admit it. She'd been hoping that this might be an opportunity to get to know someone . . . and so she'd let him goof off. She should have known he was only hoping she would do the lab work for him.

She'd been very careful in high school not to appear superior or too smart. She had never bragged about her test scores or answered too many questions in physics class, even on the days she could have given the teacher's lecture. But the boys were afraid of her anyway. She'd hoped that in college it would be different. But boys really didn't know how to deal with her, didn't realize she was like other girls in most ways and wanted to be friends.

And even her dad, someone who usually understood her, didn't understand about this. She had hated it every time her dad joked about the boys lining up at the front door when she turned sixteen. He would even quiz his young male dental patients about her in a big, jolly voice while checking their teeth. Sometimes she wondered if her dad thought girls were only valuable when valued by the opposite sex. Of course he was proud of her, but there always seemed to be that shade in his eye when she stayed home on a Friday night. And when she did have a date, he was so embarrassing, slapping the boy on the back and laughing in a big, booming voice.

She swung hard, sending the ball screaming over her head in frustration. Sometimes she felt like a square peg in a world where all the holes were round. Not everyone could be small-boned, tall, and spectacular like Morgan. Julia wanted to look good, yes, but she couldn't have her nose in every fashion magazine and recklessly waste hours shopping for matching shoes, even if her father could afford to buy them for her. How did one wrangle a date to every important event that came along? Why did she care? Why did she have to bite her tongue in class and keep track of the times she gave the right answer so it wouldn't happen too often? Why was she embarrassed instead of ecstatic when she scored 97 in a roomful of 70s?

Julia lowered her racket and dodged the last ricochet of the ball. She backed up against the rear wall of the court and slid down to a sitting position. Hugging her legs, she rested her damp forehead against her kneecaps. Her breath came in ragged heaves, her blood pulsing loudly in her ears. She noticed that her college-facility shorts had hiked up, exposing a good portion of toned thigh, and she tugged on them to cover her legs a little more, even though no one else was in the room. She leaned her head back against the cool cinder block wall and took a deep, steadying breath.

"Hey, are you going to use your last ten minutes?" A deep voice broke in as a guy's large, blonde head protruded into the court through the tiny door. Julia scrambled up quickly, grabbing her racket.

"Well, I guess I'm about done."

"Don't I know you?" he said, emerging fully into the court. Extended to his top height, he had to be over six foot five.

"Organic Chemistry," Julia said. She had noticed him before.

"Oh, yeah. Pretty tough, huh? Man, that lab was tricky."

"Yeah," she agreed. "I wish I could do it again though."

"You do?" He sounded incredulous.

"Yes. I wish I could get another crack at it." Julia added. "I would love to see if I could get it to work perfectly; I mean, that's what science is all about, precision." She immediately regretted her absurd honesty, but stuck out her chin firmly anyway daring him to contradict her.

"You sound like you know what you're talking about. I feel so out of it sometimes," he admitted. "I can't concentrate."

"Yeah, well, I'm not always in the best frame of mind either. I'm really trying to work on focusing. Maybe it'll help my chemistry grade, who knows?" She tried a laugh to lighten the situation. Though not exactly GQ, this guy was attractive, in a big-boned, Scandinavian kind of way.

Julia felt an awkward pause coming in the conversation and started edging toward the exit, not wanting to seem eager to extend the encounter. "See ya," she said, bending toward the small door.

"Hey, uh, do you want to give me a game while I'm waiting?" he asked. "My roommate's late."

She stood up slowly. "Oh, well . . . sure. But I'll have to warn you. I'm quite good for a girl."

"All the better." He swept his racket in an underhand arc, offering her the first serve.

She planted her lean, muscular legs. What was she doing?

"What's your name anyway?" he asked, just as she was about to serve. She dropped the ball, and it dribbled slowly to the corner of the court. She stumbled a little in her hurry to retrieve it.

"Julia," she replied, the blood rushing to her head as she stood up. "Julia Jeffs."

He smiled his amusement as he stepped forward, hand extended. "Ben Hammond."

His hand was large, white, and damply soft. She wondered if he saw the goose bumps rise on her arm. Returning to the server's position, she risked a smile. "Ready now?"

"Yeah." His response was drowned by the explosion of her serve, the ball hitting just behind his feet and rebounding off the back wall to the front.

"Hey! No fair! I wasn't ready." He was laughing, but he looked a bit surprised. Julia lifted her chin and looked him in the eye. If she was going to stay here, she'd stay and *play*. She let go with another killer serve, which this time he deftly returned, stepping back to give her room for the next shot.

His strokes and movements were surprisingly graceful for someone that tall. He used his long arms in extension to power back some of her sneakier shots. They played hard and long. The sweat was pouring off Julia's brow in unladylike streams. When she was up three points with two to go for the win, she felt her resolve softening. She knew guys hated to be beaten, at *anything*. It was a sure turnoff. She could let the next two barely drop, and he wouldn't know. Then he'd be up closer and would have a better chance to win. She wouldn't give him the last two.

Julia jogged up too close to the next shot, which hit the floor just beyond her. The next ball she let skim by her racket, close to the floor.

"Uh-uh," he shouted, "No way. You're not doing that to me."

"What?"

"You know . . . letting me catch up. I can do it myself."

"I'm not perfect. I wasn't . . . ." she began to protest.

"Yes you were." He looked right into her eyes.

"Okay, start again."

His serve skimmed the hair by her ear.

"Hey!" she yelled but didn't stop to argue. From years of practice, she could tell where the ball would land while it was still in the air, so he never caught her off guard. She dropped one after his skillful shot to the back corner, but cleaned up the last two, landing one toward the front wall when he was playing back and slamming the next one so fast he just missed it.

"Wow!" he said, shaking his head. "You weren't lying!"

"Of course not." She took a deep breath and pushed the damp hair off her forehead. "My dad has a family membership at the fitness center in Hunter. I used to play him or one of my brothers every week."

"Then why apologize?"

"What do you mean?"

"I mean, why miss a couple to help me catch up?"

She caught her breath. His directness left her gaping. What could she say?

"I didn't want you to feel bad," Julia admitted, looking down, feeling her pulse beat in her temples. "Most guys hate to lose." She gripped her racket tighter and looked him straight in the eyes.

"You're right," Ben said, reaching out suddenly to tug her shoulder-length hair. "But I hate it even worse when someone lets me win."

"I'll remember that," she said. Again she was edging toward the door.

"Are you going to give me a rematch?"

"Do you want to get beat again?" she flashed from her crouched position by the doorway.

"I don't mind so much when there's such a good view." He looked into her eyes and raised his eyebrows. Reddening, she jerked up, smashing her head against the low door frame. She raised her hand to rub the goose egg as she ducked through the door. The door swung swiftly shut, muffling Ben's low laughter. Outside the door Julia almost ran into a guy who must have been Ben's roommate. He had obviously been watching through the small window. She backed away quickly, but not before noticing his smirk. Julia darted across the hallway to the women's locker room, her heart hammering in her throat.

Chapter 2

The sterling silver bracelet sparkled and danced in the sun to the rhythm of Morgan's swinging step. It had arrived early, December first, wrapped up in a tiny box that had been enclosed in a larger one showing an Italian postmark. Morgan had opened it immediately, impatient and intent.

This charm is for January, Aaron had written, *and I'll send another one every month until I get home. I'll give December's to you in person.* She smiled again as she thought of the neatly written words, and turned her face to the January sun as she strode across campus.

It hardly seemed he'd been gone a year. Sometimes she still expected him to be waiting for her in the student center or the snack bar. And sometimes she felt nervous when she was standing out in the open teasing another guy, nervous that Aaron would walk up one of the slanting sidewalks and see them and be jealous.

Morgan breathed in the cold air and smoothed the beautiful wool sweater around her hips. Her mother had come through again, providing lovely Christmas gifts by staying up half of most nights out in the shop behind the house, pulling and stapling new fabric to worn chairs and couches to supplement her dad's school teacher income. The sweater was perfect for her and just matched the gray knee-length skirt she was wearing. She could be in a winter fashion ad. She flicked her long, blonde hair over her shoulder. Noticing the bracelet again, she held it at arm's length, studying the effect of the tiny "leaning-tower" charm as it reflected the winter sunlight.

"Morgan . . . Hey!" Sam Greenwell hitched his backpack onto his shoulder and jogged up to her from a nearby doorway. "What's going on?" He smiled, showing even, white teeth.

"Sambo!" she greeted. "How was your Christmas?"

"Oh, you know, a lot of relatives gossiping and arguing, a big turkey, candy canes . . ."

"Sounds fun."

"Yeah, but it could've been a lot funner if you'd been around on New Year's Eve. My mom made me take my cousin Rhonda to the stake old-people dance. Even there she should have been a wallflower. Eeek." He pulled a face.

"Well I'm sure your cousin Rhonda was grateful, Sammy. You don't know how desperate we women get on New Year's. It's slim pickings in small towns."

"And I'm the original knight in shining armor!" he said, striking a pose.

"You bet, darlin' . . . any day." She leaned against him briefly, letting her hair flick at his cheek, thinking it was a shame he wasn't just a little bit taller.

"Hey, what have you got this term?" Sam asked. "Anything brainy or are you just going to stick to all the intro courses?"

"Oh, I've got a few more intros to go," she said, laughing. "I'm actually thinking about declaring a major in the near future. Do you think I should be a librarian?"

"You? You're kidding! You don't seem like one of those dusty old chicks with foggy glasses to me."

"I can dream, can't I? Don't you think I'd look good in a bun with a pair of glasses sliding halfway down my nose? And besides, I love the library."

"Oh, brother!" he said. "I'm nervous the whole time I'm in the place, just waiting for one of those old ladies to tell me to shut up!"

"Well, you know you do have the loudest voice on campus, and you seem to think the library was made for meeting the opposite sex."

"If you go there . . . they will come," Sam chanted.

"You're crazy."

"Crazy about you!" Sam sang as he veered off down another path. "See ya, gorgeous!"

"Bye!" Morgan said, still laughing. The smile stayed on her lips all the way to the library.

A rush of warm air met her at the door, and she made her way through the noise and commotion of the first floor to the side stairs. She glanced back at a group of students talking and laughing at a near table and then turned with resignation to face the second floor. She was going to study—turn a new leaf, as her mother said.

The quiet of the second floor amazed Morgan. She could hear pages turning, people actually studying. She crossed the floor, staying close to the bookshelves. When she chose a place and swung her backpack down, she accidentally banged it into the leg of the study booth, and several students looked up from their books, irritated. She smiled an apology at them before sitting down.

The load of homework due tomorrow already seemed impossible, though she still had all night to worry about it. The wood-veneered study booths completely shut out the people next to and across from Morgan as she opened her notebook and glanced through her schedule. Two more to go today: College Algebra and Introduction to the Theater. Algebra was scary. It was so definite. There weren't any essay questions that she could brownnose her way through. Math wasn't her thing. It couldn't be helped, however. She needed the class to graduate from Hale with her associate's degree this June—if she could swing it.

Yes, graduation, and then what? She'd finally have to decide what to do. Her parents had been bugging her about declaring a major since she graduated from high school a year and a half ago. Hale was a two-year college and it didn't really matter if she just did generals right now, but she knew her parents were worried about her. They were probably right, but nothing was really very clear to her at the moment, and of course, what about Aaron? He'd be home in less than a year now. What would be the use of starting on a complicated major, classes and everything, if they were going to get married, and she'd probably have to transfer to whichever school he decided on? She guessed she'd just wait and see how that turned out. Of course there was next fall before he got home, and she should probably start taking classes somewhere . . . Morgan leaned back into her chair, rolled her eyes back and closed them.

Okay, yes, study. Morgan lifted the stack of books and her binder from her backpack. She thumbed through the French book and stroked the colorful, glossy cover. Maybe later. She opened the literature text and read a few lines from Wordsworth then looked up at the blank booth wall in front of her. She glanced around the room searching for anyone she knew.

She couldn't see enough of the blonde's hair three booths down to know if it was Chalyse Erickson. She liked her shoes though. She thought she recognized Thomas Brown's silver-tipped cowboy boots under the row behind her. He wanted to be a veterinarian. He came from her hometown—a shy, serious farm boy who blushed dark red whenever she came too near him.

She'd gone on a date or two with Thomas, though she'd been in love with Aaron even before she'd turned sixteen and could date. The first time she had felt Aaron's eyes on her, a flood of dark warmth spread from her chest all the way down to her fingertips. Of course, he'd seen her before, but she was always aware when she was the object of someone's attention.

She'd been standing around after a basketball game, killing time with a couple of her friends, when he emerged from the locker room, his hair wet and slicked back. He'd made twelve points in the game and had led the defense, holding the other team down to eighty points, even though their team had lost in the end. Morgan had felt a pricking of the hair on her neck and knew without looking that Aaron had come out of the locker room. Even though she could only see him from the corner of her eye, she felt his cool, interested gaze. It made her face heat up and her fingertips buzz. She became more vivacious, louder, and her hand raked long strands of hair back from her forehead.

For two weeks afterward she had waited confidently. She knew he would ask her.

It happened so quickly and casually that she'd hardly had time to react.

"Morgan," he'd said, rubbing the shoulder of his letterman jacket into the bank of lockers next to hers. "Want to go to a movie Friday?" He was looking down at a spot on the floor just in front of her toes. He jerked his head up and looked into her eyes. "The new show seems decent, and it's not rated R for a change."

"Yeah, great." She was amazed she sounded so calm.

"Seven?"

"Okay."

His smile with its deep dimple lit up the universe . . .

Morgan sighed heavily and surveyed the quiet library again. Then she slid a thin sheet of stationery from the pocket of her binder and began to write.

Chapter 3

Aaron glanced at the clock for the fourth time. Why wouldn't Elder Facer get up? Aaron had discreetly rung the alarm again after he got out of the shower and dressed. That had been twenty minutes ago. He couldn't concentrate on the scriptures. His companion's behavior really irritated him, but he didn't want to push it too hard. Three days ago the two had almost come to blows when Aaron had finally decided to approach Elder Facer about his recent habits. He'd prayed about the encounter for three days and tried to be tactful, but Elder Facer just exploded. He'd grabbed a fistful of just-ironed shirt and yelled in Aaron's face.

He wasn't trying to be a "self-righteous model missionary," as Elder Facer had sneeringly accused him. He just wanted to get to work.

But Elder Facer was going home in three months, and it looked like he was just going to ride it out comfortably—as long as he could stay out of the zone leader's way.

Aaron looked over at the big lump Elder Facer made in the narrow bed. He remembered the first time they'd met at a zone conference. Elder Facer was big, good-looking, and intimidating. Rumor had it that whatever basketball team he was on couldn't be beat. Aaron's companion at the time had whispered, pointing to a still-visible scar above his eye, "There's the guy that gave me five stitches! When he's underneath, watch out!"

Aaron stared at the peeling paint on their apartment wall, thinking about his last companion. He couldn't believe how lucky he'd been. Elder Cook was great! Eager and spiritual, but down-to-earth. They'd worked their tails off—getting up early, pounding the pavement, and knocking on doors. Although the Italian mission wasn't high in baptisms, their companionship had seemed to open up doors and help the people feel the Spirit. And Aaron had felt it too. Never so strongly had the Spirit poured into him as when he was testifying of the gospel in those humble apartments.

Elder Facer groaned and rolled over. "What time is it?"

"About seven thirty." Aaron tried to keep the irritation out of his voice.

"How's ol' Alma this morning?"

Aaron's eyes flicked angrily in Elder Facer's direction then back to the page in front of him. Elder Facer slowly hauled his body to a sitting position and leaned over to scratch his lower back. "Man, I feel terrible. I guess I shouldn't have stayed up so late doing push-ups. I mean, I wouldn't want to get too buff—I'm already going to have a hard enough time peeling the girls off me when I get home." He flexed, showing amazingly large biceps and flashed an obnoxious grin in Aaron's direction.

"So—what's on the big agenda today? More of that great door-knocking, I suppose? Well, let's get to it!" Elder Facer bounded off the bed in exaggeration and began jogging in place. The thin walls of their apartment rattled. It sounded as if he was about to fall through the floor.

"I'll just jump in the shower and be ready to go before you can say lickety split!" He lunged through the narrow door leading to the makeshift shower, and soon Aaron could hear his blaring baritone voice singing a love song that used to be popular back home. When he hit the high notes he gurgled an embarrassing vibrato. Aaron wondered if Mrs. Belzoni would come down and complain again.

Aaron knew Elder Facer did this just to get on his nerves. This false, jolly attitude would soon deflate to a depressed growl and then fall to silence as the day progressed. Aaron had to be grateful that today hadn't started out on the silent mode; at least he would get Elder Facer out the door today.

At three thirty Elder Jenner and Elder Facer were approaching yet another dingy apartment door. Elder Facer was pretty far into his black mood. Aaron didn't dare comment as he led the door approaches, continually getting turned down, sometimes not so gently. His Italian still left a lot to be desired, even after a year, and most contacts weren't patient enough to try to understand. He just kept going though, hoping that his perpetual motion would allow them to get a little further into the afternoon before Elder Facer copped out.

He knew that this was not the way to do the Lord's work. The Spirit couldn't be with them when their companionship was so strained, a negative pall hanging over everything they did. But how could he help it? If he kept the mission rules the best he could, at least he was moving forward. He was trying, and he knew if you tried hard, the Lord blessed you.

Elder Facer leaned on the wall beside the next door and stared vacantly across the hall. Aaron sighed as he lifted his arm and knocked, getting ready to give his door approach. They waited a moment then were finally about to go on when the door swung open.

"Buon giorno, Signore," Aaron said, smiling. A young man of maybe eighteen was standing in the doorway, a thin tank undershirt tucked into his tight jeans. He didn't look pleased. Aaron plunged forward anyway, putting all his concentration into his Italian, trying to pull the Lord's perfect message from all the strange sounding rolled r's and lilting cadences. The young man's forehead creased in exasperation, disgusted with Aaron's strong American accent.

"What? Go away! How can I listen to that?" The young man said in Italian, making wide "shooing" motions with his hands.

Aaron had stepped back, prepared to retreat, when Elder Facer suddenly stepped in and began smoothly explaining in his fluent Italian. Aaron soon lost track of the conversation; the pace turned rapid as the young man discovered Elder Facer's amazing grasp of the language. Aaron felt sick as he struggled to pick out meaning from the foreign sounds. He'd studied so much, and though he could now read Italian fluently, he just couldn't produce the sounds himself with any accuracy, nor could he understand them well, unless they were spoken very slowly. He'd never experienced this kind of a challenge. He'd been good at school, both in math and English. Actually, he'd been pretty successful at almost everything he'd ever tried. Until now.

Aaron began to sweat as he focused again on the conversation. Both men were gesticulating and pointing. He caught the word *nuovo* (new) and *bambino* and *Americano*. Aaron wasn't surprised when the conversation ended with both Elder Facer and the young man laughing. The young Italian was still smiling widely and pointing at Aaron when he shut the door.

Aaron could feel his temper rising and filling him like a black cloud. Ten paces from the door he couldn't hold back.

"What is your problem?" he exploded. "After everything I take from you, do you have to humiliate me too, and in front of a potential contact?"

"Hey, wait," Elder Facer interrupted.

"No, you wait! I have had it with you! I'm sick of tiptoeing around for the sake of keeping the peace. I don't have to take this from *anyone!*" He drove his palms into Elder Facer's chest and slammed him to the wall of the corridor, yelling the words so close to the larger man's face he could have competed well with any Italian. He then whirled around and away, in an imitation of an old football move, and tore down the hall, putting as much space between them as he could.

When he reached the outer doors on the ground floor, he turned around to see Elder Facer's large bulk coming down the hall at a run. Aaron didn't stop to think, but concentrating on self-preservation, ran out into the crowded street, around the corner, down an alley, and straight into something cold, flat, and hard.

He woke to the sound of a squeaky bicycle being wheeled slowly close to his head. He sat up with a jerk and stared into the curious eyes of a young boy who quickly looked away and then pushed his bike hurriedly down the alley. His head ached horribly, and when he put a hand up to his forehead, he discovered a large, painful bump just under his hairline.

Aaron stood up and looked around, feeling stupid. Then he saw the steel door that he'd plowed into. As far as he could make out, it was the kitchen entrance to a restaurant. Apparently it had opened at just the wrong time, at least for him.

As he stood there in the alley, it was a second or two before he realized that he was alone. Instantly guilt cramped his stomach. The cardinal mission rule: *Do not leave your companion.*

Aaron ran down the alley and back out onto the street. He couldn't have been unconscious for more than a minute. He looked swiftly up and down the street but couldn't see Elder Facer anywhere. He looked back toward the building that they'd run out of and felt again the wave of humiliation as he remembered standing there dumb by the apartment door while the young Italian and Elder Facer laughed at him.

Aaron closed his eyes briefly and took a deep breath. But it shouldn't have mattered. He had lost his temper. He'd yelled at and pushed his companion—someone that happened to weigh 220 pounds and could bench press 325. Whoa. Religion and the golden rule aside, that was a crazy thing to do. Suddenly Aaron wasn't so sure he wanted to find Facer. But, ignoring the squirmy feeling in his stomach, Aaron walked to the end of the block and stood on the corner scanning both streets.

The streets were growing more crowded as workers on early shifts filled them going home. Aaron stood up on a lamppost and tried to see over the heads in the crowd. Elder Facer was nowhere in sight. He must have run up another block.

Aaron quickly reached the next corner and again looked in both directions. He couldn't have gotten very far away so soon. Suddenly he spotted a large man in a dark suit turning up a diagonal street to Aaron's right. Relief began to flood through him as Aaron pursued Elder Facer through the thickening crowd. He began to think rapidly, hoping to come up with the right words of apology that would not lead to a black eye and a broken nose.

"Elder!" Aaron shouted and dodged an old woman with a string bag full of vegetables on her arm. "Elder!" Aaron finally got within arm's length of Elder Facer and dared to reach out and grab his shoulder. The man wheeled around and stared Aaron in the face. Not Elder Facer. He looked fortyish with a dark uni-brow running the width of his forehead. The brow lowered menacingly over his eyes as he sharply threw off Aaron's hand.

"Mi dispiace!" Aaron apologized rapidly, holding his hands out in front of his chest. "I thought you were someone else."

"Cosa?" The man didn't understand Aaron. He turned and stalked off, talking to himself and gesticulating angrily.

Aaron's head was aching so bad he couldn't think straight. He walked a few steps and sat down on an empty bench and bent over till his forehead nearly touched his knees. Aaron swung his backpack off his shoulder and dug into the bag for his planner. He sifted through the contents quickly. Where was the map? Suddenly, he could see it, remember it perfectly, sitting on top of his desk where he'd left it that morning.

He shoved his planner back in the bag and shouldered it again. People began to bump against him as he stood in the middle of the sidewalk facing the pedestrian traffic.

He would ask someone. Most people would know the street Via Garibaldi. It couldn't be too far from here. If he could get there, he knew his way home.

"Mi scusi," Aaron approached a used-clothes salesman polishing his front window with a greasy rag. "Do you know Via Garibaldi?"

"Ah, sì, sì." The older man began speaking quickly, pointing and waving his arms, nodding his head and smiling.

The only thing Aaron understood was to "go up the street about a kilometer." Aaron pulled his planner out and ripped out a blank sheet. "Can you tell me again, slowly?"

It was getting close to five o'clock. He'd been walking for almost an hour and had not yet come to Via Garibaldi. After following what he could understand of the older man's instructions, Aaron had found himself even deeper in the tangle of narrow streets. He took a deep breath and stared up into the small window of sky that was visible between the tall buildings. "Heavenly Father, help me. I am lost."

He paused for a moment trying to relax enough to let the Spirit fill him and then decided to buy a phone token so he could call the apartment. Hopefully Elder Facer had gone back to the apartment. Hopefully Elder Facer would talk to him, would help him get home.

Aaron approached a jewelry shop and stood in line behind a woman who was trying to decide between two cheap necklaces. As the conversation between her and the shopkeeper grew long, Aaron noticed a rack on the counter filled with tiny silver charms like the twelve charms for the bracelet he'd bought in Pisa and sent to Morgan.

Morgan. The memory of her intruded into his thoughts and fought for attention amid the fear and worry of his current situation.

He swallowed hard. He missed her. Especially at times like this, when things seemed hopeless, and depression like he'd never experienced before his mission descended on him like a heavy blanket. Generally he tried not to indulge in prolonged thoughts of her, trying to stay missionary-minded, trying to stay sane. He exhaled loudly.

The woman with the necklaces gave a sharp laugh of triumph in front of him and elbowed him as she rummaged in her bag for her money. Five minutes later Aaron was on the phone humbly listening to Elder Facer's instructions as he told him how to get home.

Chapter 4

"Hey, hey, how's it going?" Morgan said softly, opening her eyes from a music-induced trance. She was lying on her narrow dorm-room bunk playing the CD of her favorite ballads, *again*. Julia flipped off the stereo, dumped her backpack and gym bag heavily on her bed, and threw herself down as well.

"Good," Julia answered. "Tired though. What a day."

"Oh yeah?" said Morgan sleepily, closing her eyes again. It was four thirty in the afternoon, and the winter rays were slanting in through their single southern window.

"Yeah, I was so frustrated after my last class that I stopped and got in a great game of racquetball."

"What's so great about racquetball anyway?"

"Oh, you know, I always feel better after exhausting myself. It clears the brain," Julia said, smiling at the ceiling.

"Like your brain needs clearing!" Morgan rolled over and propped herself up on her elbow. "Check out any guys in your new classes?"

"Not really. Most of them are nothing to get excited about, like last semester. Remember Darrell?" Julia rolled her eyes, remembering the five-foot-three, greasy-haired shadow that had followed Morgan around last semester with a drooling-puppy-dog expression.

On the second of the two dates that Morgan had allowed him, he had ridiculously proposed to her, telling her he'd had an inspired dream that she was to be his wife. Morgan had felt bad about that for perhaps two seconds.

"Could you believe that guy?" Morgan agreed. "He had no idea of his league. How strange to be that unaware of yourself." Morgan stretched her long thin arms over her head, combing back her silky, blonde hair.

Julia had always envied that hair, and she knew Morgan's pride in that luscious blonde fall, even though she had never mentioned it. The color was even real.

"Get a letter from Aaron today?" Julia asked.

"Yeah." Morgan rose up halfway, reaching for the torn envelope on a shelf above her bed. "He says he's pretty fed up with his companion, but he's trying to work things out. He sent a little picture of his new area near Florence. Want to see?"

"Maybe later. I'm going to try to get a little nap in before everyone comes back. Who's home?"

"I think Trista is barricaded in her room as usual. I didn't check. Lorraine is still at dance practice. And I don't know where Cynthia and Heather are. I guess I'll try to sleep a little longer too. I'm so tired!" Morgan reached up and flipped on her stereo, again filling the room with the soft, low tones of her pop ballad CD.

Julia opened her eyes in annoyance and then closed them again. She'd been used to the music before, of course, but the two-week Christmas vacation had made her hypersensitive again. She shook her head a little to tune out the whining notes. She needed the pretense of sleep to pull a shroud of privacy around her so she could think.

She really shouldn't be doing this; she needed all the study time she could get. Mechanically she listed in her head all of the assignments for tomorrow: read two chapters in her physiology book, read Thomas More for her literature survey class, write a short essay for Art Appreciation, and work chemistry problems.

Chemistry . . . she couldn't help her mind darting back to the racquetball court. She knew it was weak of her. Her body tingled with embarrassment, like it had only happened five minutes ago. What an exit. What an idiot she was! She began drawing deep breaths to calm her body, trying to zero in on the episode, and remember exactly what she had said, how she had acted.

She had known immediately that Ben was someone she'd like to get to know. His easy, biting humor had drawn her in even while stinging. But she hated thinking about him, hated remembering her ridiculous responses; she hated the futility at the bottom of the whole thing, the hopeless knowledge that it would all come to nothing.

A past scene of humiliation rose vividly before her. James Enderby. His gray-green eyes intense. He'd moved into town the fall of her senior year and had been casually meeting her in the library for weeks, chatting, working out calculus problems with her. She'd loved his deep studious air and quiet yet chic way of dressing. She really felt he was her type. And she, her young, raw self, had begun to believe, had let herself think that maybe . . . Until one day the ax fell.

"Umm . . . Julia, I've been wanting to ask you something for a long time," he had said.

"So ask." She smiled. Her body shot up in temperature, and her breath caught in expectation.

"I've, well . . . I've really wanted to ask Morgan out. You guys are friends, right? I wondered if you knew whether she and Aaron were dating other people and if you think she'd consider going out with me." His beautiful green eyes were bright in his eagerness, his relief obvious that he'd finally done what he'd probably been leading up to for weeks.

Julia had lowered her eyes, desperate to hide the hurt, the unbelievable humiliation. She tried to make her face relax into a smooth mask, took a silent breath, and faced him. "Well, they are pretty thick." She attempted a smile. "But, I'd try her out. They date other people sometimes." *And who wouldn't die to go out with you?* she added to herself. She was glad her voice stayed steady; her hands weren't even shaking yet. And then he had stayed unendurably and discussed Morgan, how to approach her, whether Julia thought Morgan liked him at all. She had felt her insides hardening up, the tender shoots of hope dying, withering silently, drawing themselves into a tight ball.

Morgan had used the weekends Aaron and the basketball team played out-of-town to date James for about two months, laughing about him with Julia, picking apart his shyness and eager intelligence. Although Julia knew that Morgan had had no idea how she felt, it didn't matter. It had nearly killed Julia to go along with it, pretend she didn't care, try not to hate her best friend. After all, it wasn't Morgan's fault if she exuded some undeniable charm that guys fell for so eagerly.

Some people were just that way. It wasn't that she was the most beautiful girl; she didn't have perfectly even features like you'd see in a fashion magazine or flawless skin or anything like that. But she did have a great figure, and her smooth, fluid movements accentuated her graceful curves so that even shy, beautiful, studious boys could not leave her alone. It had always been that way.

Morgan and Julia had been best friends since third grade when Morgan's family moved into town from Salt Lake. They were the only two eight-year-old girls in the Hunter Second Ward, and Morgan's house had only been a block away. They had practically lived together, in and out of school, spending the long summers running back and forth along the street between their houses.

Even from that early age, there were always notes and whispers and shy little boys silently walking Morgan home while Julia walked two steps behind. In their early teens, Morgan begged Julia to sit on the other side of her at the movies where she was meeting her latest conquest. This was not dating, Morgan justified, even when a boy had asked her to "go" with him, because Julia would always come along.

Julia had often wondered in silent torment whether a boy would ever want to be her boyfriend after he saw Morgan. And yet she liked Morgan. She always had. Morgan was bright and witty and enthusiastic. And she wasn't afraid of things. Julia enjoyed taking her down a peg or two when she could and played the devil's advocate just to be a pain, but Morgan expected it and took the sarcasm head-on. Julia liked being in Morgan's life. It felt good when Morgan would confide in her, and together they would shred each situation down to the tiniest nuance.

And it was still that way. Some would probably wonder, seeing them now, how two such opposites could be friends. Julia knew they didn't have much in common, and she wasn't sure why they worked together, but somehow, their long history together—all the secrets of childhood and adventures in adolescence—bound them together in a way that wasn't easily broken. Morgan was like a sister. Sometimes Julia privately ridiculed and despised her, but Morgan was always, in an indefinable way, hers.

Chapter 5

The old door of the apartment swung inward with a loud screech, and Aaron stepped through to find Elder Facer sitting hunched over the small formica table. His triple combination was open in front of him.

"How's it going?" Elder Facer said, looking up.

"Okay," Aaron said carefully. Even though Elder Facer had sounded safe on the phone, Aaron was waiting for a loud and obnoxious response, maybe even something physical, but Elder Facer didn't move. Instead he began playing with the satin place-marker ribbon in his scriptures.

Aaron didn't know what to say. He walked over to the other rusted metal chair, dragged it from beneath the table, and sat down. He was embarrassed and dreaded giving this apology, but it had to be done.

"Hey, look—I'm sorry; I was way out of line. I'm usually not like that. I guess I just lost control . . ." Aaron trailed off. It was harder for him to explain than he'd thought it would be. He knew that what he had done was wrong, even though at the time he'd felt justifiably provoked. But that was the problem. When you were all worked up and angry, you could justify a lot of things in your mind. It was harder to make excuses the more you looked back. "And then, you know, when I saw you coming at me down the hall, well, I guess I just panicked."

"It's okay," Elder Facer responded.

"It is?"

"Well, you know, it's pretty lucky for both of us that you ran. I'm not the most 'in-control' person either." Elder Facer gave a short grin.

"I wanted to kill you. What happened to you anyway? How'd you get lost? By the time I got out onto the street you were already out of sight."

"Not out of sight really. Just out. Cold. I ran around the corner and into an alley and smack into an open steel door." Aaron smiled a little. It sounded pretty funny now.

"You ran into a steel door? And it laid you out?"

Aaron nodded slowly.

"Man." Elder Facer grinned and shook his head slowly, trying not to laugh. "That's gotta hurt."

"Oh, yeah. Look at my head." Aaron sat down and pushed his face closer to his companion. This was weird. It was the first time they'd had a reasonable, even friendly, conversation.

Elder Facer peered closely at the bump. "Whoa. And then you got lost?"

"Yeah, looking for you. After I woke up and realized I was alone."

"Hey, well, I'm sorry about that. I really wouldn't have ruined your face. Probably. Actually I'm the one who should be sorry and you know it." Elder Facer smiled widely and held out a big, meaty hand. "Forgive me?"

Aaron was amazed. He stared at Elder Facer's outstretched hand and paused a moment before taking it.

Elder Facer laughed shortly. "Hard to believe, eh? It shook me up pretty good to see you coming after me like some crazed maniac." He smiled again. "I figured I must have been getting pretty bad for someone as straight as you to lose it. I'm still not sure why you freaked out at exactly that minute, but I was pretty glad it happened after the door shut. Do you know that guy was actually interested in us? While I had him laughing and joking I asked him if we could come back again next week, and he's letting us. Wednesday at seven."

"Amazing." Aaron still felt humiliated. The fact was they'd been talking so fast that he really didn't know what they had said. He'd been hoping he was hiding it a little better.

"I didn't know what to do when I couldn't find you." Elder Facer continued. "I mean, even I felt bad about us not staying together like we're supposed to. I started getting pretty worried after about an hour, so I called the president."

Aaron's heart gave a lurch. He couldn't believe it—it was a mistake, he hadn't meant to leave his companion. What had Elder Facer told the mission president? The color began to drain from his face.

"You called the president?"

"Yeah, I told him that we got separated, and I told him why. It was all my fault, and he agrees." Elder Facer gave a small snort of a laugh. "I sort of confessed and he told me to get my act together, quick. We talked for a long time, and I'm really glad. He set me straight on a lot of things. He's a great man. The Lord did a good job when he called President Cutler."

"Yeah, he's a good president." Aaron was having a hard time handling Elder Facer's 180-degree turn. "Hey, I promise I won't come after you again," Aaron said. "It was too scary the first time! I thought for sure I was dead."

Elder Facer laughed again. "Yeah, well, you were pretty lucky. I guess the Lord was just blessing me, giving you a little speed and getting you outta sight, else you would have been creamed!" They both laughed.

Now that things were easier between them, Aaron realized he was hungry and started to get up to look for something to eat.

Elder Facer held up a hand. "Hey, wait a minute. I know I don't have to tell you why I've been such a creep lately, but I want you to understand. I haven't talked to you hardly at all, so you don't know much about me; no one out here does."

Aaron nodded and settled in the chair again.

Elder Facer licked his lips and took a breath before beginning to speak. "I came on my mission for one reason, and her name was Gina. She begged me to go for about a year and finally told me there was no way we could get married if I didn't go on a mission. I was crazy about her. I'd already proposed a couple of times. I didn't grow up all that religious, and my parents weren't thrilled when I told them I was going, but my mom tried to be supportive."

Aaron shifted in his chair; he was starting to feel uncomfortable again.

"I know it was a stupid reason to serve a mission, but I really wanted her, and I figured she was worth doing this for. It was really great at the beginning. I started to feel the Spirit and understand what the Church is really about. I couldn't believe it when Italian just started to come to me. I mean, I'd never done very well in school, so it was a surprise. But it made me feel smart, and like I could do things besides sports. But then Gina wrote me this letter. It sounded kind of weird, like she was trying extra hard to be nice. I started to panic fast, 'cause I'd seen this happen to one of my companions. The next thing I knew there was a wedding announcement in the mail. I couldn't think of anyone I knew that could be getting married. I'd never gotten a wedding announcement before in my life.

"It was her. Gina and this skinny dark-haired creep, smiling like they'd just won the lottery. And not one word telling me why, or even that she was sorry. I couldn't believe it. I started tearing around, trying to think of something to do, thinking about calling her, anything. Then I looked at the dates on the announcement. She had sent it late. They were already married.

"I looked at that little gold temple sticker on the envelope, and I just felt sick. Pretty much all I have done for the past three months is to try to get back at the world, at the Church, and anyone that's been around me. I was probably the most obnoxious to you," he admitted. "You seemed like you had everything so much in control I couldn't stand it. And when you unpacked that picture of your own gorgeous babe, I wanted to throw things. It just didn't seem fair." He ran a hand over his closely cropped hair and looked up. "But I'm ready to try now. I don't know if I'm ever going to get over her and what she did, but I'm through letting her stop me from doing what I know is right." Elder Facer blinked and stared down at the tabletop and at the ribbon from his scriptures that he had twisted into a tight thread.

"Thanks for telling me. I understand. It helps." Aaron wanted to offer some kind of comfort, tell him he was sorry, but he couldn't find more words that wouldn't seem patronizing.

Elder Facer looked up again. "Yeah, well, let's just get going and make a difference over here. I could use a few blessings."

Chapter 6

Morgan glanced behind her, pausing to turn the radio down, and then returned her attention to the large mirror. Had she heard Julia come in? She listened for a moment and then leaned into the mirror again and began to apply long strokes of mascara to her lashes. She was hoping to talk to Julia before she had to leave in about twenty minutes. Her hair had come out just right, lying in golden waves on her shoulders, reaching to the middle of her back.

Finishing with a little dark maroon lipstick borrowed from Julia's drawer, she shook her hair out and turned to admire the total effect. Her new jeans fit perfectly, accentuating her slim hips and giving the illusion of a smaller waist. The sweater was her favorite from two years ago, a soft gray-green one that sat right at the waistline. Even though her chest had filled out a little, the sweater was still a perfect fit. In fact, it was even better. She raised her arms over her head and watched the sweater rise two inches. A thin line of the soft skin of her midriff was visible. Too much? She twisted in front of the mirror, looking at her back. Her body felt alert and alive, and she arched her back and smiled brilliantly into the mirror.

Her thoughts turned to the upcoming date. David was great. He hadn't hidden the fact that he'd admired her from the start, sitting by her in theater class and waiting outside the institute after the devotional to walk her back to her dorm. He'd taken her to the movies twice, and then they'd gone to a party with some of his friends. Her stomach was tense with excitement and she felt the blood rush to her fingertips, like she used to feel just before going out with Aaron.

Aaron. Recalling his name released a small sigh from her lips and she remembered how much he liked this sweater. Sometimes she wondered if he was ever going to come back, it felt like it had been so long. But maybe David could, well, help her along a little.

"Anybody home?" Julia called out, sticking her head into the bathroom.

"Hi. You're just in time. What do you think?" Morgan whirled and struck a pose. "Do I pass?"

"Gorgeous, as usual. Do you do this to torture me?" Julia rolled her eyes.

"Of course. Do you like my lipstick?"

"You mean my lipstick!" Julia reached for the tube on the counter.

"Yes, thanks, mine just wasn't the right thing."

"I'm sure. Well, anytime. Now I'm going to have to throw it away." Julia held the lipstick over the trash can for a moment but then returned it to the makeup case in her drawer.

"Will you be serious for a minute? I want to know what you think about David? Do you think we're good together?"

"How should I know? I don't go out with him." Julia walked out of the bathroom and dumped her backpack on her bed.

"Come on, help me out. You know him." Morgan followed her into the bedroom and sat next to her on the bed.

"Well, he looks like a Greek god," Julia conceded.

"I know." Morgan flashed a big smile.

"And he seems nice. I mean, he doesn't spit on me."

"Julia!"

"And he's a returned missionary, so I suppose he's also a saint," Julia continued, pretending to be thoughtful.

"For your information he gave a talk in church last Sunday that was spiritual and brilliant at the same time. He's a great public speaker."

"Great!" Julia rolled her eyes. "I miss all the good talks. I guess it was a bad time to be throwing up." She changed to the opposite bunk and leaned her elbows on her knees. "Anyway, David's a great guy. I mean, half the dorm would die to go out with him. But what about Aaron? You're always saying how in love you are."

"I am in love with Aaron. But I'm not married to him. David really likes me, and I feel great when I'm with him. He's so nice and tall and handsome and *here*. I guess I am just a fickle little creep after all." Morgan looked down at the charm bracelet on her arm and tried not to feel the small stab of guilt. Another silver charm in the shape of a tiny cat had come last week. It was smooth and beautiful.

It reminded her how amazingly sensitive he was to her and to what would please her. After they had begun dating, he had shown her in a hundred ways that he was thinking about her. He'd talked to Julia or her mother and sisters for ideas and then would surprise her on her birthday or on one of the holidays. After a few months of dating, she began to find little notes in her locker or taped to the window of her mother's car. Once, for no reason at all, he'd set up a little round table in his backyard and had given her dinner by starlight. He had wedged his stereo speaker in his basement window, playing their song. Morgan smiled faintly. It was hard to remember it very clearly now.

"Your problem is that you're spoiled," Julia interrupted. "Aaron was a dream. No one has a boyfriend that acts like that. He was Prince Charming. It's probably like living in a vacuum now, even though you still have half the campus trailing after you." Julia took off her jacket and hung it up in the cramped closet. She opened her backpack and drew out her chemistry book and binder.

Morgan was still toying with the bracelet and didn't answer, so she continued.

"Anyway, I don't think it hurts to have a good time with someone else. Maybe Aaron isn't the only guy in the world."

"What if he kisses me?" Morgan didn't look up.

"Will you let him?"

"I don't know. I haven't let anyone so far. I've been very good at dodging. If you ever need some advice on that subject, let me know!" Morgan pushed her hair off her forehead. "Most guys are so ridiculous. They think a date wasn't good unless they get some 'lip.'" Morgan frowned at the slang term. She grabbed her purse and then turned to the mirror on the closet door. Her eyes looked large and excited. A knock sounded on the front door, and an unfamiliar little tremor of nervousness jerked through her.

"Well, anyway, see you later," she said to Julia.

"Okay. Bye."

* * *

Julia was becoming increasingly uncomfortable in chemistry class. She constantly fought the urge to turn and scan the room for Ben. She was superconscious of all her movements and felt her back burning when she sat toward the front of the room. This week she had been slipping into the front entrance of the theater-style classroom just before class so she could sit on the front row and be near the door. Coming late also allowed her to glance quickly at Ben's position and attempt to get as far from him as she could. She had become an expert at stuffing her notebook into her backpack at the end of class and was usually the first one through the doors. So far it had worked well; she hadn't yet encountered Ben.

This morning was frosty cold and she could see her breath in the air as she walked to class. Other students walking around her bent their heads low against the wind, trying to protect their faces and necks. She glanced down at her watch and saw that it was still five minutes to eight and she was almost there. She began walking more slowly, looking around her to avoid running into Ben coming down one of the slanting sidewalks. It was so cold she decided to hurry into the building and duck into the rest room until her watch said 7:58. Looking in the mirror, she decided to rub off almost all of her blush; her cheeks were red from the cold, and the pink-toned powder made her look ridiculous.

When she looked at her watch again it was eight o'clock! She ran the few steps to the classroom door and hurried to her seat. Professor Kennan was already standing up, ready to launch into the day's lecture, and he gave her a piercing glance. Her face burned. Professor Kennan had made it clear that he didn't tolerate tardiness. He had made an embarrassing example of a student on the second day of class, and people had pretty much heeded his warning. It was best to stay on the good side of the professor in such a difficult class. Julia dug in her backpack for a pen, her dark shoulder-length hair swinging across her face.

Five minutes into Kennan's lecture, the front door opened quietly again and Ben Hammond stepped through. The professor whirled dramatically and murmurs sounded through the students.

"Sir, your name," Professor Kennan demanded.

Oh, no, Julia thought. She looked down so she wouldn't have to watch and slid further down in her seat.

"Ben Hammond."

"Mr. Hammond, do you have difficulty in remembering my position on tardiness?"

"No, sir. I'm sorry. It won't happen again."

"Next time you're late, Mr. Hammond, do us all the favor of not coming in at all," the professor added.

Ben nodded, bending his head apologetically as he quickly took the seat next to Julia. Julia risked a look in his direction and could see him hiding a smile. Her eyes widened. Professor Kennan turned back to the blackboard and with an injured air resumed his lecture.

"Can I borrow a pencil?" Ben's hoarse whisper close to her ear startled her. She grabbed one and handed it to him without looking.

"Thanks," he whispered. Julia could feel his breath on her ear. She forced herself to wait a full minute before rubbing it vigorously.

She could hardly hear what Professor Kennan was saying, the noise of Ben's presence was so loud in her ears. She knew she was being ridiculous. She took a long breath and willed herself to calm down. She focused her eyes strictly on the blackboard and the long equations Kennan was reeling out. She began copying them to her notebook, writing quickly to catch up.

She was beginning to be more and more angry with herself for being so weak. When Kennan threw out a difficult question that they hadn't covered yet, the class was silent. Julia kept her eyes forward and raised her hand. She knew she would sound like a brownnoser, but she knew the answer and was going to give it. She answered correctly and gave a bit more background than the professor had asked for.

Kennan looked gratified. "Excellent."

She knew the other students would feel intimidated and resentful, but she didn't care. Why did she need their approval anyway? She answered two more questions before the end of class and still remembered to watch the clock so she was ready to stand up right as Kennan dismissed them.

She was edging out of the row of desks when Ben said, "Don't you want your pencil back?"

"Oh, yeah. Thanks." She reached out and took hold of the pencil, looking up in surprise when he didn't let go of his end.

"You're pretty hard to catch, you know, the way you come just on the dot of eight o'clock and then sprint out of here every day," he told her. "I had to be late just to find out where you would sit so I could get close enough to talk to you."

"You did that on purpose?" Julia was very conscious of the other students moving around them.

"Of course. Why not?" His eyes darted toward Kennan and he grinned. "Hey, do you have time to grab a donut or something at the student center?"

"Uh, yeah . . . I guess. My next class is at ten." Julia felt the blood rising in her face and tried to act natural. She felt an odd burning in her chest.

"Well, let's go." Ben gestured toward the door with his hand, and when she turned to go she felt the light pressure of his fingertips on her shoulder blade.

The student center was crowded with people getting a late breakfast. Julia felt intensely self-conscious with the tall blonde and tried to keep from staring up at him. She chose a bagel and cranberry juice and took her wallet out, but he insisted on paying. They found a small round table next to a wall and sat down.

Ben spread out his two glazed donuts, huge chocolate muffin, and carton of milk. He took a big bite out of the muffin and said, "I love these things. They're even fresh today. Want a bite?" He looked like he was teasing her. She looked up from her bagel with a suppressed smile.

"No, thanks."

"So how do you like chemistry?" he asked.

"I like it." She looked around the room wondering how much to reveal. She was feeling good, but it was always best to be careful.

"You should like it; you know all the answers!" He was smiling, but she still wondered if it bothered him.

"Sometimes. I'm glad if I can surprise Kennan. *You* sure did this morning. You're lucky he didn't throw you right out."

"I know, but I had to risk it." He stared her down, smiling, until she lowered her eyes.

"How are you doing in that class anyway?" he asked.

She fought the urge to tell a little white lie so he would be more comfortable. "Well, if you must know, I'm doing very well." Her voice sounded sassy and she was glad.

"How well?" he pressed.

"Excuse me, you're asking me for numbers?" She was amazed.

"How else am I going to know what the competition is like?"

Yes, that was it, she realized. He needed information. This was all related to competition in chemistry class, of course. *How dare he?* Her chest tightened, and it was hard to draw a new breath. She took another bite of bagel, chewing slowly.

"Well?" he prodded.

"Since you insist, and you've already paid for the information," she looked down at her plate significantly, "I'm at about 97 percent, and I wouldn't be that low if I hadn't forgotten the last problem on last week's quiz. I intend to be the highest in the class at the end of the semester." *What a boast!*

"Wow. I can't believe it." Ben brought his hand down heavy on the table. "I thought Kennan was impossible. Shows you what I know. I was pretty excited about my 87 percent average. I figured that was the best anyone could do. Bummer." He rubbed at his eyebrow and blinked.

"Well, I've really got to go now." Julia stood up and glanced at her half-eaten bagel. "Thanks for the snack."

"Running off again?" He looked amused and surprised at the same time.

"Well, you know me, 'the sprinter.' Can't stay still for long." Her face creased in a sarcastic smile. "See ya."

She was out of the student center before she had time to think. She saw him still sitting at their table through the window. She felt a tiny twinge of regret. Maybe she had been too hasty. He was so beautiful her heart ached. She was so embarrassed she wanted to die.

The strong muscles in her legs carried her swiftly away from him. She was furious, the anger carrying her farther and farther under the bare trees, her body responding strongly to the rhythm of her heart. She had to resist the urge to run. Would it ever be possible for her to know when somebody was sincere? Would she ever get over this ridiculous weakness that kept fooling her into thinking that a man would be seriously interested in her? Why did she want it so much? Where was her natural scorn of such a predictable emotion?

She knew she wasn't like other girls.

Her whole life, Julia had felt subtly isolated from her peers. It wasn't like she didn't have friends and relationships and that she couldn't be passably popular if that's what she wanted. It was just a feeling that she'd had as long as she could remember, that she was somehow different than others, invisibly separated from them in a way that couldn't be seen but was real just the same.

Usually, that distinction had made her feel special instead of isolated. She was sure it meant that she was somehow supposed to accomplish things that were beyond the scope of the average person's capability. She knew she cherished a shade of snobbery over this, but felt powerless to change the feeling. Sometimes she felt destined for a specific purpose, and this feeling drew her on and kept her from being crushed by setbacks like this.

She felt the old elation steal slowly through her body, lifting her past the anger and bitter humiliation, restoring her perspective and confidence in herself and the importance of her life.

She knew she was somewhat gifted, but she also knew she needed to hold to an incredible work ethic to move her past the average student. Grades were everything. If she didn't work hard and do well here, she might as well forget it. It was a race, a competition, and she couldn't afford to let her guard down and ease up on herself. Ben's question only affirmed the pressure—she was sure he could present quite a bit of competition if he wanted to, and there were others as well. There was always someone who knew more and had studied harder. She must strive to be that person.

Walking slower now, she thought of her future. She would make a difference in the world. Her work would be steady and precise; she would be respected in her field and then—she could see it—at the right moment something colossal would happen, maybe a huge discovery. It would be what she had been waiting for all her life. She could imagine her father's expression of amazement clearly, and her mother's quiet, affirming pride. She felt her strength of mind return and the shell of her resolve harden to a firm, dull sheen.

Chapter 7

Morgan sprawled comfortably in her favorite chair in her parents' living room, letting her long hair hang over the overstuffed arm. "This is wonderful. I could just lie here forever." She turned her eyes to her mother who was sitting back on the couch, leaning her head against the wall, her eyes half-closed.

"Why is it so quiet in here?" Morgan asked. "I can hardly stay awake."

"Oh, your brothers are giving me a break for once. They're emptying the neighbors' fridge this time, and Megan was so exhausted after school, dancing class, and running around the yard in her snowpants that she just collapsed. She's asleep on her bed." Her mother let her eyes close completely.

"Where's Janey? And Dad?"

"Janey's at piano lessons, and Dad went to the hardware store to buy some more screws to beef up the wooden structure of June Sanders's chair."

"She's having it done again?" Morgan asked.

"Yes, can you believe it? Blue pinstripe this time. I swear they have redecorated that house three times in the last five years. I guess that's what comes of having money." Morgan's mother drew in a deep breath and exhaled loudly, pushing a hand through her long, permed hair. She wiped the middle fingers of both hands underneath her eyes and then rubbed them along each eyebrow.

"What a day!" her mother burst out. "Cheerios and milk all over the kitchen this morning. A missing shoe made us ten minutes late for the first grade. I tried that new roll recipe and left it rising while I went to pick up Megan from school, after which I decided to do a little quick shopping, and then I ran into everyone at the store and had to talk, and by the time I got home the dough was so huge that it fell flat, but I baked it anyway and it turned into these hard little disks that the dog won't even eat. Then I remembered that I'd promised to take dinner to the Clarks tonight because Phyllis just had her fifth baby. I just now finished making them that hamburger casserole that you guys don't like, but I don't really care because I know that you are all intolerably picky, and it really tastes all right. Want to come with me to deliver the dinner in twenty minutes?"

Morgan looked at her mother and smiled. "Sure. You never change, you know." Her mother smiled back and swung her long legs up onto the couch to lie down. She lifted the tangled mass of hair off her neck and spread it out on the couch pillow. Morgan could see a smear of something along her cheekbone and the signs of meal preparation on the inside-out sweatshirt. She eyed her mother's still-flat stomach in the fitted jeans.

"Oh, and I forgot!" Her mother spoke again. "I repainted that wall in the basement that your brothers kicked a hole in. Fighting again, you know. I can't seem to get through to them." She heaved another tremendous sigh. "How's Aaron?" she finally asked.

"Are you sure you're going to let me talk?"

"Yes." Eyes still closed, her mother gave a rueful smile. "Go on, you minx."

"He seems to be doing pretty good. He's had a few companion problems lately. He kind of got in a fight a couple weeks ago."

"Really?" Morgan's mother leaned up on her elbow. "That doesn't sound like Aaron at all. He was so calm as a basketball player, even when the ref ruled against him. He didn't freak out like some of the players. Ross got benched last Friday for talking back to the ref. He's got such a hot head! But Coach Reese always forgives him pretty quick because he needs him so badly. Your brother is getting to be a crack shot, you know. You really need to tear yourself away some weekends and come and watch—"

"Mom!"

"Well, okay, but you should. We'd all like to see you more. Anyway, about Aaron."

Morgan continued. "I guess this companion of Aaron's has been really terrible, and Aaron had finally had it. And then somehow Aaron ended up running into a steel restaurant door and was knocked out cold and his companion couldn't find him and he got lost and everything. It was a pretty crazy story."

"Wow."

"I know, it seems weird, huh? But I guess they got it all patched up and things are a lot better between them now. It sounds like the mission life isn't always spiritual highs and baptisms though."

"Of course not. It's really hard out there. Even for someone as great as Aaron. I hope things start to turn around for him, you know, that he has a little success."

"I know." Morgan knew her mother was genuinely concerned for Aaron. She'd always liked him.

"How often do you write?"

"Once a week."

"Maybe you shouldn't write so often. It's pretty distracting, you know. He's supposed to have his mind on his work, not what's going on with you. You don't want to make it harder on him than it already is."

"Mom! I have to write to him. What else can I do? It is the only way we stay connected at all. I already feel like I don't know him anymore, and I'm getting really confused about our relationship. If I don't write, I feel so strange . . . like I'm floating with nothing definite to hold me down. I feel like I don't know where I'm going." Morgan suddenly sat up, leaned her elbows on her knees, and supported her head with her hands.

"Okay, but maybe just once a month, if you can handle it." Her mother sat up too. "This is a time for him to really gain the strength he needs for the rest of his life. He's such a great kid, and I know he's got a strong testimony, but he needs these experiences. These two years are a great opportunity for Aaron; he can really focus on the Lord and the Lord's work." Morgan's mother got up and dusted off her faded jeans.

"Mom, I'm not trying to hold him back. And I try not to be too personal in my letters. I've never been a whiner; you know that. I just miss him. He's the only constant thing in my life right now besides you guys."

"And I guess that means you still haven't decided on a major?" her mother asked.

"No, I haven't. I like so many things, but I'm just not sure what I'll be really good at and what I can stand studying for very long. I've thought about nursing or early childhood education, but I'm just not sure. I don't do that well in math and science, and I think nursing would have a lot of chemistry and stuff. You know I had to transfer out of Human Physiology last term."

"You should have stayed in. You could have stuck it out."

"Mom! I was flunking. I just couldn't do it," Morgan said, feeling the shame of it again.

"Julia would have helped you, you know."

"I know, and that's part of the problem."

"What problem?" Her mother disappeared into the kitchen, looking over her shoulder. "Just a minute, I have to check the casserole."

Morgan followed her to the kitchen. "Almost ready?" she asked, picking off a crusty piece of cheese from the top of the casserole and eating it.

"Hey, quit that. I'll just get the cream pie, if you'll put some plastic wrap over that salad. Anyway, what's the problem with Julia?"

Morgan sighed. "I just feel kind of inferior sometimes. She is so sure of what she wants and how she's going to get there. And Mom, she's so smart. I think she was really holding back in high school. In the few classes I've had with her, I can't believe what she knows and how well she does. I hate her knowing how dense I am." Morgan concentrated on stretching a sheet of plastic wrap as tight as she could over the glass salad bowl.

"You aren't dense, Morgan. In fact, I know you, and you're really talented. You've got a lot of things going for you. Look how you helped me with that order last week. I was so tired I just couldn't think, and you figured out the amount of fabric for that love seat so quickly. And it fit perfectly. I only had half a yard to spare, and it's a good thing not to have to waste fabric that expensive. You should see the love seat now. It's gorgeous. And your suggestion to add that contrasting braid was just what the piece needed. Sally Order is going to love it. You could do just as well in school; you are creative and bright. You just don't try like you should." Her mother thrust her arms into an old sweater and tied the belt. She tried to comb the tangles from her hair with her fingers and rubbed under her eyes again.

"I do try, Mom, but sometimes it is just so hard to concentrate." Morgan stacked the cream pie on top of the salad bowl and followed her mom through the kitchen door into the garage. She got into the car, and her mother handed her the pie and the casserole.

"I want you to do your best, Morgan, that's all," her mother said, as she reached around and fastened her seat belt. "You have so much potential, such an energetic spirit. You can do anything you want to do. The world is so wide; there is so much opportunity."

"Yeah, and you seem to try it all out," Morgan replied, balancing the cream pie and the salad on her lap and holding the hot casserole on the floor between her feet. She glanced at her mother behind the wheel and grinned.

"I just can't help it!" her mother agreed, backing out of the driveway.

* * *

Julia dug her shoulder down into her own soft bed at home and turned her back to the sunlight streaming through the crack in the closed curtains. Sleeping in was so wonderful. She couldn't imagine anything better. Okay, fifteen more minutes, then she'd get up.

A loud squeal came from downstairs followed by the mollifying tones of Julia's sister-in-law, Jenny. Someone heavy thudded up the stairs and in a few minutes clattered back down them. She could hear her dad laughing and her mother talking about sleep deprivation. After another five minutes Julia gave in to her guilt and swung her feet out of bed and onto the cold floor. A small pain rushed to her head, probably due, she thought, to the unaccustomed extra sleep. *Lazy*, Julia thought as she pulled all her hair off her face and shook it to the back of her head.

Julia was smiling when she entered the kitchen twenty minutes later with her wet hair up in a towel. She loved being home.

"Hey, look who's finally up!" Julia's brother Michael raised his eyebrows and pulled out the chair next to him at the kitchen table.

Michael, his wife, Jenny, and their two little boys were visiting from Salt Lake for the weekend. Michael looked like he was talking stocks with their dad, while Jenny ran around making sure the baby didn't get into anything. Julia's mother was at the sink just finishing the dishes.

"Well, it's not my fault that your kids wake you up at six, even on a Saturday," Julia teased her brother. "You're just jealous."

"I am! I was hoping that you'd take mercy on your poor brother and watch these kids for just one Saturday morning so Jen and I could actually get some sleep."

Julia rolled her eyes.

"Honey—do you want some pancakes?" Julia's mother pointed at the pancake griddle and reached for the mix.

"No, it's okay, Mom, you don't have to fix more just for me. I'll eat yogurt and granola or something."

"Oh, it won't take long, and I haven't even washed the griddle yet. Get yourself a plate and some silverware. There's orange juice in the fridge."

Julia dutifully got out the juice and poured herself a glass. Her poor mother. She loved it so much when everyone was home. It was kind of sad really, how hard she tried. Julia felt only a little guilty, though, when she went into the laundry room and saw her own load of whites already carefully folded on top of the dryer with both the washer and dryer working on her other clothes.

Well, she'd wash her own dishes and maybe sweep the floor.

"Julia, hey, come and sit down," her brother said.

Julia sat next to Michael, and a few minutes later her mother put a plate of slightly burnt pancakes down in front of her.

"So," Michael said, "how's Hale? How's it going? Don't you have Kennan this semester?"

"Yeah."

"Does he scare you a little?" asked Michael.

"No! Did he scare you?"

"Only when he handed out a test. Man, was he murder! But he was great on weekends. You know that mountain-biking class I took that he was in? Boy, he led the pack. And I thought I was so macho and in shape."

"So," her father began, "how are your classes going?"

"Okay, Dad, as long as I study all the time. Actually, so far, I'm doing pretty well."

"What did you think, Dad," Michael interrupted, "that our Girl Wonder would be drowning in the pressure? She's too obnoxious to be afraid of all those teachers over there." Michael reached over, grabbed her hand, and dipped it in the syrup left on her plate.

"Hey! Come on!" Julia immediately jumped out of her chair and tried to land a sticky finger on Michael's face. But Michael did have big biceps and the natural bulk of their father so she didn't have a chance and eventually ended by rinsing her hand in the sink.

"So, what do you guys want to do this morning? Anybody up for a game of racquetball?" Julia's dad already had his racket and gym bag by the door.

"Sounds good. Hopefully I can work off a few of those pancakes." Michael started bounding up and down, pulled his wife's hair as he went by her, and then took the stairs two at a time.

* * *

"So—are you going to beat your old dad today?" Julia's dad looked at her across the cab of the big new truck he'd bought last year to pull the snowmobile trailer.

"I doubt it," she replied, "but I was hoping to embarrass Michael. Sometimes I can catch him off guard, and boy does he hate it."

"I know." Her father smiled widely through the windshield.

"Hey Dad?"

"Yeah?"

"I've been putting together my applications for BYU and the U for scholarships and everything, and I have been kind of worried. I mean, don't you think I should have gone up there in the first place?"

"No." He shook his head firmly. "I think it was the right choice to go to Hale first. The guys over at Hale are the best. I've known most of them for years. Hale has professors with PhDs teaching the lower-division classes. Ask Michael what you get at bigger universities your first two years. A lot of TAs. Kids that just earned their own degrees."

"Okay, I know, I know, I was just feeling kind of insecure I guess. I want to do the right thing, have the right preparation." Julia had always felt a little worried about going to a rural high school. It seemed like kids up north had money behind them and all the advantages. She'd been more intimidated than she wanted to admit when she had faced some of those kids at educational events, but she did have to admit she'd never suffered in comparison.

"Do you know which field you are going into yet?" her father asked.

"Not really, but I'm really leaning toward chemistry. I have also thought a lot about pre-med, but I'm not sure I want to do that yet."

"What about dentistry?" He was trying to sound casual, but Julia knew he would love her to follow after him.

"Dad . . ."

"Well?"

"You're not satisfied with Nathan out there killing himself in that dental school in Oklahoma?"

"I think your brother's doing great, but there's no reason you shouldn't too."

"I don't know, Dad. Dentistry? I mean, it seems so customer-service oriented. You have to smile and be nice and make conversation." They pulled into the parking lot at the gym, and Julia unfastened her seat belt.

"That's what I like about it."

"I know, Dad, but I'm not like you. I did think about dental research." Julia reached for the door handle, but her dad didn't seem in much of a hurry.

"Research is so solitary, Julia. Don't you want to be around people?"

"Yes, but I don't want to sacrifice my career to them."

There was a pause and her father reached down to pull his bag from under the seat. He looked up expectantly. "Have you met any new people this quarter?"

She hit her head against the back window. "You mean have I been dating anyone?"

"Well, have you?" he persisted.

"No, Dad, how can I? I have to study all the time! You know that. I can't waste time anymore; this is my proving ground, and after I get these transfer scholarships and go up north, I *really* won't have any time. Why do you care so much?" She should have known it was coming and been more prepared. But it hurt, knowing he was so concerned and worried about her. Couldn't he be happy with her successes instead of worrying so much about her failures?

"I just want you to be happy, Julia. And no career, no matter how stimulating, can replace real people around you that you care about. It's the real part of living . . ." He paused as they watched Michael and Jen pull into the parking spot next to them. "Sometimes I think I've been too hard on you growing up, expected too much, pushed you too hard. You need to take some time out and have some fun right now, when you're young and you don't have so many responsibilities."

"What do you mean no responsibilities? Right now I feel like I have as much as I can handle." Maybe he thought she wasn't trying. And well, maybe she wasn't. It would be humiliating to try and fail anyway. It was much better to concentrate on the things she knew, the things she could control.

"Let's go and help Jen get the kids out of their car seats," she suggested. "And dad, I know you're just trying to help me. And well," she said, as she opened the door and walked around the truck to his side, "I do appreciate it."

Chapter 8

Julia saw the rose immediately when she stepped into chemistry class. The deep velvet red contrasted sharply with the white formica of the desktop. She froze at the door, oblivious to other students stacking up behind her. The rose was lying across the long table at the spot where she usually sat, and Ben was sitting in the next seat over. She could see a little white note attached to the rose with a white ribbon, and she felt her heart begin to pound. Was it meant for her? Should she sit in that seat? If it was for someone else, picking it up would humiliate her beyond everything.

She hovered at the end of the row of seats, her fingertips grazing the end of the desktop. She could feel the stares of the other students on her back and hear interested whispers and a long sigh coming from two girls a few rows back. Professor Kennan came into the room and closed the door, and she began to panic. Class was about to start. She finally entered the row of seats and slowly began making her way toward Ben. She was about to sit in the seat just next to the rose when Ben looked up at her with a sly grin on his face and tilted his head at the rose. Her heart lurched.

She quickly sat down behind the rose and busied herself with her backpack and notebook, but when she finally looked up she had to deal with the flower. She tentatively touched the stem and stroked her thumb over one of the thorns. She didn't dare look at Ben as she carefully moved it to the side and slid her notebook in its place.

When Professor Kennan began lecturing she took up her pen, but she couldn't concentrate. She glanced at the black letters on the stiff card:

Forgive me?
Happy Valentines Day!
Love, Ben

She felt her breath coming hot and hard and turned her head to find herself looking directly into Ben's smiling eyes. "Thanks," she whispered softly, stretching her finger to lightly touch a soft petal on the tight bud. He just smiled and placed a large hand on her shoulder, letting it rest there a minute before he took up his pencil again and turned to his notes.

Julia didn't hear much of the lecture. When it was over they packed up and she found she didn't know what to do with the flower. She passed it from hand to hand while she waited for Ben and then asked bluntly, "So, why are you asking for forgiveness?" It came out pretty matter-of-fact, and Julia wished her voice hadn't sounded so flat.

"Well," he explained, "somehow I seem to have offended you that day when we went out for breakfast. I didn't mean to bug you about your grades so much. I know it was low-class and I'm sorry. I guess it's almost as stupid as asking someone how much money they make . . . So, will you?"

"Will I what?" She was confused.

"Will you forgive me? I want you to like me again."

"Again? Who said I liked you in the first place?" She let her face relax into a sassy grin and dared to slap at his shoulder. "I guess I'll survive, but watch out, Ben Hammond, I'm not going to let up in this class, so you'd better just burn the midnight oil."

"Oh, I will, I will!" His hands went up in a mock fending-off motion. She turned to go and then turned back toward him.

"Hey, thanks," Julia said. "I love it." She held up the stem and brought it to her nose.

Ben reached out and yanked her hair, smiling. "No problem."

When they turned to go, Julia realized they were the last ones left in the room.

* * *

This February 14 was strangely mild. The watery sun filtering down through the leafless branches warmed Julia's face as she walked along this late afternoon, still holding the long-stemmed rose. She'd known that it would become limp and too warm, needing water, and though she could have taken a quick trip to her dorm room between classes, she hadn't been able to part with it. She smiled again; she still couldn't believe it, though it had been several hours. Ben liked her—he had to, didn't he? What other reason would there be for giving a girl a flower on Valentine's Day? She guessed maybe he could just be a really polite guy that had been well trained by his mother. But no. It had felt too good looking up into his eyes. She still felt a little light-headed.

When she walked through the open door of her dorm room she was overcome by the scent of flowers, and she saw that there were no less than four vases full of gorgeous, expensive-looking blooms, mostly red roses.

"Hey—what's up?" Julia called back through the apartment, but received only silence in answer. She leaned down to sniff some exquisite pink roses, fresh and cool and soft. She looked at her own drooping stem and went to the cupboard to look for a vase. Apparently, Morgan's flowers had exhausted the roommates' supply of containers, so she grabbed the Kerr jar that she had brought from home with her mother's homemade strawberry jam in it and filled it with water. She took the single rose into her bedroom and put it on top of the mini-television her dad had bought her. The February sun streamed in from the window through the jar and the water and made a pretty refraction on the wall above her bed. She lay down and looked at it.

She could hear the sound of laughter and excitement from across the hall and was sure that Morgan was over there, chatting with the neighbors, but she didn't feel like seeking her out this instant. It was wonderful, this moment, lying by herself on her bed, staring at a small rainbow reflection that came from the Kerr jar holding the flower Ben had given her. Her heart began to pound even now, and for a small minute, she closed her eyes and allowed herself to hope.

"Julia! You're finally home." Morgan bounded through the door and bounced onto the bed beside Julia. She seemed in a terrific mood.

"I don't suppose you happened to notice all these flowers?"

"Where'd you get them?" Julia knew Morgan wouldn't give up until she could give her an itemized list.

"Do you have a minute?" she giggled.

Julia rolled her eyes.

"You know those perfect pink roses? Aaron had his mother send those up from Halston Floral. Aren't they gorgeous!" She sighed and fell back onto the pillows.

"They're beautiful. Who are the others from?"

"Well, David, of course—the red roses. And Sammy sent me the red and white carnations, the silly thing, and then this guy I barely know who's in my institute class waited for me afterwards and then ran to his car and came back with more red roses and those pretty purple things and the baby's breath. I was actually pretty embarrassed because I had to think really hard to remember his name, but I guess we talk a lot in class, and he's walked me home a couple of times."

Julia could too readily imagine it. She tried not to let a shadow fall across her mood.

"Anyway, don't you think the flowers look great in here? It kind of makes up for the boring white walls, and they smell heavenly!" Morgan swirled around the room and then went to the window to let the sun shine on her upturned face.

She looked like a model, Julia thought, blonde hair falling down her gracefully arched back, the sunlight turning her eyelashes to gold. The pose went unbroken for a minute and then she looked down.

"Hey, what's this?" Morgan lifted the drooping head of Julia's rose with her index finger and turned wide-eyed to Julia.

"I believe it's a flower—a red rose to be exact," Julia said.

"Yes, but is it yours?"

Julia smirked. "Don't act so amazed. A guy from my chemistry class handed it to me. It was kind of a peace offering because he thought he'd offended me." She tried to keep her voice casual but a heavy warmth began to spread through her chest again just talking about it. She didn't want to say too much.

"What's his name?"

"Ben Hammond," Julia replied.

"You mean that tall blonde guy that said 'hi' to you in the student center yesterday?" Morgan said, sitting on her own bunk but leaning across the space between them. "Maybe he likes you."

Julia could swear that Morgan sounded slightly disappointed.

"Not much of a rose though."

"It used to be," Julia said with the hint of a smile. "Maybe it will perk up in the water.

Chapter 9

"Hey, scoot over, you guys, you're squishing me!" Morgan protested and got an elbow in her ribs and a friendly slap for her pains. She dug her fork into the crispy corner of the pan of warm brownies that Cynthia had laid on the carpet of their living room floor. She always brought a mix home from the grocery store even though she worried constantly about her figure.

"Delicious, Cynthia!" Julia smacked her lips in exaggeration and returned her fork to the pan again. "You get better at this every time!"

Morgan blew on the bit of brownie on her fork and chewed it slowly, smiling and half closing her eyes. "Oh, yeah! Just what I needed today!" She looked at the five roommates, crowded around the warm pan of brownies, brandishing their cheap, dented forks. Even Lorraine kept pace, devouring her share steadily, forgetting her shyness for once.

"Hey—" Cynthia said, through a mouthful of brownie. "I heard this great joke . . ."

Soon everyone was lying back on the floor laughing crazily, letting the stress flow out in absurd comments and hiccupping laughs.

Morgan sat up and the blood rushed to her head and she wiped the corners of her eyes as she tried to calm down. Cynthia and Heather were getting sillier and sillier and she wondered if one or both would throw up, they were laughing so hard.

Morgan quickly turned away to look at Julia who was lunging to her feet.

She patted her belly and groaned. "Oh, why did I do that! I know I'll gain five pounds! You guys made me do it! I guess I'd better jog around the dorm. Anyone want to come?" Cynthia and Heather instantly stood up and started jumping up and down.

"Let's race, okay?" Heather crouched down into a runner's starting position, letting her red curls fall over her head as she looked up at them upside down.

"Good idea," said Cynthia, crouching down next to Heather and leaning against her till she lost her balance and rolled over.

"Okay, good. But let's go into the hall to start."

When Morgan realized that Lorraine was still in the room, she stuck her head back through the door. "You coming?"

"No, you guys just go. I'll time you and be the judge."

"Well, okay. Get your watch ready." Morgan crouched down outside in the hall shoulder to shoulder with the others, infected by their mood and high spirits.

"On your mark, get set, go!"

Morgan leaped from her crouch and sped down the hall, pushing against the others until they came to the lounge. Julia moved out in front, laughing hard as she hurdled a low chair and then an end table. Morgan opened up her stride, trying to catch her, and nearly collided with a guy coming from one of the rooms as she entered the next hall. He grabbed her and held her there while Heather and then Cynthia ran past, and then gave her a good push as she started, almost causing her to fall. She shouted something back at him as she strained to catch up, willing her bare feet to fly across the rough carpet, feeling her hair stream out behind her. She passed Heather and Cynthia, fighting on the stairs, which she took three at a time till she gained the second floor. She flashed down the hall, streaming past open doors, music, voices, and she reached the second floor lounge just in time to see Julia disappear down the far hallway.

"Hey, wait! I'm still going to beat you!" Morgan called. She'd just gained the second stairwell, panting hard, ready to leap down, when Julia burst out from her flattened place against the wall. Morgan screamed so loud that she was afraid the dorm parents would come up.

"I can't believe you did that!"

"Shhh-shhh." Julia was laughing so hard tears came to her eyes. She was bending over and holding her side. Morgan smiled and took the opportunity to slip past Julia and streak down the stairs and around the landing where she entered the home stretch. She could hear Julia pounding behind her and screamed again as she felt Julia's outstretched fingers graze her back. She fell through the door and onto the couch beside Lorraine just ahead of Julia, who was still laughing between gasping breaths. Cynthia and Heather arrived together a moment later, still slapping at each other and complaining.

"I won, you snails, even though Julia nearly scared me to death." Morgan reached over to Julia to poke her in the arm with a long, strong finger.

"It was worth losing just to see you jump and scream, though I was afraid the police would show up." Julia leaned against a bank of cupboards and slid down to a sitting position. Everyone was panting hard, and as Morgan surveyed her friends, she smiled, satisfied.

"Who has enough money left to go out to eat tonight? No, Julia, I wasn't asking you. We all know you're loaded." Morgan kicked at Julia a little and listened as the other girls moaned a little over their tiny sums, but they decided to go out anyway and get salads and desserts at a little place up in the hills just out of town. Julia would spring them if they overdid it a little. Morgan knew she only had four dollar bills in her purse and a few coins that might possibly make it add up to five dollars if she was lucky. She didn't dare write another check out of her account. Her parents would have a fit. She was going home in the morning and her parents would give her cash for the next month, so it didn't matter if she spent it all. She smiled gaily and looked Julia squarely in the eye.

"I can be ready in twenty minutes."

* * *

Later that night Morgan lounged on her bed watching Julia hang up her clothes and straighten her desk.

"You don't have a date tonight?" Julia said, eyebrows raised.

"Naw. I didn't feel like it. Sammy wanted me to go to a party with him, not a real date or anything, just as a friend, but the party didn't sound that great. David went home for the weekend." It actually felt good to not have to go anywhere for a change. Morgan sighed and propped her head up on her hand.

"How's it going with him, anyway?" Julia said.

"It's good. I like him." Morgan paused for a minute and then decided to tell her. "He . . . kissed me."

Julia stood up from her crouched position where she'd been lining up her shoes. "Really." Her eyebrows stretched onto her forehead.

"What do you think?" Morgan sat up on the bed and drew her knees up under her chin.

"I don't know; did you want him to?"

"Not exactly," Morgan said. "I was trying to keep it light, you know, not too serious, but I never seem to be able to do that. If I go out with a guy more than a few times, we always seem to arrive at this point. And it's way too early, at least for me."

"Of course I don't know anything about this." Julia bent again in the closet and came out with a stray sock, which she deposited neatly into a small hamper. "But it seems the rules are all changing this year. Everyone is getting serious. It's crazy."

"I know. It's too soon. I mean, I might even think that if it were Aaron."

Julia threw her an amazed look.

"Okay, probably not. I don't know, I guess we are just growing up, getting into the big league. It's kind of scary."

There was a long pause while Julia took out hanging clothes and organized them according to size and type. Morgan was feeling strange tonight. Real life seemed like something other people did, not her. She didn't want to feel pinned down. She didn't want to decide something now that might last the rest of her life. "It's just too hard. How do I know, right now, what I'm going to want for the rest of my life? My parents are really bugging me about coming up with a major. What if I get a degree in something and then decide that it is totally *not* what I want to do? I mean, at this point, I'm not sure I want to do anything." Morgan stretched her arms up over her head and extended her legs until her feet reached across to the middle of Julia's bed.

"I don't know what you're so worried about. You know you're going to get married, probably some time next year if you wait for Aaron, maybe sooner if you don't. And then you'll have kids pretty quick, I bet. You'll be like your mother, going ninety directions at once and just managing to make everything turn out spectacular."

"Maybe. But even if I do end up like that, how do I get there? I really think that Aaron is the right guy, but David is a really awesome too. And he puts a lot of pressure on me. Is there a possibility that I shouldn't wait for Aaron?"

Julia closed the closet and moved Morgan's feet off her bed so she could sit down. "Hey—I'm not going to get into that, 'cause if I told you what to do and it didn't work out, you'd blame me, right?" She smiled and stretched her legs out onto the bed and then bent to touch her toes. "But even though you and Aaron were pretty tight before he left, well, things change, and you've got to do what you think is best for you. I mean, how do you know that he'll feel the same way about you when he gets home or will even be the same person?"

Morgan felt a sharp constriction in her chest. "What? He'd better. He couldn't dump me, not after all this time." She had never considered that Aaron might not want her after his mission. Always before she'd thought it was up to her, her choice if she wanted him or not. No, there was really no way he could dump her. Julia always went to extremes.

"Well, probably not," Julia admitted. "He'll come home and propose, and then you'll have a gorgeous wedding and live happily ever after."

"What about you?"

"What about me?"

"When are you going to live happily ever after?" Morgan replied.

"Oh, I'll do okay. I'm hoping that in about ten years some weird divorced guy with a couple of kids will think I look pretty good compared to nothing."

"Eeww. That's horrible." Morgan pushed her hair behind her ears. "Come on. You'll find somebody, probably sooner than I do." Morgan smiled and felt good for this little bit of charity.

"What if I did? What if we both did? We'd be these old married matrons."

"Yeah," said Morgan, "and then we'd have kids."

"Are you seriously going to name one of yours Salinda, you know, like you said when you were thirteen?" Julia's face broke into a smile.

"What's so bad about Salinda? It's okay." Morgan grinned. "Oh, let's think, what did you want to name yours?" Morgan assumed a pose, tapping her forefinger against her temple. "Josephine Hildegarde the Third."

"Oh, hush." Julia threw a pillow at her. "I never said 'Hildegarde.'" To Morgan's amazement, Julia blushed. "It was Josephina Catharine Rose, I believe."

They both started laughing.

Morgan looked around the small room, dimly lit by one small lamp. The red numbers on Julia's alarm clock said 1:05 A.M. She loved it when they talked like this.

"I can just see you with a little dark-headed Josephina dressed in a lab coat and protective goggles following right behind you," Morgan joked.

"Well, your little Salinda would probably be a child actor or a model or something. But not if you name her Salinda!"

They both broke out laughing again but then fell silent. Morgan thought for a moment. "Do you remember when we were ten years old and our moms finally let us ride our bikes down to the store?"

"You mean when my pant leg got caught in the bike chain?" Julia fell back onto the bed. "That was so embarrassing!"

"I know. And then you got the bright idea to stop at that gas station and ask the mechanic to help you . . ." Morgan said.

"Yeah, and he said I should step out of my pants so he could get the leg out of the chain. And you got all mad and defensive and told him 'no way,' and you called my mom. Boy, was I glad to see her."

"Me too. I was tired of holding up my end of a scary situation."

"You were so great . . . defending me." Julia pressed her palms into her eye sockets. "I was too embarrassed to say anything. And I couldn't move 'cause my leg was nearly tied to the bike."

Morgan stared at the lamp until she could see stars on the insides of her eyelids. "Well, we got through it. And things turned out okay. Maybe we'll get through all of this too."

"Who knows?" Julia said.

Chapter 10

This felt good. Aaron closed his eyes briefly. *Thank you, Father.* He smoothed back the hair above his ear as he stood with Elder Facer behind the empty chair. Marco walked in quickly and took Aaron's hand in an excited grip; then he turned and sat in the chair before them, head bowed. Marco's hair was cold and damp as Aaron and Elder Facer placed their hands on his head. Elder Facer confirmed him, giving him the gift of the Holy Ghost and pouring out a beautiful blessing upon his head. Aaron was awed at the Spirit in the room. He knew Elder Facer wasn't that eloquent on his own. When Aaron looked up, he saw the few members of the branch wiping their eyes. He felt a lump in his own throat, and his vision blurred slightly. He cleared his throat twice and coughed loudly.

Marco was radiant. He was smiling so big, Aaron wondered if his cheeks would be sore tomorrow. They shook hands again, and then the members began to press forward to congratulate him. Aaron put a hand on Elder Facer's shoulder and said without looking, "Well, big guy, what do you think about that?"

"Amazing." It came out in a croak, and Aaron was surprised to see Elder Facer's cheeks slowly dripping with tears. He wiped a large palm over his face and then stood, blinking rapidly, beaming out at the group. "The Spirit is so strong it can even use me as a mouthpiece. Man, we're lucky," Elder Facer said and then had to wipe his face again.

Since Aaron never really understood what passed between Elder Facer and Marco Pennini in the famous conversation by the door, Aaron had really felt out of it when they began teaching Marco the next week. But Marco eagerly invited them back, seeming to delight in their company. He was only eighteen years old, and Aaron had been skeptical about Elder Facer's enthusiasm toward him. Aaron had seen young men attach themselves to missionaries before, but most of them just wanted friendship and had a strong desire to be associated with anything American. It was hard for these young men to change their habits, or to even see the necessity of it.

That was where the only challenge to Marco's baptism had come. Though he'd given up his cigarettes cold turkey when they taught the Word of Wisdom lesson, and even parted with his wine after a few weeks, the lesson on chastity troubled him. They challenged him to read the whole Book of Mormon and live the gospel with all its principles, including the law of chastity, and then asked him to come to them and report whether the Lord had changed his heart.

They were afraid that he would flatly refuse to try this, but to their surprise, he accepted their challenge. They figured it would take him a month or maybe two to read the whole book if he really applied himself, and they were worried that he would just drop the whole thing without even letting them know. Elder Facer had just decided to call and check on his progress ten days later, when Marco met them outside their apartment one morning as they were just leaving.

They couldn't believe it. He'd read the whole Book of Mormon already. He said he knew it was true and that the Lord had given him an incredible experience as he obeyed and read His words. His eyes were intense and sparkling. Elder Facer asked him about his major hurdle.

"You were right, you guys, the Lord did help me—but it wasn't easy. I decided to end my relationship with Maria because if I continued to see her I knew I would slip," Marco told them. "After that, I felt so good! I can't describe it! Like my heart was burning or on fire. I knew I'd done the right thing. And man, the Book of Mormon is incredible! Such power in its pages. That section on Jesus Christ visiting the Lamanites and the Nephites—I was so surprised! I guess I'd forgotten you told me that Jesus visited America. I cried the whole way through that part. It was as if He was speaking to me, and I seemed to remember Him. It all seemed familiar. I know that your Church is true." He looked down and kicked at a discarded paper cup in the gutter. "Do you think I could be baptized, even though I have had so many problems?"

Elder Facer was smiling big. "Hey, you just let us help you fix things up, buddy!" Then he shook Marco's hand, pumping his arm up and down.

"Hey, watch it! We want him to live long enough to get baptized, don't we?" Aaron had never felt so good. The Spirit was coursing through him like liquid fire, and he knew: this was the reason he'd come on a mission.

It was a half hour after Marco left that morning before Aaron realized that Elder Facer hadn't had to translate at all for him. He'd understood Marco perfectly, even in the rapid language of his emotion. Aaron felt little bumps rise on his skin all over and paused for a minute to offer a prayer of gratitude and blink the tears back. He felt that Heavenly Father knew of him personally and understood his struggles with the language. It was a miracle in every respect. He'd been able to understand Italian speakers and do a much better job of speaking himself ever since.

Elder Facer nudged him out of his thoughts, and they both moved forward to talk to the members milling around Marco. If every day of his mission could be like today, Aaron thought, he would serve for another ten years.

Chapter 11

Julia certainly would have worn different shoes if she'd known it would snow today. The flats that she put on with her long plaid skirt had seemed like a good idea this morning—in mid-March they'd been having some pretty nice weather—but she now stood in six inches of fluffy snow. Her feet were soaked, and it was still coming down. She couldn't afford the time to go back to her room to change. She had a literature exam in an hour and still wasn't quite confident about the material. Julia's wet feet slid around in her shoes as she walked, but she lowered her head against the chilly wind and tried to get some traction on the flat soles as she made her way up the hill to the library.

Suddenly she stepped on an icy spot and her foot slipped off the sidewalk into the deeper snow on the grass. She nearly fell, and as she was standing there, arms extended, teetering foolishly, she could see Ben Hammond, coming toward her from the top of the hill. She had gained her balance by the time he reached her and was brushing the snow from her ankle. Ben was smiling widely.

"Need any help?" He grabbed her arm above the elbow.

"Not anymore. Boy, it would have been really embarrassing if I'd fallen into this mess. I'm not exactly dressed for skiing today."

"No, it doesn't really look like it." He glanced at her sodden feet.

"Thanks." The skin of her arm began to burn beneath the heavy layers of her sweater and jacket.

"Where are you going?" he asked, glancing up the hill.

"I'm just heading to the library to study for a test I have at three."

"Well, okay, have a good time studying." He released her arm, saluted her briefly, and watched her start uphill again.

Julia felt tensed up and nervous all the way to the library. She had a hard time focusing her attention on her book when she opened it at an empty table on the second floor. For a while, she kept looking up, checking out the other quiet students, glancing at an art display a few feet from her. She'd just been able to resign herself to studying and had begun scanning the first poem, checking her notes frequently, when someone sat down opposite her. She kept her head down at first, not wanting to seem rude to the newcomer, and when she finally looked up, she was looking right into Ben's eyes. She leaned back in surprise.

"Mind if I sit here?" he said politely.

"No, go ahead." Julia smiled a little self-consciously and tried to study the poem, wondering what Ben was doing at the library now, when just a few minutes ago he'd been headed in the opposite direction. She realized he might want to talk and looked up again, but he was already getting out his binder and searching for a pen. Julia forced her eyes to the poem again. Andrew Marvell. What had the teacher said about this one? She couldn't remember why she'd written this comment in the margin.

Across the table, Ben was writing in slow, even letters.

She looked through her notes, remembering something about it being a love poem, but she couldn't concentrate and found her eyes jumping to the opposite side of the table. He was still writing. The back of her neck prickled. Starting a paper maybe? This was ridiculous. How could she concentrate with him sitting there? Julia read through the poem again.

Had we but world enough, and time,
This coyness, lady, were no crime.

Ben stopped writing, opened up the rings of his binder, and removed the page. Julia kept reading.

We would sit down, and think which way
To walk and pass our long love's day.

Ben slid the paper across the table to Julia. She looked at him, feigning surprise, and took the paper, looking down at what he had written.

Will you go to the spring formal with me? I know it's early to ask, but the early bird gets the worm. Please indicate your answer below.

A broad arrow pointed down at a Yes and No, and beside each word was a box she could check. The box beside the Yes was a lot bigger than the one by the No. Julia paused a while longer, smiling, and then took her pen and quickly checked the Yes box. She then added the words:

Thanks for asking. I'd love to, though I'm not sure how much I like being referred to as a worm.

She smiled again as she slid it toward him. He took a moment to read her words and then wrote again:

April 10th. Pick you up about 6:30 and we'll go to dinner . . .

As she was reading this second message, Ben packed up his note-book and rose. He put his hand on her shoulder and said, "See ya, Julia. Hope you dry out later." Ben laughed and then walked away, leaving the note in her hands. She looked down at the poem again.

Now therefore, while the youthful hue
Sits on thy skin like morning dew . . .

She closed her eyes for a moment and thought she could see stars.

* * *

Morgan pushed both hands through her hair and winced as a hair caught and was jerked loose. She rubbed her head on the sore spot and sighed loudly, hoping to catch Julia's attention at the opposite desk in their dorm room, and then took up her pencil again. French was for the birds! *Vous, nous, voulez-vous*—it all seemed like nonsense to her now, though at first she'd been intrigued by learning a new language. She could hardly understand what Madame Paget said anymore when she was giving instructions to the class. There was a guy who always sat next to her, and she would lean over and whisper questions to him while Madame was writing on the board. For the midterm exam, Madame had threatened requiring a full five-paragraph essay on a subject to be determined—all of it in French! It made Morgan's stomach tighten up and her palms sweat just thinking of it; it was impossible that she could write something in French Madame could even understand, let alone with correct spelling, grammar, and sentence structure.

Morgan scratched at a chip of paint on the edge of her desk and looked out the window across the lawn. Two figures were walking hand in hand along the sidewalk. It looked like Sammy with that same redhead they'd seen him with at the dance concert. Morgan moved closer to the window and squinted her eyes. *Yes. Maybe she lives here in Bentwell. They look pretty chummy, smiling and laughing. Well. What do you know.* Morgan swallowed a lump in her throat and jerked her eyes away from the window.

Okay, again. She turned back to her French book. *Je voudrais faire une promenade dans le jardin. Yes, a walk in the park would be great right now,* she thought, *preferably a French park, perhaps near La Tour Eiffel.*

"Julia." Morgan scooted her chair back quickly, banging it into Julia's. "Let's walk downtown and get a drink and some fries or something. Can we?"

"Hey! You've only been sitting there for thirty-five minutes!"

"I know, but I have plenty of time, and besides, I'm getting it fine. I just need to do a little practice with my writing, *en Français*, and I'm all set." Morgan gave a confident smile that she didn't feel and reached for her wallet on the shelf above her desk. "Come on, Julia. You already know everything in that book. You're just enjoying yourself now. Quit being so selfish and come and spend a little time with your oldest friend and greatest admirer." She gave Julia a bewitching smile and began batting her eyelashes.

"Okay, let's go, but I'm coming because I'm thirsty, and you're right: I do know everything."

"Let me just run to the bathroom, and we'll be off." Morgan went to the mirror, grabbed a brush off the countertop where she'd left it, and drew it quickly through her hair a few times. She pulled a long stray strand from her sweater and dropped it onto the floor. She rubbed her face and scrubbed at the mascara smudges beneath her eyes. She was just reaching for her eye pencil when Julia stuck her head in the bathroom.

"Morrrgan, are you coming or what?"

"What the heck." Morgan gave her hair another pat. "What do I care how I look?"

* * *

"So, what time do you have the French midterm tomorrow?" Julia asked as they walked down the sidewalk.

"At ten, and then Intro to Theater at two. If I don't get an A on that one I'll know I really am an idiot."

"Pretty easy, huh?"

"Yes. You didn't take it?"

"No, I think the Honors Lit I took last fall covers that requirement. We did quite a few plays, mostly Greek though . . . you know, Oedipus and stuff."

Yeah, Morgan knew; Julia usually threw that honors bit in, grinding in her point. *Why does she always need to feel so superior?* Morgan looked toward her feet and didn't say anything.

Julia kept talking. "I've got a chemistry test at eight in the morning, and then I've got to turn in a paper for my lit class by two. The midterm is Friday. I'll be glad of the time in between to catch a few more hours of study. I have a harder time with the English classes. I guess my brain is just too analytical, and that field is so subjective. I'm worried about my paper. I nearly killed myself on the last one, but I only got an A minus. The teacher said I didn't say anything original or have any new ideas. What am I supposed to do? Reinvent these ancient essays and stories or come up with a new approach to analyzing them?" Julia looked disgusted, swinging her arms along boldly. "I have a hard time understanding the first level of meaning, let alone all the nuances the teacher wants me to find."

Morgan kicked at a small pebble on the sidewalk. *Yeah, an A minus is real rough. Hate to break it to you, Julia, but some of us would be pretty darn grateful for an A minus.* Morgan tried to keep her eyes from rolling upward as she walked along, listening to the tirade.

She began to lose the thread of the conversation as they passed the houses on the way to Main Street. A wave of irritation passed through her at the soggy newspapers, bits of garbage, and sun-faded broken-down toys littering the front yards. When she looked forward again she caught sight of some college guys way ahead of them and began focusing on them, trying to tell if she knew them.

". . . you know?" Julia asked.

"Yeah, sure," Morgan agreed absently. She thought one of the guys might be in her institute class, the one that sat back by the door. She squinted her eyes to focus better.

"Morgan, what did I just say?"

"You were talking about school and midterms and stuff."

"Wrong. I just confided in you, and you didn't even hear me. What, I'm not interesting enough anymore?"

"Sorry, what did you say? I was just watching those robins."

"I said, 'Guess who's got a date to the spring formal already?'"

"Who?" Even Morgan didn't have a date yet, though she knew of two guys that were thinking about asking her, not counting Dave.

"Me." Julia grinned.

"Really!" Now this was news. Most of the other dance dates Julia had had, especially in high school, had been engineered by Morgan, though she had been careful that Julia never knew.

"Who asked you?"

"Ben Hammond—this morning."

"Really?" Morgan said again. "Wow, Julia, he's so cute. How do you know him again?"

"He sits next to me in chemistry."

"Oh yeah. Pretty smart then too. Do you like him?" *Of course she does; what choice does she have?*

"He seems okay. It should be fun." Julia tucked a strand of dark hair behind her ear and looked up. "Amazing, isn't it? This is the first time I've ever had a date to a dance before you."

Morgan raised her eyebrows slightly. "Yeah, I'm excited for you. Maybe Dave and I will come with you guys if I decide to go with him."

"Well, Ben's got a group of friends, I think, and we'll probably go with them."

"Whatever," Morgan said lightly.

They walked into the Burger Barn on Main Street, and Morgan was glad for the warmth. She rubbed her slim arms and suppressed a shiver at the sudden change in temperature. She ordered a large fry with fry sauce and a fresh lime. She was starved, though it was only four. She ate most of the fries, unsuccessfully offering some to Julia, and Morgan held up her end of the conversation, but she couldn't quite banish the sense of dread that was hanging over her. What was she going to do tomorrow? She couldn't think.

* * *

Morgan blinked her eyes quickly to prevent the tears from spilling down her face and turned her head away from the other students as they passed her in the hall. Why had she even gone in there? She felt sick. The quick bowl of Cheerios she'd eaten for breakfast boiled in her stomach. She hadn't fully realized how much she didn't know until the crisp white paper of the test was confronting her, the directions all in clear, black *French* words.

And then she'd tried to pray, tried to find the words to call on that power that had helped her in her hardest times, but the spiritual feeling wouldn't come. She knew she hadn't done her part and couldn't ask the Lord for a miracle.

Morgan sniffed as quietly as she could, wiped her cheek, and swung her backpack up over her shoulder. She looked down the emptying hall and then back toward the open classroom door, feeling fresh tears threatening. Then, with effort, she straightened up and strode off down the hall.

* * *

It was the first time Julia had ever felt fragile in her life. Morgan had Julia perched up on black three-inch heels and had insisted on doing her hair up off her face in loosely pinned glossy curls with a few strands trailing down her bare neck. The effect was really not her, but she had to admit it was pretty. She was also triumphantly sporting the gorgeous green dress that she and Morgan had convinced her mother to buy without too much fuss.

Ben, lightly touching the small of her back or holding her hand to guide her through the dancing couples in Hale's dark old gym, gave her the kind of confidence she'd never had before. His brief touches were light and respectful and made her feel totally feminine. She smiled briefly and put a tentative hand up to touch a curl at the nape of her neck.

As they walked around the room, passing people he knew, Ben introduced her with a lift of his eyebrows, waiting for an appreciative nod from his friends, displaying her in the most blatant fashion, but she liked it. He was proud of her, of the way she *looked*, no less, and it was a heady feeling.

When they were dancing he kept his eyes on her, deep and intense. She was embarrassed by his staring and had to fight to keep from erupting in nervous laughs. She just didn't know how to deal with this. He was a great talker too, and when they sat in the chairs along the dance floor or at the refreshment tables, he listened intently over the heavy blare of the music and helped her to soften her bold edges and defensive tendency. She found herself letting out all kinds of things that she wasn't sure she wanted him to know.

Halfway through the last dance, Ben suggested they leave ahead of the crush of people. As they edged out of the crowded room, Julia brushed up against Morgan, and they briefly exchanged glances.

"Having fun?" Morgan's eyebrows were lifted and slightly amused.

"Yeah." It came out sincerely, and Julia smiled in surprise. It was the only time lately that her voice hadn't had a defensive edge to it when talking to Morgan. Julia gave a short wave as Ben tugged on her hand and led her through an opening in the crowd. Then they were outside, walking in the fluid darkness, soft and beautiful, the air cooled only slightly from the balmy 70 degree temperature of the day.

"Nice night." He tugged at her hand playfully and grinned at the moon.

"Yes."

"It makes you want to take a little walk."

"Ben, would you like to take a walk?" Julia smiled up at him.

"How did you know?" He was crisp and pressed in an old missionary suit and a powder-blue shirt that was a few shades lighter than his eyes. He'd shaved over a few blemishes along his jawline that had left little red scabs, and Julia wondered if he'd agonized over them. She didn't care; she wanted to reach up and touch the ruddy skin on his cheek anyway, but instead she looked down again and started to walk along a tree-lined path that led to the center of the campus. Her heels made a small clicking sound, and her shoulder rubbed against the rough fabric of his jacket as they strolled along.

"Are you cold?" Ben shrugged off one sleeve of his jacket.

"No, not really. It's gorgeous out here."

Ben flipped the jacket back on, and they continued down the path. Julia suppressed a small shiver, even though she wasn't cold. She could hear other people moving along the path ahead of them.

"The trees are amazing; just a few weeks ago they still looked dead, and now the leaves and blossoms are all coming out and covering up the bare bones. I don't remember noticing that before. Spring always just seemed to blend into summer." Julia looked up at the branches, and fingered a low twig that was beginning to branch out.

"Yeah, I love trees. My mom is crazy for them. She waters each one of hers every week, just letting the hose drip into their roots for three or fours hours. It takes a long time 'cause she's planted about twenty in our yard. We all tease her about it all the time, but they're beautiful . . . like you."

The words took her off guard, and her breath rushed in with a small whistle. She looked up at him quickly and then back at the sidewalk. She didn't know what to say. Ben pulled her over to a low wall surrounding the central courtyard and leaned against the edge of it. This put him at about her height. He took her other hand and sat swinging her arms together and then apart. Julia's throat felt dry.

"Did you have fun tonight?" he asked.

"Yeah, it was great. Thanks."

"It was my pleasure." Ben pulled gently on her hands and drew her to him, and Julia leaned easily forward, expecting an embrace. The next thing she knew, his lips were on hers, soft and warm. She was so shocked she jerked back, tripped on the hem of her long green dress, stumbled over the too-high heels and nearly fell. Ben tried to steady her flailing arms and flying elbows, and when she gained her balance, frustrated and completely humiliated, she couldn't look up at him. She took a step or two back from the wall, blew out a deep breath, and tilted her head back to look at the sky. She couldn't believe it.

"Come on, laugh." Ben took her hands again, and when she looked at him, he was trying not to smile.

"Oh, I can't. It's so embarrassing!" Julia pulled her hands loose, covered her face with them, and then allowed herself a sarcastic grin. "I mean, I might as well have shouted, 'Novice!' in your face. Oh, my word! What an *idiot* I am."

Ben was laughing softly now, trying to keep his voice down. "You're not, you're not," he said as her drew her in. When his head bent to her again, she was still scared, but not enough to jerk away this time, and when she relaxed, the kiss was tender and beautiful, and she could feel icy little thrills radiating through her body.

Ben gazed down at her in the moonlight. Her fingers played with the lapel on his jacket.

"I guess we'd better get moving," Ben said, looking over the top of her head toward the dance hall. Julia could hear everyone leaving the dance.

"Want to go to a movie next Friday night?" Ben asked her.

She looked up at him. She knew her eyes were shining. "Yes, Ben, I do."

Chapter 12

Dear Aaron,

Hi! Do you miss me? I sure missed you during the spring formal. I thought of our prom night, do you remember? You were so funny and so romantic and so tall, dark, and handsome in your tux. They've remodeled the old gym at Hale and put some colored lights in and a new sound system and taken out the old bleachers and brought in chairs and stuff. And someone did a great job on decorations; I think Julia knows her.

Speaking of Julia, she is sure amazing me lately. She had a date to the formal before I did! This cute tall guy has been chasing her this semester and she's so funny, she barely notices it. Imagine not knowing when a guy is after you! Well, I guess she's had little enough experience. I hope she doesn't do anything stupid and turn him off to save her pride. She's crazy. She never even talks about him, and she seems to avoid him when we're together on campus. He always has to come after her, and let me tell you, she'd better be careful, because not many of you guys can take that for very long. Your egos need feeding, right? Anyway, I try not to butt in too much, though she feels free to give me advice in her area of expertise: school.

And speaking of school, well, I think I'm going to flunk French. I just don't get it. I used to do so well in high school. Help! You won't think too badly of me if I don't graduate, will you? I can still go somewhere else and make it up and get a four-year degree in something, right? Anyway, enough of that. What about you? Do you wish you could go to a formal with me?

How's your life? Is missionary work getting any easier for you? Are you flunking Italian? I hope you're doing better than I am. I can't understand a word the teacher says.

I was impressed with your baptism. You seem to be making a difference, and you are getting so strong. I know I wouldn't do well as a missionary, but I can't help wishing I could be out there, specifically with you. Ha. Ha.

It seems like so long since I last saw you. Sometimes I can't picture your face anymore. The guys around here are so demanding. They all want commitment, and I should just make a policy not to date returned missionaries until you get back and only date the babies just getting out of high school. They don't make me so nervous, and they're pretty cute sometimes. No, don't get jealous; I have to do something, and they drive me crazy if I don't say yes sometimes. They make me so tired usually, and it just makes me remember how much fun it was to be with you, and I just want you back. We're over the hump now, anyway; less than a year left!

Keep up the good work, baby, and I'll see you soon. And you had better write more than one page next time or I'll wait a good ten minutes until I hug you when you get back!

Love forever,
Morgan

* * *

Aaron blinked a few times against the bright morning sun after finishing the letter. He was leaning over the rickety balcony that was attached to their apartment and still breathing hard from his jog back from the only decent basketball court they'd found in Italy. A cool breeze blew through his T-shirt and shorts, and he could feel the sweat beginning to dry on his body. He shivered lightly and looked at the pages again. Her writing sounded so real, it almost seemed like he could hear her talking, like she was here on the balcony with him. Aaron smiled a little and reread the part about Julia and her new boyfriend. He was really glad for her, because he understood and appreciated Julia; he always had.

Aaron looked down again, and his smile faded a little. He wasn't sure he liked the tone of this letter. It was so flirty and disturbed him somewhat. She was always throwing other guys in his face. He was used to that—their whole relationship had been that way, kind of a tease and banter, but before he'd always been able to decipher her real feelings underneath, had always been able to feel secure. Now he felt a little sick to his stomach and gulped a few times, swallowing hard. He could hear Elder Facer getting out of the shower, still singing and talking to himself in the bedroom.

A heavy longing for home descended on him. His feet felt nailed to the flimsy balcony. He stared out across the city, across the tops of apartment buildings and public monuments and past dingy strings of drying laundry. This was killing him. He couldn't do it anymore. He dropped his arm to his side and let the pages of the letter blow against his leg. These letters were destroying his focus. Morgan's words put him back in the middle of the emotional struggle, the games that boys and girls played. They made him long to get back there and try to be number one again, to win her back from all the hopefuls. And he couldn't do that. He needed to be here, to be doing the Lord's work without this kind of distraction. He shouldn't have to be dealing with these kinds of problems when he was trying so desperately to make his time over here matter.

Aaron glanced at the letter again. He was a little worried about her flunking French. Flunking? She'd always done pretty well in school before, even though she wasn't really academic. She'd always had a good head for common sense things, and she was naturally intelligent. What was going on back there? He couldn't understand it, and if he were to admit his true feelings, it bothered him. An F? He shook his head slightly and read the last paragraph again. The words seemed to belong to another world.

His own language ability had improved immensely in the last few weeks. Ever since Marco's baptism, something clicked. Italian just seemed to flow through his brain smoothly, and like a clear stream, everything seemed to fit together and find a place, without halting jerks and embarrassing pauses. He had even started to catch himself thinking in Italian, and at night his dreams ran in the same language.

He felt the gratitude swell within him for this great gift. Before his mission, he'd assumed that Italian would just come to him as part of the training. He'd heard the stories about how great the teachers were in the MTC and how the Spirit would help you to learn much faster than you could in college or anywhere else. He hadn't even expected to need to make a great effort really, but reality had hit him like a brick when he arrived here and realized how little he actually knew and that he didn't understand one word his first real Italian said to him.

And yet the Lord was there, working right beside him, helping him not to give up—only His help had been a lot different than Aaron had thought it would be. And though a clear understanding of Italian had seemed to come to him all at once, he was aware that all his study hours and obedience to the rules had formed the basis for this amazing knowledge. Aaron realized the Lord respected diligence and revealed His miracles to the hardworking and the humble.

Chapter 13

"Julia Jeffs! Sit up and take notice, baby!" A very loud voice, electronically amplified, jolted through her. Julia jerked up in bed, shaking. She didn't recognize the voice. What was going on? In a second she was at the window, with Morgan stumbling out of bed right behind her. The Hale van, painted a dark shade of maroon with gold stripes and sporting the figure of a vicious wolverine on its side, was parked below their window. The Hale van. Julia blinked her eyes rapidly and tried to focus on the figures milling around the van. There were six guys, counting the one driving the van, and three of them had climbed the chrome ladder and were standing on top of the van. Julia's face blanched, and she drew back from the window when she recognized Ben on top of the van smiling up at her.

"Hey!" said a short guy who was also on top of the van, "there she is!"

Julia tried to fall back into the room, but found Morgan behind her pressing her forward.

"Get up there, silly," Morgan hissed.

"Why? Quit pushing me!" There was a brief struggle, ending when Julia tripped over one of Morgan's cast-off shoes and fell, head and shoulders, through the open screenless window. The windowsill barely stopped her from falling. "My gosh!" She glared back at Morgan. "Are you trying to kill me?"

When Julia turned her eyes back to the street, someone was handing Ben a microphone from the driver's side window, and the next minute, loud banging music came crashing into the night.

"Wild thing . . . you make my heart sing!"

Julia gasped. Ben was singing! He stood on top of the van, dancing and singing in a slightly off-key voice, blaring into the microphone at the top of his lungs. And he was looking at her, smiling so wide it almost split her heart open. She was so embarrassed! She glanced quickly to both sides and saw Cynthia and Heather and Lorraine leaning out their windows to see what was going on. She could hear windows upstairs being shoved open and slamming doors and running feet in the halls.

Julia tried, but she couldn't keep the smile off her face; there he was, down there, acting so crazy, singing to *her*.

"You make everything GRO-O-O-O-VY!" Ben swiveled his hips crazily and leaned back, singing to the sky.

He sure was hamming it up! How did he dare? And he had on the tightest jeans, with a rolled red bandanna tied around one leg. They looked short for him too; maybe he'd borrowed them from a roommate. He also wore a black leather jacket and a tight white T-shirt, and his hair had been gelled so it would stick up spikily all over his head.

"Can you believe him?" Morgan whispered in her left ear. "He's great!"

Julia didn't say anything, but the muscles in her cheeks were beginning to hurt from her wide smile.

Two of Ben's roommates were playing air guitar and dancing crazily to the pounding music, and two other guys were miming keyboard and drums on the ground. They were all dressed like rockers, or as close to it as returned missionaries could get. One of the guys on the ground flung a long, blonde wig around on his head, and the other's hair was completely covered with a dark bandana. The driver of the van was balancing a large pair of speakers on the windowsill.

But Julia couldn't keep her eyes off Ben and the intensity with which he sang the music. He really was a terrible singer! She laughed out loud. She sang inside.

He was looking up into her eyes now, solemn and slow. "Wild thing . . . I think I love YOU!"

Did he really mean it? His friends were laughing so hard she thought they might fall off the van. As the song ended the girls in the dorm began to laugh and cheer and whistle. A few of them yelled things down at Julia.

"Julia! He's gorgeous!"

"If you ever get tired of him, send him over!"

They also yelled at the guys.

"Hey, baby!"

"Come on in! I'll open the door!"

"Haven't you guys got another song?"

And then Julia saw a campus police car turn onto their street, with its lights flashing, and all the guys dove for the van except for Ben. The driver revved the engine, but Ben ran forward to just beneath her window, and the driver shrugged his shoulders and peeled out of the parking lot, leaving Ben behind.

Grinning impishly, Ben looked up at her. "Wild thing . . . I think I love you!" He whispered it softly, almost like a caress, even with every girl in the dorm hanging out of her window. Then he whipped around and sprinted for the trees and the safety of the next building. But before he ran out of sight, he kissed his hand to her, waving jauntily.

The campus police car stopped below the windows, which began to quickly slam shut, and one of the policemen yelled over in a humored tone, "Keep it down, okay? The neighbors are complaining!" Then the car pulled away in the direction the van had taken.

"Julia! I hope they get away!" Morgan had her hand over her mouth and her eyebrows raised. A minute later Cynthia, Heather, and Lorraine burst into their bedroom, and loud knocks sounded on the outside door.

Julia fell back into her bed at the barrage of questions and the high squeals of "You're so lucky!"

Yes. Yes, she was. And she held the feeling to her, like a shield, like armor against all the other insecurities in her life. She couldn't peel the smile off her face for two or three days.

* * *

Two weeks later, Julia lay back in the dark and stared up at the blank ceiling above her bed. She was conscious of a slight panic. She was behind in all her classes. She should have started on that psychology paper tonight, but the chemistry problems had taken too long. She hadn't been concentrating in class when the teacher had explained the concept, and so she'd had to use valuable time figuring them out from the textbook. And then Ben had found her table at the library again. And though they'd tried to study, really meant to this time, they'd joked and laughed, and he'd found her hand under the table and held it a few too many times, causing her to lose track of the answer to the problem she had just calculated and even to forget what subject she had been studying. It was crazy.

The first time she'd seen him on campus after his singing debut, she'd hardly known what to say. She had stumbled over her words and blushed furiously, but Ben hadn't seemed to be in any discomfort at all. He was just smiling, and sincere, and slightly amused at her reaction. He'd taken her hand immediately though, and he'd asked her out for the weekend, both nights. They'd been seeing a lot of each other. It seemed like he couldn't get enough, and she knew she couldn't.

She'd never known it could be like this, never realized that one person could so completely take up her mind, squeezing out all her intensity and competitiveness, filling her thoughts constantly. After she'd been out with him or seen him somewhere on campus, she would go over each word he'd said, each touch, each look. She knew if someone else had been describing this feeling to her she would have thought them ridiculous. But it was true for her. He absolutely engrossed her.

She was still nervous about him though, still unsure of this new relationship. It was something she'd never experienced before. She worried that he might cool toward her and quit stopping at her library table, quit looking for her at lunch, quit stopping by her dorm room on his way home from working at the student center.

Since the dance he'd kissed her only two other times, but still she was beginning to feel less shy about it. She wanted to encourage the closeness, without appearing too forward—and without damaging her pride, which she had always been so careful to protect. She'd built such a heavy wall around her emotions and was such an expert at swallowing bitter pills with a smile on her face that she really didn't know how to act.

Julia sighed loudly and gathered her dark bob together behind her neck, leaning up in bed to free herself from the tangled sheet. Things were changing for her so quickly; it was like she'd suddenly been thrust into the channel of a swift current and she could merely touch things as she went by, seeing them always in motion, missing the present when she turned back to look at the past.

Well, she wasn't sleeping; she might as well get to work on that neglected paper. Julia threw her legs over the edge of the bed and edged past the sleeping Morgan, grabbing a couple books and a sweatshirt on the way to the privacy of the kitchen table.

Chapter 14

Aaron leaned back against the peeling wall above his short mattress, feeling the crunchy paint curls through his white shirt. He loosened his tie and unbuttoned the top button of his shirt. Elder Facer stood next to the other lumpy bed, which was crowded with his gear. His large, hard-sided suitcase lay open, and he was pawing through its contents with his broad hands.

"You know, I just don't know where to put everything. It always seemed to fit when I came over and on my other transfers. I'm so out of it." Elder Facer massaged his temples with his fingertips.

"Do you need some help?" Aaron dug himself out of the bed and stood next to his companion of three months. "Maybe you can fold some of these things down a little flatter. And tighten up these shoes. Boy, Facer, this is a mess. You're leaving here at four thirty in the morning tomorrow, aren't you? Didn't you do any packing last night? Man—I was just too tired to stay up and baby-sit you."

Elder Facer spun around and dropped onto Aaron's protesting cot. "I don't know, Elder. I just couldn't face it last night, and maybe that's why I can't focus tonight. You'd think I'd have had my stuff packed a week ago and my suitcase by the door."

"And . . ." Aaron prodded, as he continued rearranging the suitcase, sorting through the crumpled clothes and small souvenirs Elder Facer had thrown into it.

"And . . . well, maybe I'm crazy, but I'm kind of scared to go home and face my life again. I mean, even putting this whole Gina thing behind me, I don't know what I'm going to do or who I'm going to be when I get back there. Before my mission I was kind of a loser, you know, never really coming up with anything solid . . . and I guess, the point is . . . I don't really know what to do with my life now. It's all going to be so different." He sighed loudly and turned to lay back on the bed. His big feet protruded about six inches over the end of the mattress. "It's been so great, these last few months. I feel like my real mission is just beginning. It's too soon to give it up. I mean, I have known real joy, you know? It seems crazy that I have to leave now."

"I know, Facer, I wish you were staying too. We were making some real progress in this town. But hey, when you get home *things* will be different, but *you* will be so much better. You know the Church is true now. That's going to change everything for you. Don't you think your experiences out here will help you at home? And what about the Lord? He's given us the Spirit to do His work here. Don't you think He'll help you out in your personal life too? But, I understand about your being scared." Aaron smiled a little. "And to tell you the truth, I'm glad it's you and not me. I'm pretty sure I'm not ready yet."

"Thanks a lot, Elder." He reached out to slap Aaron's leg, but Aaron dodged neatly out of the way.

"Anyway, are you thinking about college? I mean, you should try out for football at Hale, or basketball, if I'm any judge of talent. You're murder underneath." Aaron rubbed at his bruised shoulder.

"I don't know. I just helped my dad on the farm after high school, trying to decide what to do, you know? And then Gina convinced me to go on a mission, and when I'd really decided, I was grateful because it gave me something to do. But now, I'm right back where I started. I'd like to play a sport, you know I would." Elder Facer shot a short grin at Aaron. "But I don't think I'd be any good at college, grade-wise. I didn't exactly shine in high school, and my dad is going to put a lot of pressure on me to be there with him out in the fields. He didn't like it too much when I decided to come out here, and the way he sees it, I already owe him two years of back labor."

"Whoa." Aaron paused a minute, thinking. "Maybe you could work something out to take a few night classes for a while, and see what you're interested in, and then after you have a plan, you could tackle your dad and show him what you want to do." Aaron's advice sounded hollow in his own ears, but he had guessed he'd better say something.

"Yeah, maybe. I've never talked to you about my family much, but my dad's real hard to handle, you know. His parents were inactive members of the Church when he was growing up. I think he's even been baptized, but he really hated it when home teachers and stuff would stop by our house and try to help us or give us cookies and junk. I mean, he was really bitter. He didn't stop me or my brother from going to church with our friends if we wanted to, because it's hard to get along in a place like Cache Valley and fit in at all without going to church sometimes and to activities and stuff.

"You should have seen the fight we had when I told him I was going on a mission. I mean, I swear he almost hit me, and I'm not so sure that I wouldn't have hit him back. We really didn't part on speaking terms, although he gave me his hand to shake before my mom took me down to the MTC. I haven't heard one word from him in two years. My mom tries to fill in for him a little, you know, tell me what he's doing on the farm and stuff. I don't know, I guess I don't want to deal with all those problems again, and I'm afraid of slipping back into that rut."

Elder Facer covered his face with his hands for a moment then continued. "You know, he used to deliberately keep me out in the fields fencing or baling hay just a few minutes too long when he knew I had a game. I would have to jog all the way to school to make it. And he didn't come to a single one of my games, and I played football and basketball all four years in high school. My senior year I was voted MVP for the region in basketball, and all I could think about when I was standing out there in the middle of the gym was that my dad wasn't there and that he wouldn't even care when he found out."

Aaron had never heard Elder Facer talk about himself this way. It was usually all jokes and sarcastic comments, or testimony when they were around investigators and members. Again Elder Facer had surprised him. Aaron suddenly realized he had been naive about the pain other people experienced. He felt, with a mild shock, the strength of what his parents had done for him, making his childhood flow on in ever-increasing opportunities and entertainments: music lessons, sports teams, vacations, holidays, science projects, church activities, campouts. And these things were only an outward expression of their love and support for him. He'd had no experience with the kind of thing that Facer was talking about.

He sat on the bed opposite Facer, leaning toward him. "Well, I know one thing, Elder. You can't back off. You'd be destroying your soul and going against everything you know. You know the gospel's true and that it changes lives and that if you follow its principles it will lead you back to our Heavenly Father. You have to make your father see it, at least see how good it is for you."

"I know." Elder Facer sat up and looked Aaron in the eye. "Thanks. Sometimes I just need a little support. Maybe I could work through the summer with my dad—you know, show him that I care about the family and want to help him, and then go down to college in the fall. Maybe Hale would be a good place, being so far from Cache Valley that I really couldn't come home on the weekends to help. And you'd be there too, when you get back, right? We can hang out together, and it'll just be 'Aaron' and 'Jim'; you know, no more of this 'Elder' stuff. Weird. Maybe it will work out somehow. I don't know. This gives me total stress!" Elder Facer rubbed a hand over his head again. "But even after all of this, I love my dad, you know, and I want him to be happy with me. I guess I still need his approval. I always did." Elder Facer sighed loudly.

"I guess we all do." Aaron bent slightly, leaning on the suitcase, and closed the latches.

Chapter 15

It was another silver charm. Morgan spread out the wrinkled twist of tissue paper from the tiny box to reveal the shape of Italy, a tiny boot that would attach to her bracelet from the upper corner. Beautiful! She held it carefully in her palm as she went into the bedroom to find the bracelet in the top of her jewelry box. After attaching the new charm, Morgan awkwardly wound the bracelet around her wrist with her free hand and stood fussing with it, straining for nearly two minutes before the tiny clasp held true.

She held her wrist up again, letting the charms dangle and twinkle in the light from the bedroom window. She loved it. Each charm represented Aaron in another way. Morgan suddenly remembered she hadn't seen a note in the small package and turned quickly back into the small dorm kitchen to look. The paper and wrappings were spread out on the table, and Morgan sifted through them quickly. She couldn't find a letter or even a short note scrawled on a scrap of paper. Morgan sat down and took the outer wrapping off the box, spreading it out carefully against the flat table. Only her address in Aaron's small block letters. She turned it over, but saw nothing. She examined the box and then began to spread the tissue paper out slowly and carefully to keep it from tearing. It was blank also. How strange! Morgan felt a lump come to her throat and blinked her eyes quickly against the unreasonable tears. He hadn't had time to write, of course. She was being silly. At least he'd sent the charm, hadn't he? Wasn't that proof enough? But always before, there'd been a page or two—at the very least a short note. He'd probably just forgotten to put it in, but Morgan felt a wave of depression pass over her, pressing down on her and leaving her weak. She walked into her bedroom and lay down on her bed, staring up at the ceiling. *Father help me.* The words echoed in her mind, but she really didn't know what she needed help for, or why.

A vision of Julia and Ben rose before her. It was the real thing with them. She knew it. This was something that would last. A strange pang of jealousy stabbed through her.

The outer door opened with a bang, and Julia's voice sang out, "Bye. See you later." The next minute she was in the room with Morgan.

"Ben?" Morgan kept her eyes on the ceiling.

"Yes. We just walked over from the library."

"How exciting."

"What's the matter?" Julia's eyes were bright and her cheeks red.

"Nothing. I got a new charm. See?" Morgan swung up to a sitting position and held out her wrist.

"Yeah, I noticed," Julia said smiling, glancing back through the open door at the pile of wrappings still sitting on the kitchen table. She took Morgan's wrist and carefully examined the tiny charm.

"Italy. Cute. How many more do you get?" Julia sat back onto her bed, leaning into the upholstered backrest.

"Eight. Aaron will be home in December."

"Wow, it's gone by pretty fast, seems like."

"To *you*." Morgan flopped back down again and began to turn the bracelet slowly around her arm, fingering each of the four charms in turn.

"You miss him. But don't worry too much. You aren't having much of a dry spell, even though one of your followers is out of the running." Julia was unloading her backpack with her back to Morgan.

"What do you mean?"

"Sammy." Julia piled three thick texts on her bed. "Come on, you know."

Julia turned now and faced her.

Morgan could feel her throat closing up. "What?"

"Well, it's that redhead of course, you know. We've seen them around campus together a lot lately. He took her to the dance concert and to spring formal, and well, I guess they've been seeing a lot of each other lately."

"So?" Morgan knew Sammy would drop that redhead in a flash if she showed any sign of real interest. After all, he'd been trailing after her for a year and a half, hadn't he?

"So, they're engaged. Didn't you hear? He asked her last Friday night, up Green Canyon, with candlelight and the whole works. His roommates cooked up this great meal and hauled it up there and served them wearing bow ties. He even picked out the ring himself. Who would have thought he'd have the guts? Quite a whopper, really . . . his dad must have more money than I thought."

Morgan's mouth was dry. She couldn't believe it. "Really? Who told you?"

"They did. Ben and I bumped into them at the library. Kind of scary, isn't it, if someone like Sammy can get hooked. We're all so young; doesn't it feel like it's kind of jumping the gun?"

"Yeah." Morgan agreed hotly. "How can he get married? And to such a little twit! I mean she can't have any brains, and we all know she gets a zero in looks with that little sweet, freckled face." Somehow, this seemed like a personal insult to Morgan, and she felt herself heat up inside to boiling. "Man, he could have gotten someone a lot better than her! I've heard she has a really annoying personality too. How old is she anyway? Twelve?"

"Probably." Julia frowned. "What are you getting so worked up about anyway? It's not like you really cared about Sammy except to tease and tan-ta-lize him." Julia smiled and raised her eyebrows. Then she looked at Morgan more closely. "Hey, don't worry about it."

"Yeah, what do I care? It's only a small defection. I would never really consider him anyway. He's fun, yes, but too short. I could prob-ably beat him up." Morgan sighed as the words tumbled forth, not really feeling their casual bravado. She felt kind of sick to her stomach.

"I wouldn't count on it. He may be short, but he's pretty stocky too."

"I know, but that's how I feel about all guys that are my height or less."

"It doesn't seem to stop you much, I notice." Julia raised her eyebrows teasingly.

"Of course not. Flies come to the honey, you know." Morgan fluttered her lashes quickly, and gracefully extended a long, tanned arm. The clowning helped a little somehow. "Hey, Julia, how about a hot fudge sundae? Come on."

"Why is it always food with you? It really doesn't seem fair." Julia looked pointedly at Morgan's flat stomach.

"I know. I guess not, but how about it?"

"Okay, why not?" Julia rolled her eyes and held out her hand to Morgan. "I guess another pound or two can't make that much difference."

Chapter 16

"Hey! He was fouled! Open your eyes, ref!" Morgan's mother stood in the middle of the crowd in the bleachers with red, heated cheeks, yelling at the referee with obvious pleasure. Morgan rolled her eyes as she walked into the noisy gym and immediately picked out her mother. She gave a small grin. Her mother was incorrigible. Her dry, frizzly hair flew in a frantic cloud around her as she dropped back into her seat. She gave her husband's broad thigh a slap and grinned into his face before she saw Morgan and began waving her arm, not realizing her whereabouts were already so obvious.

"Mom. How's it going?" Morgan asked as she sat down next to her parents on the bench, a loud blare from the speakers drowning her out.

"What?"

"I just said, 'How's it going?'"

"Good, good. Close game though." Mrs. Carter reached over her husband and squeezed Morgan's knee. "Hey, how's school going?" Her parents looked at Morgan only briefly before turning back to the game, where Morgan could see her fiery brother pushing up and down the court. Ross was eating it up, pounding to the basket, past and through anyone in his way. Score! He came away from the basket amid cheers with a smug, satisfied expression. Yes, that was Ross—headstrong, physical, and very sure of himself. He gave a short nod in their direction as he cruised up the court. Morgan was glad she didn't have to answer her parents.

"Where are the kids?" Morgan tried again to speak over the roar of the crowd.

Mrs. Carter leaned over her husband again. "Janey's babysitting Megan, said she didn't want to come, and Clint is across on the other side sitting with his friends."

Morgan's dad turned to her briefly and asked again about school, listening with only half his attention as his eyes followed the flashing basketball. Morgan managed to be specific enough to satisfy his limited attention without really answering him. She knew he meant well. Morgan closed her eyes briefly, trying to relax a little and focus her thoughts. She watched for a while, secretly proud of Ross whenever he made a good move and half-jealous at the same time.

After a while her thoughts returned to what had happened last night, to what David had said to her, the ultimatum he had given her. He wanted her to stop dating other guys. It was amazing. He'd also said he wanted some kind of commitment or a promise or something. She'd tried to stall him, to change the subject to something lighter, because she knew there was no way she could make a promise to him now, not until Aaron got back and she could see if she remembered him right. But when she didn't answer him immediately, David had said it was over. He'd said there was no way he could stand to let things continue the way they were going.

She'd pleaded with him and couldn't really believe it when he hadn't given in to her. Because she really liked David, at least it had felt like it last night . . .

But now, here, Aaron came back to her so vividly that if she squinted her eyes she thought maybe she could see him rushing down the court for a layup. A tall dark kid on the other team looked enough like him that she was able to live in her fantasy for a while, pretending that after the game she would wait for him in the front hall and he, tall and smiling, his hair shiny-wet from the shower, would take her hand. She would sit close to him in the dark car and lean her head on his muscular shoulder, and he'd ask her if she was hungry and what she wanted to eat. Later they'd come back to the dance when the gym was darkened and blaring, and they'd dance close together and once in a while Aaron would get off balance and step on her foot, and they'd sway and laugh together . . .

Morgan felt tears gathering in her eyes and blinked them quickly away. She gathered up her long, blonde hair and held it on top of her head, fanning herself against the warmth of the many bodies packed into the bleachers. She looked to where Ross was taking the ball down the court, his auburn curls dripping sweat, and she felt jealousy rise slowly in her throat. He was so confident and cocky. He knew what he wanted.

Morgan sighed loudly and looked at the ceiling.

"He's doing great, isn't he?" Her mother glanced over with shining eyes.

Morgan made an effort. "Yeah, Mom, he's like lightning!"

Later, they stood in a small family group, waiting for Ross outside the locker room, chatting and smiling at neighbors and ward members and the families of Ross's friends and teammates. Morgan's mom wanted a word with Ross before he went out with his friends or picked up one of his girlfriends. She said she just wanted to make sure what his plans were, remind him of when he needed to be home, and give him her ever-present morality reminder.

Some of Ross's teammates emerged from the locker room laughing and pushing each other. They were in a good mood after their win. As they walked toward Morgan and her parents, Morgan's mother immediately called out to them and began a teasing friendly conversation, referring to the game and some of the plays like a pro.

It was easy to join in the conversation and draw the eyes of the young men to her. Morgan felt the old excitement steal through her, the thrill of the hunt. Somewhere along the way a friend of her mother passed by, and Morgan's mother walked away to discuss a Relief Society dinner. Morgan glanced up to see her dad now some distance off, leaning against the wall and talking to the dad of one of the players about the game. Ross hadn't come out yet.

Morgan retained the young crowd of basketball players, entertaining them with her flirtatious banter. She made some sly hints, talked about their girlfriends, subtly undermining them, and soon had at least two of them ready to drop at her feet. She felt electrified and alive. She could feel admiration radiating from them like heat.

"So, what are you doing tomorrow night?" This from one of the bolder of the young guys. What a baby! But a baby with quite a bit of nerve.

"Oh, I'm going back to Hale. I've got a date."

"Oh." He looked absurdly deflated. How could he possibly think she would go out with him?

"Hey, but whenever you guys are in town, you ought to stop in to my dorm room. I'm in Bentwell block, room 15. I can introduce you to a lot of hot babes." The invitation had squared their baby shoulders and brought looks of ridiculous hope to their faces. Still, the tall one was awfully cute.

Suddenly she was aware of Ross standing just outside their little circle. He did not look pleased.

"Hey, Ross, you did a good job tonight." She went to him and punched his hard, muscular shoulder.

"Yeah, glad you could make it." Ross's voice was thick with sarcasm. Morgan smiled up at him sweetly.

"Anything for you, baby!"

"Yeah, right. Come on guys, let's go."

"See ya, Morgan. You watch for us sometime." They all chorused their reluctance in leaving her.

"I'll be counting the minutes." She laughed after them and saw Ross roll his eyes.

She watched them until they were almost at the door and her mother had noticed Ross and had run after them. Their mother pulled him aside for a minute, hugged him hard, and stood holding on to his forearm, talking fast into his ear for a good few minutes until Ross finally made his escape.

When her mother came back to join her, she was obviously displeased. She had that "I can't believe what you just did" look on her face. "Morgan, what were you doing?"

"What do you mean?"

"You know what I mean, with those boys! I thought Joey was going to have heart palpitations." They were outside now, and her mother strode along angrily in the dark, staring hard at Morgan when she didn't need to look where she was going amidst the cars in the parking lot.

"What's the big deal, Mom? I was just passing the time chatting until Ross came out, just like you."

"No, not just like me. I don't remember dripping syrup and flipping my blonde hair around, batting my eyelashes and arching my back like a little you-know-what."

"Mom!"

"Well it's true! I was so embarrassed when I turned around to see what Diane Harper was staring at and saw you putting the moves on those boys two and three years younger."

"Mom! I was just talking to them, you know, having a little fun."

"You were leading them down the garden path. What are you going to do when they show up at Hale?"

Morgan looked surprised.

"Yes, I heard that. I wasn't standing as far away as you thought. Are you really going to ask your friends and roommates to go out with them?"

"Don't have a heart attack, Mom. Those boys knew I was just having fun."

"Maybe they did, and maybe they didn't, Morgan, but what I'm wondering is why you feel the need to go after them. Does male admiration really mean that much to you? I mean, these were little boys, little not-available-to-you boys. Is that how you always react to the opposite sex? Are they all just mountains to climb?"

The words hurt her, felt like a betrayal. This was her mother, and although she was used to the motherly reprimands that had been coming at her all her life, she'd been on her own for more than a year, and it was humiliating and insulting to be treated like a baby again. Really, her mother had no right. It was her life, and her mother could just stay out of it. She fumed inside all the way home, still listening to her mother's tirade, which she knew from experience would not end until her mother felt she had done her duty. Morgan's dad sat in the front seat, nodding his head and inserting a few words here and there when he was called upon to express an opinion. Morgan stayed deadly silent and wondered why she had come home at all.

Chapter 17

He was green, almost dripping sap. Aaron walked quickly along the dirty street, trying to stay slightly ahead of Elder Spinhall in a juvenile effort to pretend he wasn't really with him. Aaron's new companion was skinny and awkward and was fond of quoting exact mission rules whenever he thought Aaron had strayed off the beaten path. Aaron began to understand how Elder Facer had felt when he'd thought Aaron was pressuring him. Elder Doyle Spinhall was definitely a letter-of-the-law man, and there was no taking shortcuts with him.

They were on their way to teach the first discussion to a forty-year-old woman they'd found yesterday. She'd hadn't let them in because she had an appointment, but said she would have a little time if they came today. Aaron privately wondered if she'd really be home, or if she had ditched them, but he'd been trying to have faith and was praying that Elder Spinhall and he could get along for long enough to teach her.

Aaron hitched his heavy backpack higher across his shoulder blade as they entered the familiar market square where Aaron had shopped for the past three months. He ran through some of the first discussion in his head, trying to feel the words, invite the Spirit. With each of his contacts, hope rose in him in these preparatory moments. He wondered if he would think back to this moment in time and think it was a premonition, that he'd known Signora Carbini would be golden, that she would commit and would embrace what he knew to be true. Aaron felt a little thrill run up his spine, and he leaned forward and quickened his pace.

A bunch of rosy grapes caught his eye on a cart off to his right. Maybe they could come back this way after giving Signora Carbini the discussion. Unconsciously he veered toward the grapes, and bumped Elder Spinhall with his shoulder. Spinhall tripped over the curb and fell sprawling into a scummy puddle in the gutter.

"Elder Jenner!"

Aaron took one look at Elder Spinhall sitting in the swampy gutter and burst out laughing uncontrollably. He could tell Elder Spinhall was really angry, but he looked so funny and outraged! Aaron actually had to wipe tears out of his eyes before he held his hand out to the elder. "Hey, man, I'm sorry. I didn't mean to bump you." He spluttered and burst out laughing again. A splash of the murky water was dripping off the right lens of Spinhall's glasses.

Elder Spinhall ignored Aaron's proffered hand and struggled to stand up by himself. The back of his pant legs to the knee and the seat of his pants were soaked with the greasy water, and his backpack and the back of his suit jacket were dotted with spots.

"You did that on purpose," Elder Spinhall accused him.

"What?"Aaron was trying hard to control another smile.

"You did." Spinhall flipped his wrists, sending a fine spray back into the water.

"Come on, Elder, why would I push you into that mess when we have an appointment in ten minutes?"

"How do I know?" Elder Spinhall held his arms out from his sides, trying not to get more greasy water on his suit. Aaron rolled his eyes and looked around. He crossed to the fruit stand and asked the man if he had a towel or a rag or something that they could borrow. He pointed toward where Spinhall was still standing with his arms out, looking frustrated and helpless.

"Here," Aaron said, tossing the large rag to Elder Spinhall. "Wipe yourself off so we can go."

"You're not serious." Spinhall's eyes bugged out behind his glasses.

"What do you mean?"

"I can't go."

"What?"

"I can't go in to Mrs. Carbini's and try to teach her the gospel after what you just did."

"Elder! You're okay. Just wipe off a little, and you'll dry while we're walking. You know it was an accident. Come on!" Aaron's eyes nearly rolled back into his head. He couldn't believe this guy.

"I can't go." Elder Spinhall was adamant.

"Come on, you can go . . . Okay, I'm sorry. Really."

"No. I just can't feel the Spirit now after what you just did. And look at me, I'm so icky." Elder Spinhall turned around, displaying himself.

"Elder! What do you want me to say? I'm really sorry I wasn't watching where I was going, but we've got to go and see this lady. We can't just not show. She'll think we're real flakes, and what do you think she'll think of the Church? Come on." Aaron was starting to get panicky. Elder Spinhall folded his arms tightly across his chest, and Aaron knew he wouldn't go.

"I can't believe you!" Aaron threw his arms up. Now they were creating a scene. A passerby gave them a strange look. They must have looked like a man and his unreasonable wife. It was bad protocol in an open street like this. Aaron grabbed Elder Spinhall's upper arm, spun him around and propelled him forward. "Just start walking. We've got to get out of here—everyone's watching." He hissed the words into Elder Spinhall's ear and was able through sheer force to get him to move a few steps.

"Okay, listen . . ." Aaron was breathing hard from embarrassment. "We'll just stop by and tell her that we can't stay today, but really want to see her another day . . . but this might ruin everything. Don't you think we could just talk to her for a minute?" Aaron pleaded, beginning to grow desperate.

"No we could not! You deliberately pushed me. You can just blame yourself. You bombed this, you know." Elder Spinhall looked up, closed his eyes and wagged his head virtuously. Aaron felt sick. They were moving along quickly now and were nearly to the building where Mrs. Carbini lived.

Aaron approached Mrs. Carbini's door feeling nervous. He glanced over at Elder Spinhall and caught the smug, self-satisfied expression on his face. He was enjoying this! Aaron paused a little, wondering if he could somehow get out of this. Then he cleared his throat and knocked.

Mrs. Carbini opened the door immediately. "Bongiorno! Avanti, avanti!" She was welcoming them in with wide motions of her arms and a big smile. Aaron winced.

"Um, I'm sorry Signora Carbini," Aaron began slowly in Italian, "but we just stopped by to tell you that we can't visit with you today. We had a little accident and Elder Spinhall needs to go home and change his clothes."

"Oh. That's okay, come in. I have a towel you can use. I don't mind." Aaron looked at Elder Spinhall hopefully. Spinhall shook his head in tight little jerks and took a step back.

"I guess he needs to go home, but we really want to come and visit you. We'd like to come back tomorrow if we could. Can we come about the same time?"

"Well, I don't know. My daughter comes to visit on Thursdays, and I don't think she would want to listen." She looked crestfallen and embarrassed. "Well, maybe it would be better if you didn't come back. I really don't think my daughter would like it if I talked to you."

"Please, Signora Carbini, we have a wonderful message of Christ to share with you. It's very important, and we care a lot about it and about you." Aaron slid a glance at Elder Spinhall. He had a frozen, uncomprehending smile on his face and was trying to look virtuous and sincere.

"What about Friday afternoon then, or Saturday morning?"

"Well, maybe. Why don't you leave me your phone number, and I'll call you when I decide about it. I am very busy most of the time."

Why was she so offended? Did she think they were making excuses? That's what it must sound like to her. Aaron got a card out of his backpack and handed it to her. He doubted she would ever use it.

"Okay, Signora, please call us. Maybe we'll call you in a few days if we don't hear from you, or maybe we'll stop by again." Aaron's smile cracked on his face as she hastily closed the door. It was over. They'd more than likely lost her. Again Aaron could feel his anger mounting, climbing and climbing, against his companion.

"Great. What do we do now?" Aaron scuffed slowly out of the building and sat down on the first bus stop bench they came to.

"Is she going to let us come back?"

"I doubt it." Aaron covered his face with his hands briefly. "How could you do that? Make me embarrass her and myself over a few patches of greasy water."

"We need to talk this out. Obviously we aren't communicating," Elder Spinhall said, moving to sit next to Aaron.

"Not on your life, Elder." Aaron shot off the bench. "I've had it with your little 'talks.' We both know exactly what happened here. You refused to teach a potential convert because you wanted to get back at me for bumping into you. For heaven's sake, won't you believe it was an accident?"

Suddenly Aaron felt exhausted. He was tired of dealing with this type of situation. When he got home he'd take his dad's jeep and drive clear up the canyon onto the skyline, and he'd take his little pup tent and a sleeping bag and a couple of books and his earphones, and he'd stay up there for a week. Alone. He was sick of working with other people and trying to be nice and work things out. It seemed like two people could never agree about anything and that other people existed only to frustrate him. How did anyone ever get married? You'd have to be with the other person all the time; didn't they get sick of each other? Well, maybe he wouldn't, not with someone as exciting as Morgan. Aaron shook his head quickly. He couldn't think about that now.

"Come on, let's go," Aaron said as the bus pulled up to the curb. He pushed his way onto the crowded bus without looking behind him to see if Spinhall followed.

Chapter 18

"I really like your family, Julia," Ben told her. "Your dad's great. Hilarious."

"Yeah, he's a little too hilarious. Could you believe him? He almost ate you alive. It's so embarrassing; it was like I'd never had a guy over before, and Dad was desperate." The words were so close to the truth that Julia looked down to avoid Ben's eyes.

"You've had other guys here?" Ben's eyes widened, and his mouth dropped in mock jealousy while his arm tightened around her shoulder.

"Well, maybe a few."

"Man, they'd better watch out. You're mine, babe."

Julia sighed in pleasure, leaning her head back on Ben's shoulder, enjoying the trapped warmth of the cab of Ben's old Chevy truck that was parked in the Jeffses' driveway. Julia smiled as she remembered the family dinner that her brother and his family had driven down for. Michael wouldn't have missed this "meet-the-parents" thing for the world. During dinner she thought she'd die of embarrassment from their teasing; but, oh, it did feel good. She wanted to hug herself. To actually deserve to be teased about this, to have someone at the table like her brother had, someone that was hers. She didn't think she'd ever been so contented.

"Julia."

"Yeah."

"How do you feel about us?"

"I love us!" Julia said facing Ben with an upturned face, hoping for a kiss.

He kissed her briefly. "Will you be serious for a minute? Our relationship, you know; do you think it's going somewhere?"

Going somewhere? What is that supposed to mean? she thought. "Ben, if you can't tell I've been enjoying myself, then you just haven't been paying attention," she told him. She blinked her eyes, thinking for a minute and then punched him in the arm, trying to lighten things up a little.

"I think you know what I mean." Ben looked out over the steering wheel toward the house.

"Do I?"

"Julia, you're being deliberately dense, which is unusual for you." He let a small grin crack his mouth.

This sounded too serious. Julia began to feel nervous

"I like you, more than a lot. Surely you know that." He appealed to her in the dark with soft, serious eyes, but she didn't say anything.

"I think I'm falling in love with you."

Julia felt like she had a live coal in her chest. He loved her? "Ben . . ." She didn't know what to say.

"It sounds crazy, I know; we really haven't been going out that long. But it's true, Julia. Almost from the first I knew. That first time I played racquetball with you I was so excited I couldn't sleep that night. You were so different and so real and so, well, cute!"

She smiled and the pressure in her chest became white-hot, almost like pain. "I felt the same way," she admitted. "Except I wouldn't let myself think about you much because I didn't want to be disappointed. You seemed too good to be true."

"How do you feel now, Julia?"

She was making this hard for him and she knew it, and it grieved her. She rubbed her index finger around in a circle on the foggy truck window. But she wanted, above all things, to be honest. "It's been amazing; it really has. Better than anything I could imagine. I can't stop thinking about you, and I even neglect my homework to be with you."

"I doubt that."

"No, really. I didn't know it would be like this. I've felt confident and happy . . . and beautiful." She looked down at this, her face growing red, and then determinedly continued. "But I don't know if this is love. I hate to admit it, but this is my first real relationship. How would I know what love is? If it's not you, you're the closest thing to it that I've ever felt . . . I want to be honest with you." She turned to him in the shadowy cab, seeing the strong planes of his face standing out against the shadows. "This is serious, and I don't want to throw those words around in the heat of the moment."

"That's just it, Julia." He looked down, and she could see him swallow slowly. "That's how they're supposed to be said. I would have told you a month ago if I'd followed my heart. I've been worrying over it ever since, but I think it's time now. If you can't honestly say that you love me now, maybe you don't. And maybe you never will."

"That's not true. I just need time." She was beginning to feel desperate, wondering where this conversation was going.

"We've had time together. Julia, I need to know where I stand. I guess I'm really talking about a future together. I need to know if that's a possibility."

A future together? Julia's mind seemed to go blank. "Of course I want a future. I want to be with you. I want us to be together. But I don't know if I can make the kind of commitment you want right now. I think I've finally decided to go to the U, but it doesn't matter if you're at BYU. Provo's not that far away, and we can drive back and forth on weekends and ride together when we come back down here to visit."

Ben brought his head up and leaned the back of it against the rear window. "But I'm not talking about just dating, Julia. I'm talking about marriage and I think you know it. I'm not proposing or anything, I just want to know if it's a possibility, if you'd consider it . . . with me, I mean."

"Well . . ."

"I mean, I'm a careful guy, Julia. I don't want to get in too deep before I know where I'm going. If you have no intention of getting serious with me, I don't want to waste any more time." His words sounded harsh and angry.

Julia felt the world swirling around her in great clouds, and she was afraid it was going to begin to fall in sharp little pieces around her ears. "Of course I'd consider it . . . in time. You are . . . so close to perfect."

Ben closed his eyes and exhaled slowly.

"But, I'm only twenty, Ben. I never thought this would happen to me now. Of course I've always hoped that I'd get married someday, but I really thought it would take a while. I want a family, but that seems years away, not something that I'm prepared to deal with now. I mean, I'm like any girl; I used to make up names for my future children and imagine what they would look like, but it all seemed so far in the future. Not now.

"Why are you doing this all of a sudden? We are having so much fun, and I love being with you. Why can't that just go on? Do we have to get all weird and serious? I'm too young to deal with this. I need to finish school. I need to grow up."

Ben raked through his thick hair with tense fingers. "Julia, what did you think was going on here? Did you think we'd just have a good time together and then say 'see ya' and go our separate ways without anyone getting hurt? Be realistic! I didn't enter into this relationship for fun and games. As much as I hate to admit it, after a mission most guys are looking to date seriously, and although I didn't think I'd find someone this soon . . . well, there it is. What can we do about it now?"

He didn't touch her again, and she realized that she'd edged across the bench seat till her back was against the door. When she didn't say anything for a full minute he said, "Listen, maybe I just need to give you some space. Maybe we both need some right now. Heck, maybe I've just been delusional lately, thinking I'm in love with you. Maybe if I was with someone else I'd feel the same way."

Julia winced at his words. Why was she doing this? Was she insane? He was everything: intelligent, spiritual, funny . . . But this was too big, this didn't fit in with her plans at all. Maybe she *had* thought of it as a game, as emotional entertainment that she could turn off when she wanted to and resume her life. She wasn't experienced in this relationship thing; actually, she wasn't used to thinking about someone else and how her actions would affect that person. She didn't know how to do this, how to tell him how much he meant to her without committing to him in a way that her head told her she'd never be able to get out of.

"Ben, I don't know what to do." Julia felt tears swimming in her eyes and she blinked rapidly, lowering her head to hide them.

"Hey, don't get upset. It's okay, we can figure this out." He put his hand out to pat her on the shoulder, but he sounded distant. "Let's just give it a rest, date other people for a while, see what we want. Okay?"

"Okay." Julia kept her head down. If she looked at him she knew she'd throw herself at him and sob in his arms, and she could do without that kind of a scene. Ben got out of the truck and walked stiffly around to her side. He let her out, and she walked past him and up the shallow steps to her home.

She had her hand on the doorknob when he said, "Aren't you going to kiss me good-bye?"

She turned quickly. "I didn't think you wanted to."

"Oh, I want to all right. C'mere." As he drew her to him his eyes seemed a little too bright and glossy in the moonlight. And when he kissed her Julia thought a rift in the universe had opened beneath them and they were falling through time and space, heedless of the future, caught up and completely consumed in the fiery present.

Julia leaned heavily against the front door after leaving Ben and had to hold onto her arms tightly to keep herself from running out after him when she heard him finally start the truck and pull out of the driveway. His retreating headlights flashed eerily in the dark entryway, and though she knew the house was full of softly sleeping bodies, she felt completely alone.

It was the only choice, and she knew it, but why did she have to make it now? They'd only been together for a couple months. Was happiness that fleeting? But really, what else was she supposed to do? Just run off and get married and give up everything she'd worked for, everything she'd dreamed of? Once she was married, then of course, she was supposed to have a family, babies. What in the world would she do with babies? She'd have to stay at home with them. Children didn't do as well in daycare, and most importantly, there was what the prophet had said about mothers in the workplace—she wanted to be obedient, as obedient as she'd tried to be all her life. She had figured her only way out of the barefoot-and-pregnant trap was to avoid marriage until she'd accomplished her goals. Sure, that was funny. Avoid marriage. She'd thought it would be all too easy.

She put her hand to her forehead. It felt hot and damp, and her breathing was still coming ragged and uneven. Could she be like her sister-in-law Jenny? Settle down quietly and have two children right off the bat? Would she be content to stay at home, supporting her man, trying to adore him, biting her tongue in jealousy, while he was off doing all the things she wanted to do? No, there was no way she could reconcile herself to that right now, even if it would gain her what she'd always thought she wanted: someone of her own. And then her heart gave a small cry, and she wondered if she'd made a mistake and indeed truly loved him.

Julia walked a few paces onto the hardwood floor of the unlit hall and then stepped onto the thick, patterned area rug in her mother's formal living room. She crossed slowly to a plush couch and fell back onto it, wearily. She didn't reach up for the light of the lamp, but sat in the moonlit darkness and waited for her hammering heart to still and slow, and after a while the burning left her chest, and her eyes stopped swimming and blurring, until finally she felt a heavy nothingness descend upon her and her fingers grew cold where they lay still in her lap. Then she rose, without a thought disturbing the stillness of her mind, and went up to bed.

Chapter 19

"Are you completely insane?" Morgan threw her backpack onto her bed and didn't even glance at it when it slid to the floor, spilling out books.

"What?" Julia asked.

"No, don't 'what' me. You know exactly what I mean."

Actually Julia did, but she wondered how Morgan had found out.

"Maybe I do." Julia looked down, though she knew she'd have to meet Morgan's eyes soon enough.

"How could you break up with the guy? I mean, he's a peach, absolutely, and he sure seemed like he was in love with you."

"You're exaggerating."

"I'm not, you idiot. You're just too dense to see what's right in front of your nose." Morgan sat on her bunk opposite Julia, knee to knee, forcing Julia to acknowledge her.

Julia looked up. "How did you find out?"

"Obviously not from my best friend."

Yes, that must be what it's about, thought Julia. "Sorry. It's not something I really wanted to talk about at the time. You know I like my space." It was more like she would have burst into tears and made a complete fool of herself if she had said a word about it.

Morgan stood up and walked to the window, watching small beads of rain roll down the wet glass. "What happened?" she asked.

"Nothing *happened*, I just thought we needed to think a little and give each other some space."

"What's all this about space, Julia? If you keep this up, soon you'll have more than enough; everyone will walk a mile around you. And I don't mind saying that I'm kind of ticked."

"Really?" Julia smiled briefly at that.

"Come on! I tell you all my ridiculous sob stories about all the stupid guys that bug me, and I plague you over Aaron and make you read his letters, and I tell you about it when my mom and I fight, and I ask your advice, but when something big happens to *you*—and I know you're not admitting it, but something that has to be terrible and hard—you don't even mention it. You act like it didn't even happen. I had to find out from a friend of one of Ben's roommates. I kind of wondered what was up when I saw Ben walking that Trudy Applegate home, and I didn't dare tell you, but now it seems that he has the perfect right to do that."

"Of course he does. Ben's a free agent. He can do whatever he wants." But Julia couldn't believe how much it hurt to hear that. Trudy was the thin, dark-headed girl she'd seen Ben talking to in the library. Her chest seized up again like she was going to have a heart attack. At age twenty.

"Don't you like him?" Morgan asked.

"Of course I like him. Ben's a great guy and he's fun. I just don't want to get too serious right now. There's still a lot I need to do, and I want to be free to do it."

"You know, there might not be another chance . . . with Ben, I mean." Morgan looked straight into her eyes.

Julia wondered what she really meant by that. "I know, and maybe that's too bad, but I've got to do what I think is right for me." Julia thought she saw Morgan's eyes open a little wider, and she felt a steel shaft sink deeper into her soul. Her voice had been clear and calm. She hadn't realized she was such a good actress. She didn't know how she was able to say that, when she felt like her insides were bleeding so badly.

Morgan turned swiftly to drop onto the bed next to her. "Actually, I don't care much about Ben, I mean, tough luck for the guy and all, but I don't know, I guess I just feel a little betrayed by this whole thing."

"*You* feel betrayed . . . ?" She could hardly believe it. "Why is it always about you, Morgan?" Julia's voice was soft, but she knew the words would pierce—she had meant them to.

"What do you mean?" Morgan asked. "What's wrong with you anyway? I mean, I've been under the impression all these years that we were friends, that you liked me and trusted me." The pitch of Morgan's voice rose. "But what is it really, Julia, a friendship of convenience? I always thought that you were teasing me with all those sarcastic comments you make, and I knew I deserved them, but did you mean all that stuff? Do you really think I'm shallow and superficial and dumb? Yeah, just plain dumb, I guess."

Morgan was really working herself up now. Julia had never seen her so insecure, and she briefly wondered why, before her own pain blocked out any budding sympathy. Clearly, Morgan was taking center stage again, playing the injured party and calling on all her ridiculous dramatic powers to make herself appear picked on and conspired against. Julia wasn't in the mood to buy it.

"Come on, Morgan, don't be stupid."

"Oh, right, right, not dumb. I guess it's stupid."

"Come on, stop twisting my words. You know what I mean. With me you just take what you get. You've always known that. And if the truth be told, *you* usually engineer yourself into the spotlight. I've always just been your trusty sidekick. And if you really want to know the truth, if you really want me to confide in you, you got it, baby. You're spoiled. You always grab the limelight for yourself and when something happens to take it away from you, even briefly, you're jealous."

"Jealous!"

"That's what I said. You can't take it that you weren't the center of this little drama."

There was a short silence that held only the sound of breathing.

"I think you really are crazy, Julia. Maybe Ben is better off." Morgan bit off the words sharply before stalking out of the room and slamming the door.

That is just like Morgan, too, Julia thought. But after a while of sitting in the same place, staring out the window, Julia began to wish she hadn't spoken so bluntly. She and Morgan had argued before, but not like this, not using hot, serious words that were sure to be regretted no matter how true they were. Julia sank down a little on her bed and rested her head against the padded backboard. She closed her eyes briefly, uttering a weak prayer, asking for forgiveness, when she wasn't sure how sorry she was yet but half-knowing that she'd been partly wrong and a little unfair and a little spiteful. She sighed loudly and then turned around to pick up the chemistry book behind her.

* * *

Morgan hurled herself into the rain and the wind outside the dorm and was halfway across campus before she realized that she'd come out without a jacket or an umbrella or her purse or any money or anything. She stopped abruptly, looked around, and pushed a lock of damp hair off her forehead. It was really coming down. Though she didn't have any of her books or her backpack she turned toward the library and half ran through the rain, arriving breathless and wet and still very angry.

Inside the entrance she thought briefly about her appearance, dragging a hand through her damp hair and wiping her fingers over the raindrops under her eyes. She leaned back a little to let her hair hang free and shook her head, spraying water all over the glass door behind her.

The Hale library was very quiet at this hour of the afternoon. She looked toward the bottom-floor lounge and then to the group of large tables next to the magazines. A few students hung around each area, looking dazed and uncomprehending in the thick quiet of the muzzy afternoon.

Morgan blew a breath of air up over her forehead and then stepped up to the first magazine rack, scanning it quickly. She grabbed the first fashion magazine that her eyes came to and sat down with a jerk at a table with a view of the front doors. She didn't open the magazine for a few minutes, but just sat back, closed her eyes and tried to think.

It looked like Julia didn't take Morgan seriously, like everyone else. Maybe Julia thought she was really just a flake after all. Maybe even Aaron was realizing it. She always got a letter from Aaron around the second week in the month. But now it was nearly the end of the month, and she hadn't got his letter. Sure, sometimes his letters had only been a couple of paragraphs, and there was that time he'd only sent the charm, but he'd never forgotten completely before.

Amazingly, in a year and a half none of his letters had been lost in the mail before either. And then on top of the no-letter thing, there was Sammy getting married and that ridiculous fight with her mother.

Her anger burned a little brighter, and she began feeding the fire. "Spoiled" and "jealous"! That was great, really, especially coming from Julia! Morgan couldn't think of two better words to describe Julia herself. She got angrier as she played little scenarios over in her mind where Julia would come to her and humbly ask her forgiveness, and she would hesitate over it a minute, like she wasn't sure, and then she would be gracious and say that it was okay. But then, of course, after that things would never really be the same again. Morgan smiled to herself and sat up a little, lifting the damp hair off her collar. She felt better now.

She was just about to open her magazine when she caught movement out of the corner of her eye. She glanced up and saw Ben Hammond at one of the magazine racks, and she watched him curiously until he looked over in her direction.

"Hey." She lifted her hand casually. Ben nodded and smiled and probably would have turned back to the rack if she hadn't leaned toward him, smiling an invitation, and said, "What're ya reading?"

Ben grabbed a magazine from the rack and came over, just like she knew he would. He sat down opposite her and laid the magazine flat on the table. "*Field and Stream.*"

"A little light reading, huh? Where are your books?"

"Oh, they're over there against the wall. I just got tired of reading chemistry and trying to write my psychology paper. I thought I'd change the subject for a minute and see if I could get back into that stuff later." He smiled a little self-consciously and glanced around.

Morgan felt an energy shoot through her and surge around in waves in her chest and her head. She felt much better.

"Uh, I guess you heard about Julia and me," Ben said.

Morgan could tell he was nervous and forcing himself to acknowledge what he thought was obvious. He began flipping the edge of the magazine with his thumb.

"Yes. That's too bad. I thought you guys were having a lot of fun together."

"Yeah, I thought so too." He looked up. He was embarrassed.

Morgan smiled again, brilliantly. "Well, I've always known that Julia was crazy, but I couldn't believe it when she gave *you* up." Morgan arched her fine eyebrows way up. "Sometimes I just can't understand her. She doesn't know a good thing when she sees it." Morgan was pushing him gently, laying on the flattery lightly like a sprinkle of powdered sugar.

"How's she doing?" Ben looked at her, transparent with hope.

Morgan felt disgusted. It looked like he was still pretty whipped over her. "Actually, she seems fine. I didn't even find out about you guys until today, and that was by accident; I was talking to a friend of your roommate. She didn't even tell *me*, can you believe it? I'm kind of mad at her right now, really."

He looked down for a minute, and Morgan couldn't tell what he was thinking. She gathered her hair up and held it on the top of her head, preening a little, making sure he looked at her before she said, "Well, I guess we'll never figure her out." She let out a long exasperated sigh. "Are you coming to the dance tonight? You should, you know." She smiled brilliantly. "And I'll even dance with you to cheer you up." She could see the teasing was working and a flame began to burn in the pit of her stomach.

"Who says I need cheering up?"

"Well, it's pretty obvious, isn't it? You're in this dark hole, moping around, not even studying. I'm not saying you're depressed, really, but it was the only thing I could think of to say to get a dance with you." She looked up at him from beneath lowered eyelashes, affecting modesty. And then she began to laugh a little, and so did he because she was being so obvious.

"You're shameless, you know."

"Yes, I know." She raised her eyebrows comically and they both laughed again. He didn't appear to mind her flirting; in fact, he seemed to enjoy it.

Chapter 20

They were knocking doors again in relative silence, taking turns at the door approaches, getting turned down and then moving on to the next door or the next building. Aaron was starting to feel like a salesman, moving from door to door, sometimes getting no more than a few words in before an angry woman or old man would slam the door in their faces. Even Elder Spinhall's enthusiasm was winding down this hot afternoon; he looked crushed and rumpled and the skin on the bridge of his nose between the heavy lenses of his glasses was pink and perspiring. Aaron jerked his gaze off that nose and turned down the hall to the next door. Elder Spinhall's turn. Aaron fixed a smile on his face as the door opened and his companion began. His mind wandered a little and caught on a remembered phrase from Morgan's latest letter. *I'll be so* RELIEVED *when you get home.*

Relieved? Relieved from what? If she'd said "thrilled" or "excited" or nearly anything else, he probably wouldn't have thought anything of it, but "relieved"? Relieved from the sheer numbers of guys that were after her? Relieved from the burden of school? Relieved to be with *him* again? He was being paranoid and he knew it. He forced his mind off her with an effort and shook his head a little in disgust as he focused on the conversation.

Elder Spinhall seemed to be making progress with a young woman in a light, cotton-print dress. She looked fresh and beautiful, the way he'd thought that Italian women would look before he'd come out here. So many younger women here dressed immodestly. Seventeen months into his mission, he was surprised at how energetic and happy this woman looked.

As Elder Spinhall asked if they could share a message of Christ with her and her family, a tiny girl poked her head around her mother's skirt. She was beautiful, with chocolate dark eyes in a dimpled face. She smiled shyly up at Aaron, and when he winked back, he set her whole face alight.

"Perhaps when your husband is at home we can come back and give you our message."

The young woman looked with strained eyes up at them and them lowered her head saying softly, "I do not have a husband."

Aaron was immediately disappointed by her answer. To teach her they would have to get one of the sisters from the branch to come along. The sister missionaries lived on the other side of Rome, and it would take them two or even three hours to travel across the city.

"Oh, I see," said Aaron. "Would you have a few minutes tomorrow to listen to our message? We'll bring a woman from our church with us too, if that's okay. I promise it is the most important message you will ever hear."

The young woman looked a little uncertain, but then her face broke into a smile. "I'm Francesca Forgonne. I will be home tomorrow at this same time. You may bring your friend and come for a few minutes perhaps."

The next day, they stood at Francesca Forgonne's door with Sister Targini, who had agreed to accompany them, her thick arms crossed over her middle and one elbow dangling a battered black purse.

Aaron was to give the discussion, and suddenly he felt a surge of fear. Signora Forgonne had seemed so receptive; he didn't want to be responsible for losing her.

Francesca Forgonne opened the door and led them to a small room that held an old sofa and two straight-backed chairs. Sister Targini spoke to Francesca in rapid Italian and then sat heavily on one end of the sofa, smiling widely. Francesca waved the missionaries into the chairs and then seated herself cautiously on the other end of the frayed sofa. The little girl pressed herself against her mother's side.

"You have a beautiful daughter, Signora Forgonne." Aaron looked at the little girl, and she flashed him another smile.

"Thank you," Francesca replied.

"Signora Forgonne, as we said, we are missionaries from The Church of Jesus Christ of Latter-day Saints, and we've come to give you a true message about Jesus Christ . . ." The words flowed on, filling Aaron as they never had before, blossoming into the beautiful truths of the gospel as Francesca's eyes grew larger and larger.

Aaron glanced over at Elder Spinhall when he'd finished and saw that he looked mellow and at ease, not at all the sharp, irritating guy that Aaron had been working with all these weeks. The light of the Spirit was on his face as well. Aaron realized he didn't feel bugged by him anymore, and he was a little surprised.

They gave Francesca a Book of Mormon and asked her to read it, and they showed her the place in Moroni 10 where Moroni says to ask God with a sincere heart to know if the book is true. She sat there calmly, taking it all in, asking intelligent questions. Aaron couldn't believe it. She said they could come back next week for the second lesson. Finally, a "golden contact" if he'd ever seen one. He didn't want to leave. The Spirit in the room was the strongest he'd felt since Marco's baptism. But he had to end it, he supposed.

"Will you read these passages and pray about them?" Aaron asked again, wanting to get a firm commitment.

"Yes, I will try," she said as she stood up. "Thank you for coming." She took his outstretched hand. "You men are different somehow," she said, looking at him strangely.

"Yes," said Sister Targini. "They are special."

Elder Spinhall jumped in. "We look forward to seeing you next Wednesday."

Aaron let go of her hand so she could shake hands with Elder Spinhall and Sister Targini.

Back out on the street Aaron looked back at the old weathered building. "Who'd have thought we'd find someone like her in there? That was amazing."

"Yeah." Elder Spinhall seemed too dazed to speak. He must have been feeling the same way.

"She was a very beautiful girl. Very good," said Sister Targini, smiling. "I and my mother will call on her also, next week, to talk. Thank you for asking me to come, Elders."

They thanked her, and she shook their hands and patted them both on the back before turning down the street to catch her bus.

Aaron and Elder Spinhall turned slowly in the other direction, to begin more tracting.

"Elder Spinhall . . ." Aaron ventured.

"Yeah?"

"I'm sorry for the way I acted the other day. I really am. I'm sure it wasn't too comfortable to go walking around in a wet suit. I'm sorry that . . . well, that I haven't made our companionship work out very well. I want to try to get along better."

"It's okay." He put a finger under his collar and pulled it out a little. "We could both try harder. I know I'm a pain sometimes."

"We need to pull together so we can feel the Spirit, so we can teach like that more often. Man, that was wonderful! I really think she'll accept the gospel. It just felt right in there."

"I know. You did a great job."

Had Elder Spinhall really said that? Aaron looked at him in amazement, and he just laughed. Aaron smiled widely and put a hand on Elder Spinhall's shoulder.

"You're all right, you know? I think maybe we're going to make it."

Chapter 21

This wasn't bad. Not bad at all. Morgan looked up into Ben Hammond's eyes as she swayed with him in the dark gym. She curled her fingers slightly into the hard muscle of his shoulder and leaned further back so she could get a better view of his face. He was so tall! She leaned back even further and nearly lost her balance, forcing Ben to tighten his hold around her waist and pull her against him. She laughed up at him and slid her hands down to grip his biceps. She shook her head, tossing her golden hair gleefully, breathing in the atmosphere of her success in a deep satisfying draft. The music pounded her ears and shook through the floor into her feet.

He was so tall it was impossible to talk to him over the blaring music unless he leaned down to her, putting his ear close to her lips. So she began a conversation, forcing him to lean close to hear her comments, again and again.

She'd played it easy, not too obvious. It was ridiculous, really, how easy it was, how well she knew them: boys, men. She'd walked past Ben first, and waved casually, intentionally heading toward a group of guys in her ward. And after talking with them for a while, she'd accepted a few dances, making sure that she led each guy to a place on the floor where Ben could watch. And then she'd disappeared for a while into the hall and the ladies room, to stand blankly around, missing Julia and her background comments as the ever-present sounding board. She remembered the tension between Julia and herself that had gone on, uneased, when she had returned from the library to get ready for the dance. They'd passed each other in the same room, but hadn't spoken, the air almost combustible with the heat of their feelings.

This made her more determined, more hardened, and more sure of herself. She could get anyone she wanted. Anyone. She knew it. If she'd wanted to break up Sammy and his fiancée, it would be easy, even now. It would only take a couple of meetings, a little bit of confession, a little mental intimacy, maybe a kiss or two, and that simpering redhead would be forgotten.

And this was easy too. Hah! Morgan thought as she danced in Ben's arms and made quick, flirtatious conversation over the strong beat of the music.

After the dance, Morgan lingered a little in the foyer, talking with a girl from one of her classes about a research paper, keeping her eye on Ben and his roommates near the entrance to the men's room.

Morgan waved as she saw Lorraine and Heather pass through the front doors, causing a pause in her conversation, and when she turned back to try to remember what she'd been saying, she caught movement out of the corner of her eye from Ben's group. Suddenly the right opener occurred to her and she hurriedly cut off the girl, saying someone was waiting for her outside. With a quick move she was able to push against the same glass door that Ben was using, and she innocently backed into him, waving to the girl back in the corner. Her eyes were wide with apology and surprise as she turned to him.

"Oh, sorry . . . Ben . . ." Another bright, swinging smile. "Did you guys have fun?"

"Yeah." He smiled back at her as they crowded out and down the steps with the last of the students from the dance. His roommates had faded back a little as expected, to give Ben some space, and she could hear a few snickers intended for Ben's ears. He glanced briefly back at them, and Morgan panicked a little, lest he slow down and wait for them.

"So how's school going? Did you get your psych paper finished?"

"Naw. I was trying to be good, you know, studying on a Friday afternoon and all, but I finally just let it go and went to the snack bar to drown my sorrows in a banana split."

"Oh, yum. You mean one of those big ones that you get to choose three toppings and three flavors of ice cream? You actually have to share those, they're so huge."

"Yeah." Ben smiled down at her. "You sound experienced."

"Of course. It's my favorite when I have a few bucks in my pocket." Morgan slapped the pocket of her jeans and edged closer to him. They were walking slowly in the direction of her dorm, and Morgan stayed close to him on the sidewalk, hoping he'd feel obligated to walk with her because they were a little apart from his group, and she'd been alone. He kept walking.

"Actually, I think that sounds awful good right now." She smiled up at him, hoping he'd suggest they stop for ice cream, hoping that he'd pay since she didn't have a cent with her.

He looked at her strangely. "Isn't the snack bar closed? Besides, I probably shouldn't have another one this soon."

Morgan knew he probably felt a little awkward and maybe was anxious not to be seen with her. But they were now well away from his group of friends and headed firmly toward Bentwell. She smiled and tried another angle.

"Oh, well," she said, pausing a little. Then, "Isn't it gorgeous out here tonight? I love it when it's so warm and dark and nice like this. You feel like you never want to go in." She spread her arms out and then turned to look at him. "What should we do? It's way too early to go home. Look at the moon." She pointed to the beautiful circle just visible between two great, old trees.

Ben stared up obediently, and Morgan took the opportunity to whirl around in front of him and walk backward so she could see him while they talked.

"Hey, let's go up to the track. I'm really fast, you know. We can race!" She began jumping up and down and jogging neatly backward. She felt strength and power flowing down into her limbs.

"Well, I don't know. Do they want us in there this late at night? Are the gates open?" He stalled a little, seeming nervous. She knew it wasn't because he was worried about the gates.

"Oh, come on, I won't embarrass you too bad. I might even let you win." She dared to grab his hand and pulled him hard in the direction of the track. He didn't resist much, and she began to wonder at her own daring. She wondered if she'd ever pulled it off this quickly before. She really hadn't ever talked to him much before the library this afternoon, and yet here he was, in the palm of her hand. She smiled again, but this time a vision of Julia interrupted her, and she felt a thread of guilt pull tight in her chest. She took two deep breaths and was able to ease it a little. Then she began to laugh to mask the feeling and she kept saying silly, chatty things to Ben, the small talk that she was so good at, that made everything seem natural and innocent.

The track gates were standing open casually, and they passed through. Morgan and Ben stepped up onto the springy, rubberized track.

"Okay, are you ready to go? Do you really want to do this?" Ben asked. "I ran track in high school, you know."

"Oh, I'm not afraid of you!" She placed her hands on her waist and squared her shoulders. Ben responded by crouching down in a runner's starting position just behind the starting line. Morgan took her place beside him and pretended to lose her balance so she could fall against him. He pushed back and she righted herself, laughing, letting her hair fall over her face as she flexed her legs and bounced her body up and down slightly.

"Okay then . . . ready, set, go!" Morgan yelled.

Ben shot ahead, seeming to take this seriously or else wanting to show off, and Morgan pounded quickly behind him, making good time but watching him pull steadily away. She was running hard and smooth. She liked the way her hair streamed out behind her, and she liked the cool, sweet air that filled her lungs. She also liked watching Ben run, graceful and athletic, his stride opening up so beautifully that she considered stopping just so she could watch him better. But then she saw her opportunity, and she stepped off the track, pushing her hardest across the grass of the football field, nearly invisible to him in the dark. Her breath was coming labored and her chest felt like it would burst—she wasn't used to this! But she could see that she would be able to catch him just before the last curve if she pushed just a bit harder. She gave it her best and stepped back onto the track just behind Ben.

He was so surprised that he slowed a little, twisting around to look at her, and this gave her the chance to push herself forward and lean on him, jumping up with her hands on his back.

Morgan caught him off balance, and he couldn't right himself. He tripped and they fell onto the grass in a rolling tumble. They were both laughing and breathing hard. Morgan smoothed the hair back from her face.

"You are such a cheater!" Ben's face looked flushed in the moonlight, and he grabbed her shoulder and shook it a little, leaving his big, warm hand there.

"Me?" She tried to look incredulous, innocent, and then burst out with another laugh. "See? I'm a great runner." She reclined easily against the grass, smilingly conscious of his lingering touch. She dropped her head back and looked at the moon briefly, aware that her moonlit profile was good and strong, and then she looked at Ben again, leaning perceptibly closer to him. He'd stopped laughing and was looking at her intensely, curiosity brushing his features. And when his eyes flicked down to her lips quickly and then back to her eyes, she knew she'd won, and she could barely keep herself from shouting. She made her eyes heavy as she moved closer, and finally shut them. And then there was a pause, long enough that she nearly opened her eyes again, but then she felt his warm lips brush hers lightly . . . and then suddenly he was gone, scrambling up off the grass. She rolled onto her back in surprise.

"Hey . . ." He wouldn't look at her. "I've really got to go." Ben wiped at his cheek and the corner of his mouth with the back of his hand. "I'll walk you home."

Morgan was stunned for a moment, but then waited for him to put out his hand to help her up. When he didn't, like he was afraid to touch her, she pushed herself to her feet slowly, beginning to feel a hard pit in the bottom of her stomach.

Ben didn't say anything during the short walk to Bentwell dorm, even though Morgan made a few half-hearted comments about the well-trimmed flower beds on campus. What was wrong with him? They were just having a little fun, after all. But she felt a little sick too, and she tried to tell herself that she had not gone too far.

When they got to the dorm, Ben shied away from the front doors and would have left without a word, but Morgan whipped up some anger out of her guilt. *Who did he think he was? It took two.* "Aren't you even going to walk me to my door?" She flung it out acidly, and she could see it stung him. He turned again wordlessly and opened the glass door to let her pass through.

He stopped about five steps from her open door though. She could hear a couple of her roommates talking quietly, and she moved up until she could see in to where Julia and Cynthia were sitting on Julia's bed. She wanted to make some sarcastic last retort to Ben where he stood, hollow-eyed and nervous, halfway down the hall, but she changed her mind at the last minute and called out loudly, sweetly, "Good-bye, *Ben.*"

Morgan was in just the right position that she could see Julia's look of shock and Ben's horror simultaneously. So why didn't she feel her triumph?

* * *

Julia couldn't take her eyes off Morgan as she stepped in through the doorway and closed the door. Morgan leaned against it for a moment, crossing her arms over her chest, a small smile of fake bravado growing in the corners of her mouth.

Julia glanced at Cynthia without turning her head to see if she had heard and then snapped her eyes back to Morgan when she saw Cynthia's body rigidly at attention, also staring at Morgan. Julia's insides slowly filled up with lead. She couldn't think what to say.

"So . . . did you guys have fun tonight?" Morgan left the door and walked, arms swinging, into the bedroom. She sat down on her bed, leaned against the backrest and wiped the back of her hand across her mouth a couple of times.

Julia's eyes were glued to those lips—full, red, and slightly amused. Still she couldn't think of any words to fill the huge void that gaped in the space between her and Morgan. She was grateful when Cynthia leaped in.

"Did *you?*" Cynthia still hadn't moved and her words had a hard, incredulous edge to them.

"Yeah, there were lots of guys at the dance, and decent ones for a change." Morgan looked directly at Julia, challenging her. "You should have come."

"Some of us are a little sick of the games." Julia hardly recognized her voice. It sounded flat and dead. The lead was stirring inside her, though, becoming a molten, angry mass. She stood up and walked to the end of the room. "How many did you pick up this time, Morgan?" Julia turned to stare at her, thinking she felt real hatred for the first time, struggling to keep angry tears from her eyes, struggling to control her shaking, her shock, and her heartbreak. It was a difficult thing to do, especially with an audience, and so she turned to her desk, opened the drawer for her car keys, grabbed her purse and a couple of textbooks and stuffed everything into her backpack, which she swung to her shoulder. As she was leaving the bedroom Morgan stood to follow her.

"Where're you going?" Morgan sounded surprised and a little uncertain.

"Home."

"Why?"

"Because I want to, you little tramp!" Angry tears began to stream down her face as she hurried to the door. Her hand was shaking hard on the knob, and her heavy backpack slipped off her shoulder. She had to jerk her arm up to keep it from falling. The tears were coming faster, with a sort of a strange sounding sob, as Julia struggled with the door handle. She finally hauled it open and fled into the hall, and then she was running to get out, barely seeing the curious stares of other girls and their boyfriends that she passed in the hall. She was bursting through the outer glass door of the building when she finally ran into someone. She kept the forward motion and twisted back to see who it was, her eyes blurring with her tears and the sudden darkness. She stopped suddenly when she realized it was Ben, looking stricken and guilty, and then another sob leaped in her throat and she stumbled back into a run, grateful she'd parked her car at the far end of the lot.

She could hear Cynthia calling her name as she willed her shaking fingers to fit the key into the lock on the car door. When it was open, she threw her bag into the back and swung into the driver's seat. She flung the car out of the parking place and raced down the lot, glancing to the right at the last moment to see Cynthia trying to wave her down and Ben beside her with his hand to his head. Morgan hadn't left the room.

Part Two

Chapter 1

Morgan wiped a rag slowly over the countertop again and released a slow sigh. It was so boring in the afternoons. She pushed a strand of hair back over her ear and surveyed the sandwich shop for another drip or smear. It looked perfectly clean and shining, something she wasn't used to being responsible for. The chrome of the old-fashioned shake machines gleamed in the sunlight. She smiled a little; there was no telling what she'd do to keep from going crazy in this little town.

She leaned over the counter until she could see the young couple in the far booth. They were laughing softly, and the guy reached over and ran his finger down the girl's arm. The girl shivered a little and so did Morgan before she jerked back from the counter in case they could see her.

So little to do. She drummed her fingers against the countertop. She was doing pretty well, considering the humiliation of her situation. But what choice did she really have? Her parents had laid down the law when they'd discovered that she'd flunked French and had done quite poorly in two of her other classes. They had been very disappointed when she'd told them she wouldn't be graduating with Julia and the others, and had said there was no point in sending her up north to a four-year school until she got her act together and decided what she really wanted. Sure, she probably could have brought them around to one plan or another, but the truth was, she didn't have one. She felt like she was in limbo. She didn't know where to go from here. She'd never seriously considered actually getting a *degree*, becoming old and studious and graduating in a cap and gown.

She'd thought of college just as something you did when you got out of high school. You got to walk around those big, leafy campuses and live on your own and have water fights in the dorms. And eventually you fell in love and married some cute guy and then you could respectably get a job as a secretary or something in an office and say you were supporting your husband through school. It was okay then to drop out of school. It was noble or something.

The problem was she was waiting for Aaron. She really was. And it was kind of hard to get her life going when he wasn't here. In fact, it was downright frustrating. Her mother had told her she'd better just live at home and retake a couple of classes at Hale and figure out a major or a career or some kind of a plan (she'd seemed pretty exasperated) before they'd think of supporting her in it. If you didn't have any money, it pretty well clipped your wings, even if you knew where you were flying off to.

Her parents had made her get a job. *And* live at home. That had been particularly humiliating, to come back and live at home when she'd been on her own for two years. Living at the dorm had been her mother's idea, even before Julia had suggested it. Though Hunter was only a fifteen-minute drive from Halston and Hale, Morgan's mother had said that she thought it would be good for Morgan to get out on her own. However, they didn't feel as willing to sacrifice financially for her when they found out why the Jeffses had suddenly turned so cool to them. You'd think she'd actually *married* Ben the way the Jeffses were acting! She tried to pretend that she didn't care about it, even to herself, but it was pretty hard work.

Julia hadn't said one word to her. Not one. Not even when she'd moved out of the dorms. Not even when she'd left town to move up to the U in August. Morgan didn't even know where Julia was staying now. That hurt, but she tried not to think about it. Like most things, if you didn't concentrate on them, isolate them, and tear them apart, they were pretty easy to bear in the long run, pretty easy to gloss over and pretend that they didn't exist.

Aaron had finally written to her and had mentioned that his cousin Lorraine and Julia were rooming together at the U. Lorraine had been accepted to the ballet program as a pre-major. It was quite competitive, and Morgan was really happy for her, if a little jealous.

Morgan's eyes stopped on a chocolate-syrup drip on the side of the dispenser, and she walked over and picked at it with her fingernail before scrubbing with her rag. The bell over the front door rang, and she turned to see a group of young men enter. Football recruits from the look of them. They were huge.

"Hi, what can I get for you?" Morgan leaned over the counter and smiled up at the first guy.

"I'll have two quarter-pounder cheeseburgers with extra pickles and a large fry and a large chocolate shake."

"To go or stay?"

"Stay."

"Okay . . ." Morgan punched the keys on the cash register. "That will be $8.75." She gave him another bright smile, to catch his attention, but she didn't need to—he was already staring at her.

The big guy put the money into her hand, and one of his friends pushed forward. Morgan turned her eyes to the next customer and bathed him in her smile, but the first guy turned around and came back. Morgan shifted her attention again.

"Hey . . . are you Morgan Carter?" he asked.

"Yeah, how'd you know?"

"Well, your name tag," his eyes flicked toward it and then back to her face, "and the fact that I lived with your picture for about four months on my mission."

"Hey, really?"

"Yeah, I was Aaron Jenner's companion. Great guy. Still waiting for him?"

"Sure. What would I be doing here if I wasn't?" She laughed and leaned toward him. He was great looking and muscular. She wondered if this was the guy Aaron had nearly been killed by. She smiled again.

"Hey, well, it's good meeting you." He turned to go.

"Yeah, except you haven't told me your name yet, so we really haven't met," she replied, sassily raising her eyebrows a little.

"Oh, yeah, sorry. I'm Jim Facer, from Cache Valley."

"Well, Jim Facer from Cache Valley, what if we got together sometime, and you could tell me about Aaron? I haven't met any of his companions yet. I'm dying to have firsthand knowledge."

The guys behind Jim started pushing him and complaining loudly.

"Sure, when do you get off?" He ignored them.

"Oh, not till about nine." She wrinkled her nose. "But at least I don't have to do cleanup."

"What if I came over and picked you up and we went over to the institute to play ping-pong or foozeball or something?"

"Okay, sounds good."

"Man, Facer, you sure work fast!" A loud laugh erupted from the back of the line.

"Hey, do it on your own time; we're starving!" another of the players yelled.

"Hey, it's not like you didn't have lunch two hours ago." Jim smiled, turned around, and delivered a swift punch to the shoulder of the guy right behind him. He responded by grabbing Jim around the neck and punching him in the ribs. Shoving him out of the way, he asked, "Do I get to order?"

"Oh, sorry." Morgan reluctantly took her eyes off Jim Facer and took down three more orders and gave them to the cook in the back.

The ends of Morgan's fingers were tingling, and she felt a little light-headed. That guy had actually lived with Aaron! She hoped he was one of those guys that talked a lot. Her heart thudded heavily in her chest.

* * *

Aaron felt like he was floating, soaring in midair. Today Francesca Forgonne had been baptized. It had taken her several months to decide, but he'd never lost hope—even when she'd gone to her priest for advice and had avoided meeting with them for three weeks. Aaron put his arms behind his head and stared up at the darkened ceiling of his tiny bedroom.

Francesca had no family. At least none that was willing to own her. She'd been kicked out of her home and disowned when she'd become pregnant and told her parents that she didn't want to marry her boyfriend. It would have been a mistake to marry him, she had told Aaron and Elder Spinhall. She knew that she didn't want to get tied up with him and pay for it all her life. For someone so young she was amazingly brave and seemed to have a mature understanding of life. She was willing to take all the responsibilities on and deal with all the hard things in order to make her life her own. She had known what she was doing when she turned her boyfriend down. She'd known she'd be on her own, and it was hard, but she was doing it.

Aaron had a new companion now, a hardworking elder from Salt Lake. Elder Spinhall had almost cried when he found he was being transferred before Francesca's baptism. He'd truly caught the spirit of missionary work with Francesca, contributing well-thought-out comments and really digging into the doctrine to answer her many questions. Aaron shook his head again in amazement. The Lord had answered his prayers. He'd led them to Francesca, and she'd been the thing that had brought them together and had kept them from petty bickering over their differences. She focused them on the gospel, and as they'd worked together toward the common goal of helping her prepare for baptism, they'd learned to get along. Aaron smiled faintly in the dark. He and Elder Spinhall had even talked at length, and Aaron had been surprised to learn that his formerly impossible companion was human like everyone else. They'd even planned to get in touch when they got back home.

Aaron surveyed their small room, still too charged up to sleep. This effort had carried him past all the disappointments and the long hours and the rigid rules. It made it all worth it. Francesca was someone who would be a good strong member all her life and who would be dedicated to the gospel. Aaron drew in a long breath of air and blew it toward the ceiling, enjoying the moment, genuinely happy for Francesca and her daughter. He closed his eyes again in a brief prayer, thanking the Lord for letting him be here, for allowing him to have this incredible experience.

* * *

"Whoa! I can't believe you! Where'd you learn to play ping-pong?" Jim grinned at Morgan before bending to retrieve the little ball from a corner.

"At home," she replied. "We have a table in the basement, and I have a very competitive younger brother!"

"How old?"

"He's seventeen, a junior in high school." Morgan returned Jim's serve, smashing the little ball into his left corner and watching it fly across the room, landing under one of the snack tables.

"Man!" Jim jogged off to retrieve the ball again.

"Don't hurt yourself under there!" Morgan teased. He looked too big to squeeze under the little table.

"Don't worry. I may look big, but I'm agile." He gave her a smile over his shoulder. "That's why coach is considering me for quarterback—second string of course. But I haven't been playing for two years, and I'm amazed I'm even on the team." He lumbered back over to her.

He didn't sound too humble about it. In fact, he looked quite pleased with himself. And cute. Big square jaw, curly brown hair. *Definitely cute*, Morgan decided.

"So, where are you living down here?" she asked.

"Over at the Bengal Apartments, you know, just off campus."

"Why not in the dorms with the other players?"

"It's not for me." Jim slammed the ball and just missed her edge of the table where he was aiming. "Dang!"

Morgan smiled and rolled her shoulders back. "That makes twenty-one for me. Too bad!"

"Hey, you didn't even say game point."

"I forgot."

"Then we get to play the point over, right?"

"Jim, do you really think you are going to beat me? You only have ten points, and I've been easy on you, really."

"Oh, quit yer braggin' and serve me the ball!"

"O-kaaay." Morgan shrugged, bent to the table and flicked the ball low over the net. She took him by surprise, and the ball bounced twice on his side of the table before shooting off toward the pop machine.

"I give up." Jim flipped his paddle up, and it landed on the table with a clatter.

"Hey, watch it! Don't break the thing." She walked over to his side of the table. "Want a soda? I'm buying."

"No." Jim had his arms folded in a fake pout.

"Come on, I beat everybody—even my brother sometimes."

"Okay, but loser buys." Jim dug into his pocket and fished four quarters from among the change. Morgan walked over with her hand out and made sure the transfer of funds involved a little contact. His hand was hot and damp, and when his fingers touched her palm he backed away a little. Still a little shell-shocked? Surely not; he'd been home for nearly four months. She curved her lips in a knowing smile.

When she returned with the soda, he was sitting at one of the little round tables.

"Do you miss him?" Jim said, snapping open his can.

"Aaron?"

"Yes, Aaron. Who did you think I meant?"

She smiled a little. "Yes."

"You guys were pretty close, I guess."

"We were." She took a long swallow of the cold drink and stared him in the eyes. "Waiting isn't as easy as one might think." She didn't want him to think she'd been sitting at home knitting for twenty-one months.

"I guess not." He looked a little uncomfortable, like he didn't know how to take her last statement.

"It's been a long time since I saw him. He hasn't turned too self-righteous on me, has he?"

"Not when I was with him. Did he tell you he nearly beat me up one day?" he asked with a grin.

"Yes. I thought it was probably you that he pushed. It's pretty darn tempting, I must say." She gave his meaty arm a token punch and swung her hair over her right shoulder. He seemed to be getting used to her proximity she noted with satisfaction.

"Have you been dating while he's been gone?"

"What do you think?"

"I think that Aaron'd have to be crazy to leave someone as good-looking as you. He should have packed you in his suitcase." Jim looked down at his soda can. He seemed a little embarrassed.

Morgan's temperature seemed to rise a few degrees. She felt a tingling in the ends of her fingers. "That's what I think!" she agreed.

"But, really, he's a great guy; we had a rough start, but it was mostly my fault. He's only a *little* annoying to live with." He sneaked a look up at her, the side of his mouth twitching a little.

"That's good to know. What's it like in Italy? Was it hard to learn the language?" Morgan kept him busy for the next half hour with questions about culture and language, denying herself, for some reason, the things she was really longing to hear: personal details that would make her feel like she knew Aaron again. She'd meant to ask questions that would paint a picture of him in the air between them. But she didn't want to anymore. Not with Jim anyway. She wanted him to see her happy and confident, in charge of her emotions, not the needy and pitiful girl waiting back home. *Jim Facer is amusing, after all*, she thought to herself.

Chapter 2

Would she ever learn her way around up here? It had seemed pretty straightforward. East toward the near mountain, west toward the mountains across the valley in the distance, north up toward Bountiful, and south back the way she'd come in August, from the Point of the Mountain. Why then was she winding around and around in this east-side Salt Lake City subdivision that seemed to have no outlet? Julia was becoming exasperated and hot in her stuffy little red car, and her nerves began to jump as she worried how much she would miss in her study group. She was already half an hour late.

It was the fault of that conniving, greasy-haired Linda Shank. Why had they not just met on campus as usual? She was brilliant, yes—Julia would give her that in a pinch—but the way she slobbered all over the guys in their group with *her* looks was beyond Julia. Two of the guys were even married, and it didn't seem to stop her much. She'd suggested studying out on her patio and having snacks, and all the men had sprung over to her side without even a discussion.

Of course food was a great motivator, even for her, but the inconvenience was considerable, for all of them, and as Julia drove the lush, tree-shaded avenues of the east bench, she barely escaped boiling over.

Maybe she should just go back to her apartment and plow through the material for the test on her own, but they were also supposed to work through the project together, and there wasn't much time before it was due. She shaded her eyes against the setting sun and decided to try down another street. Maybe she'd missed number 1236 the last three times she'd driven down that street.

She'd just about given up on the address and the study group—and that snooty Linda—when she spotted the numbers 236 on the front of a large, red-brick house overgrown with climbing ivy. This must be it. She'd risk it anyway. She parked her little car and walked up the immaculate matching brick walkway that was edged by little green boxwood hedges. She lifted her eyebrows and shrugged to herself. She hoped this was it.

When she rang the bell to the side of a magnificent oak door, inset with leaded panes, she heard it echo through the large space within. She was immediately intimidated and was almost about to turn and run back to her car when Linda opened the massive door.

"Well, it's about time!" Linda didn't look too pleased to see her. *She was probably loving it, being the only female present*, Julia thought. Linda turned to lead her into a large hall, and Julia rolled her eyes at Linda's back. She followed Linda out onto a cool stone patio, over-hung with shady vines and set with wrought-iron furniture. The other members of the group were lounging around on chairs and at tables with their books open, the pages shifting in the breeze. They were all sipping tall frosted glasses of something that looked slushy and fruity and were picking at the leftovers of the buffet spread on a long table against the house.

Well, it seemed she hadn't missed much. Julia could see that so far most of the attention had been paid to the food instead of the books. She sat down in one of the cushioned iron chairs.

"This place is ridiculously hard to find from the instructions you gave, Linda," she complained.

"Oh?" Linda smiled sweetly.

"I've been driving around for half an hour!"

"Really? We drove right to it." A small dark-headed guy to her right nodded to his friend behind him and threw an olive into his mouth.

Linda shrugged, grinning, and then sat down in a chair between the two men.

Great. This should be fun. Julia rolled her eyes.

"Have some eats, Julia." One of the guys, holding a still-loaded plate, pointed to the table with his fork, still chewing as he spoke. "Plenty left."

"Yes, Julia, help yourself," said Linda.

Julia caught a challenging note in her voice, but Julia had about had it with Linda. She ignored her and plunked her books and binder onto the little table before turning resolutely to the buffet. She piled her plate high, which wasn't too difficult with the amazing array on the table. It looked as if it had been catered. Ridiculous. Linda's social life had to be the pits if she was going to go to this much trouble for a study group.

Julia turned to the group. "What have you covered so far?"

"Oh, we're just getting started really." This from Emmet, the dark-headed olive-eater.

"Yeah, you started at the buffet from the looks of things," Julia commented.

"You bet, lady." He gave Julia a small salute with a celery stick and almost got dip in his hair. Everyone laughed.

When she finished with this plate, she'd jump-start them, she decided. They were quite keen once they got moving, and Julia reluctantly admitted to herself that she was better off with them, because they really had brains. This was the first group she'd ever been with that had actually been beneficial to her. Back at Hale she'd usually backed out of study groups once she discovered that most of the students expected her to do all of the thinking and most of the work.

Julia sat back in the iron chair and began on the exotic bits of food. The talk flowed around her but she remained quiet.

Life up here had been good so far. She'd been glad of the decision she made to major in chemistry with an eye to medicinal chemistry research or possibly even pre-med. The more she thought about it, the more she felt that she should at least look at medicine. You could really make a difference in life if you were really dedicated, and the U was the place to do it. Just being on campus and seeing all the facilities and watching the medical students and their earnestness and their tired but eager eyes excited her a little. She liked the little thrill that she felt when she came up against pure knowledge and the dedication and relentless pursuit of it.

Julia looked around her at the relaxed, joking faces of her study group, but she wasn't fooled. Underneath their ease, these people were driven and hard, as determined as she was to be the best. And yes, she was proud to be among them, even if some of their social skills left a lot to be desired. Julia shoved the last bit of a croissant into her mouth, opened her heavy biological chemistry book, and highlighter in hand, got them to work.

* * *

"Hey, you need to hose yourself down, buddy," Elder Archer told Aaron.

"What?"

"You stopped us just a little too long with Sister Forgonne. You've got to lay off," said Elder Archer, as they trudged up the stairs. Their new apartment had a great view, but four flights were four too many even when you weren't lugging anything on your back.

"Lay off what?" Aaron didn't remember talking to Francesca longer than was appropriate. "Do you think I did something wrong?"

Elder Archer turned around. "Well, I just thought that you were spending too much time talking to an unmarried sister."

"Oh, well . . . hey, I guess it's getting so a guy can't flirt with his converts around here anymore," Aaron joked, as he closed the apartment door. He shrugged off the comment and gratefully dumped his backpack onto the kitchen table.

Elder Archer began opening the cupboards and the fridge, searching for any uneaten food they might have overlooked. Monday was P-day, and Sundays had been pretty meager lately.

"If you're going to be a pain, I'll just keep the good news to myself," Aaron said.

"What good news? That Sister Forgonne is also madly in love with *you?*"

"Hey, Elder, are you serious?" Aaron was disturbed.

"Well," Elder Archer stalled, smiling, but looking down. "I just think we should be careful. Francesca is so young and attractive and everything."

"Yes, but don't you think it would be weird if we didn't stop to talk to her?"

"Yeah, I guess you're right. Of course, *senior* companion." Elder Archer grinned and bowed shortly. "Anyway, what good news?"

"Wonderful, de-licious news. Sister Carpacci invited us to dinner this afternoon at five thirty."

Elder Archer let out a whoop and danced around the table. "Man, I don't know if I can wait. Boy, that sauce of hers, *buonissimo*." He kissed his fingertips and flung his arm out, smacking the wall of the small apartment. "Ow. Hey, I guess Smith and Chevez aren't back yet. Let's short-sheet their beds."

"Don't be stupid."

"Why not?"

"They'll kill you, idiot. And you'll never know when it's coming. Smith almost got sent home for all his joking."

"Caution to the wind, you know." Elder Archer hurried into Smith and Chevez's bedroom. "That's our motto today."

"Hey, leave me out of this."

"I wasn't talking about this," Elder Archer said from the bedroom.

"What, then?"

"Francesca."

Aaron smoothed his hair back onto his head and let out an exasperated sigh. He felt a little worried. Was he talking to her too much? He liked her, yes, but he liked all the members. She was nearer his age, so maybe he felt like he had more in common with her, and it showed. Suddenly he was a little irritated. He yelled out, "Are you going to let that go?"

"Are you?" Elder Archer walked back into the kitchen, trailing a grubby white sheet. "Hey, man, I'm serious."

"So am I. But I am having trouble seeing that I have done anything worth this little lecture."

"I just think that we shouldn't spend a lot of time with her, that's all."

Aaron's eyebrows stretched up. "A lot of time with her? What do you mean a lot of time? Five minutes, ten, every week or so?"

"Well, I hear marriage is hard enough, even if your wife has exactly the same background you do."

"Marriage?" Aaron's hand went to his head in amazement. "How did we get on to that? You are totally off track here, Elder." Aaron felt like he'd missed something. This conversation seemed to be galloping out of his control.

Elder Archer continued as if he hadn't even heard Aaron. "I don't think it takes much for Italian girls to get pretty attached, you know, when handsome young Americans come along and change their lives."

"You think that Francesca is attached to me?"

"I don't know, maybe. I heard Sister Targini say that Francesca thinks you are wonderful. I'm just warning you. I guess because of what happened to my brother. He brought a girl home from Venezuela and married her in the temple." Elder Archer's face twisted a little. "He suffered along with her for about four years. She was beautiful, yes, but they were just too different. She didn't want to go to church with him because she couldn't understand, and she thought everyone was making fun of her, so he tried to attend the Spanish ward with her, and she didn't like that either because most of the people were so poor and she'd come from a pretty proud family. Anyway, she ended up going inactive and really bitter. She was so resentful of him and she wanted to go back to Venezuela, and he about bankrupted himself taking her there every year, but it wasn't enough. It was ugly, man. They eventually got a divorce, and ever since he's been a complete mess."

"Wow, that's horrible." Aaron could see why Elder Archer was so sensitive after watching his brother suffer. Maybe working with Francesca just reminded him of his brother's situation too much. Archer was afraid something like that might happen to him; perhaps Archer was the one who was a little in love with Francesca. But why was he projecting this onto Aaron? "But don't worry about me. I'm not even thinking that way. I hope that Francesca isn't either."

"Yeah, well, I figure I'm just doing my duty, trying to keep you out of trouble." Elder Archer wadded up the sheet he was holding and then patted Aaron heavily on the shoulder. "Enough said though. I'll quit bugging you."

"Thanks." Aaron rolled his eyes at Archer's patronizing tone. He didn't appreciate Archer's assumptions. He went to the fridge to examine the last apple for wormholes.

"Oh, one more thing."

"What!" Aaron cocked back his arm, threatening Archer with the apple.

"What about that girl back home that you write to sometimes? You ready to let that go?"

"Will you just get in there and short-sheet the bed?!"

"Okay," he walked back into the bedroom, "but I'm going to tell Smith you told me to do it."

Chapter 3

Ninety-three percent, in red ink, stared boldly from the front of her physics test. Julia caught a glimpse of the professor's face in profile as he moved away from her desk. There was definitely a bit of a gloating expression on his face. He'd found an error on one of her problems and was loving it. She ruffled through the test angrily, meaning to protest; she'd been sure she'd aced the whole thing when she walked away from it last week. She hadn't even worried over it the rest of the night, reworking all the problems in her head, like she usually did. It must have been some kind of a trick question, something she hadn't anticipated. There. Two flaunting red marks slashed her neat equations, and a new answer was written boldly across the original one. This couldn't be right. The professor must have made a mistake.

Oh, there. She began to feel a little sick. Archimedes' Principle; she'd forgotten to figure it in. *How stupid! No wonder he's gloating.* She must have been too confident, not careful enough. She glanced around nervously to see if anyone had seen her test, and she quickly turned it face down on the desk.

The professor had started the lecture now, but she couldn't concentrate on what he was saying. She could feel the heat radiating from her face, and her hand burned where it lay on top of the test. How could she have made such a stupid mistake? If she could do that, who knows what else she might do wrong? What if she mixed the wrong solution someday and somebody died or was horribly scarred?

The thoughts chased each other around and around in her brain until she realized she'd missed nearly the whole lecture. She glanced over at the student next to her and saw his notebook covered with numbers and equations in small, neat block letters. Her mind felt blurred, and her paper was blank. Her panic started again, and she began to have a lurching sense of guilt for missing the lesson. She'd copy Emmet's notes after class—that would be good enough. But she'd have to get him to explain them if she didn't understand, and then she'd have to give him a reason that she'd missed the notes when he'd seen her sitting there in class as plain as day. Julia's brain whirled again, and she squeezed her eyes tightly shut.

The pressure was mounting this semester, filling her like a red thermometer, and she didn't want to admit that it was hard to take. It shouldn't be, for *her*. She was meant for this, made for it. Science was her life, and was going to be her life, and she didn't want to feel the pressure, didn't want to be human like everyone else. She was different and proud of it, and she knew that some of her classmates knew it and could see her image superimposed on the future as well as she could.

Then why was it so hard to always keep it up, keep pushing and straining, keep her ears pricked and fine-tuned? There were times when she'd wake up at two in the morning and remember about a quiz that was scheduled for the next morning, and she'd creep past Lorraine and out into the living room, her heart beating wildly, to study before the sun came up. Maybe one of these times she wouldn't wake up to study and would actually be sitting there in class, dumbly, when the teacher slid the white sheet onto her desk . . .

She started when the guy sitting next to her scraped his chair back and stood up to leave. Everyone was packing up and leaving the room. Julia felt like she didn't even know where to go.

Eventually though, she stood in front of her little red car, fished the key out of her bag, and unlocked the door. She sighed heavily as she twisted the key in the ignition, flipped on the air, and backed out of the tight student parking.

She usually planned her study night in her head on the way home from classes, but today she seemed blocked, her whole head stuffed with stress and worry. She thought about running over to Michael and Jen's to see her nephews, but she decided that she probably shouldn't sacrifice the time.

Soon she was pulling into the apartment parking lot, wedging her car into another narrow space and plodding up the stairs to her room. She hoped Lorraine was home. It was becoming a little ridiculous, how disappointed she'd be to walk into their empty apartment. Sometimes it felt like she'd been alone all day, inside herself, having one-sided conversations. She closed her eyes briefly and fit her key to the lock, trying not to think about it. Maybe Lorraine would be there.

It was dark and a little stuffy in the small front room. The sun-bleached drapes were still pulled over the window and the table was bare, each of the chairs pushed in and lined up perfectly. Julia blinked a little in the dark room and then walked slowly into the bedroom to stack her books on the small desk her dad had bought her. She looked over to the single bed on Lorraine's side of the room and then up to the three large ballet posters on the wall. She smiled a little and then reached up to smooth her hand across the toe of one of the pink satin slippers in the picture. She was so glad Lorraine had gotten in up here. It was wonderful for her. And even though Julia had no inclination toward dance of any kind, she really appreciated Lorraine's talent and her immersion in her chosen field.

It took all her time, however. Sometimes they'd call practice off early, and then Lorraine would be home around four thirty when Julia got in. Then they'd either fix dinner together or go out somewhere or go shopping for an hour before Lorraine had to be back to a rehearsal or a practice session. Then Julia would study. But much of the time Julia never saw Lorraine at all until she struggled up the apartment stairs, late at night, purely exhausted. She was sweet and she tried to talk to Julia, ask her about her classes, about the people she'd met, but Julia could tell she was making a supreme effort just to sit upright most of the time. And so she would let her off the hook, and go out of the room for a minute, though her brain screamed for sympathetic ears, and when she came back, Lorraine would be asleep, curled up in her leotard and skirt, beautiful and peaceful at rest.

The sudden shrill ring of the telephone scared her so bad she banged her shin against the iron bed frame as she lunged toward the door. Hopping and rubbing the throbbing area, she grabbed the phone off the wall.

"Hello?"

"Hey, are you still alive up there? You never call home."

"Dad! I guess I'm a little busy up here, you know. I can't call you guys every night." She smiled.

"Humor us, Julia, at least once a week. You could beg for more money, you know; that's what other parents' college kids do."

"Oh, sorry, I don't want you guys to be embarrassed in front of the other parents. I'll try to be more needy." A ridiculous grin began to spread across her face. It was so good to talk to her dad.

"Really, though, are you doing okay, Julia? Classes going good?"

"Yeah, pretty much. I made a really stupid mistake on my physics test, though, and it sort of bummed me out."

"What was your score?"

"Well, 93 percent."

"93?"

"Yes."

"And you're worried about that?"

"Okay, Dad, I know I'm paranoid, but I just feel stupid when I make a dumb mistake, and I really think the professor thought it was funny."

"Maybe you should relax a little, Julia. Maybe it was funny for the best student in the class to make a little mistake."

"Okay, okay. Anyway, I'm fine. What's going on down there?"

"Oh, your mom's been canning fruit again. I don't know why she still feels prompted to do it with you guys gone. I know it costs more when you figure everything in."

Julia smiled remembering her mother's neat little canning operations with everything in its place and the "clean-as-you-go" rule as law. She never remembered her mother even having a stain on the crisp pin-striped aprons she always wore. In that kind of a test kitchen, you'd think the bottled fruit would have been edible, but she and her brothers had to choke it down politely with their dad's eye on them, making sure they didn't hurt her feelings. Maybe Julia's mother just did everything too precisely. Maybe you needed to taste the fruit and then add a little more sugar or a little less or something. Maybe Julia had a similar problem, but with life. She couldn't relax either. "So, is it peaches?"

"I am afraid so."

Julia grinned. "Have you eaten any yet?"

"No, I just told her I want to save the bottles for when I can't eat them fresh."

"Smart."

"Yes, I guess your old man doesn't do too bad." He paused for a moment and cleared his throat. "By the way, I ran into Ben Hammond the other day."

"Really." Julia's mouth had suddenly gone dry.

"Yeah, I was over at Hale, talking to the business school over there to see if they could recommend anyone for that receptionist that I'm thinking about hiring."

"Yeah, *and* . . ." Julia prompted. He was giving out lots of little details, a sure sign that he was nervous.

"Well, like I said, I ran into him as I was coming out of the business building, and he walked right over and said hello to me, like he'd been waiting or something. He sure didn't seem surprised to see me. Maybe he'd seen me going in. Anyway, I guess he was down from BYU, checking on his transcripts—something about some credits not transferring right."

"*And* . . ." This seemed a little like torture to Julia. She wished he'd just get to the point.

"Well . . . Julia, he sure seems like a nice guy."

"Dad! How can you say that?"

"You know he's a nice guy, Julia."

"Nice enough until someone flutters her eyelashes at him and swings her little hips, and then he's just a dumb male, like the rest of you."

"Hey!"

"Well, you'd have probably been the same, but luckily for Mom, Morgan wasn't born yet."

There was a little pause on the other end of the phone line.

"I know, Julia. I know how you feel . . . I guess I haven't been a very good example to you. I was pretty mad too. It's hard for me to see my daughter get hurt. I could handle it better if it had happened to me. But I've been thinking a lot about it, and well, Julia, everybody makes mistakes. You really ought to try to work it out, at least try to talk to Morgan and see her side of it.

"Dad, I don't believe you! How can Morgan *have* a side? Everything was very clear to me. She had the whole summer to come over and explain if she thought I had the wrong idea. She was guilty, and she knew it, and she couldn't face me." Julia's body was heating up, her heart thumping loudly. She closed her eyes against the fresh pain that she'd been busily burying the last few months. She couldn't do this again. She just didn't have the time.

"I know, Julia; it was bad, and she was wrong, even cruel, but you can't just let this go. You two were inseparable for more than *ten years*. You know what the Lord would want you to do. He'd want you to forgive her."

"Dad, do you think I haven't thought about that? I mean, after about the first two weeks, when I was plotting to kill her. I think, maybe I could forgive her, if I read my scriptures for about an hour every day and spent a lot of time on my knees, trying to purge wicked thoughts from my mind. But Dad, you know, I don't think I can *ever* forget what she did. How could it ever be the same as it was?" She squeezed her forehead together at the temples with her thumb and middle finger, trying to calm down.

"I don't know, honey. Maybe some more time on your knees is what you need. This is hard, and I don't have all the answers, but in my experience, if you do your best, try to do the right things and try to have the right Spirit in your heart, Heavenly Father will help you. But you have to be willing first."

Julia exhaled loudly into the phone and paused for another moment before speaking. "Oh, Dad, I'm just so tired of all this."

"I know. Well, I just wanted to call and make sure you were okay. Are you coming down next weekend? You haven't been home for a while."

"I don't think so, Dad. Too much homework, and I'm giving the lesson in Relief Society."

"You work too hard."

"Who doesn't?" she responded.

"Well, I guess I'll see you the next weekend then, for sure, or we're coming up there."

He was going to hang up without telling her about Ben. She hesitated; she hated to ask him.

"Okay, but Dad . . . you didn't tell me what Ben said to you." Her face felt hot from the words.

"Oh, yeah, boy, that was the real reason I called you." There was silence for a moment. Finally he said, "I gave him your address, Julia, and your phone number."

"Dad!"

"He said he just wanted to talk to you, just for a few minutes."

Her heart was hammering again, and she could feel a drop of sweat trickling down her spine. "I can't believe you did that."

"I'm sorry. I wondered if I should, but he convinced me. Julia, he looked so desperate. I didn't think it could hurt. But you can bet I gave him quite a lecture before I let him go."

Julia groaned. Great, just what she needed, her Dad humiliating her, telling Ben how upset she'd been.

"I've been worried about it ever since," he admitted, "and I just thought I'd warn you."

"Great, Dad. Now I'll have to live at the library—not that that's much of a change."

"Just give him a chance, Julia. Let him have his say, and then you can black his eye if you feel like it."

Chapter 4

"You were fabulous, Jimmy!" Morgan thumped his chest with one of the hands she had linked around his neck. She was riding piggyback from an intramural softball game, because she'd said her new loafers rubbed on her heels. They really didn't hurt that much, but this sure beat walking. "Have you always been able to hit that far?"

"Oh, pretty much, but I put a little weight on during my mission, kind of filled out my frame, and that helps a little." Jim Facer pulled his shoulders back and puffed out his chest, strutting a little.

"You, dear sir, are an obnoxious braggart."

"What?"

"You know, you're just a big jerk that thinks the world revolves around him." She patted his chest again. "I was just using the words of a former friend." Morgan trailed off a little, and then shook her long hair and blinked her eyes a few times.

"*Former* friend?"

"Yes." The mood seemed to slip a little.

"Sounds bad. What did you do?"

"Hey! Why do you assume it was me that did something wrong? Why can't I be the innocent injured one?"

"Because I'm getting to know you too well." Jim laughed and pressed her knee against his side with his elbow. "Anyway, apparently I'm right, so cough it up. What did you do?"

"Oh, just something stupid. And there's no way she's going to forgive me. It's a real pain, 'cause I really like her, and I got mad over something and then ran out without thinking and made a bad choice and then, well, things kind of got out of control, and it's like this huge ravine opened between us and it's totally impossible to get over it and actually talk to her." Morgan stuck out her lower lip and blew a breath over her forehead.

"Too bad," Jim said.

"Yeah, well, maybe things will change if I give her a little time. Maybe it will get easier and she'll forgive me."

"I wouldn't wait too long."

"Why not?"

"It's just not good. Not good to let things fester and grow and get all weird."

"And I guess you know pretty much everything?" Morgan teased him.

"Of course." Jim turned his head to look up at her, and she laughed at his raised eyebrows and devilish grin. He really was so-o-o good-looking. Her blood gave a jump in her veins, and she forgot about Julia and concentrated on the spiky hair on the top of his head and the feel of his warm, shifting back as he walked along.

"Okay, off you go, you little goldbricker. I bet those shoes don't hurt a bit." They'd reached the campus parking lot where Morgan had parked her dad's old rusty Honda, and Jim dumped her off his back roughly, but then reached out to steady her so she wouldn't fall. His warm fingers closed around the bare skin of her upper arm and stayed there after she'd regained her balance. He looked down at her for a minute, saying nothing, but then dropped his hand abruptly and looked off toward the mountains.

"What do you hear from old Aaron-buddy?" he asked.

"Oh, yeah, I forgot to tell you. Look, this one came last Friday." Morgan held up her slim wrist and pulled the silver chain around until she located the right charm. She put her index finger under a tiny filigree heart, and Jim bent over her wrist to examine it.

"Hey, cute."

"I know—it's so delicate." She began to play idly with the charm, twisting the bracelet around and around her wrist.

Jim picked up her wrist and began playing through the charms. "I remember these. Yeah, this little unicorn and . . . the key. I said he could put a note in with it saying that you had the 'key' to his heart, ha, ha, but I don't know if he did it."

Morgan glanced up quickly to laugh with him, but when she looked up into his eyes, he was strangely serious. Aaron hadn't enclosed a note with the little old-fashioned key, she remembered. Morgan dropped her wrist and took a step back from him.

"Hey, well, I guess I'd better get home. It's pretty much house arrest since I messed up with my friend and school and everything. My parents want me home before 10:00 on weeknights, and I'm still humoring them. I'm trying to decide what I want to do next semester, and I'll make my move then. No use alienating them before I have to."

"Smart girl."

"Hey, it was fun watching you play, and thanks for the ride." She slapped his shoulder.

"It was my pleasure." He bowed formally from the waist, and she laughed as he pivoted around and broke into a slow jog. "See you around," he said.

* * *

It was like magic, the way the equations flowed down the page in rhythm, each number and sign neat, precise, and correct. She felt like she was the master of all things, sitting here in an enclosed room in the library, smoothly working the problems to the end of the page. Finally. She felt great, powerful. The universe seemed clear to her again. Julia leaned back in her chair and tipped it on its back legs against the wall. She put her hands behind her head and stretched her back a little. Where were those guys? She glanced at her wrist and found that it was still five minutes to six. Her study group had reserved this room and planned to meet here to study for the organic chemistry exam tomorrow morning. They were going to go out to dinner late if they finished in time.

Julia's stomach growled at the thought, and she surreptitiously leaned down to her bag to break off a piece of a granola bar that was sticking out of the pocket. She chewed thoughtfully as she looked out through the glass windows into the library, watching students move back and forth as they arrived or left or browsed the shelves.

She spotted a dark head above two girls who were walking past the lounge area. *Yeah, probably Emmet, and his friend—what was his name again? John?* They were okay, friendly, and they respected her intelligence and listened to her ideas. Kind of weird though—casual and intense at the same time. She'd gotten friendly with Emmet, teasing and joking around a little. It was a platonic type of feeling, and she felt relieved that Emmet hadn't pushed it. She was enjoying the start of a friendship that she felt was based on mutual respect.

Hopefully Linda wouldn't show up. Julia didn't know if she could stand watching her simpering up to those two, trying to decide which to make a dive for. Linda acted like Julia was up there batting as well, competing with her for the single guys in the group. Julia could tell she felt threatened by anything she said to them, and Linda was constantly trying to one-up any comment she made or story she told.

It irritated Julia that someone so bent on attracting male attention of any kind could be so brilliant. Julia admitted grudgingly to herself that sometimes Linda's logic could quickly penetrate a cloudy area that they were all struggling with. But after she made a point she would raise her eyebrows significantly at Julia, as if daring her to do better, and then she'd bask in all the attention afterwards. The guys had to appreciate her quick brain—this was science, and you respected clarity and conciseness—but Linda needn't act so smug all the time.

Julia became aware that she had been staring off into space, and when she focused again the familiar features of a tall, blonde young man came into view through the window—Ben.

He was walking past the lounge, peering into the study cubicles and around bookshelves. Julia caught her breath. She sat very still in case he should catch movement and turn toward the window. At that moment Emmet and John burst into the study room, flanking Linda, who had managed to get her arms through both of their elbows. She looked ridiculously pleased with herself, and when she saw Julia, she smiled sweetly and blinked her eyes significantly a few times. Julia took this all in quickly and looked nervously at the group. She could see Ben moving deeper into the library from the corner of her eye, and she began to relax a little. He would never think of looking for her in a group study room because she'd told him at Hale how useless group study was for her most of the time.

"Getting ahead of us, huh?" Emmet clunked his backpack onto the table, unzipped it noisily, and grinned at Julia.

"Of course! Can't have you guys taking the top scores—not that I'm worried though."

"Then you should be," Linda said peevishly from across the table.

"Retract your claws, Linda." Emmet leaned over the table and teasingly stroked her hand a couple of times. Linda looked up and seemed to purr.

"Can't have you two flying into a cat fight. You've got to set me up for this test. Man, I had a look at those practice problems, and they're murder, let me tell you."

"You mean these?" Julia indicated her paper, and he glanced down wonderingly.

"Hey, you mean you've finished them?" He flipped over a couple of sheets in her loose-leaf.

"Pretty much." Julia was grateful for the screen that Emmet created as he stood over her between her chair and the window. Her heart was beating madly inside her chest, and her palms felt wet.

The other members of the group straggled in, and ten minutes later they were able to begin a really good study session. Everyone got going strong, and they were working smoothly, quizzing each other and plowing through sample problems. Linda showed everyone a trick she'd learned from her dad, who was a mathematician, and it worked beautifully. Julia almost relaxed, and there were times in the two hours that followed that she became immersed and forgot to glance toward the window every few minutes. She hadn't seen Ben again. Maybe he'd given up and gone on back to Provo.

Finally they called a halt. "Hey, we're good. Let's go down to Sizzler!" Emmet beamed around the room.

"Sizzler! Yuck. You always want to go there. What about Mexican? Isn't there that little place with the iguana downtown that has those great chimichangas?" John said.

"Hey, yeah, that iguana place. I feel like Mexican too." Linda leaned toward John, probably trying to punish Emmet for sitting next to Julia during the study session.

A chunky married guy named Rich stood up at the end of the table. "Sounds good. I'll run up and get my wife and be back down quick—she's studying on the third floor."

"So I guess I'm outnumbered. What about you, Julia? You love Sizzler, right?" Emmet glanced down at her hopefully, placing a hand on her shoulder.

"Nope, sorry, I'm not up to stuffing down all the salad I can eat. The iguana place." Julia tried to keep Emmet between herself and the window, trying to see over his shoulder into the lounge at the same time. The other married guy said he had to get home because he and his wife had plans, but Jesse, the little skinny guy with thick, round glasses who was usually too shy to join them if they ever went anywhere but the library, stood up and waited for them, licking his lips expectantly.

Julia packed up her books quickly and managed to edge in front of Emmet as they were leaving the room so as to be hidden from view of the window. Unfortunately, Emmet seemed to have gotten the wrong idea from her quickly jumping up so near him.

"Hey." He looked her up and down. "What's up?"

"Oh, nothing." Julia blushed crimson and tried to move past the awkward moment. She hurried through the door to catch up with the others, glancing back at Emmet in embarrassment. When she turned around she found herself face-to-face with Ben.

"Julia," he said.

She stopped short. She could hardly look at him; her eyes were darting everywhere but his face. She was breathing ridiculously hard.

"What are you doing here?" she managed.

"Just looking up something in the library, same as you," he joked.

"BYU's library just isn't big enough for you, I guess."

"I guess not."

Julia could feel Emmet standing behind her, waiting. She took a step around Ben.

"Julia, could we just talk?"

Julia didn't know if she could trust herself if she stayed here much longer. "Sorry, I'm meeting friends for dinner. You really shouldn't have come up here." She tried to move past him again, but he stepped out in front of her.

"Julia." He was starting to sound a little impatient, and her heart was melting, but just then Emmet stepped up behind her and draped his arm casually around her shoulders, saying, "Ready to go?" like they were on a date. Julia looked at Emmet, surprised to death, and then back at Ben, who had gone white. He suddenly stepped out of the way, and Julia walked past him slowly, starting to feel a little sorry.

"Bye." She said it over her shoulder as she turned to look at him. Ben hadn't turned to watch her leave, and he stayed silent.

Only when they'd gained the parking lot did Emmet drop his arm. "Who was that guy?"

"Someone I knew at Hale." It was really weird to be with Emmet alone. The rest of their group had gone on ahead and were clustered around a little green hatchback. It was even weirder to have to talk to him after he'd had his arm around her. She tried to edge away from him a little.

"Do you want to ride with me to the restaurant?"

What she wanted . . . what she wanted was to sprint back into the library to see if Ben was still there. The thought sprang to her mind, and she even glanced back to the library entrance, but then she was ashamed of herself, disgusted.

"Okay. Let's go over and see if anyone else wants a ride. I'm pretty sure that Jesse doesn't have a car."

Two hours later Julia put her hand to her distended belly as she climbed into her car. She'd eaten *way* too much. She slammed the door sharply, and watched Emmet's car drive off, relieved that she'd insisted that he just drop her off at her car instead of parking and opening the door for her. He really must have the wrong idea. Julia felt her face go hot, realizing that he'd thought she was making up to him, flirting, like Linda. Maybe when she'd been so preoccupied with avoiding Ben, she hadn't been as careful as she should have been.

It was stupid. She didn't want to get involved with Emmet or anybody. She'd only wanted a colleague-type relationship with him, and now it was all weird. Great. And it was all Ben's fault. She tried to be mad at him but was having second thoughts as she pulled into her apartment complex.

She knew she was really being immature, refusing to talk to him. Her dad was probably right. But maybe the pleasure she would get out of acting the ice queen, like he'd never mattered to her at all, would help the aching emptiness. Maybe it would help her to get him out of her system, if she told him it was definitely over. Or maybe not. A weak, fluttery feeling around her heart warned her that she was melting again. *Stop it*, she told herself. It was too late now anyway.

She grasped the railing and hauled herself and her backpack full of books onto the last landing and stuck her hand in her jacket pocket for her keys. She wondered if Lorraine was home from her date yet. She'd been asked out by a nice guy in their ward who was so shy that Julia had been amazed when Lorraine had told her. It would be fun to get all the details.

She froze as she realized a man was crouched down in the shadows next to her apartment door. Her hand in her pocket gripped the keys painfully. Two of the apartments in this complex had been broken into last week.

The shadow stood and stepped out into the glare of the street lamp. "I couldn't leave, Julia." Ben was looking toward his feet, but suddenly lifted his head up and looked her squarely in the eye. "You've got to listen to me."

Julia's eyes froze on the sharply shadowed planes of his face. Her heart was leaping around in her chest. She could barely form words. "Oh, really." She sounded so calm, so ice-queenish. She couldn't believe it.

"Julia, I'm not leaving until you let me have my say. I've decided that I'll just camp in front of your door and follow you around on campus until you'll do anything to get rid of me."

Julia turned her back on him and inserted her key into the lock on the front door.

"Have you got a blanket I could borrow?" he asked.

She couldn't believe him! "Ben! What's wrong with you? Can't you just let it go?" Her eyes were filling up, despite her struggle. She threw the door inward and strode angrily inside, trying to wipe her eyes while he was behind her so he wouldn't see.

"Can I come in?"

"Why not?" Julia threw up her hands in surrender and walked into the bedroom to dump off her backpack. She returned to the kitchen-living room before Ben could follow her. She took a wide stance and placed her hands on her hips. "Okay, let's have it—and hurry up, I'm tired." She knew she sounded waspish and mean, but she was so angry. She didn't think she should have to go through this again.

"I want to tell you what happened."

"I know what happened," she shot back.

"Julia! What if you just sit down for about fifteen minutes and let me talk, without interruptions, okay? Just fifteen minutes."

Julia nodded her head and walked stiffly over to the couch and sat down. Ben grabbed one of the kitchen chairs and drew it up facing her, close, with only about a foot between their knees. Julia edged down the couch a little to give herself more room. She saw Ben roll his eyes slightly when he noticed this. He leaned forward and placed his elbows on his knees, lacing his fingers.

"I made a mistake, Julia. I never should have been with Morgan alone. I knew how you felt about her, though you never really told me in words, and well, even though we'd broken up, I should have respected our relationship and you enough to stay away from her." Ben had been staring at his hands during this speech, but now looked up at her and into her eyes. Julia looked away from him quickly.

"The thing is, Julia, that I have been miserable for the last four and a half months. I feel sick about what I did, but I guess the real reason I've felt so awful is that I've realized that I have no chance with you again. When we broke up, it really hurt me. Hurt my stupid male ego, I guess, that you didn't want me. But I think I still thought in the back of my mind that there was some hope if I gave you some time. I mean, it felt so right between us." Ben swallowed heavily and paused for a minute.

"This is really hard for me, Julia. I'm proud."

Julia remained silent.

"And, well . . . I don't want to blame it on her, but Morgan is pretty friendly."

Julia snorted and rolled her eyes to the ceiling. That was the understatement of the year.

"And I was kind of mad at you, really. I thought it was okay, because I didn't care if I was doing something wrong at the moment. I felt kind of reckless because I'm not used to being rejected."

Rejected? Did he feel that way? Julia really hadn't considered the breakup from his point of view. She felt a few sharp points of guilt prick her insides.

Ben continued. "I mean, I know you said you didn't want to get serious and all that and that was the reason, but, well, a guy wants a girl to be so in love with him that nothing else matters, that she'll throw caution to the wind. It's all tied up in the whole chauvinist-pig thing."

Ben looked up at her briefly, and she felt the ice around her heart melting a little. Her heart was starting to ache too; everything about him was still so beautiful to her. She had to get him out of here before she did something stupid. Julia stood up.

"Is that it?" she asked.

Ben stared up at her in surprise. "Has it really been fifteen minutes? Were you counting?"

"I don't know. I didn't look at my watch, but it must nearly be time. I said I'd listen to you, and I have. I'm being fair. But if you're through, I'd appreciate it if you'd leave."

Ben was incredulous. Julia could see a glint of anger in his eyes.

"Doesn't any of this mean anything to you, Julia? Didn't you care at all? You could have fooled me."

Julia went over to stand by the door, and she opened it without saying a word. She was starting to feel panicky. Her heart was dripping all over the floor. She didn't know what would happen if he didn't leave soon.

Ben stood staring at her for a moment longer and then strode past her and through the open door. But before he could reach the stairs a tortured question burst from Julia's lips.

"Did you kiss her?"

Ben whipped around and locked his eyes onto hers. There was a long, heavy pause. When he didn't say anything, tears gathered in her eyes, and she tried to blink them back, hating them and her weakness, but soon they were spilling silently down her face, and her chest was burning and splitting from the pain. A choked sob rose in her throat, and she turned from him blindly, to get through the door, to put it between them. But then she felt his hands on her shoulders. She tried to jerk away, but he pulled her to him anyway, wrapped his arms tightly around her shoulders, and pressed her face into his chest.

"I hate you!" she said tightly.

Ben brought his hand up and stroked her hair.

"I know."

Chapter 5

"I don't believe I'm getting transferred! Man, things were just going good around here. We have that Paccinni lady and her son, and that old couple, the Farones." Aaron threw his hands in the air. "I was really hoping they'd let me finish my mission here."

"Hey, you know about transfers. It's happened to you before," Elder Archer said.

"Yeah, well . . . shoot." Aaron pushed the hair back over his head, making it stand on end.

"And I guess we won't mention the real reason you're upset."

"Which is?" Aaron stared him down. He wouldn't dare start that whole 'Francesca' thing again.

"That you're leaving me, of course." Elder Archer squinted his whole face in a smile.

"Of course." Aaron smiled back mockingly, but he felt cold and hopeless and depressed, maybe more so than he had at any other time on his mission. Since that conversation with Archer two weeks ago, Aaron had been very careful about Francesca. In fact, he'd barely spoken to her at church and at the branch activity. It made him mad that he had to be worried about staying away from her. He had seen in her eyes that she didn't understand. Aaron looked away from Archer and walked out onto the iron fire escape, closing the door behind him.

He couldn't believe he had to leave Rome. The transfer had come so suddenly and without explanation. It was hard to leave everything that he had built up here.

He was being sent to Napoli, the place all the missionaries hoped to avoid. He'd heard in Napoli they only had about fifteen active members, and some of those were only semiactive. He'd met two guys that had spent a few months in Napoli, and they hadn't had anything good to say about the area. It was dirty and crime ridden, and the people spoke a dialect that was difficult to understand. An all-around kind of a scary place as far as Aaron could tell. Aaron blew a long breath toward the alley below, emptying his lungs. Boy, he'd thought the last few months of his mission were going to be great, the best. It just wasn't fair. He didn't expect to always have it his own way, but man, maybe just once!

He could hear Elder Archer knocking around in the kitchen, slamming cupboards and stuff, and Aaron turned slowly, realizing that if he didn't get in there soon, they'd probably get gluey oatmeal again for breakfast, and man, he could do without that today.

* * *

Two days later at around ten o'clock, just a half hour before he was supposed to be asleep, according to mission rules, Aaron was quickly stuffing his suitcase: socks, T-shirts, shorts, jeans, three pairs of shoes, shoe polish, overcoat, shaving kit, souvenirs, journal, post-cards, paper, envelopes. Aaron looked around the small room quickly then hauled his heavy dress bag out of the closet and threw it over the end of his bed. He pulled out the ten white shirts, the pair of two-pant suits, and the hanger he had his ties draped over, and he care-fully fitted them all inside the dress bag, which bulged and pulled at the zipper. Then he took them all out and took five of the shirts off their hangers, and looking at the crisp collars and sleeves regretfully, folded them up and pressed them into the side of his suitcase. Then he replaced the other shirts and the suits.

He was trying, desperately, not to think, not to think at all. *Don't go there.* He told himself. *Just keep packing, keep looking forward, close your mind.* He squeezed his eyes shut tightly to keep the image from reappearing, but it didn't work. Again he replayed the scene from this afternoon in President Cutler's office.

"Elder, good to see you. Sit down." President Cutler shook his hand firmly and then waved him into a chair in front of his desk. "I've been thinking this over and I thought that I should speak to you about your transfer."

Aaron had been silent and smiling, unable to imagine what was coming. He'd heard rumors that he was going to be called as the next assistant to the president, though he'd always shrugged them off. He tried not to let the rumors get to his head, but the thought of serving with President Cutler was exciting.

President Cutler sat down, leaning his elbows on the desk and lacing his fingers, and then paused for a moment before he spoke. "I think that you should know that Elder Archer spoke with me last week during his interview. And part of his conversation concerned you. Elder Jenner, Elder Archer was concerned that you were getting too involved with a convert, a young woman named Francesca Forgonne."

The words sent a shock through him. He felt sick. He couldn't speak, couldn't defend himself.

"I am aware that this is his private opinion and that through talking with other elders in the area and with the branch president, this may or may not be true . . ."

Aaron drew breath to defend himself, but President Cutler held up his hand for silence.

". . . but, I decided that the best thing to do is to transfer you, get you out of a potentially dangerous situation. Even if the implications aren't true on your part, the fact that others think they are gives the wrong impression of what missionaries are supposed to be like."

Aaron's whole body was hot with embarrassment and humiliation. How could Elder Archer have done this to him? It wasn't true, but after this kind of a suggestion, no one would believe him. Not even President Cutler.

"I want you to know, Elder, that I know there's a very good chance that absolutely nothing happened and that your feelings are only what they should be. Sometimes different people have different perceptions of the same event. You have been a great missionary here in Rome, have done a great deal in the service of the Lord. The people in Napoli need this kind of service as well. They need enthusiasm and the strength of the Spirit I know that you can give them. You can make a difference down there. I know that it is a difficult and unpopular area, but that's all the more reason for sending you there. Are you willing to try?"

Here he paused, without giving Aaron the opportunity to return to the accusation and attempt to defend himself. "I . . ." What could Aaron say? "Of course I will do my best, President."

"I knew I could count on you, Elder. And I hope, with the Lord's help, we can put all this unpleasantness behind us."

And that was all. Aaron stood by his open suitcase staring unseeing at the wall of his apartment.

Aaron glanced over at the other bed. Archer was snoring loudly, his foot sticking out of the blanket at the end of the bed. Aaron had said nothing to Archer after talking to the president. He didn't think he could trust himself. He felt like the wind had been knocked out of him. He had liked Archer most of the time. He searched around in his mind for an excuse for Archer, trying to look at it objectively, but any way he twisted it, getting him transferred was a low thing to do.

Before he could stop himself, Aaron reached out and gave Archer's foot a sharp slap. "Elder!"

"Hey!" Elder Archer sat up in bed suddenly, blinking. "What's going on?"

"Why did you do it?"

Archer rubbed his eyes, and Aaron could see his brain trying to focus.

"You told the president I was getting too involved with Francesca. Admit it."

"What?"

"Don't play dumb. Elder, you stabbed me in the back. What did I ever do to you?" He threw his hands into the air and slumped back onto the bed, his back to Archer. He wondered if the whole mission was talking about it. He felt sick to his stomach. He placed a hand over his belly and wondered if he would throw up.

"I just did what I thought was right." Archer still sounded half-asleep and resentful.

"How could it be right, Elder, if it wasn't even the truth," Aaron said, gritting his teeth against his anger.

"You were better this last week at church. But I talked to President Cutler before that. I was just looking out for you."

Now that was rich. "What?" Aaron whipped around. "You must live on another planet! Francesca was a convert to me. She was my friend, just like any of the other members."

"Yeah, but she was young and unmarried and good-looking." Archer swung his legs over the edge of his bed.

"What about you? You liked her. You talked to her, and you aren't getting transferred. Weren't you in danger too?"

Archer didn't answer.

"Well . . ."

"Jenner, you've been here longer. And besides, I have kind of sensed a chemistry between the two of you."

"What?" Aaron was breathing hard. "*Chemistry?* Elder, you were imagining things. *You* were mistaken."

"I'm sure you see it that way, Elder. But, again, I just did what I thought was right."

How could Archer defend himself? What could Aaron say that would make anything different?

"Hey, come on. It's better this way. You'll be out of the situation, you know; you won't have to worry about Francesca, and you can concentrate on the work." Archer began to scratch at the sole of one of his feet.

It got worse and worse. Aaron stood up and started grabbing things out of the top dresser drawer, cramming them haphazardly into the suitcase. "So, what happens to you then, with me slinking off to Napoli with my tail between my legs." Aaron's voice was bitter, but he didn't care.

"Actually . . ." Archer cleared his throat and paused.

Aaron looked up.

"Actually, the president is making me AP."

Aaron's chest froze. Fingers of ice protruded into his veins. Archer's eyes slid down and away from him. It seemed like time stood still for a moment. "Oh," Aaron breathed. There was nothing else to say.

After a while Elder Archer went to sleep again. Aaron was almost finished packing. He'd cleared off his desk and walked past the banged-up dresser numbly, trying not to think or feel. Bending down to pick up a sock, he caught sight of something wedged behind the dresser. He eased it out and froze there in his crouched position. It was Morgan, framed in the polished cherry-wood frame that she'd given him that last night. Aaron sat back against the foot of the bed, feeling the cold marble floor through his flannel pajama bottoms. He balanced the frame on his knees, looking deeply into her eyes. What if someone told her about this? What if his parents found out? He closed his eyes against the pain and humiliation. He pressed his forehead up against the glass of Morgan's frame as the tears slid over his cheeks. He hadn't cried since he was twelve.

When he opened his eyes they rested again on the picture of Morgan. Did he even know her anymore? He seemed so isolated at this moment, apart from any relationship he'd ever had, like he was floating in space. He'd only had time to briefly reply to her last few letters, which seemed really strange now. But the work had been going so great!

He went to his suitcase and opened a binder and rifled through the letters jammed in the front pocket. He grabbed the top, most recent letter. He looked at the postmark in the corner. *Whoa, nearly a month ago.* And he hadn't written back or anything . . . THE CHARMS! Suddenly he was digging among the souvenirs in his suitcase and came up with a small box. There were still *four* charms in the box. How stupid! He hadn't sent one last month.

Aaron grabbed the binder with the envelopes and rushed out into the kitchen, slamming the things down on the kitchen table. What could he wrap them in? He started to open and close cupboards swiftly, looking for the small cardboard box that had held Elder Chevez's returned watch. A restaurant had mailed it back to him when he'd left it last week. There it was. Great. The packing was even okay still. Hurriedly he wrapped two charms in a twist of paper and placed them in the box, smashing in some more of the paper to cushion them. He took out a plain piece of lined paper, grabbed a pen from the counter and wrote her name. His hand was shaking. What could he say? He began tapping the pen against the wooden table.

I'm sorry I didn't send one last month, Morgan. I guess I got busy. Don't be mad at me. He paused for a long moment, racking his brain, and then quickly wrote: *All my love, Aaron.* He couldn't think of anything else. How could he explain? It was impossible. Before he'd felt justified in putting off the letters, because he was immersing himself in the work, like he was supposed to be doing. But now his lapse seemed incomprehensible to him and almost surely offensive to Morgan.

He remembered Morgan's sassy grin and silky blonde hair now with amazing clarity. The thought of her was wonderfully comforting. She would be there when he got back, waiting. All this wouldn't matter to her; she would understand. She knew his heart, and his history, and she would be his future.

Chapter 6

Morgan was half an hour late again tonight. Her little gold watch showed 11:06 as she flipped her dad's Honda into park and turned off the lights. But even so, she lingered in the dark car, not wanting to go in and face everybody and explain everything. A bunch of girls that she'd met in the dorm last year had gotten together with some of the football players and had decided to go out to the lake to roast marshmallows, and since they'd seen her with Jim Facer a few times, they asked her to come with them. She'd driven Jim and his roommate out in the Honda, and they had run around and waded in the lake and stuffed themselves with marshmallows, chips, and pop. It had been pretty silly and had gotten worse and worse until Morgan suspected that some of the football guys had been drinking, which disgusted her.

She'd dragged Jim out of the group and interrogated him about it. He thought they probably were. He said that a lot of the guys on the team were total jerks and that it was hard to be around them so much and try to keep his head straight and keep up his standards. But they were together so much with practice and road trips and meetings and everything that it was hard to make friends elsewhere.

Jim had told his roommate to find another ride home, and he and Morgan had begun the walk around the lake to her car . . .

Morgan pulled the keys from the ignition, but leaned back into the seat and closed her eyes. It was another month, and Aaron hadn't sent a charm *again*. Five weeks ago she'd had a kind of half letter, asking about Julia and then telling about how great everything was in Rome with the investigators and the success they were having and about how the Lord seemed so close to them.

It wasn't personal at all, didn't refer to her in any way, or ask what she was doing, and she felt so selfish, and jealous at the same time and ashamed. The Lord hadn't seemed close to her for a while. She felt outside of everything. Her family had been used to life without her during the two years she'd lived in the dorm, and though they'd moved a single bed back into her old room with Janey, she felt like an intruder in her own home. She went through the motions in school—and she was actually doing a little better, passing—but her heart wasn't there, and she felt like she was spinning her wheels, still at Hale, still at home, while everyone around her was growing up, moving on, fulfilling their dreams. She shook her head in frustration. Depression was swallowing her again, covering her in blackness.

She remembered feeling the same despair and longing tonight, walking along in the darkness, stumbling along the same path she and Aaron had walked together so many times. Aaron had seemed so close tonight that she'd almost thought that the tall shadow walking beside her was him, and then she tried to believe it, wanted to believe it, convinced herself almost desperately . . .

She didn't know what was the matter with her. Was Aaron that wonderful? Was he the only guy in the world? He was in *Italy* for heaven's sake! And she hadn't seen him for ages. For all she knew he'd turned into some zealous nerd and would quote scripture to her continually when he got back. Really, he'd probably gone off the deep end, probably wanted to extend his mission and wouldn't adjust to life when he got back. He'd be completely changed from the boy who used to take her breath away when she looked at him, who used to cause her heart to plunge and dip and burn . . .

It wouldn't be the same. But what if it was?

The vision of Jim, shadowed by a fluttering aspen tree, staring down at her in the starlight, caused her chest to tighten again. And she'd reached out to him, rested her hands lightly on his forearms, assuming the intimacy, knowing what would happen and pretending all the time that it was that other night with someone a little slighter, a little darker, someone with a fall of dark hair hanging over his forehead, hiding the depths of those expressive eyes. And when Jim's arms had closed around her she shut her eyes and gave herself up to the vision, the deception, which grew earnest and convincing and almost on fire when he touched her lips.

* * *

Elder Jenner,

How's it going, man? So I guess you're out of Rome finally? Time for a little change, huh? What's it like down in Napoli? Are you having much luck tracting? I've heard that it's tough down there. Do they have a place to play basketball? First things first, right? Anyway, you haven't got much time left before you can come back here to Hale and show me the ropes. Or maybe I'll have to initiate you, you know, post-mission life can be a challenge. Ha, ha.

Things are good here. Yes, the good life. I've even seen a fair amount of playing time. Can you believe it? I guess the coach thinks I'm all right. I guess you had a pretty good idea, steering me toward Hale. Good for me, that is.

Well, anyway, I think I'm okay in my classes too, 'course I'm not acing anything, but I'm not doing too bad. I've found someone that motivates me to study. I got a B on my biology test last week. Not too shabby, eh? Seriously, if I can really do this school stuff, it would help me out a lot. I've kind of been thinking about coaching high school basketball or football or P.E. or anything, and I think you need to be able to teach another subject too to get your certificate. Maybe I could get something up in Cache Valley, if I'm lucky, and then help my Dad on the side. It seems like things might be looking up for me.

That's another thing. It's the real reason I wrote, I guess. Man, this is hard to say, but I've got to be straight with you, more than anything. I have really wondered if I should write about this or just keep my mouth shut and see what happens when you get home.

I met Morgan down here. She was working at the little burger joint on Main in Halston, you know. And, well, we got together to talk about you. She was really keen to hear about the mission life. She loved the story about you beating me up. She made me tell it a million times!

Well, things have changed between Morgan and me lately. Aaron, I didn't mean for things to go this way. I tried to stay away from her for a while, and I tried to just be her friend, you know, big brother, but it seemed like she was always in the same place as I was, and well, you know how she is.

I guess I didn't want you to find out from anyone else. I know this is the worst. Especially seeing that you helped me through the whole Gina thing, but man, I just couldn't help it. Morgan is pretty hard to resist. I'm sorry, buddy, but well, I think she's the ONE. I'm grateful now, that Gina dumped me. Because, you know, she doesn't even compare.

I guess there's nothing more to say. Probably you won't talk to me again or anything. Or maybe you'll look me up and black my eye.

Your friend still (if you can believe that),
Jim Facer

* * *

Morgan tripped a little as she came out of the fine arts building, clutching a binder to her chest. Boy, was she lucky! She had barely scraped by on the French test this time, 78 percent, but hey, she wasn't complaining. That was a C+ or something, right? That was okay. So far she was passing just fine if she could get over the finals that well. Madame Paget had nodded to her a little when she laid the corrected test on her desk, like she approved. Maybe she knew Morgan had been studying this time. And she had . . . of course not as much as her mother would like.

A lot of the time at the library she'd sit down on the first floor with her book open and people she knew would pass by and sit down and chat for a bit. And more often than not she would see Jim there, and he would ask her about something from one of his classes, like whether she'd taken the class and from which teacher, and she'd fill him in on all the gossip about the professors and tell him which classes were easiest and how to avoid the hard professors. And then she'd slap him on the shoulder and tell him to quit wasting time and that he'd better study or he'd flunk out. And then they'd sit there semi-quietly for about half an hour, and Morgan would really study, go over her French verbs and maybe try and work some of the algebra equations. (She hadn't *flunked* College Algebra, but her mother didn't seem to think a D was the best thing to have on one's transcripts.)

And so far it seemed to be working pretty good. Sometimes her dad helped her with the algebra if she couldn't get it. It was about the first time she'd ever asked him for help with her homework. Julia had always been so available and so full of all the answers that it hadn't occurred to her that maybe her parents would know something.

It was an ugly day, gray and blowing. The flash of Julia through her mind took her off the small high that she'd been on from the decent test grade. She wondered if it would ever quit bugging her. Why couldn't she just move on? The wind reminded her of a day like this when she and Julia were about eleven. It was Halloween, and they were both dressed like gypsies and freezing to death because they wouldn't wear coats or gloves or anything that would cover their costumes. She smiled.

Her hair blew back off of her face with the changing wind and billowed out behind her shoulders as she hurried toward her dad's little car. He was pretty great to give it up and ride his bike to the high school. It was only two blocks, but still, she should give him more credit.

Morgan grabbed the keys out of her jacket pocket and opened the car door, watching the charm bracelet on her wrist swing and dance. Now there was something to smile about. She'd had a five-week dry spell with nothing from Aaron. Five very ugly weeks, and then these two charms had arrived at the same time about two weeks ago, packed into this tiny box with a short and very stiff note. She'd been so relieved to see the box and the little note that tears had stood in her eyes for a few moments before realization flooded her. It was like a makeup, throwing the two in together.

He'd forgotten to send one. Why? That hurt a little. Of course she knew he was busy and that sometimes you were just caught up in everything going on around you, but still . . . The charms were beautiful though. She fingered them thoughtfully. The little silver figures stretched nearly around the bracelet now. She'd left two spaces when she'd attached the last two, being hopeful, she supposed, that Aaron's memory would improve. She wasn't quite sure that she forgave him for the lapse; in fact, it felt kind of weird now, and she wondered if he thought of her as a duty to be fulfilled, a previous engagement, an obligation.

She shifted an old fast-food bag stuffed with garbage off the passenger seat, and in doing so she caught sight of the edge of an air-mail envelope under a stack of advertisements.

Morgan swiftly fished it out and saw that it was an unopened letter from Italy with a recent postmark. Her dad must have left the mail in the car again, like he was always doing. Mom had missed several of the bills because of him. But man, he could have told her! How long had this letter been sitting under that pile of junk?

She slit the letter with her forefinger and quickly scanned it, hungry and eager for words from Aaron, in spite of her recent disappointment. Her heart had begun to beat a little faster, and then as she read, a white-hot searing began in the center of her chest and spread to her head and her hands as Aaron's stiff and formal words sank in. *Oh, no. Jim! What did you do?*

Her stomach turned, and she wondered if she would throw up. And then anger began to fill her. Quickly she threw the car into reverse and slammed out of the parking place, speeding up the lot and out onto the street. She glanced at her watch: five o'clock. He'd just be getting out of his afternoon practice, ready to head over to the cafeteria for dinner. She could probably just catch him. As she sped around curves and paused at a couple of stop signs, she wondered briefly if she'd get pulled over, or maybe even hit one of those bold students who stepped self-righteously out onto the crosswalks just as a car was about to barrel through. She didn't care though. It didn't matter. Nothing mattered at this moment as much as getting to Jim.

She was cruising along the practice field, coming up on the stadium when she spotted Jim's large bulk, sauntering along in the direction of the cafeteria with a group of players. Morgan hit the brakes hard and pulled over to the side of the road, almost landing the front tire in the deep gutter at the side of the road. The car jerked to a stop, and she leaped out, leaving the door open, and darted across the field. When she got to him, she was breathing so hard from the hundred-yard dash that she couldn't speak immediately.

"Hey, Morgan, what's up?" Jim draped an arm casually around her shoulders and beamed at the group of guys who had stopped to see what was going on. "Why's your face so red?"

Morgan stepped quickly out from under Jim's arm and turned to face him angrily. "Why did you do it, Jim? I can't believe you!"

"What's wrong, bay-bee?" drawled a recruit from down south who was standing behind Morgan. She whipped around.

"You just shut up and stay out of it, Dorry!" She felt like her eyes were going to pop out of their sockets.

"Uh oh, big boy Jimmy, looks like your babe don't want to play today. I'd just get on out of here if I was you." All of the players erupted into loud guffaws, and Morgan stared into Dorry's big fat face and felt like she would kill him.

"How 'bout if I just slap your fat face for you? Huh? You big, dumb . . ."

"Hey." Jim grabbed her shoulders and pulled her back from Dorry. "You boys better get on to dinner. She's a cat on fire today!" Jim grinned again, still not getting it, thinking she was just playing. She let the others get a few paces away from them before she ground out under her breath, "Get your hands off me."

Jim's hands jumped from her shoulders as if he'd been burned.

"Hey, what's the matter?"

She could tell before turning around that she was now coming in loud and clear.

"You! You idiot!" She pushed at his massive chest with both hands. "What did you do to me?" The blood was pushing so madly at her temples that she put her hands to the sides of her head to steady it.

"What are you talking about?" He said it quietly, softly, like he knew what was coming.

"You know what's going on, you dumb jerk." Morgan brandished the letter she was still clutching in the air.

"Oh." Jim looked down at the grass and exhaled noisily. "Yeah, well, I had to do it, Morgan . . . and I knew you wouldn't like it, would want to tell him yourself."

"Tell him what?" But Jim talked on, like he hadn't heard her.

"But I couldn't be sure that you would do it, that you would let him know. And, well, Aaron is a great guy and a good friend, and I just couldn't stand for him to be over there, thinking he was coming back to you. I thought it was important to tell him the truth. Give him time to get used to it."

"JIM! There's nothing to tell!" She was screaming at him now, attracting the notice of several girls who turned their heads toward them curiously. "How could you do this to me! I'm in love with *him*, and now he hates me, because of you!" Tears of rage and frustration were streaming down her face. "I've waited a long time, Jim, a very long time, and now, when he's nearly home, you've ruined it all!"

She was sobbing now. Making a big scene. Somewhere in the back of her mind a little voice was urging her to get hold of herself, to retain a little pride, control her anger, and she listened for a minute, trying to be rational. She looked up at Jim, who was still staring at the grass, and wiped at her cheeks savagely with the back of her hand.

"So all this was nothing?" Jim's words were so low she barely heard them over the beating of her heart. "You and me . . . it didn't mean anything?"

"Jim! We're just friends, don't you know anything? I was just passing the time, waiting, you know. I never *asked* to be kissed; I was just trying to be nice to you! You couldn't really think that there was something between *us*. You've got to be out of your mind!" She was panting a little with the speech, and only barely aware of the venomous words as they poured from her lips. It didn't matter. He deserved it. He'd ruined everything. She felt her world crumbling around her as her anger wound down, and she sat down suddenly on the cold grass in the middle of the field and drew her knees up to her chin.

Jim stood perfectly still for five slow minutes, and she kept waiting for him to say something, but in the end he just turned around and walked back toward the stadium. Morgan watched his broad back until he opened the door to the locker room and disappeared from view.

Chapter 7

"So, I guess you guys have made up your little lover's quarrel, and now it's on to bigger and better things?" Julia's brother Michael lifted his eyebrows suggestively across the table. Julia glanced at Ben seated to her side and then up at Jenny, her sister-in-law, who was trying to kick Michael under the table. When she didn't say anything, Ben tried to cover.

"Sure, why not."

"Of course, yours lasted a little longer than most. We had our little tiff before living happily ever after, didn't we, Jen?" Michael smiled over at Jenny whose eyes were widening. She was still searching for her husband's shin under the table. "Jenny was jealous of the girlfriend I had before my mission. This girl came back through town to see her younger brother at Hale, and we went out as friends, and then she invited me to go to a wedding reception of one of the roommates she'd had at Hale who we both knew. I went because I thought it would be fun to see some of the old Hale crowd that I knew before my mission. It wasn't a big deal and the girl was just being friendly, but Jenny had a fit, if you can believe that coming from such a mild-mannered person as my wife." Michael indulgently laid a hand on the back of Jenny's head.

"Hey, don't tell me that girl . . . what was her name? Goldy or Candi or Brandi or something?"

"It was Ginger, and you know it."

"Okay, Ginger." Jenny gave a little smile. "Anyway, don't tell me that *Ginger* asked you out because she was dying for a friend. She was after you, trying to get something going again."

"Oh, she was not."

"Mike, girls usually don't ask a guy out if they're not interested."

"Well, maybe not." He gave Julia a wink and took a long drink from his sweating water glass.

Julia watched this interchange with interest and relief. Yes, get him talking about himself. Maybe he'd lay off. She took a bite of Jenny's homemade lasagna. This was one of the few times she'd seen Jenny stirred up about anything. Maybe she did have a few opinions under that milquetoast exterior.

At that moment Julia's nephew, Collin, dumped a bunch of blocks over his little brother's head. The two-year-old began wailing and Jenny jumped up and lifted the child into her arms as she gently chastised Collin. Julia's eyes rolled a little. That Collin, darling as he was, was being spoiled out of his mind. When his mother turned back to the table with the baby on her lap, Collin turned to Julia with a mischievous grin. She winked at him.

"This lasagna is great!" Ben was searching for something to say.

"Yeah, Jen. It's wonderful," Julia echoed.

"So, anyway," Michael began again, "what was up with you guys?"

Julia stared at him significantly from across the table, but he pretended he didn't see her and focused on Ben.

"Well . . ." Ben looked uncomfortable.

"I got jealous, of course, just like Jenny," Julia said quickly, avoiding everyone's eyes as she looked down at her plate and speared a bunch of green beans.

"So your eye had been wandering too, huh Ben?" Michael was acting like an idiot and Julia could tell he knew it, but he was having too much fun to stop. "What's her name?"

Ben looked from Michael to Julia for help, but Julia still wouldn't look up from her plate.

"Well, it's kind of complicated, really."

"Oh?" Man, she was going to let Michael have it! He'd better just mind his own business.

"Michael!" Jenny leaned over in front of his face.

"Well, I'm just teasing them. Can't I have a little fun?"

"Maybe you should just mind your own business, buddy," said Julia, still trying to signal to him with her eyes.

"Hey, I have a right to know where my future brother-in-law's eyes are wandering."

There was a small silence.

"That's a little premature, don't you think?" Ben said, looking steadily into Michael's eyes.

"If you say so." Michael held his hands up like he was fending Ben off, still daring to smirk a little.

"Hey, how about dessert?" Jenny passed the baby to Julia and stepped over to the fridge, bringing out a beautiful cheesecake with raspberry sauce dripping over a chocolate crust. When she placed it in the middle of the table, Julia could see molded chocolate leaves mingled with fresh mint arranged in a cloud of whipped cream.

"Wow! That looks delicious!" Ben looked over at Julia, the relief plain in his face.

"Jenny, how long did you spend on this dinner, and who did you get to tend your kids while you did it?" Julia asked.

"Oh, it didn't take that long. I did some of it last night when Michael was home, and then the kids take a pretty good nap in the afternoon."

"This is just gorgeous. I could never do this." Julia accepted her plate and shifted the baby to her left knee so she could eat.

"I can take him," Jenny said when she finished serving the cheesecake.

"No, it's okay." Julia liked the feel of the baby's curly hair grazing her chin as she leaned to take a bite.

"You sure have cute kids," Ben said.

"Yeah, we like them," said Michael, leaning down to his cheesecake eagerly.

* * *

They'd driven down to a park not far from Michael and Jenny's, and Ben had stopped the truck and rolled down the windows a little. Julia smiled at him and scooted across the bench seat beneath his arm. Ben's arm tightened around her, and they sat for some minutes, saying nothing, watching the people in the park.

"We've got to talk about it, you know."

"Why?"

"It's going to come up all the time now, and besides, I don't think I can stand it like this."

"Like what?" Julia shifted around so she could see his eyes.

"You know, this whole tiptoeing act that I've been doing. I've been so afraid of you. But it can't go on. Not really."

"But why, Ben? We're happy, aren't we?"

"Well, yeah, but I just can't exist in a void with no past and no future. I'm a planner, Julia, in case you didn't realize. I like to know what's going to happen with my life. And I'm having a hard time visualizing the next few years."

"Well, what about school? It will take years and years to get your MD, and I've got a few years left too, if I do my master's and maybe a doctorate. Why do we need to get all stressed out about relationships? Let's enjoy right now, mark time, be happy."

"I can't do that, Julia. I really can't. That's not what I was brought up to do. Neither were you."

"Okay." Julia brought air into her chest until it hurt and then let it go, fluttering a neon flyer on the dashboard. "Just give it all to me. Lay it on the table."

"Oh, great. That's a good way to put it." Ben took his arm off of her shoulder and grabbed the steering wheel with both hands. He paused for quite some time, and Julia was about to prompt him to continue, when he finally spoke.

"I love you, Julia. And I hate saying it here, like this, along with your demand to know what I'm thinking about us. But . . . it's a fact I can't ignore. I love you. So much that I couldn't make myself stay away when you dumped me. I knew it would be better to leave you alone, but it was killing me. I can't think about the future without you in it. I need to know if you're going to be there, or if you're going to decide two years down the road that your career goals are more important than I am. I'm going to be a family man, Julia; I'm going to do what the Lord wants me to do, raise a righteous family. And if it's not going to be with you, you'd better tell me now so I can find someone else. I guess it's that simple."

Julia groaned inwardly. It wasn't that simple. Not at all. It was a heck of a lot different for women. Maybe she just thought too much.

Maybe she should just go with her heart and let things work out how they would. But she couldn't. Too much was at stake.

"I want to do what the Lord wants me to do too, Ben. I've been trying to do it all my life. But it's complicated for me. I've been raised to believe I can do anything . . . that I can be an astronaut if I want to, or president of the United States. And I really believe it."

"I know."

"Do you really? Do you really see what a commitment here could cost me?" Julia couldn't bring herself to name what they were really talking about. "It is so different for you, don't you see? *You* can have it all. *You* can have this quaint little family in a house in the suburbs and walk away from it at eight in the morning and have a professional life and your colleagues and lunch in the cafeteria with the hospital director. You can progress and learn more and become a specialist and get fat and complacent on your steady reputation. And then at five you can pull into that suburban driveway with the basketball hoop over the garage, and you can shoot a few with your oldest son and come into the kitchen, where your dinner is ready, and kiss your wife and your little girls. And then you can go over to the church at seven and work with the young men or the scouts or something else, and you can feel really good about your life."

"Julia I know, I . . ."

"Your sacrifice is nothing compared to mine." She was breathing hard by this time, her chest rising and falling. "But the big problem is . . . the big problem is that I love you too. Enough to give up everything for you. Enough to be that wife with your kids in that little house in the suburbs." She colored at this, embarrassed that she'd named the unnamable between them. "But I am so scared . . . so scared that everything I am will die, smothered in that little house crowded among all the little houses just like it and all the young mothers and their darling babies piled upon one another. And I just don't know. I don't know if I could give up all that I am and remain sane and still be the person you love.

"It is so hard, because I feel like my very being, all that I am essentially, is a *paradox*. I know the Church is true, I feel it strong in every breath that I take, but yet I cannot find my place within it. My devotion fights with my strong, capable mind. At my age, it seems like I have two choices: get married if the opportunity presents itself." She dared to smile a little here. "Or go on a mission. I'll be twenty-one in a couple of months. And neither of those options offers me what I really need—an outlet, a place to use my talents. I have them, though I'm not musical and I don't dance and I can't sew or cook. I get math problems, I get equations, I get trigonometry and chemistry and physics. I see numbers in my head and I can figure quickly and easily and I can memorize and I can do well." She bent her head toward her chest. Silent tears began making their way down her face, and she blinked rapidly, angrily, embarrassed by them and herself. Maybe she was just being selfish; maybe other girls were more dedicated to the Church, more willing to sacrifice. But she didn't think so. It seemed like it was easier for them. It was pretty easy to give up what you never knew you wanted.

Julia looked up then into Ben's surprised and compassionate face.

He said two words, "You're right," and then folded her into his arms.

When her cheek was on his chest and she could feel the warm, steady beating, she knew she would give it all up. Here and now it was worth it, and whatever she may feel next month or next spring or next year didn't matter, not as much as this moment. Right here, right now was the only place she belonged. She couldn't argue with this, even though tears were still running down her face, and she could feel acutely the pain of her dying dreams.

"We'll work it out," Ben said.

"What?"

Ben pushed her from him and stared into her eyes. "We'll work it out, Julia. We'll find a way for you. There's got to be something. There is no way that I'm going to let you waste your talents. You *are* brilliant, and it can't be right to let all of that go. Heck, I might as well admit it, you're smarter than I am!"

"You finally noticed," Julia teased.

"Hey, I'll admit it this once, but don't expect to hear that ever again. If you quote me, I'll deny it."

She laughed then, loud and thoroughly, getting a little hysterical with relief at the end. Ben joined with her, delighting her with his rich, sincere laugh.

"Yeah, but Julia." They were calming down a little now, but still ridiculously happy. "I think you're underestimating yourself."

"What do you mean."

"You'd be a great mother."

"Why do you say that?"

"Well, look at you with your two nephews. You love them. You try to hide it sometimes, act like they're a pain, but you know you adore them. It's obvious, and I've only seen you with them a couple of times. Give yourself a little credit."

"Maybe I need to explore my many talents," Julia said.

"Maybe you need to quit seeing yourself in only one dimension. You are more than just your brain, you know, and anyway, don't you think that you'd actually use your intelligence in child-raising?"

"I don't know; I've never tried it. It really doesn't seem to be very scientific."

"Does it have to be? I mean, look at your sister-in-law; she's pretty with-it." Ben took her hand. "She had that whole dinner timed perfectly, and both the kids were clean, and the house looked great. And she'd just finished doing that whole Young Women thing. You don't think all of that takes a little brain power?"

"Well yeah, of course," Julia said. "But Ben, I don't have her kind of talents. Have you ever eaten anything I've made? I'm kind of like my mom that way."

"Your mom is great."

"I know, but we both have this total lack of talent in the home-making area." Julia grimaced.

"Well, what about raising you." Ben took a lock of her hair and curled it around his finger. "It seems to me she did a pretty good job."

"She was a great mother. Perfect almost, if you didn't count the cooking." Julia smiled.

Ben leaned over and kissed her cheek. "But don't you see, Julia, she did what she did for you, and for the Lord, not because it was her favorite thing to do. And don't you think that she's happy?"

"She is probably the most peaceful woman I know."

"You see? We'll find you that peace. Who knows? You may be able to have your cake and eat it too."

Chapter 8

Aaron lined the two new letters up even with the edge of his desk, which was really just an old door supported on each side by a couple of crumbling stacked bricks. He swept up the brick crumbs at least once a day, because he couldn't stand the grit when he was walking around the bedroom with bare feet.

He pushed the top corners of the letters together slightly until there was a uniform one-inch strip of brown door between them. He didn't believe either of them, didn't want to. He sighed again and took a quick look at his new companion, a very quiet greenie, who was writing furiously and already had two written, addressed, and stamped letters stacked neatly on the edge of his broken-down desk. Aaron returned to the two pages, trying to focus his eyes.

Aaron—
Please, you've got to believe me! Nothing happened!

Morgan's handwriting was large, hasty, and passionate. He could almost hear her speaking through the words.

I don't know what delusion Jim is suffering from, but there is nothing between us. He's just a lonely returned missionary, thinking every girl that smiles at him is in love with him.

Aaron was pretty sure that Morgan always did more than smile at the guys. He guessed that Jim probably just couldn't help himself.

He's just mixed up, that's all. Yeah, we're friends, just because I loved hearing about you so much. It was fun talking to him, because he told me a lot of things about you that I didn't know. If you could have seen how I licked up those crumbs of information!

It's been really hard without you, you know, but I've always known I would wait for you. Aaron, I've never even been tempted by another guy, not seriously.

Yeah, right. She must have been giving some pretty mixed signals, thought Aaron. If he knew anything about Jim, he knew he was honest. And he didn't see Jim as the kind of guy that would think a girl was in love with him if she wasn't acting like she was.

I really hope you'll understand this, that you'll forgive me, although there's really nothing to forgive. Aaron, I love you! I know I haven't said it before, because, well, I was afraid. I didn't want to say the words, but I know now. I know it for sure! There's nobody like you, Aaron. You understand me. I know you still do.

Please say everything is all right again. Tell me you believe me. I won't make it unless you do.

> *All my love,*
> *Morgan*

Curiously, her pleading affected Aaron not at all. His heart seemed like stone. He didn't even feel sorry for her. Maybe he should, but he didn't.

He turned his eyes to the other letter and with difficulty, relaxed his jaw where he'd been gritting his teeth together. It ached.

Aaron,

I guess you win after all. I just wanted to put the record straight. Morgan still wants you. Nothing happened between us, I guess. Nothing to her, that is. It looks like I'm just a big, dumb, love-starved RM. Lucky me. No. Lucky you.

> *Jim*

Aaron knew Morgan had led Jim on. Probably just like she'd done with half a dozen other guys over the last twenty-three months. And then when Aaron had sent her that crazy, tearing letter, the one that he'd written before he could control himself, when he was still so angry he could break her neck, she'd gotten scared. She'd probably told Jim off good. Probably hurt him a lot too. She wasn't really that sensitive to what others were going through. Aaron had always known that in the back of his mind.

This was all so crazy, so stupid. Why didn't things work out like you thought they would? Why did he feel so dead inside? He'd won, right? She didn't really like any of those other guys. Jim's letter proved that. But it just didn't feel right, none of it did. Yes, he understood Morgan; he knew her. And it was too bad. It really was.

* * *

"So, where do you go from here?" Julia's dad's voice came clearly through the phone.

"Dad, I'm just so confused. I know what I want, yet the two things I want don't seem to fit together."

"There's got to be some sort of a compromise. Have you prayed about it, Julia?"

"Not really," she admitted.

"Why not?"

"I know the answer I'll get."

"Oh?"

"Yes," Julia said.

"So now you really do know everything."

"Dad, if I pray about whether I should have a career or be a wife and mother, I know what the Lord's answer is going to be."

"Don't you believe in individual revelation? I mean, everyone isn't the same. And have you even asked if Ben is the right guy for you?"

"Dad, if I'm going to marry someone, it's going to be him!"

"You seem very sure."

"Well, about that, I am. I don't have to ask the Lord. I already know." And she did.

"Julia, you think you've met the guy you should marry. I'd say you'd received a witness. And yet you're still questioning. Why?"

"I just can't give it all up. I mean, sometimes I think I can, because it's so wonderful when I'm with Ben, and I think that nothing else matters. But then when I can be rational again, I know that if I sit and watch Ben going through medical school, struggling, succeeding, I will be so jealous—jealous enough to ruin everything."

"Julia, a woman only has so many childbearing years," her dad told her.

"Hey, I'm only twenty years old," she protested.

"I know, I didn't mean that. I meant that there is time for you to do everything that you want to do. Life is long. I mean, you can get your education now, and still have time for babies and family, and then after that, still have the career that you want. Everything will work out for you if you try to include the Lord in your life and obey Him. Don't you believe that?"

"Yes, I do. But I'm so rebellious, and so selfish. It's hard to get over that."

"I know. But you will. You're still immature in some ways, although you seem to think 'you've arrived.'"

"Dad!"

"Well, Julia, there's a lot that you learn as you get to be as old a guy as I am, and one of the things is that everything is not such an emergency and that there is time, a lot of time, in life and that you don't need to determine your whole future in a few months. You can leave things open, work on them later, see what develops, leave room for change. Your feelings might even change too."

"That's the exact opposite of what you've told me my whole life. Plan ahead, prepare well, work hard, be smart, think. And I can't stop doing that now. I just keep thinking and thinking and thinking, trying to figure a way out of this mess, a way to have my cake and eat it too. Because I really want him, Dad. I really do. If I'd been able to pick out the perfect man, honestly, it would have been him. All right, well, he's not as serious about life as I am, and there are one or two other things that bug me like why he stuffs garbage behind the seat in his truck instead of putting it in the garbage can . . . and he wears this one shirt that is just horrible sometimes, but really, in everything else, he's the best. I can't believe my luck. And I know I'd die if he married someone else."

"I know. We've already been a little ways down that road." He paused. "Have you talked to Morgan yet?"

"No. I feel bad about it, and I do miss her. I didn't realize how much I talked to her, how much stress she relieved. But I just can't get over it, you know, what she did to me, and on purpose too. I have no doubt in my mind that she intentionally went after him to get me back. Dad, sometimes, even now, I wake up in the morning feeling that something is wrong but not being able to remember quite what. And then I remember; and it's her, her betrayal, and I feel sick—sick that I don't have her anymore and that I never will. Anyway, thanks for letting me talk."

"No problem. Just try not to be too stubborn, Julia. So, when are you coming down for Thanksgiving?"

"I'll probably come with Michael and Jen on Wednesday. It'll be better than driving myself. I can sleep."

"Are you bringing Ben to dinner?"

"I don't know. Maybe." She smiled.

* * *

Later that night after she'd finished three hours of study, Julia decided to wash the dishes even though it was Lorraine's turn. Lorraine had been working so hard lately, practicing more and more and hardly eating. Julia wondered if she would actually disappear one of these times, she was already so thin. She worried about her getting mono or something. She was always exhausted and had deep black circles under her eyes.

Julia stacked the dishes in the drainer and wiped off the countertop. Then she unpacked a bag of groceries she'd bought earlier in the day on her way home. She took out a box of crackers, a couple of cans of ready-to-eat soup, and a package of peanut clusters and propped them up on the counter. She ripped a page off a notepad and quickly scrawled a note.

Lorraine—
Eat something, will ya? Hope everything is going well at practice.
Julia

Julia taped the note to one of the cans of soup and then put away the rest of the groceries in the cupboard. She looked at the phone. Maybe Ben would call. She stared at it for a few seconds and then gave up. She knew he was probably still at the library or something.

When she'd changed and brushed her teeth, she sat up in bed and grabbed her scriptures from the nightstand. Sitting cross-legged, she found her place in Alma and stared at the chapter heading for a couple of minutes. The scriptural quad felt heavy and good in her lap. Even just from opening the book she felt a rush of peace that couldn't exactly be described. She needed this closure every night. It was something that she'd learned about herself when she'd moved out of her parents' home. Sure, before she'd read on her own, filled in the squares on her seminary reading charts faithfully, and tried on and off to really study, but when she'd moved out after high school and had been away from the comfort of home, somehow she'd nearly always found time to read.

But as she began the chapter, unease began to fill her. Julia's mind jumped back to the conversation she'd had with her dad. Didn't she want to do what the Lord wanted of her? She'd been obedient her whole life. The gospel was true. Was there anything more important than that? A flash of guilt stabbed through her. Ben was a good man, young as he was, and Julia knew he'd get even better. Shouldn't she want to be his wife and raise good, righteous, responsible children, even more than she wanted a career for herself? But what of her talents? Surely they were God-given. How could she have been given the specific mental gifts that she knew were hers for no reason?

Julia squeezed her forehead between her middle finger and her thumb. It was so hard. Julia flipped to the topical guide and looked up the word *obedience*. Tonight, instead of a chapter in Alma she needed specific inspiration. As she read down the scripture descriptions her brain snapped together and her sharp analytical side kicked in. She quickly looked up the passages that seemed to apply to her situation.

If ye be willing and obedient, ye shall eat the good of the land . . .

Julia underlined the words with a bold red stroke.

Not everyone that saith unto me, Lord, Lord, shall enter into the kingdom of heaven; but he that doeth the will of my father . . .

". . . doeth the will . . ." Julia murmured under her breath.

Blessed are they that hear the word of God, and keep it.

Julia's fingers flew as the Spirit filled her. She came to the listing of 1 Nephi 3:7 and without reading the description quickly turned to the page. She knew what it said. She took a deep breath and released it slowly as she read Nephi's amazing declaration of faith.

I will go and do the things which the Lord hath commanded, for I know that the Lord giveth no commandments unto the children of men, save he shall prepare a way for them that they may accomplish the thing which he commandeth them.

Nephi knew. Did she? Didn't she believe the Lord would help her if she obeyed? Could she find the way the Lord had prepared for her?

* * *

Morgan had absolutely stuffed herself. And her only regret was that she felt bloated, big as a tick, though, glancing down, she saw that her stomach still looked flat and sleek in her favorite pair of jeans. Morgan licked the back of the gravy ladle before putting it in the sink and pinched a hunk of leftover mashed potatoes off the pile before putting plastic wrap over the bowl and jamming it into the already-stuffed fridge. The Carters were all here again this year, and Morgan's mom was being gracious and amazing, though their house was too small for the thirty-two people who showed up. They'd had to clean out the garage, put out a couple of space heaters and set up two long church tables that they'd borrowed from the ward.

The kitchen was hot and stuffy, and Morgan leaned over the sink to open the window a crack to let in some cold air. Aunt Shelbie bumped into her from behind, and Morgan nearly lost her balance and fell into the sink.

"Sorry, honey."

"It's okay."

Aunt Shelbie moved her large bulk out into the dining area, dodged three chasing children, and bent over the large table to continue clearing it. Mom and Grandma were scraping plates into the garbage can near the bar. Morgan looked around for the next thing to do, to move all of this along and bring the holiday to its end, like everything else, but suddenly it was too much, and she just couldn't do it.

The women and Aunt Jean's new, obedient husband were cleaning up and talking in the kitchen. The men and older boys were sprawled in the living room, on the couch, folding chairs, and on the floor, and the ten children were running in and out of the house and both rooms. Morgan swiftly crossed to the kitchen door and escaped out into the garage and then into the backyard. She crossed to her mom and dad's work shed, waving away her sister and little cousins who begged her to have a hula-hoop contest with them.

It was dark and cold in the shed, and Morgan didn't turn on the fluorescent lights overhead, but walked over to the wooden work bench and cleared a place for herself with a forearm. She turned around and hoisted herself up to sit on the scarred plywood, edging over so the last of the afternoon light would fall on her right side, warming her just a little.

Morgan sat there, freezing, staring at the dust motes as they danced across the beam of light coming through the small window. Aaron hadn't written her back. Not even to say it was really over. He was getting back in three weeks, around December 15.

She would see him. She would convince him. Nothing could hold her back. And he would remember her. It would be all right then, wouldn't it?

She sat still for a long time listening to the kids playing in the yard. And then finally she walked over to her mother's unfinished project, Melanie Harper's threadbare gold couch, and picked up a tool and began prying old nails out of the frame.

Chapter 9

Julia pushed against the heavy classroom door with her back and swung into the teeming hall, feeling a great rush of relief overlay her exhaustion as she put one foot in front of the other and moved on down the hall. The semester was over, finally! She'd just written in her last formula and then checked through the Organic Chemistry final for errors. She wouldn't be making any dumb mistakes this time. Any missed points on that final would come from honest ignorance!

She felt sweaty and hot from all the pressure and the elevated temperatures of the unevenly heated chemistry building. She pulled on the front of her shirt to fan herself a couple of times. Up ahead in some ugly green lounge chairs she could see Emmet, John, and Linda trying to convince each other that they'd aced the final. Julia quickened her step to join them.

"Yeah, I don't know. I guess we'll have to wait and see." Emmet glanced up. "How'd you do, Julia?"

"I'm not sure. I think I knew most of it. A couple of the problems were pretty rough, though, tricky, and I couldn't seem to remember what I'd read about it in the book, though I know I'd seen the answer. But hey, it's all over now, nothing we can do about any of it. And I feel exquisitely FREE!" Julia stretched her arms up over her head and grinned broadly at her classmates. "Anyone up for a little celebration?"

"Where to?" said Emmet, still a little hopeful, though he'd seen Julia with Ben a couple of times during the last month. Julia hadn't talked to anyone but Lorraine about Ben, so Emmet didn't know.

"We could just go over to the student union and get something."

"Sure, let's go, but you might have to carry me. I stayed up all night." John winked at Julia and came over to put his arm around her briefly, leaning with all his weight and almost making her knees buckle.

"Hey!" Julia pushed him off, smiling. She didn't even care that Linda rolled her eyes and gave her a dirty look when John touched her. Boy, it was so good to be done. The relief was absolutely exquisite. She couldn't wait to go home and pack and pick Ben up in Provo at seven. Then they'd have three blessed hours alone together in the car on the way down to Halston. He would stay for a couple of days at her house before catching a ride down to Cedar City with his second cousin who was at Hale.

Jesse, the skinny guy with the thick glasses in their study group, approached them.

"Hey, Jess, we're going for a little celebration, want to come?" Emmet looked over Jesse's head and raised his eyebrows at Julia. Julia was glad that Jesse was gaining a little confidence and was coming with them a little more. The guy needed a little bit of social life. He still lived at home and he was twenty-four, getting his second major. Julia gave Emmet a "be nice" look, and they all headed toward the outer doors.

"Did you hear Dr. Jorsht talking to those pharmacology majors?" John pushed the glass door open and held it as the rest of them walked through.

"Yeah, it kind of makes you want to change your major. Man, there are some great opportunities." Emmet turned to Julia.

"Yeah, but I guess standing behind a counter like a clerk all day would be a drag." Julia shrugged her shoulders. It didn't seem very scientific to her, just handing out a bunch of pills.

"Probably," Emmet replied. "Still, all those working internships, and man, a little bit of cash! I only get seven bucks an hour cleaning up after all you slobs in the lab. And I'm in danger too. Who knows what kind of caustic mistakes you guys make." John pushed Emmet in the shoulder, and Emmet fell into Linda, who smiled.

"But, hey, it is something to think about," Emmet continued. "I'm about sick of scraping along. Every time we go out to eat I have to starve for two days to make up for it. I'm a poor man." Emmet looked at Linda, who didn't seem to mind financially destitute men, especially if they were breathing. Julia rolled her eyes, not thinking anyone would notice, but Jesse happened to look at her in that moment, and a small grin appeared on his face. Julia shaped her lips into a silent "shhh" and winked at him. He grinned even more.

"Would you guys quit stressing out? We're done, aren't we? Don't think about anything else, okay? I mean, we may never go back." Julia stretched her arms wide.

"Boy, you're in a good mood." John looked at her suspiciously. "What did you do, ace us all out on that last final? Stretch the curve up? I think we're going to have to kill you."

Linda looked like she really would. "She's just relieved, glad to have it over, aren't you, Julia?" Linda smiled thinly and arched her black brows.

"Sure, you know me. I usually go to pieces during an exam."

"Anyway, how about it, is anyone changing to pharmacology with me?" Emmet looked back at the group expectantly as they walked along.

"Would you just give it a rest? Everyone knows you are way too gung-ho in chemistry to sit behind a counter at Wal-Mart and try to reason with old people." Julia breezed past him and pushed through the door to the student union. In the short distance to the snack bar she decided. Definitely a hot fudge sundae. One had to celebrate, right?

* * *

Back at her apartment, feeling a little guilty after eating the huge hot fudge sundae, Julia pulled her suitcase out from under the bed and began filling it from her closet and drawers. She tried to pick the things that looked best on her, though she couldn't say she had the best taste that way. Morgan had always told her the truth about the way she looked, whether she could handle it or not, although usually she had ignored her, hadn't cared much. But now . . . she tried not to think about what Morgan would say.

She pulled out the things that were the newest and any that she'd had recent compliments on. She caught a glance of herself in the small mirror above her dresser and then moved closer. Her dark hair needed a cut. It was a little too long and messy looking for the blunt style it had been shaped into. She shook her head. She'd been ignoring herself a little lately, being so immersed in her books and spending all that time in the lab. Some days she left the apartment at six fifteen and didn't look in the mirror again till she was brushing her teeth at eleven or twelve at night.

She ran her fingers through her hair, wondering if she had time to wash it. Boy, it really needed a cut. Morgan would never let herself go like this. She'd spend her last dollar at the beauty salon. But of course she wouldn't be dividing her time between the library and the lab either. Julia smiled a little. It still hurt to think about her though.

In a little less than an hour Julia had stopped for gas, bought a yogurt and a banana to make up for the sundae, and was cruising down I-15. She'd washed up and combed through her hair a little, had even gotten out the curling iron to see if she could do anything, and had put on a little mascara, lipstick, and perfume. Her heart had begun to beat faster even now, as she drove up the hill, past the prison, and around the Point of the Mountain. When she was feeling like this, there could be no argument. Everything seemed wonderful and bound to turn out well. She glanced down at her open backpack on the seat next to her, wondering why she'd even brought it. Her organic chemistry book had bounced out and was lying on the floor of the car.

She was probably okay on that final, right? She probably would get an A from the class, though she wasn't sure. She'd worked hard enough. She wondered how the others had done. Emmet hadn't had much time to study with them lately as he was trying to balance two jobs and a huge load of credits. He couldn't afford to go slowly in his education because he didn't have the luxury of leaning on his parents for everything as Julia did. The only job Julia had ever had was cleaning offices for her dad or catching him up on secretarial work when he was between employees.

Maybe that was why Emmet was thinking about the pharmacology major. Was he serious? It had never even occurred to Julia as an option, but she guessed it would be something to him to be able to work somewhere, doing something that would help him toward a degree *and* actually get paid enough to be able to eat and pay for a room without getting another job. And the work was so flexible too. There were places like Wal-Mart or Kmart that kept their pharmacies open later so you could do something during the day and work too. Julia could see and appreciate the practical side of pharmacology. And she guessed it was plenty challenging, at least from the schooling end of it. She knew a couple of pharmacology majors from one of her classes who were brilliant. And there were so many opportunities for work. You could practically live anywhere . . .

Julia's mind focused intensely on the subject, like it was a test question, and by the time she pulled off the freeway on the University Parkway exit, toward Provo, she was smiling widely and tapping her palm on the steering wheel in time to the radio.

* * *

Well, he was ready. Aaron's suitcases stood stacked near the front door, his overcoat and backpack on the chair next to them. He couldn't believe it was time. Not already. Aaron ran his hands through his short hair and looked around the tiny apartment blankly. He was just waiting for his companion to finish shaving. This one was very precise and thorough about everything, and if things weren't just right, well, Aaron just had to wait until Elder Nielson fixed them. It was okay though; they'd done pretty well together, done their jobs, and had quite a bit of success here in Napoli, though they hadn't baptized anyone yet. Aaron hoped that Elder Nielson would see at least two of their current investigators baptized in the next few months, if he stayed that long.

Aaron slid the back window up and put his leg over the sill. The iron fire escape felt a little bit wobbly under his feet, and the landlady had warned them about it, but they'd been out on it a lot anyway. It was still dark, and pretty cold, but Aaron didn't feel it as he looked out over the city in the greying dawn. The battered rooftops and strings of neglected laundry were muted shapes against the slowly rising sun and reflected a beauty and uniqueness he would never get over. It was beautiful, this place, for all its poverty, and suddenly he was afraid that he'd never see it again, never walk through the streets and smile at the kids and buy that mouth-watering Napolitan pizza at the corner store. His eyes began to water, and he wiped at them quickly.

The work here had been a great relief, really, like a healing balm, helping him to get his perspectives into focus. He was so grateful to the Lord. There was so much help available if you wanted it.

Funny, he couldn't regret that it wasn't Rome. He couldn't regret being sent here. Though a lot of those bad stories about Napoli were true on the surface, he'd found so much here to love. The narrow, winding streets, though poor and rough, held a kind of charm he couldn't describe. And the people, they'd seemed to open their arms to him. He guessed that since they didn't have as much as the people in Rome, they had less to lose. He'd had a great rapport with these people and a deep respect. And even though none of their contacts had resulted in baptisms yet, he felt with a sureness that his time here hadn't been wasted. He didn't feel that sense of frustration that had come over him many times during his mission when so much rejection had flattened him. He knew that the Lord was molding him, directing his mind, purifying his soul. Aaron bent his head in gratitude. Would this be the last day he would feel like this?

A kind of beautiful anguish closed in his throat as he thought about his two years in Italy. A kaleidoscope of faces, scenes, and feelings shifted through him as he stared out into the greying dawn. He'd built up so much over here, so much that was good. The Lord had helped him and had been at his side even in his worst moments. He'd picked up the Napolitan accent almost effortlessly. The Lord's gift of the language that could now flow through his mind and fill his heart would be lost back in the States. How many Utahns spoke Italian?

A gentle breeze blew over his face. He turned to look back through the open window, into the lighted apartment. No sign of Elder Nielson.

He looked down into the still-dark alley, barely making out a cat winding its way between some old cardboard boxes and the rusty dumpster. Suddenly his mind shifted, and though he was still looking at the cat, he thought of home, seeing all those familiar things again, all those people he loved. He thought of school and work and water-skiing and basketball, and wondered how he would fit in there again. And he thought of Morgan. He shivered slightly. Aaron knew it was silly, but he was afraid to go home.

Chapter 10

Ben had already stayed at Julia's house a day longer than he'd planned because Julia had begged him to. They figured out that one of Ben's sisters was traveling down for the holidays and had room for him, so they let the cousin go and stole the extra day to be together. It was still a few days before Christmas and they'd decided to try ice-skating at a small pond up in the foothills. The weather had turned cold suddenly, and everything had frozen. Julia had rummaged through some old boxes in the basement and had found old skates that the two of them could squeeze their feet into.

She remembered when she and Morgan used to string the skates around their necks and ride up to the pond nearly every afternoon that really cold year when they were thirteen, convinced that they might be good enough someday to skate in the Olympics. She winced at the memory and smiled ruefully, remembering that it had taken nearly an hour and all their energy to shovel the snow off the ice that first afternoon. They'd been too tired and a little discouraged at the rough surface of the ice to skate much that day. But they hadn't given up.

Julia sat squashed down in her dad's comfortable wing chair, staring up into the many lights of the Christmas tree, waiting for Ben to get back from the gas station. He was going to take her on a ride. She smiled and hugged herself. The last three days had been the most wonderful in her life. No contest. In fact, she didn't even recognize herself. She hadn't thought or worried about anything the whole time. The future and the past didn't seem to exist for her. She would find herself thinking that she'd look back on this time and long for it, long for this feeling, this excitement again.

She and Ben had shoveled all the walks in the neighborhood one morning when an inch of snow had fallen, feeling virtuous and high-spirited in the brisk air. Later they'd hopped on a hay wagon full of the youth from her ward, and Julia had sung Christmas carols with a vigor and glee that had shocked and pleasantly surprised Ben. They'd had hot chocolate at the church and then walked home in the cold air and stood under the frosted willow tree while Ben picked the straw from her hair and touched her cheek and kissed her . . .

She laid her head back in the soft chair and closed her eyes at the sweetness of it. She'd always scorned romance . . . oh, but when it was happening to her! Ben was ecstatic too. She could tell. She would look up into his blue, blue eyes, and it seemed she could see forever—and she wouldn't even feel embarrassed, staring at him that way.

"Hey, ready to go?" Ben's voice jolted her out of her thoughts.

Julia jumped up, grabbed her coat, and intentionally bumped into Ben on her way out the door.

"Be good, you two," said Julia's dad from the doorway, trying to look stern.

"Don't worry, Dad."

"Okay, but don't be gone too long. Your mother is in the kitchen trying to make apple crisp to have a little later. I'd better go help her."

"Yes, you'd better."

"And Ben," Julia's dad added.

"Yes, sir?"

"You have to eat it," he warned solemnly.

"It's that bad?"

"It may be; we just don't ever know for sure. But pretend you like it."

"You got it." Ben saluted.

"And Ben," Julia's dad said again.

"Yeah?"

"You be careful with my girl."

"Of course, sir."

"Dad!" Julia complained.

"Well, I was young once too, you know. I know how it is."

"You are so embarrassing." Julia smiled at him, exasperated, but somehow unembarrassed.

"Okay, see ya."

And then they were alone.

Ben helped her into the truck and then ran around to his side. "Tired?" he asked.

"Yeah, I guess, a little. We stayed up too late watching that movie."

Ben smiled and rubbed one eye. "Yeah, and I haven't really recovered from those all-nighters during finals. Man, what a workout."

"Ben, you're crazy. If you would just plan a little you'd have plenty of time to study without staying up all night. That can't be good for you."

"Well, it seems like the only thing to do sometimes."

"You poor baby." Julia smiled and scooted a little closer to him. They were winding up the frozen canyon now, the dark air pressing in on the little truck, the headlights flashing briefly on lightly snow-dusted pines and rutted, frozen mud. A peaceful quiet descended on them and they grew silent, yet content. And it wasn't awkward. It felt like love.

Julia let her head drop a little onto Ben's shoulder. The next thing she knew she was jerked awake by a large bump and Ben slamming on the brakes and skidding to a stop on the frozen road.

"Shoot! I think I hit something." Ben twisted his head and upper body to stare out the back window at the dark road behind them. "It was too small to be a deer, but maybe a fawn or a fox or something."

"A fawn?" Julia stared out the back window too. She could see a dark shape in the road. It had started to snow in large, fat flakes.

"I'd better go out and check on it."

"Oh, yuck."

Ben bent over and took what looked like an old pair of gloves from beneath the seat. When he tried to grab the door handle to let himself out, he missed it, fumbling with the catch. Julia could see his hand shaking in the dim light and her eyes widened. Was he scared? Or did he just not relish dragging the bloody body of a wild animal off the road? Understandable. Or maybe he just felt bad. In some ways, he really had a tender heart. Julia smiled at the thought.

Ben disappeared around the back of the truck, and Julia remained facing forward, preferring not to watch. It happened all the time when you lived in a rural community, but still, it was too bad and pretty gross.

He was taking a long time. Julia began tapping her fingers on the dashboard and was just about to turn around to see what was going on when Ben stepped into the beam of the headlights about five yards in front of the truck. What was he doing? Julia put her hand out for the door handle, but stopped when Ben turned to face her and suddenly dropped to his knee. The falling snow shimmered in the beams of the brilliant headlights and lay down gently on his head and shoulders.

"Julia," Ben yelled, throwing his arms wide, "WILL YOU MARRY ME?" He smiled nervously and rocked a little unsteadily on one knee, but he was so beautiful.

Julia began to laugh in short chokes and then felt tears slipping down her cheeks. She opened the truck door and leaned out. "What about the fawn?"

"Will you forget about the fawn? There is no fawn!"

"Well, fox then."

"There's no fox either, for heaven's sake. I made it up."

Julia was still laughing quietly and crying silently. She sat back down in the truck, leaving the door ajar.

"Hey, I'm serious, you know!" He dug into his jacket pocket and produced a velvet box which he opened with shaking fingers.

"Will you marry me?" he asked again.

Julia put her hand to her throat and drew in cold air until she thought her lungs would burst. Every detail in the truck came into sharp focus for her and time hung in the air, quivering and unnatural like an icicle about to fall to the ground and smash into a million pieces. She tried to dredge up the steady logic that had always been ready on the surface of her mind, but another sob rose instead and suddenly she was bolting from the truck and charging Ben, knocking him to the ground in her embrace and looking into his face, inches from her own while the snow fell on both of them.

"You know I will, Ben. You know it."

* * *

Aaron knew it was the right thing to do, the sort of thing that he wouldn't be ashamed to tell his children. In fact something that he might want bring up when they got older and had troubles of their own. It was honest and forthright and showed that he was a man of integrity, not a ridiculous boy, and it would make everything easier in the long run for him; he knew it.

But why then was Aaron sitting with his jeep parked halfway down the other side of the street from Morgan's house with his hands sweating on the steering wheel, itching to turn the ignition and race off down the street?

Aaron could barely see her front door beyond a fat pine tree which he hoped hid his jeep from view, and he tapped the wheel a couple of times, trying to calm down.

This was hard and ugly, yes. But it had to be done, and he couldn't put it off any longer. He'd already been home for three days, and he was making himself sick over it. His mom kept bringing him stuff and telling him to lie down and sleep off his jet lag, but he was so antsy he thought he would explode if he didn't do something, if only to stop his mind doing mental gymnastics trying to think of an easy way out of this.

This was so different from the way he'd thought it was going to be. He had dreamed of the moment he'd see Morgan again. He would never have believed this empty, ugly feeling could replace the excitement and thrill of the prospect of being with her.

Aaron took a deep breath and reached down for the package on the other seat. He owed her this, at least, and clutching it in his sweaty palm, Aaron swung down out of the jeep and walked across the street. Bits of ice crunched under his feet, announcing loudly his measured steps toward her house. It wasn't too late; she hadn't seen him yet. He could still make it back to the jeep and run away from this, and someday when he was, say, forty, he could rationalize it by saying that he'd been too young and immature to know it was the right thing to do. After all, Morgan basically knew the score, didn't she? He didn't *really* have any obligation to her, not after what she did.

Suddenly the thought of Francesca and Elder Archer's accusation appeared in his mind and he tried to push it away. What if someone told her about that? He would seem so hypocritical, and there was no way that she would know the rumor wasn't true.

Aaron stopped walking for a moment, pausing just behind the big pine tree and then cursed himself for his ridiculous sense of duty as he forced himself to walk on, stepping in front of the tree, exposing himself so he couldn't turn back. Soon he was on the front porch, ringing the bell.

"Why, Aaron! What are you doing here? I didn't think you'd be back till after Christmas. What a surprise! Come on in." Morgan's mother held the screen door wide and ushered him in, patting him soundly on the back. "Morgan didn't say, she didn't tell me any—" Morgan's mother stopped abruptly and swung around to face him.

Aaron could tell that she knew there'd been trouble. He felt his cheeks burn.

"Anyway, glad you're back."

"Thanks, Sister Carter. Is Morgan here?"

"You know, she's not! Can you believe it? You leave a girl for two whole years and then you come to see her, and she's not even here. Pretty fickle, huh!"

Morgan's mom grinned widely at her own joke, clearly not realizing that it certainly wasn't funny to him. Maybe this was going to be even harder than he'd thought. Obviously, Sister Carter thought he was coming to make up with Morgan.

"Well, I guess I'll come back then." But he knew he wouldn't. He reached out toward the screen door eagerly, glad that he could assuage his conscience without actually having to do the deed. Maybe the Lord was watching out for him.

"Hey, no, stay. She's just down at the Burger Barn, working, but she got off twenty minutes ago, I think. She'll be here any minute. You just sit on down." She pushed him onto the faded sofa where he'd sat with Morgan so many times. The musty odor filtered up to him and made him feel like he'd never been gone and he was waiting to take Morgan to the junior prom again. He began to sweat under his armpits.

Morgan's mom sat in a dining room chair across from him and was just about to start talking again when Ross walked into the room.

"Hey, Mom, did you iron those khaki pants yet? I'm taking Melissa to . . . Hey, Aaron! Buddy! When did you get back?" Ross crossed the room to shake his hand and then pounded him on the back.

"How was Italy, man? You sure are lucky, getting to go to a cool country like that. I bet they'll send me to South Dakota."

"If you don't watch out, they won't send you anywhere. You better shape up, young man." Morgan's mother was smiling, and Aaron could see that Ross was still the "golden boy" in the family. Morgan had always complained that he could do no wrong as far as his mother was concerned.

Ross sat down on the arm of the sofa, and they both started interrogating Aaron. Aaron answered them easily enough, but his ears were pricked for a car engine, and he kept his eyes on the door.

When she came in, her blonde hair swinging, it took his breath away. It felt like time froze for a minute and held her standing there, staring at him. He'd forgotten how arrestingly beautiful she was in person.

"Aaron!" she exclaimed.

"Hi."

Morgan didn't say anything for another minute and neither did anyone else.

"Quite a surprise, isn't it, Morgan?" Her mother took her forearm and pried the jacket she was holding out of her arms and the keys from her clenched fingers.

"Did you know he was coming, Mom, and didn't tell me?" Morgan moved her eyes briefly from Aaron to stare at her mother.

"No. He just sailed in here, pretty as you please, about five minutes ago."

Aaron glanced at Ross, perched on the arm of the sofa, and saw the big Cheshire-cat grin on his face as he looked back and forth at the scene. Aaron was glad someone was enjoying this.

And then the sunshine turned on.

"Well, Aaron, when did you get home?" She was walking toward him, smiling and happy and the slightest bit teasing, just like he remembered her.

"Oh, a couple of days ago. I've really had a lot of jet lag. It's been hard to get used to the time change." He felt awkward and wanted to stuff a sock in his mouth. He wanted to run for the door and never see her again.

"Really?" He could tell she was disappointed but was trying to hide it. Of course this wasn't like they'd planned. She'd wanted to meet him at the airport with his family. He'd wanted her to, when they'd planned it. It was pretty hard for her to take, he guessed, that she hadn't even known which day he'd be home.

Mrs. Carter pulled Ross up off the couch and began dragging him toward the kitchen, signaling furiously with her eyes.

Morgan was close to him now, smiling up at him, and the room was empty. He knew he should hug her, that she expected him to. He put his arms around her awkwardly, meaning to pull back quickly, but she melted into him, slid her arms up around his shoulders, and linked them around his neck. And he couldn't help, just for a moment, inhaling a breath of her, sweet and pungent and so familiar. He couldn't think, not now; he could just have this moment . . .

"I'm glad you're home," she murmured into his neck in her soft, throaty voice, and it was then that the shower of ice water came down upon him again. This was how she sounded to everyone else. She was doing it to him now, using her body language to get her own way, to get him to forget about everything, to hypnotize him into forgiving her. He couldn't do it, and he didn't want to. Aaron pulled away abruptly, and her arms fell in surprise against her sides.

"Morgan, we need to go somewhere and talk." He didn't relish saying what he had to say with all the listening ears in this house.

"Okay."

* * *

"So you won't even give me a second chance then," Morgan said, looking out across the frozen park a few blocks from her home that Aaron had driven to for privacy's sake.

"I just don't think that it would change anything. Not for me."

Morgan turned quickly to strike the tears from her eyes with the back of her wrist. She wrapped her hand around the iron support that held up the park pavilion and kept it there, hoping the feel of the cold metal would freeze her, numb her so she couldn't feel.

"Aaron, I . . . I know that what I did hurt you, but you've got to believe that I didn't mean for it to go like it did. Jim just didn't understand. I was just being friendly, you know?"

"It doesn't really matter now, Morgan," he said. He looked tired, old, and it panicked her.

"What do you mean?"

"I mean, I can't, that's all. Too much has happened that we can't take back."

"You mean what you *think* I did. Listen. You had to know I was dating guys. Did you think I wouldn't? Did you think I would be able to not have friends?"

"Well . . ."

He appeared to be considering it. She pressed the advantage.

"Okay, I did date. I dated a lot of different guys, and I got close to some of them. But you have to believe me, Aaron. I always wanted you. And I'm here, aren't I? Unattached, waiting?" Her words were coming fast and thick, her desperation mounting. He had to understand in the end, didn't he? Was he just trying to make her suffer?

"Morgan, you just can't change some things. I guess I'm not secure enough to take all the attention you get from other guys, whether you want it or not. I want a girl that has eyes only for me."

"Aaron, I do, I . . . just give me a chance."

Aaron's eyes scanned the park, and he looked down into his hands where he was turning and turning a small brown box. He looked up at her. "I can't."

She couldn't believe it, not really. Somewhere, behind all of the depression and the pain of the last month, she'd thought he would forgive her in the end. She'd been sure that when she was able to see him, talk to him face-to-face, things would be different. Back in her living room when he'd put his arms around her she'd felt him softening, and relief had begun flooding through her. But now, looking at his face, cool and impassive, she knew it was really over.

"Here, I brought this last one." Aaron handed her the small package wrapped in brown paper.

The package was still warm from the heat of his hand, and she wrapped her fingers around it and held it a minute as if weighing it. She knew what was in it, of course. Aaron was trying to be so noble, so gallant, doing the right "missionary" thing. Now she wished he'd been a jerk and ignored her, had not had the courage to see her again.

The tears were coursing down her face now, but she didn't bother to wipe at them or even turn her head as she stared down at Aaron. He sat stone still on the edge of the picnic table, his face expressionless, and didn't even flinch when the wind rushed around the trees and caught him full in the face.

"Thanks," she said finally.

Aaron looked toward his jeep. "Well, I guess I'd better be going."

"Okay." Her heart lurched and her breath was coming in painful bursts.

"Do you want a ride home?"

She didn't say anything, because she couldn't. She couldn't take her eyes off the little brown package.

"Are you okay?"

She raised her head with effort and looked at him one last time. "Yeah, it's okay, you can go. I think I'll just stay here for a few minutes, you know, then walk home."

"Okay." Aaron put his hand out toward her like he would touch her, but then decided against it. He turned and began walking quickly over the frozen grass.

Morgan stood there, staring across the park in the opposite direction until she heard his jeep start up and pull away down the road. She took a deep breath and then sat down at a picnic table. She stared at the box in her hands for a long time before unwrapping the paper, opening the box, and drawing out the last silver charm. It was a while before she recognized the flowing cursive of the word, *amore.*

Part Three

Chapter 1

Afternoon quiet soaked through Morgan until she wondered if even her heart had slowed its beating, her lungs holding the air longer and longer, though she wasn't asleep. She began counting between breaths of air, trying to get to twenty-five before taking another breath. A short stab of pain flashed through her head where it rested against the wall above her bed, and she winced slightly and drew in more oxygen.

She hadn't moved for about an hour. Her crossed ankles had begun to ache from inaction, and she wanted to shift her back to a more comfortable position against the wall, but she didn't think she could summon strength to her muscles against the blackness that lay like lead full-length on her body. She couldn't even cry.

She wanted to. She wanted to sob until her throat ached and her eyes puffed out and her breath came out shuddering and pathetic, but her body stayed closed in and clenched, like her mind.

The warped bedroom door suddenly opened with a twist and a shove, and her mother walked into the room, smoothing the back of her hair and blinking her eyes. Morgan looked at her expectantly, but her mother didn't say anything, just walked over and sat on the edge of the bed next to Morgan and put her hand on Morgan's knee.

They sat there for a moment, quiet and still, and then Morgan sighed and reluctantly uncrossed her legs.

"Pretty rough, huh?"

"I'm okay, Mom. You didn't have to get up from your nap and come in here."

"I know, but it was pretty hard to sleep when I knew you were in here sitting like this."

"Mom." She could barely utter the word.

"I know; it's terrible. Do you want Ross to go over and deck him? Or maybe I could—I'm mad enough. I knew that big mess with Jim would upset him, but I really thought he would understand. I thought he'd want to work things out with you. It just kills me to see you hurt like this."

Morgan forced her lips up into something like a smile to show her mother she appreciated the motherly defense, and then she sighed again and made herself talk.

"You were right, you know. You always are."

"You sound disgusted."

"I am. I mean, I think I know things and what's best and what's right for me—I should be old enough by now—but it looks like I just have no clue, you know, about myself and people around me. And it makes me mad that you were right. I don't want you to be right all the time, Mom. I mean, I think it's keeping me from growing up."

Her mother smiled. "I'm just older, and I can see things better from way up here. I did a lot of stupid things when I was young. I still do a lot of stupid things. I worry so much about the way I raise you kids and if I'm making you weird because of the way I am, but I just can't seem to change myself, even though I try. But it's the trying that counts, Morgan. If we give it our best effort, maybe we'll be able to make a little headway, you know?"

"I can't believe I was so stupid, Mom. I mean, at first I was really, really mad at Aaron; I wanted to kill him. But I've thought about it way too much, and it hurts to admit it, but I know I was wrong. I just didn't realize it. Mom, I can't tell when I'm going too far!" Morgan knocked her head back against the wall in disgust. "I mean, look at the stupid thing that happened with Julia. I wrecked everything, and it's just now that I can see that, and it's really hard for me to admit it, you know?"

"I know." She reached out and put her hand on the back of Morgan's head. "I guess you're kind of like me."

Morgan leaned her head back into her mother's hand and closed her eyes to keep the tears back.

There was a long silence, which her mother finally broke.

"I wasn't ever going to tell you this, Morgan, but I think, maybe, that you need it, that you'd understand." She sighed and nudged Morgan a little to scoot her over. She lifted both legs to the bed and leaned against the wall next to Morgan.

"Mom, I'm going to fall off."

"No you're not. Anyway, the fact is, I think you inherited a lot from me. Ross did too. Personality-wise, I mean. You both have this sort of charisma that attracts people to you. Not that you don't look good too, but I think you both have that excitement and vitality about you that makes people want to be around you, you know?"

Morgan nodded a little.

"I was that way too. Maybe more so. When I was your age I felt all-powerful. I could make people do whatever I wanted them to do, even my parents. Anyway, it went to my head, eventually. Of course it was bound to, and I began to feel like I could get away with anything. I could have had any boy I wanted at any time, and I'm not just saying that. And, things didn't really change after I was married."

"What do you mean?" Morgan asked.

"Well, I married your dad really young. He was very handsome, you've seen the pictures, and was great at playing hard-to-get—you know, he acted like he didn't care. He seemed so cool and untouchable, but what I didn't know was that it was all just inexperience and shyness. He didn't know how to act around girls, so he just avoided us as much as he could. Anyway, for some reason I got fascinated with him. I mean, he was the only one that didn't seem to respond to my charms, you know, stop dead in his tracks, with his tongue lolling out.

"And, of course, when someone could resist me, well, that made them all the more irresistible to me. Pretty soon I was going out of my way to be where he was. I even signed up for a class he was taking that I didn't need. Anyway, I got him in the end, kind of wore him down, and he asked me to marry him. At the time I felt incredibly victorious, like I'd won the lottery or something. But, Morgan, the fact was, I just didn't know him. I'd been so busy trying to win him, I didn't consider what I'd do when I got him."

"But Mom, Dad's a great guy, you know he is; it couldn't have been that bad." This sounded to Morgan like one of those nice little stories that was intended to teach her a lesson or make her feel better or something. But it had nothing to do with her. Mom and Dad were still married, weren't they? And you'd never get her to believe that her mother wasn't happy. Not the way she still sat on Dad's lap in front of everyone, and he liked it even though it embarrassed him.

"Hey, just wait a minute, I'm getting to the relevant part. I had a pretty hard time after we were married. We were still going to school and sometimes it felt exactly the same as before I was married. I would forget sometimes. And your dad was so serious. Not fun and exciting all the time the way I had pictured it.

"I met a guy in one of my classes. He was so cool! Dark hair, slicked back just a little, you know, a little James Dean–ish, with that slouch and that attitude. I don't know what was wrong with me. One day in class he kept looking at me, and I looked back. He passed me a note asking me to go to lunch with him, and I felt beautiful and excited and alive. I looked down at the ring on my finger, and then twisted it and took it off. I didn't know that your dad was standing in the doorway waiting for me. One of his classes had been cancelled, and he'd decided to splurge and buy me lunch in the cafeteria. He saw the whole thing.

"Mom!" Morgan was shocked.

"I know." Morgan's mother rubbed her middle fingers over her eyebrows in a characteristic gesture. "I looked back toward the door just in time to see your dad turn and run down the hall. I grabbed my stuff in the middle of class and ran after him, sick at heart, but I couldn't find him. I don't think I would have really gone with that boy. I wasn't crazy. But all I know is that I was considering it."

"Mom, you were married in the temple! How could you even consider it? I mean, even I . . ."

"Even you. You mean you would never have done such a thing? How do you know, Morgan? That's my point. The way you treat boys and your friends and yourself doesn't magically change the day you decide to get married. Anyway, he was gone when I got home. It was the middle of a week, the middle of a quarter, and he'd just taken the car and driven down to his folks'. He wouldn't take my calls. I don't know what he told his parents, but I couldn't face them for years. He was gone for three days." Morgan's mother looked down at her hands, tightly clasped in her lap. "And I died in those days. I was never the same after that. Finally, life was serious to me. Life had rules. You obeyed them or you suffered and made other people suffer. I prayed and I prayed so hard for forgiveness. I was so sorry that I had been ungrateful, hadn't appreciated your dad and other people around me. It was like my wake-up call. And I never, never did anything like it again. And even though he came back on Sunday afternoon, and we talked, it took a long time before he trusted me again. It was painful Morgan, for a long time."

Morgan was silent, taking this in. She felt kind of a shocked vibration running through her, a buzzing in her head.

"But Morgan, I want you to know, I love your father, more than anything. And I did back then, only I was immature. I'm so grateful he gave me a second chance, and I have never given him a reason to doubt me again."

It was incredible—that her mother could do that. Morgan could hardly comprehend it. "Mom, but the temple marriage—didn't that mean anything to you? I mean, I can't believe it. That's terrible." Morgan knew she sounded self-righteous, but her own flirtation was perfectly legal, if a little disloyal. It wasn't the same thing at all.

"My old habits were too strong, Morgan. Flirting was the way I gained recognition and self-confidence. Let's see . . . do you know someone else who has this problem?"

"Yes, Mom, of course, but I would never . . ."

Her mother interrupted her. "Morgan! You already have, almost. Can't you see? You ruined your oldest friendship because of it; you destroyed your relationship with Aaron because of it; and you hurt that missionary companion really bad."

"Mom, I don't think he . . ." she started to protest.

"Yes he was, Morgan. If he thought you were 'the one,' what you did killed him. Come on, wake up! You have the same problem I did, that undeniable attraction, and the power that comes with it. You hurt people just so you can feel good about yourself. And you've been indulging in this sort of thing for years. Going after Ben wasn't the first time you've walked on Julia. It's been part of your relationship for a long time; she was just a tough little cookie until you finally found her weak spot."

"But Mom, I wasn't trying to do that. I had a great time with her all these years. I love her . . . you know that, Mom." Morgan started to cry.

"I want you to think, really think, Morgan, because I love you, and if you don't change you're going to have a really hard life. Any relationship you have will be in danger, because you aren't sincere, and you won't give enough of yourself to make it work. Here you are so upset about Aaron, but the fact is, I'm pretty sure that things would have gone bad if you two had gotten together. You've been getting worse these last two years, focusing more and more on yourself . . . Oh, honey, I don't want to make you feel worse, but I've always believed that the truth has to be told. You've got to realize, Morgan. You see that, don't you?"

"I guess, I . . ."

"And Morgan, you've got to think about the consequences to yourself. How do you think your selfish actions are affecting your spirituality? Do you think you can continually hurt people and retain the Spirit in your life? Can you kiss several different guys at once and not lose your sensitivity to the respect that you should have for your own body and for others?"

"Mom, I didn't kiss them at the same time."

"You know what I mean. Leading someone on and kissing them without commitment is wrong. It hurts the guy and it hurts you, even if you may not be able to feel it at the time."

Morgan rubbed her eye. She felt horrible, but she knew her mother was right. But, how could she do what her mother was suggesting? Remake herself overnight? It seemed hopeless. But she was glad that her mom had come in. She had helped her up a steep hill, and now she could see over it to the other side. She could feel the concern and love radiating from her mother, and it relieved her.

"Maybe I'll be able to do it, turn myself around. After all, you did it, right?" Morgan asked.

"Yes, even me," her mother confirmed. "Your dad was never charming or brilliant or flashy or anything like that, but he was so strong and good, capable and kind. I've been very blessed. And you can be too."

"I know . . . thanks, Mom."

"Morgan, the Lord loves you. Let Him help you. Open your heart." She winked and then turned, sighing as she walked out of the door.

If possible, Morgan felt even worse now than when her mother had come in, but it was a different kind of pain. One that made her want to change. She rolled over onto her pillow and sobbed.

Chapter 2

The sun shining on Aaron made him feel better than he had felt for a few days. It was unusually warm, and Aaron had taken his parka off and thrown it into the backseat of the jeep. The cool air and blinding sunshine reflecting off melting snow braced him up and made him feel alive. He liked the warm feel of the leather-covered steering wheel beneath his hands and the comfort of his old pair of hiking boots and worn jeans. He'd retrieved his favorite flannel shirt from his sister's closet, with her screaming her head off, and it felt soft and familiar against his neck.

Aaron smiled a little and pushed the hair back on his forehead. Already it was longer, growing back into the style he'd liked before his mission. It was amazing how quickly everything seemed to close down around him again, like he'd never been gone. He breathed in deeply and squinted his eyes against the bright light.

He'd come into Halston to buy a couple of Christmas presents, although he'd basically brought everyone something from Italy. He wanted to get his niece and nephew a couple of extra things, though heaven knew they didn't need them. Everyone in the family spoiled them to death as the only grandchildren, but he couldn't help trying to be the favorite uncle.

He was cruising around the college, sightseeing a little, when a bunch of guys stepped off of the curb in front of him and lumbered across the road. He had to stand on the brakes hard to keep from hitting them. Some of them turned and grinned at the sound of his brakes, but it was the guy in the middle who caught Aaron's attention. Facer! He hadn't seen him, and Aaron was tempted to just drive on. He hadn't written Facer back after his last letter, and this was the first time he'd seen him since getting home. His foot was on the gas pedal when Facer looked up at him from the trunk of the car he was opening. His eyes showed instant recognition, and he nodded slightly. Aaron, determined to meet this head on, pulled into the next available parking place along the road and jumped out of the jeep.

"Facer! Hey." Aaron took a rough jog around a parked car and slowed to a walk. He stuffed his hands in his jeans pockets.

"Looks like you're back," Jim said.

Jim had toned up a lot since Aaron had last seen him, maybe lost a few pounds. His face looked lean and hard.

"Yeah, I flew in last week."

"Are you still jet-lagged? It took me about a month to shake that off and feel normal again."

"I'm doing okay, I guess. My mom won't let me stay up past nine thirty, and I'm humoring her," Aaron smiled, "so I guess that's working."

"Good."

"Yeah, well . . ." Aaron looked around, trolling for something to say. "You guys heading home?"

"Yep, we hung around for the weekend to go to a party that one of you locals was having. But now, I am DONE." He boomed the last word in a football-player yell. Aaron was a little embarrassed, but the guys behind him yelled, "Yeah!" and made hooting noises.

"That's great. How'd you do with grades and stuff, do you know?"

"Yeah, I know all right. I was doing okay at first, even pulling B's in a couple of classes, but things slid off a little around Thanksgiving time. I didn't do so good on my last couple of tests, so I am now praying that I brownnosed the teachers enough to pass. Heaven knows I tried." He raised his eyebrows, smiling suggestively, and began looking around to find his audience, but they had moved off and were walking back into the apartment building.

"It's good to see you. I hope everything's going well."

Facer cracked a sarcastic grin. "Oh, well, you know me, everything's sailin', moving sweet."

Aaron was trying not to feel guilty. None of this was his fault. He really liked Jim still. He wanted to help him. Maybe that was forgiveness?

"Maybe we can get together sometime next semester, you know, double-date or something?" As soon as the words were out Aaron couldn't believe he'd said them.

"Oh, yeah sure. Let's just do that. Should we both get a date? Or maybe we can just share Morgan." Jim turned around and shoved a duffle bag deeper into the trunk, slammed the lid down, and began walking around the car, back toward the apartments.

Great. Aaron let him go because he didn't know what he could say. Maybe some things couldn't be fixed. But it was a shame, a great shame.

How could this be happening? Aaron wasn't prepared for this, although he should have been. A few scenes from Italy flashed through his mind: the endless nights of tracting, the time he and Jim tried to make homemade pasta from a branch member's recipe, the night before Jim went home . . .

He looked up at Jim's retreating back and knew he couldn't let it end this way. Not with Jim so bitter.

"Hey—Jim!" Aaron jogged up to the open door.

"Yeah?" Jim leaned back against the glass door and turned his head to listen to a conversation that was going on inside the lobby.

Aaron was embarrassed. Maybe Jim wasn't the same anymore. All the football and everything. He looked back at his parked jeep.

"Yeah?" Jim said again, this time with a belligerent hint to his voice.

"Are you guys leaving right now?"

"No, in about a half hour. I'm taking a couple of guys up to Salt Lake. One of them went out to visit a girl and isn't back yet."

"I was just thinking . . . maybe . . . do you want to go for a ride in my jeep? You know . . . you could meet my parents, maybe we could drive up the canyon a ways." Aaron felt like an idiot, like he was asking for his first date. There was no way Jim would do it. But, Aaron had to ask; he didn't want this mess to be his fault if he could help it.

"Well, I don't know." Jim stepped outside and let the door swing shut. "I don't know if those guys will want to wait. We were going to get pizza or something."

Aaron could tell he was thinking about it, and he felt relieved and kind of surprised at the same time. "Come on. You can't give me an hour after what we went through together? My parents would love to meet you, and we can grab a sandwich or something. And I think Jodie's home."

"Your sister?"

"Yeah, remember I told you she was going to start at Hale fall semester? She graduated from high school last year."

"I wonder if I've seen her around."

"Maybe."

After Jim got into the jeep, things seemed a lot different. It was like he changed from the big, braggy football player into the guy that Aaron had learned to love and respect on his mission. He seemed deflated though, and after a few comments about the weather, fell silent during the short drive.

"Thanks for coming."

"Yeah, well . . . it's okay." Jim looked around absently, searching for something to say. He picked at a loose thread in the old upholstery on the jeep seat. "This yours?"

"Yeah. My dad helped me buy it after I graduated from high school. It was six years old then, and a guy across town sold it to us for a pretty good deal. And even though my sister's driven it around while I've been gone, it's still pretty solid, although not such a smooth ride anymore."

"You go four-wheelin' much?"

"Yeah, with some of the guys, but most girls don't like it. One time I took Morgan, with the top down, and she thought the whole time I was going to roll it, and she got splattered with mud . . ." The smile was still on Aaron's lips when he realized he was being stupid again. He couldn't believe it! He looked over at Jim, who was staring straight through the front windshield. "Hey, sorry about . . ."

"No, don't worry . . ." Jim held up his hands. "I gotta get used to it."

They drove in silence for about two minutes.

"You know I broke up with her?" Aaron said, glancing at Jim quickly.

"You did?"

"Yeah."

"Why? Are you crazy?" Jim's voice was low and he turned away, looking out the passenger window.

"I don't know; I guess I just couldn't handle it, you know, everything she'd done. I just couldn't look at her the same way I used to. I realize what she did to you, Jim. It wasn't fair."

"Yeah, well, I should apologize to you. I never should've let it go as far as it did. I felt kind of crummy the whole time, like I was stabbing you in the back. But half the time, well, I felt like I couldn't help it, like it was just meant to be. And then . . . when I realized she'd just been playing with me, I couldn't believe it. It almost felt like that whole Gina thing again, plus I'd betrayed you into the bargain. I was stupid, I guess. I kind of let my classes slide . . . and I'd really been doing good. I started hanging out with some of the wilder players just to show how angry I was."

"Hey, man, I am sorry. It must be pretty rough to go through that again."

"When am I going to be able to handle stuff like that?" Jim hit the dash with his closed fist so hard that Aaron worried about the old vinyl cracking.

"I mean, I can't fall apart every time someone disappoints me. I shouldn't have let it get to me so bad."

"How could you help it?" Aaron drove into town and turned off Main Street toward his house. "There's just something about her. I was determined to break it off totally with her once I got home, but when I saw her, I almost couldn't do it." A slight shiver jerked through Aaron's body. "There's just something about her. I mean, she's beautiful and everything, but she's got something else too."

"I know. I still can't believe you broke up with her." Jim looked Aaron full in the face and grinned for the first time during the ride.

Aaron pulled into his driveway and stuck his hand out to Jim over the gear shift. He took Jim's hand tightly and gave it a firm, missionary shake and said, "Well, we're here."

"Mom?" Aaron called through the house as he led Jim through the front doors. There was a muffled response from the back of the house, and then he heard a door slam, and his mother came striding down the hall.

"Mom, do you remember Elder Facer, from my letters? I just ran into him in Halston."

Aaron's mom looked at Jim and smiled. "Well, yes, of course I do. Nice to meet you." She put out her hand, and Jim shook it briefly. "It's great to have you here. Aren't you going to school at Hale now?"

"Yes, I started this fall."

"And don't you play football on the team?" She looked at Aaron for confirmation.

"Yeah. I was lucky to get on the team."

"How do you like Hale?"

"It's seems like a good school. I like the small-town feeling."

Jim was looking kind of embarrassed, and Aaron was sure his mother would keep asking questions, possibly embarrassing ones, so Aaron changed the subject quickly. "Hey, Mom, where's Dad? And Jodie?"

"They're around here somewhere. Are you guys hungry? There's stuff for sandwiches in the fridge, and I went to the bakery yesterday and got some of that nice brown bread you like. Go ahead and fix sandwiches, and I'll go and find them."

Aaron led Jim into the kitchen, and they sat down at the bar.

"Nice house."

"Thanks. It still seems huge to me after what I was used to in Italy. I can't get used to how big everything is around here. We don't appreciate it enough." Aaron opened the fridge and started pulling things out and lining them up on the bar in front of Jim.

"I know. It is such a shock to come back. It's like you don't remember it right or something. I remember thinking how wide the streets were when I first got back."

"I know. It's weird." Aaron got out two plates, glasses, and knives, pushed them across the bar and walked around to sit by Jim. "Dig in."

"Hey—are you making one for me?" Jodie said, coming up the stairs from the basement. "I'm starving."

Aaron smiled widely, knowing she'd be embarrassed when she saw he wasn't alone.

"I—oh." Jodie came into view and turned bright red. "I was just . . ."

"This is Jim Facer, from my mission."

"Hi." Jodie's smile seemed frozen on her face.

"Nice to see you again."

"Again?" Aaron said.

"Yeah, well, we ran into each other at the institute one day, right?" Jim stood up and leaned a hand against the bar. He suddenly had that confident, lady-killer look on his face that Aaron remembered from his early days as Jim's companion. What was going on here?

"Right," Jodie said.

She looked over at Aaron and widened her eyes slightly, trying to signal him, but Aaron wasn't sure what she meant. He raised his shoulders a fraction of an inch. Jodie turned her back on Jim as she rounded the bar and rolled her eyes at Aaron in exasperation. She got out a plate and a glass, and when she looked up to begin making her sandwich, the red was gone from her cheeks, and she flashed a smile at Jim that seemed totally different from any Aaron had ever witnessed. Again Aaron was amazed at the change in his little sister. He'd never even thought about her in this way before, but man, he had to hand it to her, she was a good-looking girl—all that thick dark hair with the same olive complexion Aaron had. Aaron looked at Jim suspiciously.

"Was your violin okay?" Jim said still looking at Jodie.

"Yes, thank heaven. My parents would have killed me if something had happened."

"What happened?" Aaron was wondering how Jodie's violin had anything to do with anything.

"I tripped and fell flat on my face walking out the institute door when . . . is it Jim?"

Jim nodded.

"Well, when Jim was holding the door for me. I was carrying my violin, and it flew out of my hand and crashed down on the sidewalk. I was lucky that I had it in the hard case. Jim helped me up and grabbed my books and stuff for me. I was so embarrassed; I really hoped I wouldn't see you again so soon!" Jodie put her hand up to her cheek, which was turning red again.

"Oh, sorry. I guess I'd better go then." Jim half stood up from the stool, teasing her, and then of course she told him to stay and after that, Aaron was pretty much in the background of the conversation.

Chapter 3

Of course, Julia wasn't convinced, not all of the time anyway, but really, who could be, who could see the future and who knew what was "right" or if there really was a "right" thing out there for her? Sometimes she thought that that kind of thinking was maybe a way of copping out, of putting the responsibility for everything on Heavenly Father and not taking enough of it yourself.

She was concentrating so closely that she nearly missed a stop sign as she drove out of Hunter on her way to Halston.

She'd talked with Ben, of course . . . about everything, and she'd made it clear to him where she stood even though she was ridiculously in love with him. Pharmacology maybe wasn't what she'd thought of at first, but it was a vehicle; she'd finish her schooling right now, and when they had children she could work a few hours in the evenings when Ben was home, if it seemed like the right thing to do.

Studying pharmacology would give her something in common with Ben in his pre-med studies and later in medical school. They'd be a team. She'd talked it all over with Ben, and she felt right about it even if it wasn't her first choice. Later when the kids were all in school, she could pick up research and chemistry again if that was what she wanted . . . and things would work out.

She'd never let Ben go now, not after the last few days and then his proposal. It was so intense, the mad longing that she had for him. He'd only been gone two days and already she was beginning to feel physically ill. She wondered a little if love wasn't a sickness, something that one just couldn't help. She'd had to get out of the house, away from the phone, because it was driving her crazy wondering if he would call. She'd already talked to him for a half hour last night, but she just couldn't get it out of her mind that he might call today just for fun, to hear the sound of her voice again . . .

She could feel a ridiculous grin on her face. How could she go on like this? She pounded the steering wheel and stepped on the gas. She had a long list of orders for the Burger Barn from everyone at the house. Her dad had given her a fifty to pay with and said to buy herself a shake if she wanted one. He was so incredibly pleased with the engagement, even going so far as to say that he had gotten them back together—and she'd smiled and let it pass because he'd never change. But maybe he figured she could afford the calories in a shake or two now that she'd "captured her man." It was laughable. Did he imagine that she'd never let a french fry pass her lips the entire time she'd been away to college?

Julia pulled into the parking lot at the Burger Barn and swung into an empty space. She had turned the motor off and put her hand on the door handle when a sudden thought shook her. Morgan! What if she was working? Immediately she began to sweat. She could feel her armpits becoming sticky and her forehead hot. She didn't know why she hadn't thought of it the instant her dad had asked her to go. Was she crazy?

She leaned heavily back into the seat and dropped her hand into her lap. It was just that they'd gotten food from the Burger Barn so often on weekends and when her mom was going to be gone. After all, it was nearly the only place around for fast food, and luckily it was pretty decent. Mom had had her hands full cooking for the Jeffses' Christmas Eve dinner, so of course her dad had stepped in and suggested Burger Barn for lunch. Her nephews and brothers had cheered. But she couldn't go in there. There was no way. Absolutely no way.

Julia looked into her rearview mirror and tried to see inside the window. *Is that a girl behind the counter? What are the chances that she's there right now, on Christmas Eve day? No way would Morgan take an inconvenient shift like that, especially since Aaron is home by now. No, that must be the owner's wife, kind of thick around the hips, with that frizzy orange-colored hair. Saved!*

Julia pushed open the door and stepped out of her car. She reached back in for the list and her wallet, feeling incredibly relieved.

It was too bad it was such a big deal. She hated being on pins and needles the whole time she was home, trying to avoid Morgan. Sunday had been horrible, trying to dodge her in the hall at church and predict which Sunday School class she'd attend.

The air in sandwich shop was warm and thick with grease. Ahh, the smell of comfort food! Julia walked up to the counter and eyed the rows of candy bars under the glass.

"Hey, Julia! How're ya doing?" the owner's wife, Ruth, asked pleasantly.

"I'm good, thanks."

"What'll ya have today?" She whipped out an order pad, complete with carbon copies, and poised her pen over it.

Julia smiled and then slid her list toward Ruth. "My dad's written everything down. I'm afraid it'll take you guys a half hour to make up all this stuff. We've got the whole crew down, and Mom's busy cooking for tonight."

"Well, then, we'd better get cooking. You guys had better fill on up before you have to face it." Ruth raised an orange eyebrow and winked slyly. Everybody knew what a terrible cook Julia's mom was. Of course, no one ever let her know.

Ruth quickly transferred the list to two and a half sheets on her duplicate pad, which she ripped out and painstakingly separated. She grabbed the originals and slid each into a clip on a metal ring above the window that opened into the kitchen area. She spun the wheel and said, "Order to go, Hal, and on the double for Dr. Jeffs!" Then she stepped around to push through the swinging door to the kitchen.

"Oh, Ruth?" Julia called.

"Yeah, honey?"

"I guess I'll have a hot chocolate while I'm waiting. And can you put a little of that marshmallow cream on the top?"

"You bet. And how about a cherry too?"

"Sounds good." Ruth was a woman after her own heart.

Julia thanked Ruth and took the steaming styrofoam cup into the empty dining area to wait. She sat in a booth next to a window and bent to take a cautious sip of the steaming drink. When she looked back up from the hot chocolate she was looking straight into Morgan's eyes.

Julia gave a little jolt and slopped scalding hot chocolate onto her hand and the table.

* * *

Morgan had seen the whole thing. How Julia had pulled briskly into the parking lot and had gone to get out of the car, and then how she'd stopped and had sat there for about five minutes, probably wondering if Morgan would be in here. Morgan had seen her adjusting the rearview mirror and peering into it, trying to decide who was behind the counter. And then when she'd recognized Ruth, Julia's relief had shown on her face and in the way she'd walked across the little parking lot. And she'd been so breezy and cheerful with Ruth. You'd think she'd won the lottery or something.

Morgan had hoped she could hide; she'd pulled herself back further into the corner booth where she'd been filling salt and pepper shakers, and had kept her head down, but when Julia had walked over to sit down only two booths down—they were the only people in the place—Morgan knew she'd have to face the whole thing. So she kept her eyes up and waiting. It was a relief, really, now that it was happening. She'd been planning to go over and see Julia, to walk the few blocks to her house, but she'd felt shy for the first time in her life, and embarrassed, and she didn't know what to say that would make a difference to Julia.

It was ridiculous the way Julia jumped when she saw her sitting there. She must have fried her hand with that hot chocolate, and now she was standing up, flapping it and grabbing for the tin napkin dispenser, trying to act like it didn't hurt.

"Hurt yourself?" Morgan asked. She might as well get the whole thing over.

Julia flashed her dark, proud eyes up.

"You might have a burn, you know; that hot chocolate machine gets the water pretty darn hot."

Again, nothing, just fidgeting with the dispenser and wiping up hot chocolate off the table, ignoring her red hand.

Morgan stood up. "Do you want me to get you some ice water?" She was standing close now, about a foot away from where Julia sat.

She didn't know why she was pushing so much. She walked over to the counter, flipped it open, grabbed a large cup, dug it into the ice bin and filled it with water. She was back at the table before Julia could wipe up the whole mess and leave. She sat the cup down in front of Julia and slipped into the booth on the other side. Julia flashed her another indignant look and put her hands into her lap.

Morgan smiled. Julia was so stubborn. Well, she could be stubborn too. She'd just sit here and watch Julia let that hand burn rather than admit it hurt at all. A lot of pride there, whatever she said. When Julia looked up again Morgan raised her eyebrows and smiled a little.

"You are such a pain!" Julia said and thrust her hand into the water for a minute before gingerly removing it to examine the red area.

"Yes I am."

Chapter 4

Morgan and her mother had made all the arrangements. They'd spent a couple of days in Provo, staying with her mother's cousin, while they looked over the campus at UVSC, talked to a counselor, and registered for classes.

Now as the big trees slid by on the Provo streets, all the excitement of the last few days evaporated. When they pulled up in front of the old apartment building where they'd found an inexpensive room, Morgan was sure she would hate it. She sat still for a full minute, staring at the dingy yellow brick and the dirty piles of melting snow.

"All set?" her mother said, looking over at Morgan and opening the creaky Suburban door.

Morgan got out and helped her mother open the rear doors of the Suburban. All her things were crammed into the back, and it looked as if there could be an avalanche any minute.

"You have a real genius for packing, Morgan. Look at this mess!" Morgan's mother gestured sharply to the pile. "I'll just take this first box, and you catch anything else that falls. Do you have the key in case your roommates aren't home?"

Morgan produced the key from her jeans pocket and showed it to her mother, hoping that her roommates weren't home. She'd only met one of them when she looked at the apartment last week, and she wasn't sure what she thought of her.

She'd always felt confident around strangers, but suddenly she wished that Julia had been able to come up with them and help her move in. They'd talked that day at Burger Barn, and she'd confessed and apologized and coaxed Julia into making up, but she still wasn't confident enough of her footing with her to ask her to come and help. Besides, Julia and Ben were looking for apartments today too. They were getting married midsemester and were hoping to find something between Provo and Salt Lake so that neither of them would have a long commute.

Morgan hadn't realized she would feel so alone.

Morgan's mother removed a large box, and Morgan grabbed a laundry basket full of shoes, which they hauled around to the ground-floor door. Her mother knocked sharply with her elbow, balancing the box on her knee, and Morgan was just about to put the basket down and get out her key when the door flew open. A tall girl with long, shiny, dark hair posed in the doorway. She was beautiful.

The girl looked at them with a kind of vague contempt, her eyes half-closed, and then said, "Oh, you're the new roommate," and stepped out of the way.

"I'm Morgan's mother; nice to meet you," Morgan's mother said, without putting down the box. "Which room is open?"

"She's in with Valerie, in the last bedroom, across from the sinks." The girl pointed down the hall, then returned to the small living room and curled up on the sofa.

Morgan turned to her mother, followed her down the hall, and entered an incredibly tiny bedroom with rough wooden bunk beds on one side and a cramped closet on the other. Morgan's mother looked at her and rolled her eyes silently, pointing back down the hall. Morgan widened her eyes and nodded in answer, but strangely felt like she was going to cry. This place was horrible, worse than she thought. They barely had space to put the box and laundry basket down on the floor, and when she looked around, Morgan wondered whether she'd come into the right room. The entire closet was packed with clothes. There were skis and poles stacked behind the door, suitcases and a flat box crammed under the lower bunk bed. The surfaces of the small dresser and the windowsill were covered with CDs, books, and stuffed animals.

"So where do we put all this stuff?" Morgan said, totally at a loss.

"Maybe that girl told us the wrong room," her mother whispered. "You should go ask her."

"Me?" No way was she going to go out there and look stupid in front of that glamorous girl.

"Well, you're not a baby, and you've never been very shy before."

"I know, but . . ." Morgan looked around her again. "I'll just go and peek into the other rooms."

Morgan walked quietly down the hall and caught a glimpse of the girl in the living room examining her painted fingernails. She looked quickly into the next room down the hall and decided it was even more stuffed than the last. The end room looked less crowded and more organized and after looking around for a minute, Morgan decided that this must be the room she was supposed to move into. She wasn't sure, though, and finally decided she'd have to go talk to the "roommate." She looked down the hall in her mother's direction, hesitating a minute, and then walked quickly into the living room.

"Uh, did you tell me the right room?"

The girl looked up, blinked rapidly, like she couldn't believe Morgan was talking to her, and then looked back down at her nails. Morgan waited for about twenty seconds, feeling disgusted, and tried again.

"Hey, I think that you must have told me the wrong room. The one on the other side looks like the one I'm supposed to be in." She waited again. "The one by the sinks must already have two girls in it, it's so crowded."

The girl sighed and looked up at Morgan critically. "No, that's the one. It's just crowded because Valerie has tons of junk. That's why the other girl moved out. The room on the far end is mine. My parents are paying double so I can have my own room. Next semester I'm getting out of this dump and moving into a condo with some friends from back home."

"Oh." Morgan didn't know what to say. Great. She went back to *her* room.

"Did you hear?" she said to her mother, who had opened the box and was pawing through it.

"Yes. Sweet little thing, isn't she?"

"Oh yeah. Darling. 'My parents are paying double . . .'" Morgan said in a whiny whisper, flipping her hair behind her shoulder and shaking her head.

Her mother looked up with a short laugh and glanced toward the doorway. "Well, you'll just have to get rid of some of your stuff or let me take it back home."

"But Mom, I need my stuff, or I wouldn't have packed it. This is *not* a cool place."

"I know. It's even worse than the place I stayed in when I was up here at BYU, if that's possible, but you'll just have to make the best of it. Maybe next semester you can look around and see if you can find something better."

Morgan and her mother spent the next hour carrying stuff in and squeezing things into the closet and onto the shelf above it. They moved some of the other girl's vases and figurines and put Morgan's alarm clock on the windowsill. They squeezed Morgan's backpack with the new books in it into the narrow space between the bunk bed and the wall, but they didn't know what to do about a drawer for her underwear and pajamas, because all four drawers in the dresser were smashed full of clothing. Finally they just left Morgan's suitcase on the floor under the window and put anything they couldn't hang up in that.

"Well, okay . . . Your classes start Monday, right?"

"Yeah."

"I locked your bike out there to the railing in front of the door. Don't forget to lock it up every time, or your won't have one, and we can't afford to buy you another one."

"I know."

"And you'll keep looking for a job?"

"Yes, Mom, but I think that shop at the mall will probably hire me. I've just got to go down there again because I didn't know the phone number here."

"Well, okay . . ." She'd already said that. "I've got to get going then. Ross's game starts at seven, and I've probably got to get something for everybody to eat first."

"Okay." It was hard not to feel like she was being abandoned.

"Well, walk me to the car," her mother said.

They walked out to the Suburban, and Morgan told her mother she was all right and waved her good-bye. And then, it was ridiculous, but Morgan suddenly felt that she couldn't bear to walk back into that apartment alone.

* * *

"Well, I don't know, really," said the girl seated beside Aaron in the jeep. She looked into the backseat, gave a little jump, and giggled with her friend. Aaron tried to smile and grit his teeth at the same time. This situation was impossible, and it had only been half an hour.

One of the dorms was having a "buddy dance," and this girl, Marcie, had asked him to be her date. He'd only talked to her a couple of times in Music Appreciation because she always sat behind him, but now he regretted ever looking her direction. She was a freshman, of course, but then so was his sister, Jodie, and though Jodie got on his nerves sometimes, she was nothing like this. Again, Marcie laughed at something her friend said from the backseat, and Aaron again smiled politely. He took a curve in the canyon road a little sharply, and Marcie squealed and laughed and punched him in the shoulder.

"Are we almost there?" she asked.

"Oh, yeah, the restaurant is just up here."

"And you're sure it's good?" said Marcie. "And not too expensive? Because, of course, I'm paying." She patted her little black purse and giggled again.

"Sure, it's all right." It was all Aaron could do to answer her back. He wasn't really sure what was so terrible about her; he'd been out with silly girls before, and Marcie wasn't bad looking or anything, but this nearly amounted to torture! It was probably because he'd been on two similar dates in the last three weeks since school had started.

Aaron parked the jeep, got out, walked around to the other side, and opened Marcie's door. The other girl's date did the same thing. He was a guy Aaron didn't know, but he looked pretty grim too. As they were walking into the restaurant Marcie managed to grab Aaron's hand and entwine her fingers tightly with his. She looked up at him, smiling, and Aaron had the wicked desire to snatch his hand away and shove it in his pocket, but he endured politely. The whole time they were waiting for a table she kept his hand, occasionally patting and stroking his fingers with her free hand. Aaron bit his tongue and didn't say much, but Marcie didn't seem to mind and kept chattering away with her girlfriend, giggling every few sentences.

He supposed she must be nervous, but he wasn't feeling too charitable just now and didn't feel too sorry for her. He was just about to say that he needed to go to the men's room, to get away from her, when the hostess appeared again and led them to their table. When they sat down Aaron pried his hand away and gratefully picked up his menu.

Marcie asked him a question and waited, looking up at him. Aaron hadn't been listening and he stared blankly at her, trying to think of a plausible answer. Finally he said, "I'm sorry, what . . ."

"What's your favorite food?" she asked again.

"Oh, I don't know . . ." He looked at her again. "Uh, I like pasta, you know, being in Italy and everything." He surveyed the menu and remembered that neither the spaghetti nor the lasagna was very good here. "But I think I'll have the steak."

The other date said he'd have the steak too, and Aaron asked him about himself and managed to start a little side conversation over the voices of the two girls, trying to pass the time. The guy spoke readily enough, and it sure seemed to Aaron that he was enduring too.

He nodded at something Marcie said, and she patted him on the shoulder.

He felt bad. He was being uncharitable—he should give these girls a break. They were probably very nice people, good Church members and all that. They probably had talents and ambitions and dreams, just like he did. And their parents probably loved them and hoped they would find a religious and responsible man to share their lives with.

He began to sweat, and he could feel his muscles tighten in his neck and shoulders. How could he fit into that mold? It was what the Lord wanted of him . . . to choose one of these girls eventually and then settle down and have a family. But how could he do it if everyone was like this? If his face always felt cracked from smiling and being pleasant, and he felt all itchy and annoyed inside? This couldn't be right.

The waitress finally brought their food. She smiled at him and placed the heavy plate of steak, baked potato, and mixed vegetables in front of him. They all tried their food and asked each other if it was good, and Aaron nodded and chewed with the rest, relieved that at least the food was okay and he could be sincere about that.

When he'd drunk the last of his water, Aaron looked around for the waitress. "Does anybody else want more water?"

"Oh, yes, I'm so thirsty. Can you see the waitress?" Marcie looked up at him, obviously pleased that he'd spoken to her.

Aaron felt a stab of guilt and turned his head quickly to survey the room. The dining room was nearly full tonight, mostly with couples.

"I don't see her anywhere. She must be in the kitchen. I—" Aaron stopped short. His eyes caught on a fall of long, blonde hair. The girl was sitting at a table for two across the room. She had her back to them. Morgan. He couldn't help it; her name leapt to his mind. "I can't see the waitress, I . . ." He paused. The girl shook her head again and leaned in close to her date to whisper in his ear. The guy put a hand on her back. Aaron's chest burned and the palms of his hands began to sweat.

"Aaron, silly, she's right over there." Marcie nudged him with her shoulder and pointed to a booth just next to theirs.

Aaron tore his eyes from the scene across the room and looked at Marcie, embarrassed.

"Are you okay? I can ask her for more water if you don't want to." Marcie giggled with her friend.

"No, I'll get her." Aaron waited for the waitress to look in his direction and then lifted his hand and asked her for the water. When the waitress was gone he looked back over at the table across the room. The couple was getting up, ready to leave. The guy helped the girl on with her coat and then cupped his hands around her neck to pull her long hair free of the coat. The intimate gesture made Aaron sit stock-still and feel cold all over. He clutched his water glass convulsively and tried, unsuccessfully, to look away.

The couple turned to walk out the door, and Aaron saw with a shock that it wasn't Morgan after all. Just a girl that looked a lot like her with that same beautiful hair. His heart was pounding. Still, Aaron's eyes followed the couple from the room, and he felt resentful when the guy put his hand on the small of her back to guide her through the door.

"Hey! Do you know those guys?" said Marcie's friend, nodding toward the door.

"Uh, no. I, uh . . . That guy kind of looked like one of my mission companions," Aaron lied.

"Oh, well, anyway . . ." Marcie resumed her chatter, and Aaron sat silently, staring at a knot in the wood paneling just over her head.

Chapter 5

"No, no, definitely not the purple. Really." Morgan pushed the swatch of material away from her with a grimace.

"But it's the one my mom likes the best." Julia retrieved the piece of fluid crepe and ran it through her fingers again.

"Well, maybe if it was a different shade, say a periwinkle . . ." Morgan envisioned the color in her mind and compared it to a silver or perhaps a gray green.

"What is *periwinkle*, for heaven's sake?"

"You know, kind of a blue-purple color, but I would say you'd want a very pastel shade of it if you were to mix it with another color for the decorations and the dresses and everything." Morgan considered all this in her mind. She was excited. The wedding would be beautiful. And Julia's parents would spare no expense, especially in view of all the circumstances. Morgan would just come up with some great ideas, and then Julia could convince Sister Jeffs . . .

"Hey, let's go down to that fabric and craft store and look around, and then we can go to the mall to look for matching dresses. Are you having little girls?" Morgan gathered the pictures and catalogs that they'd been looking at off the kitchen table and stuffed them into a folder.

"Well, Nathan's baby is only a year, but I know my mom wants something for her, and Ben has a couple of nieces. I think they're about four and six. It would be cute to dress them up. Ben wouldn't say I had to, of course, but I think he would like it. When I met his sister she seemed pretty gung-ho about the whole thing—you know, asking me colors and everything, so I think she's probably planning to get them new dresses even if I don't have them in the line. Of course my parents would pay for them. Look." Julia stood up and pulled a credit card out of her back pocket. "Dad said to get whatever I thought might be nice for the wedding, and if Mom didn't like it, we could always take the stuff back."

Morgan looked at the card and felt a flash of jealousy. It would be great to be able to get whatever you wanted. She thought of the new jacket that had just come into the shop across from the boutique where she worked.

"Let's go. It is so great to have your car, though my thighs are getting mighty toned riding my bike everywhere." Morgan flexed her thigh and looked at Julia. "Soon even you will be jealous."

"What do you mean? I've always been jealous." Julia laughed, brushing too-long bangs out of her eyes.

"Come on, Julia. You have always had much buffer legs than I have, all that jogging and racquetball. When are you going to get your hair cut?" Morgan flipped a bunch of Julia's dark hair as she walked past to pick up her purse on the counter. She was feeling good today, comfortable, almost like old times. "I'll take you to this place in the mall close to the shop where I work. There's one girl that does a pretty good job."

"Sounds good."

Both girls turned as the apartment door opened, and Morgan's roommate walked in.

"See ya," said a deep voice from outside.

The tall, dark girl winked and waved at a guy just visible through the half-open door.

"Are you going to the fireside tomorrow night?" he said hopefully through the door.

"Oh, I don't know, probably not. Maybe I'll see you." She smiled again provocatively and closed the door, nearly smashing his fingers as she did so. She waited until she saw him walk past the window and then commented to the room in general. "I can't get rid of that one." Then she looked around and noticed Julia. Her eyes narrowed a little, and she looked at Morgan as if for an explanation.

"Vanessa, this is Julia, my friend from home. She's up at the U."

"Oh." Vanessa looked at Julia for another few seconds and then without saying another word walked past them into her room.

Julia arched her eyebrows and looked at Morgan.

"I know," Morgan said in a whisper. "She's always like that."

"What's her problem?" Julia said, opening the front door and waiting for Morgan to follow her out.

"Who knows? It's probably that she's spoiled and too good-looking for her own good." Morgan thought of all the guys that were in and out of the apartment, trying to gain Vanessa's favor, and was surprised that she didn't feel jealous. It all seemed a little immature and stupid, all the games Vanessa was playing.

"That's an interesting statement, coming from you."

"What!" Morgan turned around on the sidewalk to confront Julia.

"Well, if the shoe fits."

"Hey, now, you know you forgave me, and I am trying to change. I haven't been on one date since I got here; I'm serious."

"You? Come on. Let's have the truth."

"No, really." Morgan realized with a shock that it was true. Maybe she should be a little worried. Was she that different to guys up here?

"Okay, maybe not dates, but how many guys have walked you home and asked for your phone number, or fought to sit next to you in class, or just happened to drop by to tell you they'd had a revelation that you were to be their bride?"

"None, Julia. And even as I'm saying it, I find it hard to believe." She gave Julia a smart-alecky smile and turned around again, heading for Julia's little red car in the parking lot.

"What's the matter, lose your touch?" Julia asked.

"I don't know, maybe. I've just been really busy with school and working and everything. And biking around takes a lot more time than you'd think. And it's freezing too."

Julia inserted the key into the driver's side and popped the lock to let Morgan in. Once in the car Julia looked at Morgan skeptically. "Well, it *is* pretty hard to believe." She placed her left hand on the wheel and faced Morgan without starting the car. "I know it's been awkward with what's happened and everything, but don't think you can't tell me things. Sometimes I can understand what you did, and I'm over it, you know. And I know that, well, I wasn't there for you when . . ." Julia looked out through the windshield and paused. Morgan knew what she was going to say. ". . . well, when Aaron came back and things didn't work out." Julia looked back at Morgan quickly and then down into her lap.

Morgan felt her throat closing up and struggled to pull enough air into her lungs to make a response. "It was my fault . . . everything that happened." She looked at Julia so Julia could see that she was sincere.

"Yeah, but I know that it's been pretty rough for you anyway. Okay, you did dumb things, I mean I could have strangled you, but . . . still, Ben and I are together after all, and . . . I hate to have this happen to you."

"Thanks."

"How are you feeling about it? I mean, is it getting any easier?"

"You mean honestly?" Morgan was still unsure how close they were to their former footing. For most people she would put on a brave face and say that Aaron and she had grown apart, that they had both wanted the breakup. But . . . if she was trying to reform and she really wanted Julia's friendship again, she shouldn't hold things back. She never had in the past.

"It's hard, Julia, still. Things just aren't the same for me anymore. I guess I'm more human than I thought. And I guess I really hurt myself more than anyone."

Julia nodded her head once and then said, "Did you know that Aaron's sister, Jodie, is dating his old companion now?"

"You mean Jim Facer?"

"Yeah."

"Oh. Really? She's kinda young . . . cute though." It was hard not to feel a pang of distress over the news. Her old self was still a part of her after all. She paused for a moment, and Julia started up the car. They were out of the parking lot and onto the street before Morgan spoke again. "I guess you know about all that stuff with Jim too." She had to ask—she hoped the whole thing hadn't become common knowledge.

"Well, yeah." Julia concentrated on the traffic. "You know how things get around in Hunter."

"All of that is hard to explain, even to myself," Morgan said. "The only thing I can say about it is that it all had something to do with

Aaron. I mean, I felt like if I could find a substitute for him, even for a little while, that it wouldn't be so hard." Morgan paused to gain control over her voice. "Does that sound totally stupid?"

"Not really, but I think it's hard for most people to understand. Don't you see that it's like, well, using people to make yourself feel better?"

Morgan could tell that Julia thought she was walking on eggshells, trying to understand. But she was giving Morgan a pretty broad hint, even one that bordered on accusation, and it was a moment before Morgan could convince herself not to be offended. It almost seemed now that it had been someone else moving in on Jim, betraying Aaron. She just remembered it happening so naturally that she hadn't even thought about it at the time, aside from a few feelings of guilt before kissing Jim. Why had she done it? Maybe she was so good at faking people out that she'd even fooled herself. It was amazing how clear she could see it now, how disgusting her behavior seemed.

"I know. You're right," Morgan admitted. "I just don't know how everything happened so fast. I really don't see myself as that kind of a person. I mean I never used to be . . . it just . . . I don't know." Morgan raised her hands up, as if to explain, and then let them drop back into her lap. She felt slightly resentful toward Julia for bringing it up again. Maybe she hadn't really changed after all. Maybe she *was* that vicious girl that would steal her best friend's boyfriend and date her missionary's former companion—anything to feed the insatiable ego. She felt afraid of herself, afraid of the future.

"Hey, you made a mistake." Julia looked over her shoulder before changing lanes. "Maybe more than one."

Morgan looked up into Julia's mischievous grin.

"But you aren't a bad person. You know that. I've known you my whole life. I know who you are. And you're not the only one who makes mistakes. I'm so glad that you finally made me stop being such an idiot and quit ignoring you. I was really stupid. It's so great to be back together like this again and having you plan the decorations for the reception. I could never imagine getting married. I never really let myself." Julia's eyes widened. "But there's no way I could go through this with anyone else. You're like . . ." she trailed off, turning her head to look out the window, ". . . my sister."

When she turned back to look through the front windshield she was blinking hard. Suddenly Morgan's own eyes were swimming. How could Julia forgive her like this? It was incredible. She now saw the enormity of the thing she had done to Julia, the betrayal. Her stomach gave a sickening twist. And Julia, she was being so great. This was true forgiveness, like the stories you read in Church magazines and hear about in Sunday School. This was the real thing. Morgan gulped down her tears and said, "I am so sorry, Julia."

"I know." She paused, and her breath came out with a rush. "So am I. We'll get over this, you know." Julia pulled into a parking space at the craft store. "Things change and life goes on." She smiled lightly, wiped her eyes, and got out of the car.

"Yeah, I guess . . ." Morgan took a deep breath and smiled again and followed Julia into the store.

* * *

Aaron turned the wheel swiftly to avoid a large mud-filled hole and then pulled up short on the brown grass at the side of the road. He leaned his seat back until he could feel the sun on his face.

It was beautiful today. It felt like spring. If he sat still, low like this, out of the breeze, he could feel the sun beginning to warm his body. If he sat still enough, maybe it might penetrate to his brain . . .

A long minute went by as he sat in the jeep, trying to clear his mind of all the pressure in his life. He could hear a few cows in a distant field and the sweet, short burst of a bird's song. He breathed deeply for a few minutes, thinking that he might even fall asleep, but then his eyes blinked open again, his breathing grew shallower, and his knee began to bounce against the seat in a nervous tempo. He sat up, realizing it was no use, and bent to double knot his running shoes.

His body was throbbing with tension. He felt keyed up and anxious, and his brain kept darting from one thing to another: classes, career, mission memories, girls. He thought of a stupid argument he'd had with his dad that morning and then remembered the mounting irritation he'd felt when Jodie had walked Jim to his car and Aaron had been unable to stop looking at the clock . . . ten minutes, fifteen, twenty-five . . . She'd come back in looking dreamy and ridiculous.

Aaron leaned against the hood of the jeep and stretched first one calf then the other. He grabbed each ankle to stretch his quads and then crossed his legs and bent down to touch the tips of his running shoes. He started the stopwatch his parents had given him for Christmas and moved out onto the dirt road in a slow jog. After only a few strides he found himself speeding up, moving faster and faster down the road. Soon he was flat-out sprinting, and though he'd meant to pace himself for a five-mile run, it felt good to let himself go . . . flying faster and faster down the slight incline of the curving road. His muscles straining, his blood pumping, springing through his veins, the oxygen filling his lungs, he found himself wondering if he was breaking records.

When he got to his old one-mile marker, a large post in the barbed wire fence that ran next to the dirt road, he stopped and bent over, heaving, and then remembered to check his watch. 5:10. It was one of the fastest miles he'd ever run! Wild! He couldn't believe it. He smiled in pleasure. All those times in high school when he'd been running against the best milers from other 2A schools, he couldn't get himself much under five—his fastest was 4:55—and now he'd done a 5:10 the first time he'd been running since he'd been back from his mission. He hadn't timed himself in Italy—he had mostly just done slower, longer runs for exercise—so he didn't know how he'd done this. It was probably just a fluke, just a result of keyed up nerves and the springtime and well . . . he took a deep breath, trying to steady himself . . . of frustration.

Aaron straightened up and began to walk slowly down the road again, hands on hips, still breathing deeply. Nothing felt right anymore. The first few weeks off his mission, he thought he had everything figured out, that he wouldn't be one of those fish-out-of-water RMs. He'd registered for classes, confident that engineering was what he wanted, slipped back into the easy relationships with his family, had found a couple of his old buddies to hang out with, and had made his peace, or what he thought was his peace, with Morgan. Now he wasn't sure.

Ever since he'd seen that girl in the restaurant, he'd been plagued by thoughts of Morgan, obsessed. Even though he knew she was in Provo, he worried that he'd see her on a weekend and then was unreasonably disappointed when he didn't. It was crazy. What was he thinking?

He *had* seen her one time—at the park by her house. He'd just been driving by, running down to the store for his mother, when suddenly his eyes had stopped on two figures on the distant playground. He'd known immediately that it was Morgan. She was on the swings with her youngest sister, laughing and clowning.

Aaron had remembered the Saturday afternoons when Morgan brought Megan along on their dates. The whole Carter family was in love with the little girl, and Morgan was no exception. She would treat her and tease her, help and play with her . . . Morgan's hair glinted and swung in the spring sunlight as she spun Megan around on her shoulders. Aaron had put his foot on the brake and had to physically restrain himself from joining them. His natural place seemed to be with them; it felt so wrong to just drive by. And so he'd compromised, had stopped by the side of the road and watched them where his jeep was half-hidden by a row of bushes.

Memories of Morgan flooded him, nearly filling him to the top with longing. She was amazing to be with, witty and fun, energetic and sometimes so sweet. Aaron shut his eyes and shook his head swiftly.

He wiped the sweat off his forehead and onto the leg of his shorts.

Lately it seemed like he was jealous of everyone. When he'd see a couple on campus, holding hands, laughing, talking, he resented them. He thought how unfair it was. He even sometimes thought they must be faking, that they couldn't possibly be having that much fun. They were just in love with love. They were young and stupid. And then he would feel this frustration, this boxed-in energy, and he would imagine running and running and running . . . Maybe that's what had got him the 5:10 today—mental preparation.

Aaron started jogging again, holding himself down to a slow pace, thinking that maybe he'd go another mile before turning around. He was tired from the sprinting, but his body felt good, better in fact. He should come out here every day.

He just couldn't seem to relax anymore. He spent any free time he had after school, homework, and his part-time job kind of wandering around aimlessly, and Sundays drove him crazy. Sunday had been his busiest day of the week on his mission, but here . . . even though he attended his meetings, spent time with family, read scriptures, and wrote in his journal, the day was interminable.

And sometimes in the evenings, when he knew he should go to bed early, his body wouldn't shut down. He didn't want to pick up a book after doing homework all day, and watching TV had seemed stupid and pointless since he'd returned from his mission, though he remembered watching way too much when he was younger.

Everything seemed just like that, like he was battling his way through new experiences every day that seemed familiar but just didn't make sense anymore. It was like he was on the outside, looking in through distorted, wavy glass. He knew what he was seeing, what was happening, but he couldn't fit himself into the picture.

And the future—it seemed impossible to contemplate. He couldn't see himself in the role of a young father, a man with a good job and a family to support, but he couldn't see himself doing anything else either. What was there? What was out there for him that would make everything come together? Life just seemed . . . empty.

When he reached the big tree at the bend in the road, his two-mile marker, he resolutely touched the rough bark with a swipe of his hand and turned around to complete his circle.

Chapter 6

"Really, it's kind of strange."

"She can't be that different." Ben said as he and Julia arrived at the apartment door.

"Well, she's not really different. I mean, Morgan is Morgan, but it's like she's softer. She put the key in the door of the new apartment and pulled the knob toward her as she turned it. The door opened, and still standing outside, she turned to face him. "I think she's trying now. She's serious. It's kind of weird. And she seems pretty organized, kind of like she was when she was on the student council in high school. It's like she cares about something again. Besides chasing guys, I mean."

"Well." Ben leaned against the brick wall to the right of the door. "I hope you're right, and she is changing. Girls like her, as good-looking as she is . . ."

"Ben!"

"Well . . . she is—you know that. And it takes nothing away from you to say it." He smiled and took her hand. "Girls like her, chasing guys all the time, well . . . they usually turn out bad. Pretty soon guys figure out how many others they've been making out with, how fickle they are, and cute or not, they don't want them."

"Man, I hope that doesn't happen to Morgan. She doesn't deserve it, you know, though sometimes it's hard to see it. Underneath all the selfishness, she's a good person; she's fun and creative and talented. And she's really good with people, when she's not trying to attract every male in sight. But really, Ben, she is softer now, and she says she hasn't gone out with anyone the whole time she's been in Provo. Do you think that's true?"

"Sounds unlikely."

"And she's got this job at this kind of decorator store at the mall, and she's doing her homework and everything. She's also got this terrible roommate, a real snob, but gorgeous, that's doing the same kind of thing with guys that Morgan's been doing all her life. I think Morgan sees how bad she is and realizes that she was like that."

"Maybe. It sounds hopeful." Ben paused and then went on, "You know, I am so proud of you—amazed."

"You are?" Julia looked up surprised. "Why?"

"She really betrayed you . . ." He paused, smiled, and swung her hand up and back. ". . . and now you are concerned for her happiness. You are incredible to have forgiven her. And me."

"Well . . ." Julia smiled with pleasure. "It was hard for a long time, but now I feel so much better, not stressed out, like a weight has lifted off me. And I have to admit it's great having her back. There's just something about being around her that's exciting. And she's so comfortable to be with. I mean, I know her so well, I know what she's going to say and, most of the time, what she's thinking. I really hope we can get back to how it was before. It's still a little awkward." Julia moved closer to him and let her head brush against his shoulder.

"You know, Julia, it's probably never going to be the same as it was."

"Why not?" Why couldn't things be the same after a while? Julia really thought that her forgiveness would soon blend into forgetting, or at least not feeling the hurt, even slightly. It was easier for her with Morgan in this new situation, kind of vulnerable and alone. But as soon as Julia thought this she felt a stab of guilt that maybe her forgiveness was conditioned upon Morgan's humiliation. Maybe she couldn't have forgiven her if Aaron had come home and adored Morgan and they'd been engaged and everything had turned out wonderful for Morgan.

"Well, after we get married . . . *I* am going to be your best friend." Ben grinned. "At least I'd better be."

Julia turned to face him, letting the conversation about Morgan drop. She looked up into his eyes and smiled slowly. "Well, that's true," she said in a low voice, backing toward the door. "I wish I could ask you in."

"Well, it won't be long now. Pretty soon you'll be trying to get rid of me." He took her hand and kissed it gallantly and then turned and ran down the steps and out to his truck.

Julia held her breath, watching him, until he pulled away and moved down the street.

* * *

It was raining hard as Morgan pumped her bike up the incline to her apartment building. The rain poured from an ugly gray sky and ran in a torrent down the gutter at her right. Head down, Morgan concentrated on the white line at her left and on moving as quickly as she could. Her thighs screamed their pain the last couple of feet as she pushed herself up the hill and began turning into the driveway of the parking lot. She gave one last final shove on the pedal as the bike took the corner, intending to coast down to the bike rack, but instead the wheels slipped on the wet pavement and she went down, scraping across the pavement and landing in a heap against the curb.

Morgan lay there for a moment, head on the curb, and let the rain pelt her face. She didn't need this today! Man! She sat up and saw her backpack lying in a large puddle, the expensive books inside soaking up water. She tried to jump up and grab it, but only succeeded in tripping on the bike and landing with a thud in the same puddle. She splashed at the water in fit of temper and grabbed the pack and her bike and dragged them both to the bike rack where she dumped the bike, kicking it in a parting shot, and stomped off to get out of the rain.

She slammed the door and leaned against it, dripping and exhausted.

"I saw your little show out there in the parking lot," Vanessa said from her place on the couch. She was perfectly groomed, her black hair shining in the lamplight, her long red nails flicking through the magazine on her lap. "It was quite amusing, actually."

She allowed a sarcastic smile to crack her perfect porcelain veneer and then looked down at the magazine again, ignoring Morgan completely.

Morgan walked past her and into her empty bedroom and closed the door. She opened her backpack and drew out the wet books and papers. Her copy of *Business World* was soaked, and when she care-fully opened it several of the pages came apart in her hands. It had cost one hundred dollars! She sat down on the floor and leaned against the wall, letting the book drop. She laid her head on her knees. All of her emotions erupted, and she sobbed, semiconscious that Vanessa could probably hear her in the other room, but unable to stop the flood of pain and loneliness.

She'd been trying so hard, but everything was so different up here. Sure, aside from Vanessa, her other roommates were nice to her, but they already had friends or boyfriends, and they weren't around very much. All she did was go to class and go to work and study. She didn't even have a calling in the ward, even though she was there every week. It was like she was invisible or something. She'd never realized how much she'd relied on the people around her to make her happiness. When they were gone, well, it was just her and her work. Before she'd just skipped the work and had gone to find something to make her feel better.

But she'd told herself she wouldn't do that this time, even if she could. She had to succeed up here; she *had* to. What else was left?

Morgan pushed her wet hair off her face and then cleared a place on the windowsill and propped up her book to dry in a vain attempt to save it. She looked out the window at the rain and felt another wave of anguish. She crossed to the door and locked it and then fell to her knees in the middle of the floor.

Father in Heaven . . . her mind searched for words to describe her pain, but found none; instead, fresh tears flowed down her cheeks as she struggled to form the thoughts into coherent phrases. Minutes went by, but still the only images that rose to the surface of her mind were those of inner pain and turmoil. She saw Julia's face as she real-ized that Morgan had betrayed her; she saw Jim walking slowly back to the locker room after she'd screamed at him; and she saw with clarity the silver charm of the word *amore* lying in the palm of her hand after Aaron had left the park.

She tried to ask for forgiveness, but still she couldn't find the words. She didn't know how long she'd been here in the middle of the floor; the pain felt like forever. But then she began to feel a lightness, a warmth growing in her chest, and suddenly she knew that the Lord loved her. *She knew it!* The feeling grew until every part of her body was glowing with it. Even with all her weakness and sin, the Lord loved her, her own true self. And He knew her intentions and her heart and everything that was good about her. He could forgive her, and He could help her. Morgan took a big breath, opened her eyes, and stared into the room. She felt clean and alive, if a little weak. She rubbed her eyes and suddenly a phrase from the scriptures came into her mind . . . *And lo, I am with you* . . . The words echoed in her ears. She didn't want to move in case this feeling would leave, but it didn't. It stayed with her the whole night and into the next day and helped her begin to build again.

Chapter 7

"Okay, well, see ya in about an hour then." Jim's voice projected into the kitchen.

"Okay," Jodie answered him.

"Do a good job up there; make me proud. Play it better than anyone else."

"Jim—it's not about playing better than everyone else. It's about blending and sounding beautiful as a group."

"I know."

"I'd better go or I'll be late."

Aaron tried not to listen to Jodie and Jim saying good-bye by the door, although they'd only be apart for an hour. He rolled his eyes at a short silence and tried to put his hands over his ears before he heard anything that would make him sick. Too late. The sound of a soft smack and then another reached him where he was sitting at the table with his books. He shook his head and dove back into his engineering problems.

Jim came sauntering back into the room. His cheeks were red and his eyes bright.

"So, are you ready to check out the Jazz game yet?" he asked Aaron.

"In just a minute. I've got to work out this one problem still." Aaron looked at the figures on his notebook paper, and his eyes glazed over. He'd already been at this for an hour and a half. It was murder. After a few stabs at his calculator, rechecking some of the calculations, Aaron finally discovered his error and was able to finish out the problem. He looked up to where Jim was still standing.

"Done?"

"Not really, but close enough." Aaron shut his book on the five remaining problems, hoping that getting up at five thirty in the morning would give him enough time to finish before his class at eight.

Aaron grabbed the remote off the couch and turned on the game, but for once Jim wasn't leaning forward eagerly, following the moves of the players. He sat at the other end of the couch with his arm across the back, looking somewhere over Aaron's head.

"What's the matter? The Lakers don't do it for you this year?"

"What?"

"LA too boring for you?"

Jim glanced over the back of the couch toward the kitchen and then down the hall, as if making sure he wouldn't be overheard.

"Didn't Jodie tell you my parents are eating out with friends before the concert?"

"Oh, yeah, I guess. I . . . well . . . I just wanted to ask you something."

Aaron could tell this was probably something he didn't want to discuss. He turned toward the TV. "Yeah?"

"I know this sounds stupid, and I sure as heck shouldn't be asking you. But man, you know everything about it, so I basically have no choice. You know?"

Aaron was afraid he did. "Yeah, I guess."

"I was just wondering . . . man, do you think I have a chance with Jodie? I mean a real chance? I know I'm not in the same league with your family, and your parents have been really nice to me and all, but they probably want Jodie going out with a guy that comes from a more stable LDS family, a guy that's more academic and everything." Jim paused for a moment and a loud buzzer sounded on the television. "Even myself, I can't really see Jodie with an ex-football player, high-school coach kind of guy."

"Jim, for heaven's sake, you know my parents like you, and if you can't tell that Jodie's completely infatuated, then you *are* stupid." He turned back to the game to watch the Lakers score right over Malone's head. "Did you see that? That was really disgusting. When are the Jazz going to wake up!"

Jim ignored his shouting. "I know they like me as a person and everything, but what about long term? I know this sounds crazy, 'cause we really haven't been dating that long, but I don't want to get into anything again unless I think I've got a real shot."

"Jim—why do you have to get all serious right off the bat with everyone? I mean—give it a few weeks. Why do you feel all this pressure to decide right away? Can't you just have fun? Just look what happened with Morgan for instance—you could have saved yourself a lot of heartache over that if you'd just waited for a few months until I got home to see what happened." Aaron didn't know why he was feeling so mean. He really should have been understanding over this whole thing, and at least sensitive enough not to mention Morgan . . . He tried to take his thoughts off her and began concentrating on the game again.

Jim didn't say anything for a long time. He didn't even react when Stockton hit a jumper just outside the three-point line.

"So *that's* it," Jim said, nodding his head wisely.

"Oh, what!" Aaron exploded. "What's it? Suddenly everyone knows everything about everyone."

"You're still in love with her."

"What do you mean? With who?"

"Morgan, of course. And you're kind of blaming me and the world in general." Jim shifted a knee up onto the couch. "And we've been taking a lot lately from you."

"Really." Aaron's face froze for a moment in a sarcastic grimace.

"Yeah. You're kind of a grouch, you know. And you were so weird on those dates when we doubled with you. You didn't even try with those girls, and they were pretty decent."

"Oh, sure." Aaron was beginning to feel a little guilty. He'd thought he'd been hiding his irritation with life a little better.

"You still like her. Admit it," Jim pressed.

"I was done with her before Christmas. She's just not someone I can be with anymore."

"Can't you forgive her? I mean—it's not like you didn't have some straying thoughts yourself."

"What?" A brief vision of Francesca and Elder Archer crossed his mind, but Jim didn't know about that and Aaron wasn't about to enlighten him.

"I met a guy named Josh Archer last weekend when Jodie and I went up to Provo."

Aaron stiffened.

"We took a couple of girls from the orchestra with us and picked up their dates in Provo. This Archer guy was one of the dates. We went out to dinner, and he and I got to talking about our missions, you know, that we both went to Italy and everything around the same time. And then we started talking about companions and realized that we'd both had you. Well, I guess you know Archer. He couldn't keep his mouth shut and pretty much told me everything about you and Francesca."

Oh great. Perfect. Yes, Aaron knew Archer. His face felt hot, his stomach sick and mortified, and he was no longer paying any attention to the game. He pictured Jodie and Jim and Archer—the group of them—all clustered around the table, laughing at him. How could he set the record straight? He was especially embarrassed about Jodie thinking that. Maybe she'd say something to their parents. Maybe she already had.

"Well, Archer is quite a blabbermouth. The whole thing happened in his head. He was just starved for some type of gossip to spill."

"You mean you didn't really feel attracted to this girl, what was her name?"

"Francesca. Yeah, well, I noticed her, of course. She was sweet and young and pretty. But I wasn't *attracted to her* in the sense that you mean."

"Yeah, well, that's not how 'Elder' Archer tells it. He said you had to be transferred out of Rome over it."

"Yeah!" Aaron yelled, standing up. "That's because he told the mission president I was getting too involved with a convert—he made this whole *chemistry* thing up just because she was attractive, young, and unmarried. Can you believe that? It was horrible. I think he did it so he could be AP. Man!" He slammed the couch pillow he'd been holding. "I thought I'd forgiven that guy!"

Aaron stood there clenching and unclenching his fists, the blood pulsing madly through his veins. He couldn't believe Archer was telling that story around. I mean, he'd still thought the guy had some honor. He'd been a good missionary.

Jim went on. "All right. All I'm saying is this: can't you under-stand Morgan a little after having that, well . . . *experience* of being attracted to someone else?"

"Don't you believe me?" Aaron looked around the room. He was so mad he wanted to hit something. The frustration of the last two months began to explode. He looked at Jim intensely for a moment.

Jim started to laugh.

"Hey!" said Aaron.

"Do you know that's exactly how you looked in that apartment building just before you shoved me and went barreling off down the hall?"

Aaron smiled a little.

"I think you wanted to hit me, just a little, a minute ago."

Aaron shifted his weight. "Maybe . . . but I am definitely not that dumb." He eyed Jim. "Could you have gotten any bigger?"

"Oh, I'm not all that buff." He flexed his bulging muscles and grinned. "Come on, calm down. I know Archer is kind of an idiot, and he was showing off in front of those girls. But I thought, you know, maybe it would help you to think about giving Morgan another chance."

"How can it help me when I didn't do anything wrong. I was completely innocent!" Aaron threw his hands in the air. "I can't believe we're talking about this. I can't believe you, of all people, want me to take Morgan back."

"Aaron, I don't really care if you take her back or not. Man, I just hate seeing you in pain."

"You just want me all goggle-eyed and blissful like you and Jodie. You guys make me sick."

"She is so great. Can I just tell you? I mean, I know she's your sister, but, oh yeah, she is pretty sweet."

Aaron made a gagging noise and then turned off the TV. "Ready to go to the concert?"

"You bet."

Chapter 8

She was actually excited about this! Morgan swept a couple of books off the kitchen table and laid down the mat board she'd bought. She retrieved a bag from just inside the door and began to take things out and arrange them on the board.

It had taken her days to put this all together, but finally, she was sure she had it right. She arranged three paint chips to one side and then looked around her quickly, trying to remember what she had done with her scissors. She ran into her bedroom and then back out to the kitchen, finally finding them in the third of the kitchen drawers. She picked up the first swatch of fabric and was about to cut into it when she decided she'd better get a ruler and make sure she cut it even. Back to the set of drawers, rummaging, and then to the table again with a pencil and a ruler, slightly out of breath. She marked lines for a large rectangle on the back of a tan, sisal-like fabric and then carefully cut it out. She laid it against the gray-green mat board next to the three paint chips and felt a thrill again. She knew she'd been right about the fabric for the major upholstery in the room she was planning for her interior design class. She then drew a heavy piece of black and white fabric from the bag. This one she worried about—she'd stood around in the fabric store for about thirty minutes agonizing over it. The pattern was bold—black and white stripes in a chevron design—it had almost a zebra-print look to it, though the zigzag chevron was traditional enough to tone it down for what she wanted. She turned it over and marked it with a ruler and cut out a somewhat longer rectangle than the tan sisal and placed it on the board under the first fabric.

Morgan stood back and studied the effect with half-closed eyes. Did it blend enough?

Just then the door opened and Vanessa and a couple of guys came in. They were laughing and Vanessa was flirting like crazy. She stopped short when she saw the books on the floor.

"Why are my drama books on the floor?" she said, looking up at Morgan.

"Oh." Morgan looked to the floor and remembered pushing them off to make room for the mat board. One had fallen open and a few folded papers had spilled out. "Sorry, I wasn't thinking." She bent down to gather the papers and stack the books. She stood and handed them to Vanessa.

"I don't know who you think you are, pushing my things off the table. You aren't the only one who lives here, you know." She rubbed an imaginary scuff off the cover of one of the books and tossed her head.

Morgan saw the two guys exchange uncomfortable glances and felt embarrassed and angry. Vanessa could never seem to let anything go. She apparently felt it her duty as a superior human being to point out all faults. Because she was paying double, it seemed like she felt she owned the apartment and thus had first priority to all the community spaces.

"Sorry." Morgan looked back down at the mat board and her materials. It worked out better if you just ignored her and let her have her little tantrum. It wasn't worth it to descend to Vanessa's level. Though, to be fair, Morgan knew she shouldn't have pushed the books off.

Turning to the two guys, Vanessa said, "I'll just go put this stuff in my room. *Some* people don't respect personal property. You guys can sit down. I'll be right back."

She hadn't introduced her two friends to Morgan and so left an uncomfortable silence behind. Morgan took a couple more things out of her bag and then looked up at them and smiled. Vanessa was taking a long time. The dark-haired guy stood up and walked over to Morgan.

"What are you doing?"

"Just working on a project for my interior design class. We are supposed to design a room, and this board is going to show all the paint choices, the fabrics for upholstery, and window treatments, moldings, accessory colors, and so on." She picked up a couple of pieces of molding that she had had the hardware store cut for her and stacked them together to study the effect.

"Sounds cool."

"Yeah, I really like the class. Though it's scary sometimes. This is only our midterm project. For the final we get a four-by-eight-foot wall and we're supposed to pretend it's a corner of a room and paint or wallpaper it, put up hangings, whatever we want. Then we get to pick a chair and a side table from the class supplies or we can bring our own. And then, of course, pictures, accessories. My teacher also wants full drawings of the room, complete with furniture and any colors and fabrics that aren't shown in the 'corner.' It scares me to death." Morgan smiled and looked up at him and noticed he wasn't bad looking. "Are you in school?"

He began talking about his accounting major and how tough it was. But Morgan was only half listening. She was marveling at herself. Why wasn't she going after him? He was obviously interested, smiling and throwing out lures, saying maybe they should get together sometime. Why didn't she feel that excitement, that need to make the conquest? She looked down at the materials on the table in front of her and fingered a piece of the smooth molding. It would be sweet to take this guy from Vanessa, and though Vanessa was beautiful, she was much too big a brat. It would be easy to transfer his affections, though probably the other guy was the one that was really interested in Vanessa. But did she care? He looked like a nice guy, and maybe if he asked her out and Vanessa wasn't involved—she'd never double with Vanessa—she might go.

He said something about which ward they were in and then asked her name.

"Morgan Carter."

"Hi." He held out his hand. "I'm Brad Layton."

"Nice to meet you, Brad." And she really felt that. It was "nice" to meet him. Nice, and that was all. She wasn't churned up, her heart rate hadn't increased, and she didn't feel any tingling or anything. She smiled suddenly and realized he hadn't let go of her hand. She took it from him just as Vanessa was coming into the room.

She looked suspiciously at Brad standing over Morgan at the table, and then said brightly, "Hey—I thought you guys were going to take me out for ice cream." She walked over and put her hand through Brad's arm and started pulling him toward the door.

Brad looked back at Morgan and said, "Do you want to come too? I think I can afford to buy another ice cream."

"Oh, she's too busy. Can't you see? All crafty and sticky." Vanessa looked at the fabric scraps on Morgan's lap and then at the bottle of rubber cement Morgan hadn't even opened.

"Yeah, I really need to finish this right now. I've got to go to work at six. Sorry—sounds fun though."

Brad waved to her, and the three of them left. Morgan entertained herself for the next few minutes by imagining how she would have acted if she'd gone. She would have pretended that she and Vanessa were best friends and said all sorts of things to make Vanessa mad. She might even have asked to borrow her hairbrush or something in front of the guys. Vanessa would probably have handed it over, trying to make a good impression and look generous, but she would be murderous underneath. Morgan laughed a little in the empty apartment and then turned back to the design plan. It would be great if she could actually paint the molding . . .

The next night at the shop, it was nearing eight thirty, and business had slowed quite a lot. A woman with a young girl still loitered at the back of the shop, picking over the clearance items, and a young BYU-ish couple walked down the aisles, window shopping.

Morgan stood at the counter and straightened a group of artificial forsythia stems in a crystal vase next to the cash register. She was tired tonight, and sometimes had to shake her head a little to clear out the fuzziness.

Her classes were demanding. She'd been at the library late last night and had struggled home, nearly falling off her bike again. She knew she shouldn't be out alone at night. But sometimes she didn't know what else she could do. Her mother had been on her to take the bus at night, but it didn't always fit her schedule. Besides, she kind of liked the feeling of doing this all on her own, of handling things. She'd thought she had it all together at Hale, had thought that she was living her own life and standing up as an adult, but she'd been wrong. Nearly everything that had happened during the last six months, all the bad things anyway, had come about because of her immaturity, her need for someone else to always shoulder all the responsibilities, take all the blame.

She liked the new feeling. She liked herself. Finally, finally she could see clearly enough to focus on her dreams. The Lord had helped her. She wasn't just some shallow head of hair bent on makeup and nail polish and boy-chasing. She didn't think other people could see the difference, but strangely, that was okay. Maybe she deserved that. She felt a growing inside her, a changing that opened a pathway to her soul.

The last few years the tide of flattery, the flood of compliments had swirled enticingly around her and had kept inching up her body until everything she really was had nearly drowned in it. Her heart had been so submerged, so slogged and soaked with images of herself, that it had ceased to function normally.

And now, only now that the tides had receded, could she begin to massage that shrunken vessel and coax it to begin a labored beating.

In this new place she wasn't worshipped, wasn't pushed into the center of the universe. Her ultimate failure, losing Aaron, had caused her to stop vying for that center, for the spotlight. Maybe it had humbled her enough that she didn't even have the same effect on the new people she met. And she didn't see them in the same light either, as people to conquer, to measure against herself. It was a relief and a cleansing. She could begin to forgive people for their faults, which she could never quite do before. She still liked praise and attention. Who didn't? But now she mostly got it for what she did, not for what she looked like, and she found that the buzz from those compliments lasted much longer, and she didn't need to continue to fish around, hoping to draw more comments from male lips.

Last week her boss had asked her to try her hand at window dressing, as their usual designer had a big job somewhere else and couldn't redo the display for two weeks. Morgan had been so excited she couldn't sleep. She kept going over the possibilities, tried to remember everything they had in the shop that might lend itself to a fresh spring layout. She asked if she could buy six yards of sheer lime fabric she'd seen at the store and then had hung it in the window in wispy folds. Next, she spent two hours coming up with a lighting angle that would simulate a sunrise reflecting off the fabric. She moved a couple of white wicker chairs into the window with a low white coffee table and a clear glass bowl holding a few silk tulips bending gracefully at different angles. She added a floral pillow and draped a soft, faded-looking quilt over one of the chairs.

And after all her work, the next night she'd had the exquisite pleasure of standing at the cash register, watching shoppers pause to admire the display. She'd even walked by it a couple of times herself when she'd been on break. This kind of success filled her like nothing else had. Her boss had praised her a number of times over the window and had promised her another shot at it soon.

Morgan leaned back a little to catch a glimpse of it now and could just see the back of one chair and a little of the quilt. She smiled and drew in her breath until her lungs were full.

Chapter 9

This was something they would always talk about, this moment. Julia and Ben paused just inside the temple doors after their wedding, ready to go out and face the crowd of happy, laughing faces, ready to begin their life together.

Just a short time ago, inside the temple, all of her doubts and worries had disappeared, seemed ridiculous, childlike. The seriousness and the reality of what she was doing didn't flatten her but sat on her shoulders like a golden cloak. And when she knelt across from Ben and looked into his eyes—she'd never forget that moment—everything seemed to open up for her, the future, the past, the present. It all lay before her in unending folds receding and receding but never losing focus.

As soon as they came out the temple doors, they were swamped with relatives, hugging and kissing them, laughing and smiling. Everyone had a camera. If Julia had ever wondered what it felt like to be a fashion model, now she knew. She and Ben seemed pinned to the doors. Every time they started to move out toward the crowd, someone else would yell, "No, no. I need another picture," and then the flashing would begin all around them again.

She glimpsed her mother, her Aunt Beth, her dad, and her brothers in one flash, and then saw Morgan, Lorraine, and the kids coming up the ramp when she looked the other direction. Everyone was milling and laughing and joking, and she kept looking up at Ben (in fact her neck hurt from doing it) just to see how he was taking it all. His face was pink, like he was a little bit embarrassed, but he was smiling from ear to ear.

Finally they were moving down the stairs to meet the real photographer waiting for them on the road. But then Michael pushed to the front.

"Hey!" He held his camera up near his chest. "I want to get one of them kissing in front of the doors."

"Mike," Julia said. Her cheeks hurt, and she was trying not to smile. "Come on. We've got to start with the real pictures."

But Ben turned to her and then glanced toward Michael. "Well, I think Mike's got the right idea. Some things have just got to wait." He reached for her with a gleam in his eye and kissed her right in front of everyone. Julia couldn't help feeling embarrassed, but she was deliriously happy at the same time. Everyone laughed and clapped.

"I do believe you've got a blushing bride there," Mike said, grinning, moving away just in time to avoid Julia's playful slap.

"Oh, I've missed it." Morgan's mother came rushing up the ramp, teetering on high heels, trying to unzip a camera bag. "Go back over there a minute, okay? And do it again. Kiss her, Ben. I gotta get a shot of this."

The crowd groaned and laughed and moved back toward the door. Ben said he didn't know if he could be as convincing the second time, and as they replayed the scene both of them were struggling not to laugh.

"Oh, that's perfect. Thanks," Morgan's mother laughed with them.

Finally they were out in the sunshine walking toward the steps in front of the tall doors that would be one of the photography points. Ben squeezed her hand, looking into her eyes, and she felt another thrill travel through her. Would she ever get enough of this?

The group of people around them seemed to grow. The photographer was trying to get the crowd's attention in all the confusion so he could get a few group shots, but no one was cooperating very well.

Julia and Ben reached the steps and obeyed the photographer's instructions for positioning. Julia let her mother and Morgan fuss with her veil and was relieved that she'd chosen a simple dress without a huge train to drag around. When Julia's mother went to gather up her side of the family for a picture, Morgan stayed and hugged Julia and then Ben.

"I am so glad, you guys."

Julia could see tears standing in Morgan's eyes as she looked up at them, and the sincerity in her face touched her so much that she had to blink a few times herself.

"You are just so . . . well, perfect together," Morgan said, "and I wanted to tell you again, both of you, that I am sorry about everything stupid that I did and that I am your friend for life. Which means," she added with a saucy smile, "that you're going to be seeing a lot of me. Maybe more than you'd like. But," her eyebrows lifted wickedly, "I'll try to respect your privacy."

"Well, you'd better come see us. I just hope we won't be too boring for you, you know, an old married couple." Julia looked briefly up at Ben and then hugged Morgan again. She felt like she'd already hugged more people today than she had in the last fifteen years.

And then there were pictures, and pictures, and pictures. Julia was surprised that she didn't tire of it, didn't tire of being in the spotlight. But in fact, she was having the time of her life. She couldn't remember another time when she'd felt so wonderful, when the Spirit had been with her so solidly and for so long.

The photographer finally folded up his tripod and said he would meet them at the reception. Both sets of parents and the few siblings that had stayed gathered up their things and moved toward the parking lot. Julia's mother said she would meet Julia back in the temple to help with her dress. They would need to pack it carefully so it would be ready for the reception in about five hours.

And then suddenly they were alone again, Ben and Julia, together and away from the crowd.

"So . . ." Ben's blue eyes looked down at her. The sun was behind him, his face in shadow. "Was it that bad?"

"No . . . nothing I couldn't handle," she grinned.

They laughed and then Julia gave a short scream as she felt her feet leave the ground.

"Ben! Put me down! You're going to drop me in my dress and there will be grass stains and Morgan and my mom will go crazy." She looked into his eyes then put her arms around his neck. Glancing over his shoulder she noticed that her brother and Ben's oldest sister had turned around and were getting their cameras out again.

"No, I won't," he said. "I won't ever drop you again. You are mine—no, don't look at them, they'll probably take pictures for the rest of the day, and," he laughed, "I want you to remember *this* day and *this* moment and *these* words: I love you, Julia, and nothing you can ever do now or in the future will change that. I'm going to be there right beside you until the end of time." He looked at her for a long, floating moment and then kissed her with a tenderness that took her breath away. She could faintly hear cheering in the background over the roaring of her blood pounding in her ears.

She was still a little dizzy and panting when she said, "And I love you, Ben, forever."

It was crazy, but she wasn't scared anymore. She knew life wouldn't be easy; everyone had told her that. But at this moment it was hard to imagine.

* * *

"What can we help you with, Morgan?"

It was Julia's mother, looking a little stressed out as she walked across the cultural hall dressed in her "grubbies," which for her translated into a button-down shirt and crisp jeans that looked suspiciously as if they'd been ironed.

"Well . . ." Morgan looked around for something that Julia's parents could help with without ruining the effect. "Oh." Morgan's eyes came to rest on a group of antique silver and clear glass vases and containers. "Could you fill all those up with water? The florist should be here with the flowers in a few minutes."

Julia's dad came up and put his arm around Morgan with a squeeze. "It's so great to have you with us again, I have to tell you." He winked at Morgan and then whispered, "It was almost like I'd lost one of my kids."

Morgan smiled at him and laughed. "Hey, I felt the same way."

"I'm serious though, you know. Now, all we have to do is get you married off."

"Trying to get rid of me already?"

"You just make sure you get someone as wonderful as Ben. I am so glad Julia finally quit being so silly and took a good thing when she saw it."

"Me too. I was hoping she would realize that guys like that don't come along every day. They're great together." Morgan looked down again at the silver gauze she was arranging down the buffet table and twisted one of the white Christmas lights through a hole she'd made.

Mr. Jeffs nodded at her and then walked over to carry vases to the kitchen.

Morgan was excited. It was going to look amazing, she could already tell. And she absolutely *loved* those vases. She'd been all over the Wasatch Front searching in thrift stores and garage sales for old-looking silver plated bowls, urns, jars—anything that would hold flowers. She loved the antique feeling they gave, and when they were filled with the blue hydrangea blossoms that she had ordered, they would be fabulous.

Morgan bent over and plugged in the row of lights arranged under the silver gauze on the buffet table. She stood back to look and decided it needed a little more height. She added another block of wood under the tablecloth, and it looked just right. She laid some of the silver serving platters on the different levels and then grabbed two of the biggest silver urns she'd found and placed them also on the table. When she had the fern fronds from the florist tucked in here and there and the catered food and drinks were on the table it would be perfect, absolutely. She blurred her eyes to get the effect of everything blended together and then brought them slowly to a sharp, clear focus.

Morgan stood still a moment and felt the thrill come over her again. It was amazing, this feeling—that you could feel this good over something you'd done. Maybe this was how Julia felt when the teacher told her she was the smartest student in the class. But no one had to tell Morgan. She just knew. You *know* when you're good at something, when you make a difference. Why had it taken her so long to find that out?

Everything was nearly ready. The cake was coming in half an hour, the tables just needed the vases with the flowers, the caterers would be here at five thirty, and Morgan's dad was almost done bracing up the backdrop support where it hadn't stood up last night. It wouldn't take too long to arrange the flowers and drape the columns she'd borrowed, and then she could do the table where the guests signed the book . . .

The guests . . . She knew she would have to face him again tonight. In fact, she was still high-strung from seeing him across the room at the wedding breakfast that morning. Julia had apologized for having to invite Aaron and his parents, but his parents did belong to the same dinner group as Julia's parents, and they'd gone to dinner every third Friday *for years* . . .

Of course Morgan had understood, and she knew perfectly that Julia couldn't leave Aaron out, not when he was living at home and had been friends with Julia and all of them for so long . . . but it had been humiliating. She'd been trying not to think about it, trying to be sane and strong, but now she felt heat on her cheeks, and she closed her eyes briefly and swallowed.

After all, he could at least have acted like he was her friend. He could have talked to her the way he did to Lorraine and some of the other kids they'd all been friends with in high school. She'd been willing to put a brave face on and act natural and friendly, but he hadn't given her the opportunity. Every time he'd looked in her direction his eyes had seemed to skip over her, like she wasn't even there.

She'd thought that finally she was returning to normal, that finally she had accepted that she wouldn't have him. She'd gone through it all in her mind hundreds of times, hadn't she? And every time she'd tried to be mature about it, she'd realized with a heavy heart the justice of the whole thing. After all, it wouldn't be fair if she were to have him now after what she'd done. Where was the justice in that? She'd schooled herself not to expect mercy.

Then why was the blood racing in her veins, her heart like a hot coal in her chest, at the thought of seeing him?

"Uh, Morgan?" Julia's mother was standing at her elbow, nudging her lightly. "Isn't that the florist?"

Morgan looked toward the door and saw two people carrying buckets of flowers. "Oh, yeah." Morgan shook her head to clear her thoughts and smiled apologetically before moving to receive the flowers.

* * *

Aaron pushed a comb slowly through his hair and stared at himself in the mirror. He'd seen her at the wedding breakfast of course, busy and smiling amongst a group of friends. But he'd been very careful to stay away from Morgan. It was just too weird. He'd been on pins and needles the whole time.

He straightened his tie and smoothed back a stubborn lock of hair. The lunch hour had been extremely stressful, so what was he doing standing here, in front of the mirror, getting ready to go back for more at the reception?

He heard his parents calling for him as they prepared to leave and in another minute heard Jim arrive to pick up Jodie. Still he paused, wondering if it would look too obvious if he said he had a headache or something and had to stay home.

The muscles tightened in his stomach as he remembered Morgan eating with a group of their friends at the end of the table. She'd been witty and alive, but somehow different. She'd looked . . . well, lighter. It was hard to describe it. Aaron had watched her closely when she wasn't looking his direction. It was funny, but she'd seemed more like a part of the group, less like the center. There seemed to be a new mellowness about her . . .

Aaron shook his head and took a deep breath before turning off the bathroom light and heading out the door.

* * *

When Aaron walked into the old second ward cultural hall, he was amazed. It had been completely transformed. The fluorescent lights overhead hadn't been used, but instead lamps, spotlights, and twinkling Christmas lights glowed from every corner. And man, look at that buffet table! All sorts of fancy looking food was piled on shiny platters, and there was even a fountain that spouted a purplish punch. It looked wonderful. It was too bad that his stomach felt so sick. He could have made a meal of the buffet.

"Whoa, this place is amazing. I guess the Jeffses *do* have money." Jim and Jodie walked in behind Aaron and stood looking around. Jim nudged Aaron and said, "Did you see the food?"

"Yeah, but it's too fancy for you. No cheese puffs or greasy pizza."

"I think I'll try it out anyway." Jim pretended to move from his place in the long reception line.

"Hey, get back here." Jodie pulled at his arm and an embarrassing little tussle started.

Aaron rolled his eyes and stepped up closer to his parents, who were handing over the gift and bending to sign the reception book. He took a deep breath and looked up to the head of the line: Julia's brothers and a couple of other guys in tuxes, Ben's parents, Julia's parents, the bridal couple, looking ridiculously pleased with themselves, and then . . . man, did *she* look gorgeous. He felt a jolt go through him.

Morgan was standing next to Julia in the reception line. She had her hair piled up on her head, exposing the long line of her neck. One loose strand reached down just beneath her chin, and she kept pushing it back behind her ear as she shook hands and hugged people.

Aaron's heartbeat was coming in hammers, each blow exploding in his ears as they moved closer and closer up the line.

Jim made a loud comment that Aaron didn't hear and then pushed him from behind, laughing. Maybe he could get through this if he just smiled quickly and skipped past Morgan then went on to the next bridesmaid, Lorraine, to talk about school and everything. It would probably look pretty natural, and no one would notice. Jim and Jodie would be talking to Julia and Ben and admiring the dress and all of that. But what about shaking hands? He didn't see how he could get out of it—it would be too obvious, and he didn't want her to be embarrassed.

He could feel sweat gathering in his palms. He shouldn't have come. But there'd been no way out of it—friends of the family and all that, and plus Jim would have bugged him to death, would have said it was true—that he was still in love with Morgan. Seeing her at the wedding breakfast had been enough to make him sick all day.

The line surged forward and his parents were beginning to shake hands with Julia's brothers. Aaron cleared his mind and took a big breath.

And then—yes, he was doing good—calm, smooth, normal. He was talking to everyone, even laughing, shaking hands, just avoiding looking too much to the left. It was going to be okay. Julia looked great, better than he'd ever seen her, but he couldn't trust himself to say so. He just hugged her and made some sarcastic funny comment, and then when the conversation died a little prematurely, Julia gave him a nervous look, her eyes flicking quickly to his left, obviously waiting for him to move on.

He did it quickly, looking into Morgan's eyes only briefly and grasping her hand in a loose clasp so he could let it go . . . smiling fakely, nodding his head, and all the time burning and burning inside.

Lorraine looked a little puzzled, but hugged him and kept him there for a few minutes when he was really hoping to get through the next sisters-in-law and nieces as fast as he could and make a run for it. Why had he let his parents convince him to come in their car? He could walk home, but they lived out of town a ways, and he knew how stupid he would look to other guests that were driving away from the reception if he was walking down the road in his shirt and tie. Probably no less than five people would stop and ask if they could give him a ride, and then they would ask him why he hadn't waited for his parents, and then, well, he didn't feel like making up stories to disguise his feelings right now.

He walked over and stood next to his parents in the buffet line.

Much later, he still hadn't been able to get away. His parents were involved with a group of their friends, laughing and talking around a big table, and then he himself became caught up in a group of high school and college friends with Jim and Jodie. He was now thoroughly enmeshed, trying to be a smart aleck and joke with the rest of them.

He could see the line was breaking up and people were drifting around. A group formed around the cake with the bride and groom, and though Aaron elected to watch from his table, he caught himself smiling a little. It did look like fun. He wondered what was going through Ben's mind right now. He wondered if he was scared at all.

Morgan was there with her camera, catching all the angles. She looked like she was having a great time. A couple of guys came up to her, eager to start a conversation, but to Aaron's surprise she just smiled at them and said a few words and then turned back to Julia and Ben and the cake. The guys waited a few minutes, thinking she would turn back around to resume the conversation, but she didn't.

She just kept snapping pictures and laughing with the others. Disappointed, the young men turned to the back of the crowd. There was something weird about the interaction, something different, but Aaron couldn't quite put his finger on it.

Julia shoved cake into Ben's mouth, and Morgan rushed forward with napkins for both of them. It was easier to look at her now, not so alarming. Maybe he was getting used to it.

A few minutes passed, and Aaron decided to get up and try another chocolate éclair from the buffet. He was just putting it onto his plate when he heard Morgan's name from a couple of ladies ahead of him.

". . . all this? With no help? Come on. What is she, maybe twenty or something? They probably hired a decorator from up north and Morgan just helped set up."

"No, really. I was talking to her mother, and you know how she likes to brag about her kids. Morgan is majoring in design up in Provo, and she convinced the Jeffses to let her handle it. She organized *everything*: the flowers, the caterer, the cake. And she did *all* the decorations herself. I think her dad helped her to build the backdrop, but all these vases and the lights and the colors and everything were just her. I even heard Gloria Jeffs saying to someone that she would hardly even let the family help set up."

Aaron moved away after that and didn't hear anymore. *Morgan* had done this? It was incredible. He'd never seen anything this elaborate or classy around here before. It wasn't just some homemade thrown-together thing. He'd heard people commenting on it all night.

He looked over at Morgan again where she was talking to Julia and Ben and laughing with the group around the wedding cake. Julia's mother was cutting slices and handing them around and Morgan was holding a piece on a napkin up to her mouth, trying not to spill any on the long, flowing dress she was wearing. The dress clung to her curves when she was still and floated and danced around her every time she moved. She choked a little at something somebody said and then jumped back as a piece of cake from her napkin fell to the floor. Aaron smiled a little and then looked away.

He'd nearly eaten the last of his éclair when the group around the cake started moving toward his table. Jodie and Jim sat down, and

Lorraine and Julia's brother Mike . . . and Morgan. They all kept talking and laughing and eating as Aaron struggled to swallow his last bite.

"Hey—the cake's pretty good, you missed out, man." Jim elbowed Aaron in the ribs and took another huge bite of cake. "You can probably still get some if you go over there, you know."

"It's okay, I'm about sick as it is. I got in line up there at the buffet at least three times. They're probably going to kick both of us out."

"Not me, I'm too darn entertaining." Jim gave a huge grin and then put his arm loosely around Jodie's shoulders. "Hey, Aaron," Jim looked back toward the door, "I think your parents just left. Are you going to get a ride with us?"

Aaron quickly turned toward the door and then looked around the room. *Great. What were they thinking?*

"Oh, yeah, I guess. I knew I should have brought the jeep. You don't mind, right? You don't have any plans, do you?"

"Well, you know I have plans, boy, but I guess I'll drop you off. There's this guy over there who's in one of my classes that I want to talk to real quick and then we'll get out of here."

Jim pulled Jodie up and was across the room before Aaron could say anything. Mike stood up and ran to grab his two-year-old, who was pulling the tablecloth off the cake table. Lorraine had turned sideways in her chair and was talking to a couple of ladies that he didn't know, and so when he looked up, all he saw was Morgan. She was looking at him too, but looked away immediately.

This was ridiculous. He was a grown man, wasn't he? He could at least be nice.

"How's it going?"

Morgan looked up at him quickly, the surprise in her eyes. "Good. And you?"

"Oh, I'm okay. School's tough and everything. You know, busy."

"Yeah."

There was a short silence, and Aaron felt the blood pulsing in his temple. "Hey, I heard you did all this? It's great, amazing."

"Thanks. I really had a good time doing it. I'm working at a place in the mall in Provo, and the manager has let me do a couple of design projects for her. I'm really excited about it. I got some of the ideas for the reception from things in the shop, and I wanted to do this for Julia. It turned out really well, even if I do say so myself." She smiled up at him and a gleam of the old mischief appeared.

Aaron's heart jumped. "Well, man, you deserve to brag it up. I'm really impressed, Morgan." When he said her name his throat went dry, and he felt a blush creeping up his neck. He looked down and away and waited for a few minutes.

"Well, what about you? Are you going to work for the sprinkler place again this summer?"

"Yeah, I guess, unless I can find something better to do . . ."

And the talk between them kept on, stupid things, sane things, things she would say to anybody, polite conversation, yet it was all intensely interesting to Aaron. The old jokes came up, and the stories. He felt rooted to his chair. He couldn't move his eyes from her, couldn't turn his head to the right or the left. He felt hot in the pit of his stomach, yet a calmness surrounded him and his mind relaxed for the first time in months.

"Oh, shoot." Morgan had stopped in the middle of a sentence and was looking around. "Ross was supposed to wait for me and take me home to change. I've got to come back and start cleaning up. I wore these silly high heels and my feet are killing me." She swept back her dress and revealed silver high-heeled sandals and long, slim feet.

Aaron remembered how beautiful he had always thought her feet were.

"He's always running off." Morgan was trying to look exasperated. "Do you see him anywhere?"

Aaron looked around. "No." He realized that Jim and Jodie were also gone as well as most of the rest of the crowd. Had Jim left him with Morgan on purpose?

"Did Julia and Ben already leave?" he asked.

"Yeah, only about twenty minutes ago." She laughed a little.

There was an awkward pause.

"Oh, well, you know, I'd like to give you a ride home, only I have a little problem myself."

"And what's that?" Her eyes were sparkling, smiling . . . dancing.

"Well, my ride left me too."

She laughed, and they both got up from the table and moved toward the door. Julia's mother came out of the kitchen, already changed from her formal dress.

"I'll go and change and be right back, okay?" Morgan called to her.

They were walking side by side, together again. Aaron was super-conscious of the few people left in the room and wondered what they were thinking. What was he thinking? What was he doing?

It was dark and cold outside, but neither of them said anything as they began walking in the same direction. A tiny chiming caught his ear. He looked down and saw his bracelet on Morgan's swinging wrist. He caught his breath and felt a tightening in his chest. Had she been wearing it all night?

"Didn't you bring a coat?" Aaron said.

"No. I didn't think I was going to have to walk."

"Oh, well, I guess I'll just walk your way, if you don't care, just so you won't be alone."

"Okay."

She was so different, yet somehow exactly the same. It was uncanny. Aaron was sweating in the chill air under his sports jacket.

"Hey, do you want this coat? It was kind of hot in there." He took it off and offered it to her.

"No, I don't want you to be cold. After all, I was the dumb one . . ." She looked into his eyes in the moonlight, and somehow they stopped walking.

"No. It wasn't just you." Aaron's breath was coming fast and hard even though they'd only walked three blocks.

"Here. You're going to freeze." Aaron put the coat around her shoulders and pulled it close under her chin. He drew one of his fingers lightly along the back of her neck to free from the collar the strands of hair that had fallen from the twist on her head. She closed her eyes and he felt her tremble. He was standing so close; his lips were two inches from her forehead. When she looked up at him a tear was running down her right cheek.

"Morgan . . ." His voice sounded hoarse in the stillness. "Do you think, well, do you think that we could be friends again?"

Morgan looked down and didn't say anything. He was in agony. "Listen, I know how I hurt you, and I really don't have any excuse, but . . ." He took a deep breath; his heart was hammering. "I still love you. I guess I just never got over you. I . . ." What could he say? "Well, I hope you can forgive me."

There was a long silence, and he didn't think he could bear it. And then she looked up at him and moved the smallest bit closer. Tears were running down both her cheeks now. He put up a shaking hand and wiped under one of her eyes with his thumb and then slowly bent to her lips.

When he drew away from her, she put her arms up around his neck and whispered softly into his ear, "I love you, Aaron."

It was just what he wanted to hear.

About the Author

Taunia Luster Bean grew up in Ephraim, Utah, and attended Snow College. She earned a degree in English literature from Utah State University and worked as a technical writer before taking up the art of child raising. Taunia enjoys reading, writing, home decorating, and volunteering at her children's school. She currently resides in South Jordan with her husband, Terry, their four children, and two cats.

Excerpt from

THE LONG ROAD HOME

Seventeen-year-old Reese Clark's blue eyes widened with delight when Stacy Jardine walked into the small kitchen of her home in Roy, Utah. Reese self-consciously ran a hand down the back of his thick black hair, wishing he had spent more time with his own appearance. He had lost track of the time playing basketball at a friend's house as they celebrated their high school football team's homecoming victory earlier that afternoon. Reese's mother had finally called to remind him that he needed to shower and change before picking Stacy up for the homecoming dance. There had barely been time for that when he arrived home.

"I told you Stacy had dolled herself up for this dance," Ann Jardine beamed.

Nodding in agreement with Stacy's mother, Reese continued to gaze at his date for the evening. Wearing a maroon prom dress he knew she had borrowed from a friend, Stacy was gorgeous. The floor length dress had a high neck and long, lacy sleeves. Modest but elegant, the gown accentuated Stacy's slender waistline. Reese's eyes traveled to Stacy's face. Naturally beautiful, she hadn't used much makeup, only a hint of base to cover two small blemishes on her chin, a touch of rouge on her cheeks, and a trace of eyeshadow and mascara to accent her dark brown eyes. Her long, brown hair had been swept up in the back with pearl-draped barrettes. The sides of her face were framed by loose curls.

"Wow," Reese whispered as he pulled at the snug maroon tie he wore with the black tuxedo he had rented for the evening.

"Go stand next to Reese and I'll take your picture," Ann insisted, grabbing her camera from the kitchen table. "Now turn sideways.

Stacy, turn your face toward me. Reese, quit looking so stiff," Ann laughed. "Relax, and put your hands around her waist. There, that looks more natural. Good. Smile," she encouraged, taking another shot with her camera.

"Mom," Stacy said, glancing at the clock, "we're going to be late."

"Maybe if you hadn't spent so long in the bathroom, you'd have more time now," Stacy's younger brother teased.

Stacy stuck her tongue out at the sixteen year old. "Behave, Brad."

"I could say the same thing to you two," Brad countered.

"Now, Brad, that's enough," Ann said, reaching for a lacy white shawl that had been draped over a kitchen chair.

"Don't worry, Mrs. Jardine, I'll be a perfect gentleman all evening and have her home at midnight," Reese promised.

Ann smiled at Reese, then pointed to the plastic box he had left on the kitchen table. "Aren't you forgetting something?" she asked.

He followed her gaze to the table. "The corsage," he exclaimed. He carefully pulled the arrangement of tiny white roses, accented by baby's breath and green fern, from its transparent container and held it out to Ann. "Could you pin this on Stacy? I'm terrible at this sort of thing."

"I'll do it!" Brad volunteered.

"I don't think so," Stacy refused. "You'd probably skewer me on purpose. If you wanted to pin a corsage on a girl, then you should've asked someone to the dance yourself," she added.

"Maybe some of us think it's silly to waste that kind of money on a girl," Brad said, grinning.

Reese winked at Brad. "When the right girl comes along, it's worth all the money in the world."

Ann began a coughing fit that lasted several seconds. Reese glanced at the concerned look on Stacy's face. He knew how worried she was about her mother's health. Ann had smoked for years and now endured a persistent cough.

"Are you all right?" Stacy asked in a subdued voice.

Nodding, Ann retreated to the kitchen sink, grabbed a plastic tumbler, and filled it with water. She took a long sip, breathed deeply, then set the glass on the counter and hurried to the fridge. "Don't forget his boutonniere," she said, pulling out the small plastic box.

Stacy slipped an arm around her mother's slender shoulders and gave her a quick squeeze. Reese overheard the whispered thanks that passed between the two and smiled. Ann and Stacy were close, bonded through shared trials that had nearly torn their family apart. Stacy's father had been an abusive alcoholic, so Ann, Stacy, and Brad had learned to depend on each other for comfort and support. Larry Jardine's costly habits grew progressively worse until Ann had given him an ultimatum. His disappearance from their lives a short time later had almost come as a relief, though it left tender wounds that never seemed to fully heal.

After the divorce, Ann had moved the three of them into a small house they could afford to rent. She worked two jobs—as a clerk in a local grocery store during the day, and at a video store at night—to keep them afloat financially. Stacy spent three afternoons a week cooking at a nearby drive-in after school. Brad did his part by working part-time at a local garage and helped Stacy straighten things at home. Pulling together, they were surviving this latest chapter in their lives. Reese admired their determination and envied their close relationship.

Ann returned her daughter's squeeze. "You two have a good time tonight," she said, handing the rose boutonniere to Stacy.

Stacy nodded, then walked to where Reese was waiting and pinned on his flower.

"Did she stick you, Reese?" Brad inquired.

"Nope," Reese replied, shaking his head at Stacy's brother.

"You guys aren't very entertaining," Brad complained.

"That'll come later," Reese said, invoking a look of dismay from Stacy and Ann. "I didn't mean it like it sounded," he stammered, turning a deep shade of red. "I meant when we get out on the dance floor."

"I think I'll be watching out the window tonight when you bring Stacy home," Brad laughed.

"I don't think so," Ann said as she helped Stacy with the shawl. She tied it in place, draping the knot down the front of her daughter's borrowed dress. "Have fun," she said as Reese walked Stacy to the door.

"We will," Reese called back.

"I'll bet," Brad sang out, wiggling his eyebrows.

"Mom!" Stacy complained.

"Already taken care of," Ann said, signaling that Brad had gone far enough.

"Sorry about that," Stacy apologized as Reese helped her onto the porch. He closed the screen door, then escorted her to the green sedan he had borrowed from his parents.

"Wait until my family has their turn," Reese sympathized. "This will seem mild."

"We're going to your house?" she asked excitedly.

Reese nodded, enjoying the sudden sparkle in her dark eyes. "That's where we'll end up for dessert," he explained. "Since there are six couples in our group, we decided to have a progressive dinner. We'll have one course at each guy's house."

"This sounds like fun," Stacy commented as Reese helped her into the car.

"Better than a fancy restaurant?"

"Much," Stacy replied.

"All righty then, let's be on our way," he said, making sure Stacy's dress was tucked inside the car before closing the door.

* * *

"Here you are—finally," Janell Clark sang out as the six couples invaded her home later that evening. "I thought you said you'd be here around seven," the attractive blonde added, directing her gaze toward her son, Reese. Truthfully, she was relieved they were late arriving. It had given her a chance to thoroughly clean the house after a crazy day of running errands. It had also given her enough time to change into a dark pair of dress pants, a cream-colored blouse, and a matching sweater. Her short hair had been styled in a flattering fashion, swept back at the sides and curled on top. Her bright blue eyes sparkled with delight as she studied the becoming but modest gowns the six girls had chosen for this special night. With today's fashions, that was a major accomplishment.

"We were beginning to wonder if we needed to send the search and rescue out to look for you," Will Clark added, glancing at their son.

Janell laughed at the look of mock indignation on Reese's face. With that expression he looked so much like Will. Nearly the same height, father and son were close to six feet tall. Their hair was the same color, though there was a difference in the amount of hair they had. Reese's short hair was dark and thick, unlike Will's hair that was thinning on top and greying at the sides.

"We're only an hour late," Reese teased, leaning to kiss his mother's cheek. "It took us longer at each place than we had figured."

"I see," Janell said, closing the front door. She turned for another look at the dressed-up teens. "You all look great."

"I'll say," Will agreed. "I'll go grab the video camera. We need to preserve this rare occasion—it's the first time I've ever seen Reese in a tux," he said, hurrying from the room.

A chorus of dismay echoed in the entry way as Reese began leading everyone into the dining room for dessert. Janell slipped an arm around Stacy's waist as they followed behind the small crowd. "You look beautiful."

"Thank you," Stacy replied in a hushed voice.

"Are you having fun?"

Stacy nodded. "Reese's friends are so funny."

"Reese thinks he's quite a comedian himself," Janell replied, releasing Stacy as they approached the table.

"I know," Stacy whispered.

"Know what?" Reese asked.

"Never mind," Janell responded. "Now, who's ready for dessert?"

"Bring it on," one of Reese's friends encouraged. "What are we having?"

"Strawberry cheesecake," Janell announced, enjoying the delighted murmurs that circulated the polished oak table. Turning, she stepped back into the kitchen.

Stacy followed. "I'll help you," she offered.

"I'd appreciate that," Janell said, opening the fridge. She placed the large cheesecake onto the counter and motioned for Stacy to grab the small paper plates she had set out earlier. "Just don't get any of this on that gorgeous dress," she cautioned. "I'd feel terrible."

"So would I," Stacy agreed.

"Tell you what, I'll dish it up and you can hand it out, how's that?"

"Sounds like a plan."

"I found the camera! It was buried under a pile of clothes in the laundry room—something I suspect Reese knew all along," Will announced as he walked into the dining room with the camcorder.

Reese shook his head in protest, but the mischievous look in his blue eyes revealed the truth.

"Now, everyone, act natural," Will encouraged. "Where's Stacy?"

"I'm helping your wife," Stacy replied from the kitchen.

"Hurry. I'm not sure how long this battery will hold out," Will said, moving around the table for a better shot.

"I can't believe he's filming this," Stacy whispered to Janell.

Janell smiled at the young woman her son had been friends with for nearly a year. "I can. We have a collection of interesting footage from every event this family has participated in since he bought that camera three years ago. Some tapes I've threatened to burn."

Stacy giggled. "Mom's the same way . . . I mean . . . we don't have a camcorder, but she's always taking pictures of me and Brad. She took several tonight before Reese and I left."

"I'd like a copy of those," Janell said as she began cutting the cheesecake into small, squared sections.

"Sure. Mom always gets double prints."

"I'd be willing to pay for reprints if you want to keep the extra shots," Janell replied. She glanced at Stacy. "So, how are things going?"

"Tonight?"

"In general," Janell responded. "I haven't had a chance to visit with you for a couple of weeks."

"I know," Stacy said as she set the plates near the cheesecake, spreading them out on the counter. "It seems like all I do anymore is go to school, work at the drive-in, and stay up late doing homework."

"Are you keeping up okay?" Janell asked, concerned.

Stacy nodded. "Who needs sleep?"

"We all do," Janell counseled. "Are you still taking those honors classes?"

"Sad but true."

"Is it worth it?"

"I think so. I'm hoping to get a scholarship. That's the only way I'll be able to go to college."

"Where's that cake?" Reese hollered from the dining room. "The crowd is getting ugly in here!"

"It's coming," Janell called back, her blue eyes twinkling with suppressed humor. "Well, so much for small talk. Guess we'd better feed the starving masses." She placed slices of cheesecake onto the small paper plates as Stacy took them into the dining room. When Stacy came back into the kitchen for the final serving, Janell handed it to her. "What would you think about coming over for dinner tomorrow after church?"

"Sure," Stacy accepted.

"Great. I assume Reese is picking you up for church in the morning?"

"He said it depends on what time we get home tonight," Stacy said, laughing at the look of mock horror on Janell's face.

"So help me, if he doesn't get you home by midnight—"

"He promised my mother that he would," Stacy interrupted.

"Well, he'd better," Janell exclaimed. "I don't know, though. You look like a goddess tonight, so I'm a little concerned."

"Don't worry, I'll keep Reese in line," Stacy promised.

"Good girl," Janell replied.

"Stacy? Did you lose your way?" Reese hollered.

An amused look passed between Janell and Stacy. "I'll be right there," she called back. "Persistent little thing, isn't he?" Janell observed. "You'll have to watch out for that."

"I know," Stacy agreed before moving into the dining room to join the other teens.

* * *

Dancing in Reese's strong arms across the crepe-papered gym, Stacy wished the evening would last forever. Twisted strands of blue and white hung from wires that crossed the dimly lit room, giving it an ethereal quality. After enjoying several slow songs, Reese led her to the refreshment table for a glass of punch. Making their way through the crowd, they spied two vacant chairs and sat down.

"I thought maybe we could use a break," Reese said, sipping the fruit punch.

Stacy nodded. She returned a wave from one of her friends, then smiled at Reese.

"Are you having fun?"

"Yes," she bubbled. "Are you?"

"Let's see, I recently consumed the best meal I've had in a long time and I'm with the most beautiful girl in the world. Yeah, I'd say I'm having a good time. I do have a confession to make, though," he added.

"What's that?"

"This monkey suit is the most uncomfortable thing I've ever worn in my life!"

Stacy laughed. "But you look so good in it."

"Really?" he replied, puffing up. "Well, as Dad always says, maybe we'd better preserve this moment for our future posterity. I don't think the line for pictures is getting any smaller, so we might as well get this over with."

"*What* future posterity?" Stacy pointedly asked as Reese reached for her empty paper cup.

Reese wiggled his eyebrows. "Time will tell," was his only reply before he helped her to her feet and led her across the large room.